ST. MARTIN'S

MINOTAUR

MYSTERIES

"This book is a true delight. Chock full of wry observation and propelled by a compelling plot, *The Cold Blue Blood* is classic Handler. As for characters Berger and Mitry . . . they better come back and visit again; they're the best buddy team to come along in years."

—Jeffery Deaver, author of
The Blue Nowhere and *The Empty Chair*

"Mitch is a terrific character, full of passion and sensitivity . . . The New York color is perfectly rendered, as is the Connecticut salt. Here's hoping for many more stories of Des and Mitch."

—*Booklist*

"Can a tough African-American cop with a soft spot for feral cats find happiness with a nice Jewish boy who says he does his best work in the dark? Here's hoping that Handler . . . explores this question in more first-rate puzzlers."

—*Kirkus Reviews*

"Definitely an odd-couple team we look forward to seeing more of in future installments of this delightful new series."

—*Denver Post*

ALSO BY DAVID HANDLER

The Cold Blue Blood

AVAILABLE FROM
ST. MARTIN'S/MINOTAUR PAPERBACKS

THE
HOT PINK
FARMHOUSE

DAVID
HANDLER

St. Martin's Paperbacks

ISBN: 0-312-98704-8

Printed in the United States of America

St. Martin's Press hardcover edition / November 2002
St. Martin's Paperbacks edition / November 2003

St. Martin's Paperbacks are published by St. Martin's Press, 175 Fifth Avenue, New York, NY 10010.

10 9 8 7 6 5 4 3 2 1

FOR EARLE C. DRAKE,
A WISE AND GENTLE SOUL

THE
HOT PINK
FARMHOUSE

PROLOGUE

This wasn't supposed to happen.

She had made a solemn promise to herself about sneaking around in the night this way: Never again. I will not treat another man's wife this way. I will not treat myself this way. But there was a mighty big problem with such a promise, she had discovered. It lasted only until it was put to the flesh test by a certain man, the right man, *him.* And then it went flying right out the window, along with shame, self-respect, and sanity.

I am not in control of myself, she realized as she steered the rocket-fast Porsche down the narrow, twisting country lane, its twin exhaust pipes burbling in the after-midnight quiet. *I am a bad, bad girl.*

She parked on Frederick Lane, a few houses down from the little inn, well away from its parking lot, and closed her door very softly when she got out. Sound carried in the village. And it was important that no one hear her coming to him in the night. No one.

The stars were out and she could see her breath in the light of the full harvest moon. There would be a frost come morning, first of the season.

She did not lock the car. No one who grew up in Dorset did. The newcomers locked theirs, of course. Sometimes, in the night, she could hear the alarms going off when raccoons jumped onto their fashionable Land Cruisers. What an intrusive, hostile sound that was. But she could not knock the newcomers. She would not have been able to stay here in her lovely little village, earning the kind of money she was earning, if it weren't for them and their kids moving in.

Fallen leaves crackled under her feet as she strode softly toward the darkened inn. The earth smelled of rotting apples, a sweet, moldy aroma that reminded her of when she was a little girl on the farm. As she walked, she thought she heard somebody else's footsteps in addition to her own. She paused, her ears straining, but now heard nothing. Her ears had been playing tricks on her. She resumed walking, her heart beginning to race with anticipation. It was after midnight and she was up to no good and she knew it.

This time her eyes were wide open.

They hadn't been that first time, back when she was working as an au pair the summer after her freshman year of college. A wealthy Park Avenue couple had rented themselves one of the big summer bungalows overlooking the Sound. Two darling little girls they had. The wife was a society skeleton with a hyphenated name and an overbite. And Stephen was a grave, sensitive dreamer who yearned to write sonnets but traded in hedge funds because this was what was expected of him. How tragically romantic he had seemed. And sooo handsome. And then his hyphenate wife had to leave for Kennebunkport when Mumsy took ill. She moved into a guest room to see to the girls. And she and Stephen had talked and talked into the night. There had been soul-baring and there had been tears. And it had happened right there on the living room sofa. Three times, quickly in succession.

The poor man had been positively starved for her, she had told herself.

At summer's end she had followed him into the city and their affair had continued in a succession of hotel rooms. She became something of an expert on the relative merits of their various accommodations. The mattresses at The Plaza were the firmest, the club sandwiches at The Carlyle the tastiest, the towels at the St. Regis the most luxuriant. After their trysts, she would ride home on the Metro-North commuter train, asking herself if these seasoned suburbanites could tell by her bruised lips and sated, dreamy countenance that she had just been ravaged by a married man. The career women stared at her with such flinty disapproval, she swore they could. The middle-aged businessmen, they just stared.

And then one day they were caught by his wife's best friend as the two of them came out of the Waldorf. And she discovered that Stephen had done this many times before with many different young girls and she was not special and there was nothing poetic or glorious about it at all. She'd just been having a tawdry affair with a lying creep who should have been treating his wife, his children and any number of sweet young college girls a whole lot better.

That was when she swore it would never happen again. And it hadn't. There *was* one boy, a boy she would have given everything to, but he broke her heart and she sealed it shut after that, and there was no one.

Until now. Now she could not help herself. She simply was not strong enough. Everyone who knew her thought she was incredibly tough. She was, in fact, weak. She was just very good at hiding it. Possibly, this was the one thing in life she was best at.

So every night she came sneaking to him like this, breathless with anticipation and desire.

The innkeepers locked the front door after midnight. But they kept a key to the kitchen door under a flowerpot on the back porch. She knew this because she had waited tables here in high school. There were very few jobs for teenagers in a village like Dorset. Every reasonably presentable girl in town had pinned up her hair and donned the blue gingham jumper at one time or another. It was a rite of passage, just like the prom-night kegger on White Sands Beach.

After she'd returned the key to its hiding place she slipped off her shoes and tiptoed barefoot through the kitchen, hearing the hum of the big refrigerators. It was still warm in there from dinner, and the scent of roasted duck lingered in the air. She passed through the swinging doors into the darkened dining room, careful not to bump into the tables that were set for breakfast. Up one step to the main hallway, past the sitting room to the curving staircase. It was a grand old three-story house, a sea captain's house. There were eleven guest rooms in all. Up the stairs she darted, quick and light-footed as a girl, knowing it was wrong. Not caring. That was the truly crazy part—not caring.

No lights showed under any of the doors. The guests were asleep. She could hear snores coming from the second-floor front room—an elderly Jewish lady from Brooklyn, he'd told her. The old dear sounded like a French-Canadian lumberjack. Up to his third-floor rear room she ran, tapping on his door.

He immediately flung it open and she was in his arms and he was kissing her mouth and eyes and neck and it had never, ever been like this before. This intense. This feverish.

She broke away, gasping for breath. "My God, you are a total madman."

"I'm just a sad case," he said, his eyes gleaming at her in the light from the bedside lamp. "Haven't you heard? Everyone says so." He pulled her inside, closing the door softly behind her. The room was small and cozy, with a canopied bed, a rocker, a lovely old wardrobe cupboard. "I thought you'd never get here."

"I had a little car trouble."

He wore boxer shorts and nothing else. He wanted her badly. She could see this plainly.

"Well, that answers my first question," she said tartly. "How you feel."

"Terrific," he answered exultantly. "Today was the best thing that's ever happened to me. Well, second best . . ." His hands reached for hers. "I was lying here thinking you weren't going to come. I didn't know what I would do if you didn't."

"Perhaps what you need is a hobby," she teased him. "Have you thought about making your own jams and jellies? Or whittling? There's a grand old tradition of Yankee whittlers that goes all the way back to Ralph Waldo—"

He plunged his mouth down upon hers, his hands flinging

her skirt and sweater off her. She wore nothing underneath. Naked, she leaped into his arms. He carried her to the bed, pulling her up and over on top of him, kneading her breasts with his hands.

"*Ohh . . .*" she cried softly as she felt the exquisite agony of him inside of her. The canopy bed creaking under their weight. In fact, the whole bedroom floor creaked—God help whoever had the room directly below them.

"*Ohh . . . Ohhh . . . Ohhhh . . .*" As he buried himself deeper and deeper in her. "*Ohh . . . Ohhh . . . Ohhhh . . .*" As she raised herself up and down upon him . . . "*Ohh . . .*" As she felt herself going and going . . . "*Ohh . . . Ohhh . . . Ohhhh . . .*" Until at last he exploded within her and she collapsed upon him, quivering all over.

"Do you have any idea how beautiful you are?" he whispered in her ear.

"I don't mind you telling me, if you feel like it."

He felt like it, he felt like it.

Then she got busy straightening the covers around them and they lay there under the quilt, snuggling.

"I'm not liking this," he confessed. "What we're doing."

"I'm not either. But if it feels this good, it can't be all bad, can it?" She let out a soft laugh. "That sounds just like a Sheryl Crow song."

"I wouldn't know. I never pay attention to lyrics."

"You don't? But how can you tell what the song is about?"

"What's to tell? They're all about the same thing—love that's starting, love that's ending. Good love, bad love, *love*."

"Okay, if our love was a song, who would sing it?" she asked, immediately feeling stupid. It was a high school date question.

He was silent a long moment. Was he carefully considering his response, or was he just asleep? It was only when they began to talk this way that she began to wonder if they had anything in common at all.

"Okay, I'm thinking Bonnie Raitt," she rattled on. "Or maybe Sarah McLachlan. How about you?"

"I guess I'm thinking more along the lines of Roy Orbison."

She cupped his chin in her hand. "Oh, honey, it's not that bad, is it?"

"This has got to end. I have to leave town."

"You can't leave," she protested, hearing the desperation in her voice.

"It's too risky."

"There are people who go through their entire lives without risking anything. We don't want to be like them, do we?"

"But both of our lives could be totally ruined."

"So we'll leave town together. She'll let us go. She'll come to her senses. We just have to give her time."

"And then what?" he asked miserably.

"And then we can start a new life," she said, not even believing her own words. The utter and complete hopelessness was washing over her now, too. It was only their passion kept it at bay.

So they reignited it, much more slowly and tenderly this time. And there was this and only this. And it was so much better than it had ever been with anyone else. Until they were spent once again, and the despair came creeping right back, like a chronic pain that could only be dulled with stronger and stronger drugs.

They did not sleep a wink, not wishing to lose a single precious one of their stolen moments together.

The kitchen staff generally trickled in at about five-thirty to begin breakfast. Not wishing to encounter anyone, she kissed him good-bye shortly before five and tiptoed back down the stairs and out the kitchen door into the pre-dawn darkness, her clothing disheveled, hair a mess.

The village was still asleep. No dog walkers were out yet. No joggers. No one. It was quiet and calm and cold.

Shivering, she scraped the thin layer of frost from the Porsche's windshield and jumped in and started it up with an indiscreet roar, wishing it weren't *quite* so loud. Quickly, she steered her way back up Frederick Lane toward home, tearing past an enclave of precious antique houses that dated back to the early seventeen hundreds. They were set far back from the road and surrounded by lush green meadows and mossy stone walls. Many of them overlooked the Connecticut River. One by one the adjoining meadows were being transformed into building sites. Giant new prairie palaces with many wings and turrets were springing up alongside the lovely old houses, dwarfing them. Often, as she passed by these new showplaces, she made unkind remarks about them under her breath. But on this morning, as she turned north onto Route 156 and floored it up into the farm country, she was so lost in thought she barely noticed them.

It was no good and she knew it. Because his wife would never let him go. Because it was an illicit, unbelievably tacky small-town romance, and no good ever came of those. Because all three of their lives would be destroyed.

No, she was not tough. But she was stronger than he was. So it was up to her to do the right thing, the adult thing, the *smart* thing. End it. Right now.

As the dawn light came, the autumn leaves began to emerge from the darkness in their red and orange splendor. This was her favorite time of the season, just before the peak color, when there was still a good deal of lush green foliage remaining on the trees to offset the flaming color. At Winston Farms, a blanket of frost lay over the pastures, sparkling. It was as fragile and serenely beautiful a sight as she had ever seen.

Her turnoff onto Old Ferry Road was just beyond the Winston Farms feed troughs, where the cows were busy enjoying their breakfast. It was a hard left turn, and it required her to come nearly to a complete stop, even in the nimble roadster. As she did so, downshifting, she glanced at the dashboard clock. It was five-twenty. That left her just enough time to shower and change and start breakfast. Sleep? That would have to wait until after work, when she'd be able to close her eyes and take a deep breath and—

She barely saw the flash. It came from somewhere up in the rocks across the road. But this fact barely had a chance to register in her sleep-deprived brain. And she never did *hear* it because by the time the sound reached her, the car had already exploded and flipped over onto the hay trough, where it and countless bales of hay and several poor, unwitting dairy cows erupted in a fireball that rose over a hundred feet into the dawn sky.

The very last thing on earth she saw was that flash. It was the brightest light she had ever seen. Just like staring right into the sun. And then she *was* the sun. And she didn't have to worry about their relationship anymore. Or about anything else.

The very last thing she thought was: *This wasn't supposed to happen.*

But it had.

And now there would be hell to pay.

CHAPTER 1

Autumn's arrival meant the onset of headless mousey season out on Big Sister Island. Or at least it did in Mitch Berger's little corner of it.

Shortly before dawn, Mitch's rugged outdoor hunter, Quirt, deposited a fresh head-free corpse on the welcome mat of Mitch's antique post-and-beam carriage house and meowed to be let in. And meowed. And meowed. Upstairs in his sleeping loft, Mitch reluctantly stirred. Next to him on the bed, Clemmie, his gray-and-white short hair, did not so much as open an eye. Not even a hurricane could rouse Clemmie. In fact, with each passing day, Mitch was becoming more and more convinced that she had been genetically altered into a meat loaf.

Yawning, Mitch padded barefoot down the narrow stairs into the living room and waddled to the front door, flicking on the porch light to find one orange tabby who was immensely proud of himself and one white-footed field mouse who was missing his or her head.

It definitely took some getting used to as a morning wake-up call.

Quirt immediately made straight for the kibble bowl. The mouse stayed outside. Later, Mitch would bury him. Her. It. A small ceremony, nondenominational. Right now, he put the coffee on, watching Quirt chew his way steadily through his breakfast. Quirt had been a feral stray until he was six months old, same as Clemmie, but the two could not have turned out more different. Quirt remained a sinewy outdoorsman who did not linger inside unless it was raining. On those rare occasions when he would consent to sit in Mitch's lap he'd squirm and wriggle and make this unbelievably strange noise in his throat that sounded more like Gorgo, the monster that rose from the ocean's depths, than it did a pussy cat. Clemmie, on the other hand, never went outside, never stalked anything more threatening than dust and spent so much time in Mitch's lap that he sometimes felt she was attached to him by Velcro.

Mitch had not actually chosen to adopt either one of them. The new lady in his life was one of those kindhearted people who rescued feral strays from supermarket dumpsters and she had, well, forced them on him. But now that they were settled in he could not imagine life without them.

While his coffee brewed, Mitch shaved and put on a baggy fisherman's-knit sweater, rumpled khakis and his wading boots. Then he poured himself a fresh hot cup, topping it off with two fingers of the rich chocolate milk that came in glass bottles from a dairy in Salem. He stood there sipping it contentedly and watching the purple-streaked dawn sky through the big windows that looked out over Long Island Sound in three different directions. A few fishing boats were heading out. Squadrons of geese flew overhead, honking. Otherwise, it was so quiet he could hear the water lapping at the rocks outside his door.

This was his first autumn in the cottage on Big Sister, a family-held island off Dorset, the historic New England village situated at the mouth of the Connecticut River halfway between New York City and Boston. The summer people were gone now, the kids back in school. The water was bluer and colder, the sky clearer and spiced with the smell of wood smoke. Migratory barn swallows and monarch butterflies filled his trees by the thousands, pausing to feed on insects before they took off again like a cloud for the Carolinas. With each passing day, the afternoon shadows grew longer and longer.

Mitch was the only one on the island who was not a Peck by birth or marriage. Right now, he was also the only one in residence, which meant he could enjoy the rare luxury of playing his beloved sky-blue Fender Stratocaster as ear-splittingly loud as he pleased. There was a decommissioned lighthouse on Big Sister, the second tallest in New England. There were four other houses on the island besides Mitch's, forty acres of woods, a private dock, a beach that Mitch alone used, tennis courts that no one used. A rickety wooden causeway connected it to the mainland at Peck Point, a preserve that belonged to the Nature Conservancy. Paradise. It was a Yankee paradise.

For Mitch Berger, a pure-blooded New York City screening-room rat, it was also a brave new world. He had taught himself to garden. Bought a palm-sized pair of bird-watching glasses and well-thumbed copy of Roger Tory Peterson's *Field Guide to Eastern Birds*, a high-low thermometer, barometer, tide clock, and a rain gauge that was calibrated to one-hundredth of an inch. He yearned for a telescope, too, but worried that he might turn into one of those unshaven old geezers whom he'd seen around town with egg-yolk stains down the front of their Mackinaw bib overalls, the ones who kept bees and railed on to total strangers about the virtues of the flat tax.

Still, he was really looking forward to the Leonid meteor shower on November 16.

At age thirty-two, Mitch was lead film critic for the most prestigious and therefore lowest-paying of the three New York City daily newspapers. He was also the author of two highly entertaining film reference books, *Shoot My Wife, Please* and *It Came From Beneath the Sink*. Mitch loved what he did for a living. He especially loved this time of year in the film calendar. The bloated, over-hyped idiocy of the summer blockbuster season had been put to bed. He had been revived by the quirky talents on display at the Toronto and New York film festivals. And now he had several clear weeks before the Christmas screenings to spend out here on *They Went Thataway*, his woefully overdue guide to Westerns, which explained the discs, files, books and video cassettes that were heaped everywhere.

Last night he had e-mailed news of this to his editor at the paper, Lacy Mickerson. Mitch fired up his G-4 and logged on to see if she had replied. She had. Her response began with two well-chosen words: *As if*. Because Lacy knew perfectly well the real reason Mitch wanted to be out there. She continued: *But if you insist on playing small-town boy, how about that Cookie Commerce article?*

This was in reference to the so-called Serious Fun Edict devised by the new executive editor, who was encouraging staffers to branch out into other sections of the paper. The Knicks-beat reporter, for instance, recently got a chance to spend an entire fun-filled day hanging at the U.S. Supreme Court with Ruth Bader Ginsberg. Mitch was being steered toward the food section by Lacy based on something he'd mentioned to her at lunch one day.

His e-mailed response to her on this day: *Still searching for a hook*. Which was newspeak for: *Go away and leave me alone*.

He shut down his computer and started in on his morning chores. Scooped up that headless corpse with a garden trowel and buried it out behind the barn with the others, wondering what an archaeologist would make of this site in five thousand years. Headed down the path to the island's beach with a trash bag. Trudging along the sand, alone except for a family of cormorants, Mitch dutifully picked up the plastic bottles, Styrofoam cups and beer cans that had washed ashore from the fishing boats in the night. People, he had discovered, were absolute pigs.

He returned to his cottage, puffing slightly, and went to work with a rake on the leaves that had fallen in his beds, relishing the physical activity. Mitch was a big guy, just over six feet tall, burly when he was in shape, pudgy when he was not. Since his job called for him to spend every working hour in the dark on his butt, he could morph into the Pillsbury Doughboy if he was not careful. Being out here kept him in tip-top shape. The biceps under his *Rocky Dies Yellow* tattoo positively rippled. Okay, maybe it didn't really ripple, but it *was* a biceps.

He dumped the gathered leaves into a wire enclosure where they would quietly rot into mulch. Then he put on his work gloves and cut back the honeysuckle and wild blackberry vines that were threatening to engulf his whole house. These invasive predators he could not compost—he loaded them into the back of his bulbous, kidney-colored 1956 Studebaker pickup and tied a tarp over them. Mitch paused to cut a generous bunch of fresh white Japanese anemones from his garden, then hopped into his truck with the flowers and went toodling off across the rickety wooden causeway toward town.

The leaves on the old sugar maples that lined Dorset Street were turning a million different glorious shades of orange. John the Barber was out early sweeping the walk in front of his shop. Bill the Mobile Vet was stocking the medicine drawers in his truck outside his house. Over at the Grange Hall a hand-lettered sign announced that performances of the Dorset Players' fall production of *Bye Bye Birdie* were under way. The volunteer fire department was running its annual cow-chip raffle—first prize was a thousand dollars. Lew the Plumber was busy hosing down one of the fire trucks. He waved to Mitch. Mitch waved back. Rita, who worked behind the counter at the drugstore, was taking her morning power walk. She waved to Mitch, too. And, if he had cared to stop, would no doubt have asked him how he was making out with his jock itch.

Outside Center School, the charming circa 1912 elementary school located directly across Dorset Street from town hall, there were countless red SAVE OUR SCHOOL ribbons and green WE CARE ribbons festooning the trees. Center School was the focus of a heated local controversy. There were problems with its ventilation system—kids had complained of mold-spore-related respiratory problems last year, as well as nausea and headaches. Concerned parents, most of them the newer arrivals in town, had denounced the school as a health risk. This group, which called itself WE CARE, wanted

Center School to be replaced by a new high-tech school that would be built on forty acres of woods on the outskirts of town and be able to hold twice as many students. Their SAVE OUR SCHOOL opponents, most of them folks who had grown up in Dorset, merely wanted the existing school to be renovated and upgraded.

The issue would be settled in a special election on November 1, when a thirty-four-million-dollar bond issue to finance the proposed school was scheduled for a vote. For a town with a year-round population of less than seven thousand, it was a major financial undertaking. It was also a referendum on the very future of Dorset. Opponents were sure that if Center School got torn down it would strip the village of its small-town character. They also believed a giant new school would open the door to rampant suburbanization. Their mantra: *If the school doesn't grow, the town can't grow.* Proponents argued that those who opposed the plan were living in the past, not to mention cheap, selfish and sadistic for putting Dorset's kids at risk for the sake of a little charm.

The issue was pitting neighbor against neighbor. Tempers were flaring. No one was neutral. The nine-member school board was itself sharply divided—five members were for it, four against. Dorset's longtime school superintendent, Colin Falconer, was against the plan, pitting him directly against its biggest backer, school board president Babette Leanse, a sharp-tongued new arrival from New York. A prominent architect, Babette Leanse was married to Bruce Leanse, the most famous real estate tycoon not to be named Donald Trump. The Brat, the New York tabloids called Bruce Leanse, who was busy bulldozing hundreds of acres of Dorset's farmland and forest to make way for new designer mansions.

Mitch opposed the new school. He liked Dorset the way it was. That was why he had moved here—because it *wasn't* suburbia. But he was aware that he might feel different if he had kids. And, after losing his beloved wife Maisie to ovarian cancer, Mitch was well aware of something else: As hard as it might be to hold on to the past, it's even harder to hold on to the present.

He stopped in at the market to shop for Sheila Enman, a retired schoolteacher who had just turned ninety and couldn't get out much anymore. Mitch bought her a box of Cream of Wheat, milk, eggs, a half dozen bars of bittersweet chocolate and several gallons of the Clamato juice she loved. Also a jumbo-sized tub of sour cream, which she would go through in less than three days. The old girl went through sour cream so fast, Mitch wondered if she bathed in it.

On his way up Route 156 he dropped the stuff off at her house, an amazing old mill house built out over the Eight Mile River directly in front of a waterfall. Sheila had lived there since she was a girl. Her kitchen door was unlocked, her bedroom door shut. She wasn't up yet. Mitch stowed the groceries and put the anemones he'd cut for her in a vase on the kitchen table. She'd left money for the groceries on the kitchen counter, not to mention his payment: a sandwich bag filled with her homemade chocolate chip cookies. Sheila's chocolate chip cookies were the finest Mitch had ever eaten—big and chewy and filled with gooey chocolate chunks. He marketed for her twice a week in exchange for them. Reputedly, Sheila also made a killer lemon meringue pie, but Bob Paffin had that franchise all sewn up. Dorset's white-haired first selectman still shoveled Sheila's walk for her whenever it snowed, just as he had done back when he was in high school, in exchange for one of her pies.

Mitch was discovering that this kind of payment system was the invisible commerce that held Dorset together. Cookie Commerce, Sheila called it. Lacy wanted him to write about it. Mitch was tempted. He had already written a lighthearted piece for the travel section on Dorset, as well as a longer, more sober article for the Sunday magazine on the disappearance of one of Big Sister Island's residents. He found the place quirky and intriguing. And he had always admired the way one of his idols, E. B. White, had written about the life he'd found on his saltwater farm in Maine. Maybe this was something he could do, too. A way for him to grow as a journalist now that he'd ventured out of the movie theater and into the sunlight, stumbling and blinking. Then again, writing about people whom he knew as friends was something entirely foreign to him. He wasn't sure he felt comfortable with that idea. That was why he'd put Lacy off.

That and the fact that he really, truly had no hook.

He jumped back in his truck and continued up the narrow country road to the dump, munching contentedly on one of his cookies as the morning sun broke brightly through the autumn foliage. The cookies were all gone by the time Mitch got there. First he backed up to the brush pile and unloaded his vines and brambles, then he eased the Studey over to the green Dumpster where folks deposited their metal items. A picker's paradise. Mitch almost always came home with something choice. In fact, he'd furnished his whole house at the dump—his desk, bookcases, chairs, lamps, lawn furniture—the works.

On this particular morning, he was not alone. Another man had descended the ladder to the bottom of the bin and was sorting his way through the things that people had left behind. He was an old man, well into his seventies, with a scruffy white beard and a wild, uncombed mane of hair. He wore a beat-up black leather jacket, filthy corduroy trousers and work boots. His vintage motorcycle, complete with sidecar, was parked nearby, leather helmet and goggles hanging from its handlebars.

"It's no mm-rr-McDougal's House of Horrors," the old man growled up at him. "But it'll do, wouldn't you say?"

"Excuse me?" Mitch responded, frowning at him.

The old man sported a mouthful of crooked teeth ranging in color from yellow to brown to black. He sounded as if he were gargling lumpy mashed potatoes. Plus he reeked of whiskey. "Well, you're Mitchell Berger, aren't you?" he demanded, staring up at Mitch with eyes that were shockingly clear and blue and lit with intensity.

"Why, yes. Yes, I am."

"Sure you are. Recognized you from mm-rr-your picture. Only writer worth reading in the whole damned paper. Rest of 'em are a bunch of bed wetters and suck-ups. Well, did you or did you not write that *Abbott and Costello Meet Frankenstein* was your all-time favorite Halloween film?"

"I-I did . . ." Mitch stammered, stunned. It had just hit him. He had not happened upon just any old wino. The old man standing down in that bin was Dorset's most famous and reclusive resident, Wendell Frye, the man who had single-handedly redefined modern American sculpture. Andy Warhol had transformed a Campbell's soup can into art. Wendell Frye had done the same for the automobile hub-cap. His towering, breathtaking scrap-metal sculptures graced plazas and parks throughout the world, his name echoing alongside that of Alexander Calder, Isamu Noguchi and Ellsworth Kelly. He was a giant, a genius. He was also someone who hated prying eyes, publicity, critics and virtu-ally anything to do with the art world. Wendell Frye hadn't granted an interview in at least twenty years. If the art critic from Mitch's paper somehow got a chance to meet him she would, well, plotz. And here Mitch was standing in a Dump-ster talking to him about Abbott and Costello.

"Must have seen that movie fifty times," the old man muttered, fishing an unfiltered Lucky Strike from a rumpled pack in his leather jacket. His hands were huge and knobby and scarred. He lit his cigarette with a battered Zippo lighter and pulled on it deeply, setting off a cough that seemed to rumble up from the pit of his stomach. "I love when they're searching for the mm-rr-monster down in Dracula's dun-geon. Those wonderful slimy walls and cobwebs." He seemed quite chatty for a recluse, Mitch couldn't help but notice. "And then when part of the wall swivels around and Bud finds himself in that secret chamber with Karloff."

"Strange," Mitch spoke up.

"It's hilarious is what it is!"

"No, no. I mean it's not Boris Karloff playing Franken-stein's monster in that movie. It's Glenn Strange."

Wendell Frye peered up at him, befuddled. "You're kid-ding me."

"I never kid about credits, Mr. Frye."

"Christ, don't call me *that*." The great artist seemed genuinely hurt, as if he'd extended his big hand in friendship and Mitch had slapped it away. "It's Hangtown."

"Okay, sure," Mitch said, smiling at him. "As in a Hangtown Fry—bacon, eggs and oysters, am I right?"

"So you know your eats, too," he said approvingly.

"You don't get a shape like mine by nibbling on rice cakes and parsley."

"I sure do love that movie." The old geezer was still talking about Abbott and Costello. "Love dungeons and secret passageways of all kinds."

"If that's the case, then you ought to check out an old Charlie Chan picture called *Castle in the Desert*."

"Is that the one where Douglass Dumbrille wears that mask over one side of his face to cover his scars?"

Mitch raised his eyebrows, impressed. It wasn't often that the name Douglass Dumbrille came up in conversation anymore. Not even in the critic's section on the flight back from Sundance.

Hangtown flicked his cigarette away and went back to pawing through the trash bin. "You mm-rr-might enjoy my house. It's rigged with all sorts of secret passageways and chambers. They used to hide slaves there back in the days of the Underground Railroad. Emma Teasman owned it then."

"The poet?"

"That's the one. My great-grandmother. Mind you, I've made a number of modifications and I've put in . . . Aha!!!" he exclaimed suddenly. He'd found himself a bent-up old rooftop television aerial. It must have been eight feet high when it was intact. It was still plenty large. "A monument if ever I saw one!" he proclaimed, hoisting the ruined aerial up in Mitch's general direction.

"A monument to what?" Mitch grabbed it by the other end and yanked it up onto the ground.

"To when the one-eyed monster was king," Hangtown replied, starting his way slowly up the ladder out of the Dumpster. "It's not anymore. That damned Internet's the big boss now. Point and click. Point and click. Now the nincompoops are buying crap they don't need without even getting up off the sofa. Hate those damned computers. Only good thing about 'em is they killed television—except for *Celebrity Deathmatch* on MTV, of course. Ever watch it?"

"You bet. Martha Stewart removed Sandra Bernhardt's inner organs with an ice cream scoop last time I saw it."

"So you have cable at your house?" the old man inquired slyly.

"Why, yes. Don't you?"

"Nope. Still aren't wired out by us." Hangtown reached the top of the ladder and climbed out, wheezing. He was a big, lumbering old man, at least six feet three, and he had a lot of trouble moving. "I'd love to get me a satellite dish. But then I'd never do a thing except sit and watch old movies all day. Hey, what are you looking for down here anyway, Big Mitch?"

"A bucket to hold my kindling."

"Hell, got some old copper apple-butter tubs in my barn. Fix you right up."

"That's awfully generous of you, Hangtown."

"The hell it is. You'll pay me for it."

"Why, sure," Mitch said hastily. "How much did you have in mind?"

"I need you to take this aerial home for me. Won't fit in my sidecar."

"You've got yourself a deal," Mitch said, glancing admiringly at Wendell Frye's antique ride. "That's quite some old bike."

"It's a 1936 Chief," Hangtown said, as the two of them deposited the aerial on the tarp in the back of Mitch's truck. "Manufactured right up the mm-rr-road in Springfield by the Indian Motorcycle Company. Found her in a barn in Higganum a few years back. Cylinders still had the original nickel plating." He climbed slowly on and donned his leather helmet and goggles, cackling at him. "*Spiral Staircase* was another good one. Remember that eye in the peephole? Man, that's the good stuff! Who was the villain in that?"

"George Brent."

"George Brent! Whatever happened to him?"

"He died."

Hangtown shook his huge white head at Mitch. "Wish people would stop doing that. Makes me wonder if it might happen to me someday."

"You think it won't?" Mitch found himself asking.

"I don't *think* at all, Big Mitch," the great artist roared, kick-starting the bike's engine. It caught right away, spewing clouds of thick exhaust in the morning air. "*Thinking* is what kills you. Christ, didn't you know that?"

CHAPTER 2

Ohh . . . Ohhh . . . Ohhhh . . .

They were at it again up on the third floor. Those damned Sealy Posturepedic gymnasts in the room right above hers. They'd been humping away up there nonstop every night for the past week, that bed of theirs shaking like a washing machine in its final spin cycle.

Ohh . . . Ohhh . . . Ohhhh . . .

Whoever *she* was, she was not quiet. Her love cry was plaintive, the cry of a sad young girl. As for *him*, Des hadn't heard the man make one single sound yet. Assuming that it even was a man up there. Because if there was one thing Des Mitry had learned so far in life, it was this: Never assume.

Ohh . . . Ohhh . . . Ohhhh . . .

Thoroughly wide-awake now, she flicked on her bedside lamp and fumbled for her heavy horn-rimmed glasses, the ones that were forever sliding down her nose. It was 4 A.M., according to the clock on the nightstand, and more than anything in the whole wide world she wished she were in her own bed in her own home. But that was not possible—the renovations on her new place still hadn't been completed. In fact, every single aspect of the job was taking twice as long as the contractor had said it would. She knew this was normal. But knowing it didn't make it any less aggravating. Besides, it was just plain impossible to get comfortable in a new job in a new town when everything she owned was in

storage and she was sleeping—make that *trying* to sleep—in
a strange bed. Even if it was a damned canopied bed.

Ohh . . . Ohhh . . . Ohhhh . . .

The inn was fine, really. Except for those damned
X-games upstairs, of course. But they weren't the real reason why she was awake. After four years at West Point, Des
could sleep through a carpet bombing. No, it was the wondering. Wondering if she'd made the right decision when she
gave up a job she was good at to chase after something she
really loved, but—let's face it—might be no good at at all.
Wondering about this new, highly unlikely relationship she
was in with a pigment-challenged man who sometimes
made her feel as giddy as a schoolgirl and other times just
plain scared to death.

It was entirely possible, Des realized, that this was the
happiest she'd ever been in her life. It was also entirely possible that she had completely lost her mind.

Ohh . . . Ohhh . . . Ohhhh . . .

She got up and put on her sweatpants and started in on
her homework exercises. A succession of hand and wrist
studies by Dürer to be copied out of Robert Beverly Hale's
Anatomy Lessons of the Great Masters. Des was studying
figure drawing two evenings a week at the world-renowned
Dorset Academy of Fine Arts, one of the only institutions in
America that still taught art the same painstaking way the
Renaissance masters had learned it—line by line, stroke by
stroke, with serious attention to craft and a refreshing absence of baloney. One night a week they worked with a
model, the other they studied perspective and anatomy. Paul
Weiss, her professor, was so serious about anatomy that he
had taken them to the morgue at Yale–New Haven Hospital
to watch medical students dissect cadavers. Not that Des had
needed to tag along. She knew what was underneath the skin
only too well—violent death was what had driven her to the
drawing pad in the first place. In fact, when Paul got a look
at her portfolio of murder victims he became so disturbed
that he fled the studio and vomited. When he returned, looking exceedingly pale, he'd asked her if he could show her

portfolio to some other faculty members. She let him, naturally. Now they all stared at her, wide-eyed, when she strode the corridors with her drawing pad and tackle box filled with charcoals.

They did not know what to make of her. She was not like the others.

Ohh . . . Ohhh . . . Ohhhh . . .

Seated on the edge of the bed, she went to work diligently replicating Dürer's intricate hatchings and cross-hatchings. She worked in pencil, focusing her considerable attention on the flexor tendons of the palmaris longus, transfixed by how, *somehow,* each line articulated tendon and sinew and bone, how the human wrist slowly came to three-dimensional life on the drawing pad in her lap. It was sheer magic.

And, God, was it ever fun.

Shortly after five she heard a door open upstairs, then a low murmur of voices, followed by light footsteps on the stairs. A woman's footsteps. The moaner was leaving. Des could get back to sleep now, if she desired. But she was so totally into her work that sleep was the farthest thing from her mind.

At six she stowed her homework, did fifteen minutes of stretching and made her bed, pulling the corners tight. The housekeeper would happily have done that for her, but Des did not feel right about having someone else pick up after her. It was her bed. That made it her mess. When she was done she put on her New Balances and a fleece pullover and headed downstairs.

Outside, the early-morning air was crisp and clean. She inhaled it deeply, enjoying the country quiet, her eyes still seeing the lines and shapes from her drawing pad in the dewy meadow before her. She walked, her stride swift and sure. Des was six feet tall, lithe, long-stemmed and high-rumped. When she wore tight jeans she could cause fender benders. Up Frederick Lane she strode, past the historic homes that backed up on the Connecticut River. One narrow dirt drive led its way back to a goat farm, another to a llama ranch. Occasionally, there were new houses, houses so huge and gaudy that they stuck out like the gold teeth in a gang-banger's mouth.

A milkman passed by in his delivery truck. He waved to her. Otherwise, she saw no one. A mile up the road she turned in at Uncas Lake and made her way around it to her new place. It was a snug little two-bedroom cape on a hilltop with a great view of the lake and, best of all, incredible light. The living room, where she intended to set up her easel, had skylights and floor-to-ceiling windows. And it was hers. All hers. Gazing at it, Des positively tingled with excitement.

This is my house.

The price had been right, too. Of course, it had needed a whole lot of work. A new roof. New kitchen. New furnace. New wood floors, plaster, paint. Plus the back deck was all rotted out. A young contractor named Tim Keefe, who was Dorset's assistant fire chief, was handling the whole thing. She'd hired Tim because he knew the local workmen, and she was way too busy.

Trouble was, so were they. Everything was half-completed. The roofers, who were supposed to have been done a week ago, still hadn't even finished stripping the old shingles off. In place of a roof she had a festive blue tarp held in place by two-by-fours. She unlocked the front door and moseyed inside, fearing the worst. And encountering it—her floors had not been polyurethaned yet either. Damn. Tim would never be done by Friday. She had hoped to be all moved in by then—Friday was the Deacon's birthday. This could get complicated, she reflected anxiously.

Way complicated.

By seven Des was back at the inn eating her Grape-Nuts with banana and skim milk in the quaint dining room. She still wore her fleece sweats, since once she got dressed for work she scared the hell out of people. As she ate she found herself glancing around at her fellow guests, wondering once again about the identity of her indefatigable upstairs gymnasts.

It had been a gradual process of elimination. The first night she'd heard them, a young power couple from New

York had been staying there, eager to impress everyone in the place, especially each other. Des had been positive they were the ones, but they left the next morning and the X-games continued. Next her suspicion had fallen on a honeymoon couple. The man did look like a computer nerd, and his bride was as plain as milk, but appearance was no measuring stick for ardor. Age was, however, and the honeymooners were well into their sixties. Des doubted that they could keep up such a torrid pace night after night, Viagra or not.

Now that she'd heard those light footsteps on the stairs this morning, her suspicions fell elsewhere—on two single men who had been staying at the Frederick House all along.

One was Colin Falconer, the school superintendent. If Des had been told that Colin was the town pastor, she would have believed it. He was a gentle soul in his early forties, with a shy, kindly manner. Very tall and thin, almost stork-like, with cheeks like polished apples and neatly brushed ginger-colored hair. Behind his rimless glasses Colin's eyes were earnest and sincere. He was very popular with the kids in town. Played the banjo at school assemblies. Took the Cub Scouts out to Peck Point to see the piping plovers. Colin was also an ardent environmentalist who rode his bicycle to school every day, dressed in a tweed jacket and corduroy trousers, a jaunty red knit scarf wrapped around his throat. Colin was staying at the Frederick House because he and his wife, Greta, were presently separated. Des was not up on the details.

The other single man in residence was someone Des did not know. He was a big, weather-beaten man in his thirties, muscular and ruggedly handsome, with uncombed straw-colored hair, crinkly blond hairs on his big arms and no wedding ring on his finger. He looked as if he did some kind of outdoor work. He also seemed very chilly and standoffish. He did not smile or say good morning when he came down for breakfast every morning, generally clad in a polo shirt and jeans. Just sat there pecking away at the small laptop computer that he brought down with him every morning, his eyes rarely leaving its screen. Des did not like his face. It was a hard face, a user's face. Her money was on him. Possibly he was bonking one of the housekeepers or waitresses. He was certainly the type that a pliant, not-too-bright small-town girl would go for.

"*Nu,* did your roofer finish yet?" Bella Tillis plopped down in the chair opposite Des now, dressed in a sweatshirt and knit pants.

"Girl, I am not even going to answer that," Des grumbled back at her.

"You know what your problem is, Desiree? And I say this with nothing but love in my heart . . ." Bella paused to pour herself some herbal tea from the pot on the table. "You are too nice."

"So that's it," Des said, smiling at her.

Bella was a short, feisty, entirely round widow from Brooklyn in her seventies with four grown children, eight grandchildren and nine million causes. She'd lived next door to Des in Woodbridge. After the breakup with Brandon, Bella had rescued her. Brought her homemade mushroom-barley soup. Dragged her out on her feral-cat rescue patrol every morning. Des quickly became ardently devoted to saving the strays—it is a known fact in pet rescue circles that people who are trying to save stray animals are really trying to save themselves. Staking out supermarket dumpsters together in the pre-dawn cold, the two of them had become unexpectedly close. Bella was her best friend now. "If you want results," she declared, stabbing the air with a stubby finger, "you've got to kick some *tuchos.*"

"I try to treat people with respect."

"You see, that's where you're wrong. Tim's not *people.* He's a *contractor.*"

"What's up with you today?" Des asked, to get her off of the subject.

Bella took a loud slurp of her tea and sat back in her chair, shaking her head in disgust. "I'm looking at more places, if I can get a realtor to return one of my calls." When Des relocated to Dorset, Bella decided she would, too. Her house in Woodbridge was on the market, and she was in town house-hunting. Or trying. "But I'm getting nowhere fast. I *finally* got through to that realtor on Dorset Street, that Takai Frye. Know what she did when I told her my price range? She laughed at me. Can you imagine the nerve?" The waitress brought Bella her All-Bran and berries. Bella thanked her and got busy with it. "What kind of a name is Takai Frye anyway?" she demanded, munching. "Sounds like a Polynesian fast food dish. No, no, this is hopeless. If I pay the going rate for what they call a starter home around here I'll have nothing left to leave my grandkids. Not one penny."

"So why don't you just rent something?"

"I can't. There's nothing. And what landlord would be willing to put up with our cats?" Bella presently had nineteen boarders looking for good homes—eight in her garage, eleven in her basement.

"The cats can come live with me," Des assured her. "And so can you. My guest bedroom is yours for as long as you like."

"Desiree, I appreciate the offer. Truly, I do. But rooming with you is not an option. For one thing—and I can tell you this because we have no secrets from each other—I snore in the night. Late in our marriage, Morris took to sleeping in Abe's room at the far end of the hall, *with* the door closed, *wearing* earplugs. Besides which, you're young and gorgeous and you're in love with a nice Jewish boy who treats you like a princess."

"Um, okay, I think you're confusing us with another couple."

Bella raised an eyebrow at her impishly. "Am I? How so?"

"Well, for starters, the aforementioned L-word has not exactly arisen."

"Well, something has," Bella cracked. "Or should I say *someone*."

"Bella, you are being bad today. Better ease off of that All-Bran."

"My point is you don't want some fat old broad around the house when you two want to have wild sex on the kitchen floor at one o'clock in the afternoon."

"Okay, now I *know* you're confusing us with another couple." Des finished off her cereal, dabbing at her mouth with her napkin. "Actually, we aren't even a *couple* yet, per se."

"Tie that bull outside, as we used to say on Nostrand Avenue. Are you seeing anyone else?"

"You know I'm not."

"Is he?"

"Not if he wants to remain among the walking and talking."

"So what's the problem?"

"Who says there's a problem?"

Bella didn't respond, just stared at her intently from across the table.

Des sighed. "The problem is that I am *so* not in control of my emotions."

"Congratulations. That means you're someone who's in love."

"*Or* a candidate to be a serial killer. Bella, this is a vastly more insidious creature than I've ever encountered before. The man keeps doing deplorable things to me. Like when I was packing up my house last week, feeling bluer than blue, he shows up out of nowhere with a bunch of wildflowers he'd picked from his yard. You know what he said to me? He said that they reminded him of the color of my eyes in the candlelight. Shut up, that is *so* not fair . . ." Come to think of it, they *had* ended up on her kitchen floor that afternoon. "I mean, no one is that sweet. I keep waiting for the other shoe to drop. Which you know it will. If he's human. Only, he's *not* human. He's straight out of one of his horror movies— The Stepford Boyfriend. Except he doesn't cook, unless you count that damned American chop suey of his, which I sure as hell don't."

Bella reached across the table and grabbed Des's hand in her Vulcan death grip. "Listen to me, Desiree, all men are animals."

"Tell me something I don't already know."

"Some are wolves. Some are asses . . ."

"I repeat, tell me—"

"Mitch Berger is a bunny rabbit."

Des instantly softened, her face breaking into a silly smile. "Isn't he? I just melt into a puddle when I'm around him."

"Do you want to know what your problem is?"

"Aside from the fact that you're breaking my hand?"

Bella released her. "You have no faith in happiness. People without faith are lonely, bitter people, my dear. You are not such a person. Tell me, it's not the sex, is it?"

"No, that part is fine. More than fine. The best."

"Speaking of which . . ." Bella leaned over the table toward her. "Any idea who our moaner is?"

Des glanced at her sharply. "You can hear her, too?"

"Tattela, they can hear her in Flatbush."

"Good morning, ladies," interjected Colin Falconer, who stood there before them with a shy smile on his long, rather pinched face. Colin wore a pair of birdwatcher's glasses around his neck and clutched a brown-bag lunch. The innkeepers made one for him every morning. "What a pretty time of year, is it not? I thought I'd ride out to Peck Point to see the terns before school."

"I took a nice long walk myself before breakfast," Des responded, smiling up at him. "It was beautiful."

Colin lingered there, his tongue flicking nervously across his thin, dry lips. "I'm guilty of having a terribly awkward question for you," he murmured at Des.

"Go right ahead."

"I was wondering . . . That is, are you hearing *noises* in the night?"

"Do you mean like animals?"

"Of a sort," he said, reddening.

"You, too?" Bella exclaimed, beaming at him conspiratorially.

"I haven't slept all week," Colin blurted out. "It's so unsettling. I don't suppose it would be appropriate to have the innkeeper ask them to enjoy themselves a little less . . . enthusiastically."

"It's not as if they're breaking any laws," Des said, her eyes falling on that blond hunk of muscle seated by himself across the room, tearing into a plate of blueberry pancakes and sausages. She couldn't tell if he was hearing what they were saying or not. He gave no sign of it. "I guess we'll just have to live with it."

"I guess we will," Colin said ruefully before he headed out the door to fetch his bike.

It was time for Des to get moving, too. She went upstairs and stripped and jumped in the shower. She didn't take long in the bathroom. She kept her hair short and nubby these days, and had never been into war paint. Never needed it, really. She had almond-shaped green eyes, a smooth complexion, a wraparound smile that could melt titanium.

Her charcoal-gray trousers were cut full for comfort. The contrasting stripe that ran down the outside seam was royal blue with yellow piping, same as the epaulets on her light gray shirt. Her necktie was that same shade of royal blue, her tie clasp gold, her square-toed oxfords black and gleaming. She tucked her shirt neatly into her trousers, found her horn-rimmed glasses on the dresser and wiped them clean and put them on. Then she unlocked the dresser drawer that she kept under padlock and key. Inside was her crime girl kit—her nameplate and badge, her eight-pound black leather belt complete with radio, her holstered Sig-Sauer semiautomatic weapon.

The last but by no means least thing Des put on was her great big Smokey the Bear hat. Armed, dressed and dangerous, Resident Trooper Desiree Mitry of Dorset—formerly Lieutenant Desiree Mitry of the Major Crime Squad, the highest-ranking black female homicide investigator in the entire history of the Connecticut State Police—headed out the door to perform her first official duty of the day:

Directing traffic outside of Center School.

CHAPTER 3

Hangtown led Mitch home on Dunn's Road, which twisted its way through a cluster of old, family-run dairy farms. These were genuine working farms, complete with silos and animals and fragrant smells.

And they were an endangered species.

Even over the flatulent *putt-putting* of Hangtown's vintage motorcycle Mitch could hear the big bulldozers flattening a nearby stretch of forest. And then he could see them—they were like giant, grotesque yellow insects devouring the landscape in starved bites. A tastefully lettered billboard announced that this soon-to-be ex-forest was soon-to be "*Sweet Hollow Farms, a Bruce Leanse Concept for Living*, featuring 23 Grand Manor homes." Mitch had seen the glowing ad for the development in his paper's real estate section. Each home, it promised, would enjoy its own seven-acre wooded parcel, classic architecture, handcrafted detail. Floor plans ranged in size from 5,800 to 7,600 square feet.

Prices *started* at $1.35 million.

As the great Wendell Frye wheeled past the workmen on his Indian Chief, cutting quite the raffish figure in his leather helmet and goggles, several of them waved and gave him appreciative thumbs-up.

In response, he treated them to a good look at his own upraised middle finger.

Dunn's Road ran into Route 156 at the crossroads at Winston Farms. Hangtown crossed over onto Old Ferry Road, scooting past the proposed site of the new elementary school. Mitch followed. Just before Old Ferry Road ran smack into the Connecticut River, the old man turned in at a private dirt road called Lord's Cove Lane, sending a flock of wild turkeys scattering. Lord's Cove bumped its way a half mile or so deep into the woods before it broke into a clearing marked by two twenty-foot-high totem poles made of junked personal computers stacked one atop the other and spray painted Day-Glo orange.

As they passed in between these they were met by a forty-foot-tall grasshopper made of fenders and hubcaps, a Wendell Frye creation that stood guard over several acres of meadow filled with junked cars and buses, stacks of bicycles, airplane propellers, dinged-up aluminum garden furniture, bedsprings, rain gutters—a virtual junkyard, or it would have been if it weren't also home to dozens of immense, half-completed Wendell Frye mobiles and whirligigs that had been left to rust in the tall weeds along with everything else.

Around a bend they approached a rambling center-chimney colonial that backed right up onto the river, affording it a panoramic view across the marshes all the way to Essex. The house had been added on to numerous times and painted the brightest shade of pink Mitch had ever seen. Or maybe it was just that he'd never seen a historic home that was painted hot pink before. An ancient, tan-colored Land Rover was parked out front, alongside a Toyota pickup and a spanking-new red Porsche 911 Turbo.

A German shepherd started streaking toward Hangtown's motorcycle from the front porch, barking with unbridled glee. Two women immediately came out of the house, gesturing frantically at Hangtown, who waved and kept right on going, the dog sprinting alongside of him. Mitch followed. The dirt road took them past a row of sagging one-room cottages, past apple and pear orchards, past a fenced meadow with sheep. Past a chicken coop, a pigsty, a vegetable garden.

They finally pulled up alongside a huge old barn, which

was also painted hot pink, the shepherd hopping into its master's sidecar, tail thumping.

"This is an amazing place," Mitch marveled as he got out of his truck.

"You should see it after the first snow," Hangtown wheezed, yanking off his helmet and goggles. "You'd swear you'd gone to heaven."

"You believe in heaven?" Mitch asked him.

"Of course I do, Big Mitch. All children believe in heaven."

Mitch dropped the tailgate of the truck, the big dog sniffing at the cat scent on his legs. Back at the house, one of the women started determinedly across the meadow toward them.

"Not that any of this is really mine," Hangtown went on. "My granddad married into it. Plundered himself a local girl with good Teasman bloodlines and no damned sense. Hell, she mm-rr-married an *artist*." Wendell Frye was a third-generation Dorset artist. It was his grandfather, an eminent landscape painter, who founded the Dorset Academy. His father, also a fine painter, ran it for many years. "There's eight hundred acres in all. My dad nearly lost it to the tax man when I was a boy, but it's still ours. And it'll stay ours as long as there's enough fools out there who'll pay good cash money for my contraptions. The developers would love to get their hands on it. All they see is the dollar signs. Me, I see what granddad saw—the freshwater tidal marsh with osprey and great blues, the eagles nesting in our cliffs. He used to come out here from the city every summer to paint them. That's what those cottages were for," Hangtown explained, waving at the little bungalows. "Painters lived in 'em. Nowadays, I've got Jim Bolan in residence. You'll like Big Jim. A part of him died in 'Nam, but he does honest work with his hands. Been helping me with my contraptions since he got out of prison. These old hands aren't what they used to be."

The antenna was not heavy, just clumsy. They eased it out of the truck and started toward the barn with it, Mitch wondering just exactly what Jim Bolan had been in prison for.

"Got my two beautiful daughters living here, too," Hangtown added. "They can do any of the farm chores need doing. I taught 'em to hunt, fish, change a tire, you name it. Moose—not a soul calls her Mary Susan—Moose took to it more than Takai. Does most of the farm chores. Now Moose is the one for you, if you want to plant your seed in some fine, fertile soil. She'll make you jump through hoops for it. She's a full-time practicing virgin, but she's—"

"Hangtown, I'm really not looking to—"

"A big healthy brown-skinned girl, just like her mother was. Loves children. Makes all of her own clothes, pickles, bread. Can slaughter a pig. Hell, she could probably take out your appendix on the kitchen table if she had to."

"It's already out," said Mitch, reflecting on just how different it was in Dorset than in the city. Here, he regularly came in contact with people who could *do* things. In New York no one knew how to do anything except express their opinions, loudly.

"Mind you, Takai will catch your eye first," Hangtown pointed out. "Get your blood to boiling."

"She's the realtor, right?" Mitch had seen her sign on Dorset Street.

"She's a serial destroyer of men, is what she is. Nothing but teeth and claws. Stay clear of her, Big Mitch. Her mother was half-Japanese, half-Hawaiian, and all she-devil. I married Kiki after Moose's mother, Gentle Kate, got sick and passed away . . ." Hangtown's lined face broke into a sudden scowl behind the beard, his piercing blue eyes very far away. "Then I lost Kiki, too."

"She died?"

"She left us. Died out in California. Kiki's death . . . it was very sudden. I raised the girls myself. It's just been we three for a long, long time."

They made their way inside the big barn now and dropped the antenna on the dirt floor next to an old potbellied wooden stove. Mitch gazed around in pure, wide-eyed wonderment. He was actually inside Wendell Frye's studio, the very place where the master created his works of art. It was like being inside the cluttered workshop of a gifted and mad Santa Claus. There were tin snips, cutting tools, shaping tools and welding torches of every conceivable type on his workbench. There were bins filled with hubcaps and fenders. There were deep-sea-diver's helmets, boat propellers, copper pipes and elbow joints, bales of wire, rolls of copper flashing. There were mobiles in the shapes of birds and animals and planets hanging from the beams overhead. A ladder led up to a loft where there was even more stuff.

Mitch was enthralled. "How will you use this?" he asked Hangtown, meaning the antenna. "What will it be?"

"I collect things," the old master replied, shrugging his heavy shoulders. "And I collect ideas. Sometimes the two connect up, sometimes they don't. I have very little say in the matter. Most people don't believe me when I tell 'em that. I'm sure you do."

Mitch nodded dumbly, wondering why Wendell Frye had so much confidence in him. They'd known each other less an hour. Now he heard footsteps approaching.

"Father, where have you *been*?" a young woman demanded from the doorway.

"Foraging. And now I'm going to show my friend around."

"Well, you'll just have to show him around later," she lectured him, as if he were an unruly child. "You'll be late for your appointment."

Hangtown waved her off. "Moose, my dear, say hello to Mitch Berger, an honest writer and one hell of an Abbott and Costello fan. You might consider taking him into your bed. You could do a lot worse."

Moose was a tall, strongly built woman in her early thirties. She had her father's piercing blue eyes. A face and hands that were weathered by outdoor work. Ash-blond hair that was gathered up in a bun. Her homemade denim jumper and wool cardigan lent her a dowdy, Swiss-peasant sort of look. She was not homely but she was not exactly pretty either. She had too much chin and way too many worry lines. She seemed like someone who was accustomed to carrying a considerable burden. Possibly Mitch had just met him.

"You'll have to forgive my father, Mitch," she said, gripping his hand firmly. Her manner, like her gaze, was direct and no-nonsense. "He's of that age where he says whatever comes into his head, just like one of my second graders. He's always wandering off, too. Father, you *can't* just take off without telling us. Jim's been waiting to take you to the doctor."

"Now where are those apple-butter tubs . . . ?" Hangtown muttered, ignoring her completely as he clumped his way over toward the loft ladder. "I always pay my honest debts."

"Father, you were supposed to be in New Haven at eight o'clock. Father, be careful up there! Father . . . ?"

"Damned doctors," Hangtown groused as he made his way slowly up the ladder. "What's he going to tell me I don't already know? I need a new hip, two new knees. Got to stop smoking and drinking—if I don't I'm going to die. Well, guess what? I'm going to be taking myself a nice long dirt nap any day now, and there's not a goddamned thing anyone can do about it except grab a shovel."

"Please don't talk that way," she said fretfully. "You know I don't like it. Father . . . ?" Moose followed him up into the loft, sighing with exasperation.

As the two of them began thudding around up there Mitch heard another set of footsteps approach. And now Wendell Frye's other daughter came striding across the dirt floor toward Mitch, who immediately drew in his breath.

Takai Frye wasn't just pretty. She was exotically, stunningly beautiful—without a doubt the sexiest woman he had ever been face to face with in his life. And he was someone who had interviewed Uma Thurman. Takai was uncommonly tall, slim and long-limbed. And decidedly Asian, with gleaming slanted eyes, silken skin, a perfect rosebud mouth and a face that was all angles and planes and cheekbones. She wore her jet-black hair cropped at her chin, her nails long and painted black. Her thumbs were unusually long and narrow, more like index fingers than thumbs. She wore a shearling jacket that must have cost three thousand dollars over a black turtleneck sweater, stirrup pants and ankle boots. She carried a black leather appointment book in one hand, a cell phone in the other.

"Well, well, I have to admit you're a cut above the usual skeegie characters the old man drags home." Takai spoke in a clipped, somewhat mocking manner, as if there were invisible quote marks around everything. She possessed major attitude. Clearly, she was used to being smarter, richer and prettier than anyone else she came in contact with. "At least in outward appearance you are," she continued, circling Mitch as if he were a farm animal at auction. "You've shaved, run a comb through your hair. You have a decent, relatively clean sweater on. You're amply fed . . ." She poked him indelicately in the tummy with a talon. "More than amply, in fact." Now she gave him a final once-over, a probing examination that seemed to scan the size of his IQ, bank balance and sexual equipment. "Yes, I would say you're a cut or two above his usual dump crowd."

"In Dorset we don't say 'dump,'" Mitch pointed out. "We say recyclable waste transfer station."

Takai drew back, raising an eyebrow at him haughtily. "I suppose he promised you that you could stay in one of the cottages for as long as you like, free of charge. And that one of his two—count 'em two—lusty daughters would make passionate love to you in the night. Cook you a hot breakfast. Mend your filthy socks. Well, forget it, Buster Brown. None of that is ever going to happen."

"The subject of bearing my round, healthy children also came up. At least I think it did—he mentioned the word *seed*."

Takai peered at him suspiciously. "You don't *sound* like his usual swamp Yankee either. I'm beginning to think that we have a case of mistaken identity."

"In movies, they call this a meet-cute," Mitch said. "Honestly, I just brought an antenna home for him, is all. And I already have a home of my own on Big Sister, an apartment in New York, a job, a book contract, an investment portfolio and . . ." Mitch trailed off, wondering why he was trying to justify himself to Takai Frye. She'd instantly gotten under his skin, that was why. "And I know how to mend my own socks."

Overhead, Hangtown and Moose were still thudding around in the loft, sending trickles of dust down upon them.

"Wait, I know who *you* are," Takai exclaimed, switching her thermostat all the way from icy to toasty warm. "You're Mitchell Berger. I've *heard* of you. Christ, who hasn't? You're one of our local celebrities. I'm Takai. It's so great to finally *meet* you. And I'm really sorry if I seemed bitchy, but Father needs protecting." She pulled a slim black leather card case out of her jacket pocket and handed him her business card. "When you outgrow that starter cottage of yours, and you will, call me, okay? I'm the number-one property mover in town."

"I'm not going anywhere," Mitch said, shaking his head at her.

"Nonsense," she insisted, looking at him through her eyelashes. "There's no room there for you to expand."

"I don't want to expand. My goal in life is to get smarter, not bigger, and I . . . Why are you staring at me like I have three heads?"

"Do you have *any* idea what would happen to our society if everyone were like you?" Takai demanded.

"Yes, we'd all be a lot better off."

"Wrong! Upward mobility is the American dream. God, if everyone was *happy* with what they had, our economy would utterly collapse. We'd have breadlines." Her cell phone rang now, cutting her off. "Yes, yes?" she barked into it. "Fine, not a problem. I'll show them where to plant it . . . I know . . . I'll be right there. Ten minutes." She shut it off and turned back to Mitch, shaking her pretty head. "You have no idea how demanding these new power nesters can be. They want it all and they want it now. My God, they think nothing of spending fifty thousand on a trophy tree. A *tree*."

Mitch couldn't tell if she was disgusted by this or awed. Possibly she was both. He also found himself wondering about her. With her looks, famous name and obvious ambition, Takai Frye could write her own ticket in New York, Los Angeles, anywhere. Why was she still here in sleepy little Dorset?

Hangtown was making his way back down the ladder now, clutching a battered copper bucket in one hand. "Don't let princess sell you a house, Big Mitch."

"He won't," Takai objected, pouting. "He's decidedly un-American."

"I know, that's why I like him." Hangtown handed him the bucket. It was solid and heavy, and would fetch real money at an antique store. "That do the trick?"

"Perfectly, but are you sure you can spare it?"

"He has seven more just like it up there," Moose said wearily, descending the ladder. "Father, you have to leave right now or you'll be late."

"I guess that tour will have to wait, Big Mitch," Hangtown said apologetically. "Hey, how about tonight? Can you come over for dinner?"

"I'd like that very much."

"Outstanding! Bring a girl. You got a girl?"

Takai let out a sharp laugh. "Of course he does, Father. Haven't you heard?" Clearly she had.

This was the downside of small-town life, Mitch reflected. Being talked about behind your back by people you didn't even know. "As a matter of fact I do, but she's tied up tonight."

"Too bad," said Hangtown. "Come stag, then. Maybe you'll get lucky."

"Father!" scolded Moose.

A crusty old hippie appeared in the barn doorway now. He had a graying ponytail, a wisp of a beard, eyes that were bloodshot and suspicious, skin that was sunburned and leathery. Cords of muscle stuck out on his wrists. It was impossible to place his age. Mitch guessed he was somewhere between fifty and sixty-five. He wore a filthy denim jacket, torn jeans and oil-stained work boots. In a sheath on his belt he carried a large knife. "Let's get it on, Chief," he said to Hangtown in a rasping voice. "Else we won't beat the rush-hour traffic over the bridge."

"Not you, too," Hangtown said sourly. "Say hello to Mitch, Big Jim."

"How ya doing, man?" Jim Bolan, the ex-con, said guardedly.

"You got our smokes, Big Jim?" Hangtown asked him.

"In the truck," Jim responded, shooing the old man out the door. "Let's go, Chief. C'mon, c'mon . . ."

And out the barn door they went, followed closely by Takai, who was in a hurry to see a man about a tree.

Mitch was left there alone with Moose. "I don't really have to come for dinner," he said. "I don't want to impose on you."

"No, not at all," she said quickly. Now that it was just the two of them, she seemed a bit uncomfortable. "You're invited. Please come."

Mitch stood there looking around at Wendell Frye's workshop. "I'm having a little trouble believing that this is really happening."

"That's a common misconception. My father's not as reclusive as everyone thinks. He's simply reached a point in his life where he believes that very few people are worth knowing. He's eighty-three years old. He has no time left to waste. And he has an instinct about people. I call it his smell test. Most people fail it. You passed."

The two of them headed back outside. The old Land Rover was still parked in front of the historic hot pink house. The pickup truck and Porsche were gone. The Porsche was Takai's, not that Mitch had doubted it for a moment.

"It sure is pink, isn't it?" he said, gazing at the house.

"Father likes to do the unexpected. That's what passes for normal around here."

"How come I passed?" Mitch asked her.

"I don't know," Moose replied. "And I probably know that man as well as anyone. The only thing I've ever been able to figure out is that he can't stand anyone who's selling something."

"But everyone is selling something, don't you think?"

"Yes, I do," she said, turning her gaze on Mitch. There was a scrupulous absence of sexuality in her gaze, especially compared to her sister. Or maybe because of her sister. "What are *you* selling, Mitch?"

CHAPTER 4

It was the high schoolers in their Jeep Wranglers who were her biggest headache, Des had come to discover as she stood out there in the middle of Dorset Street with her orange reflector vest on, making her official presence felt.

They were just so jacked up on their hormonal energy and deafening suburban hip-hop that the posted speed limit of twenty-five felt like a baby's crawl. Most of them were doing forty when they hit the high school driveway and that was simply not acceptable, because both the high school and middle school were located directly behind Center School. Dozens of school buses were pulling in and out. Soccer moms in minivans were dropping their kids off. More kids were arriving on their bikes and . . . well, it was a major public safety situation.

Speeding tickets? She'd tried that, but tickets didn't mean a thing to these kids in Dorset. Their parents just paid the tickets for them, same as they paid for everything else. Out of sheer frustration, she'd resorted to this—standing in the damned street—holding some of the traffic up, waving some of it on through, trying to keep it under control and moving. Knowing full well that if the Deacon saw her out there like this he would have himself a stroke.

Christ, all I need is a pair of white gloves and a whistle.

In all honesty, becoming a resident trooper was a bigger adjustment than Des had anticipated. She hadn't just changed jobs—she'd changed careers. She was in community relations now, not law enforcement. Her role was to be a liaison between the state police and this stable gold-coast community that was home to more millionaires per square mile than East Hampton. She handed out free trigger locks for handguns, signed off on fender benders, made sure the kids got home in one piece from their keggers on the beach. If a break-in went down, she picked up the new digital handheld radio that connected her to the Troop F barracks in Westbrook and they took over. Anything hot, Westbrook called Major Crime Squad Central District headquarters in Meriden, her old crew.

Not that she'd had a single hot call yet. In fact, the only ongoing crime problem she'd encountered was a roving late-night gang of high-spirited local boys who liked to spray-paint erect penises on store windows and proudly sign their work—they called themselves the Mod Squad. Lately, they'd also taken to stealing things out of unlocked parked cars. The town fathers were not amused, and Des was under tremendous pressure from First Selectman Paffin to nail them. She was finding leads hard to come by. It was not easy building trust when she was still finding her own way—especially in a village with such a pigment-free population. Face it, Des saw only one face of color all day long—her own in the mirror. Not that anyone had acted unfriendly toward her. It was a very polite town. They respected the uniform. They respected order. It's just that she was *different*. Plus she was a young single woman. She was not going to cultivate local relationships in her off-duty hours by hanging at the barbershop or the fire house swapping fish tales. No, she had to find a new way, a way that suited her.

And fast.

On this particular morning she was presenting DARE awards to a classroom full of Center School second graders. When she was done with traffic detail she unlocked the trunk of her cruiser, stowed her reflector vest and removed one kid-sized DARE baseball jacket and five stuffed animals—the Drug Abuse Resistance Education mascot was a fuzzy lion named Darren. Then she slammed the trunk shut and started up the bluestone path to the front doors.

Center School was a beautiful old building of white-washed brick and granite with a slate roof. There was no metal detector at its front doors. No bars on its windows, no gang markings on its walls. It was a throwback. Which, Des supposed, was why people had such strong feelings for and against it.

She went inside, her big leather belt creaking, and started down a corridor lined with class photographs and Halloween art projects. It had been a long time since she'd been inside a grammar school. It was the smells that struck her the most, those forgotten childhood smells of finger paint, glue and heavy-duty floor cleanser. The principal's office, where she got directions to Miss Frye's room, had a knee-high drinking fountain outside the door. It was a bright, sunny classroom filled with tiny desks for tiny, tiny people. A motto written in big blue letters stretched across the wall over the black-board: A GOOD BOOK IS A GOOD FRIEND.

Miss Frye's second graders were scrubbed, alert and excited, although Des couldn't help but notice that most of them still had their jackets on. Three big windows were thrown wide open and two fans were circulating fresh, chilly morning air throughout the entire room. Miss Frye herself wore only a dowdy cardigan sweater over a blue denim jumper. She was a strongly built farm girl with muscular flanks and a gentle, natural manner with the children. Des wondered if she was one of *the* Fryes.

A photographer from the little shoreline weekly paper was already there, waiting to snap a picture of Des posed with the winners of the class's DARE slogan contest. The five runners-up received Darrens. Ben Leanse, an unusually small boy with an unusually large, bulbous head, got the baseball jacket for his winning slogan: DRUGS ARE FOR SICK PEOPLE.

Miss Frye had chosen the winners. Des was merely there to make the presentation. Mostly, it was a chance for her to interact with them in a setting they were familiar with.

Young children needed to find out that police officers were people they could talk to. Plus Des was exceedingly aware that these sheltered, affluent small-town kids had spent very little time around anyone of color. She wanted them to realize that she was not an alien from a galaxy far, far away.

So, after the photographer took off, she hung out, seated there on the edge of Miss Frye's desk, twirling her big hat in her long, slender fingers.

"Boys and girls, Trooper Mitry has been kind enough to give us a few minutes of her time this morning," Miss Frye said, as they gaped at Des from their desks. "Can anyone tell us what a resident trooper does?"

"Make busts," the Leanse boy spoke up promptly. Poor little guy had a gurgly, adenoidal voice to go with his huge head. "Take down bad guys."

"Ohhh, pumpkin head . . ." a boy in the back row gurgled mockingly, drawing snickers. And an icy look from Miss Frye. "Pumpkin head . . ."

"*Sometimes* I arrest people," Des said. "What else do I do?"

The other kids began to jump in now: "Gunfights and—"

"Car chases!"

"Break down doors and beat people up—"

"Speeding tickets. My dad got one."

"My daddy's pickup truck got broken into," an angelic little blond girl spoke up. "The Mod Squad stole his nail gun and spray-painted a great big wienie on his windshield." This drew more snickers. "You gonna catch 'em?"

"We're working on that real hard," Des replied, pushing her horn-rimmed glasses up her nose. "Do you know what else I do? I help people. That's my job. So if anyone ever has a problem, don't be afraid to call me, okay?"

"You ever kill anyone?" the Leanse boy piped up.

"Ohh, pumpkin head . . ."

"Ricky, stop that!" Miss Frye said sharply.

"I never have, no," Des responded, shifting so she could get herself a good look at the taunter in the back row. Ricky was a classic schoolyard-bully type—a fat, no-necked kid with a flattop crew cut and outthrust jaw. Also one helluva black eye. The last kid he'd tangled with had clearly gotten the best of him. "Most of us never have to fire our guns. It's not like on television."

"How come a lady is a policeman?" asked the angelic blond girl.

"Well, I was a lieutenant in the Army, first. After the cold war ended I decided to join the state police, just like my father." The Deacon was deputy superintendent, the second-highest-ranking man in the entire state. And the highest-ranked black man in Connecticut history. "How about you, Ricky?" she asked, making eye contact with him. "Anything you'd like to ask me?"

"Yeah," he said, his brow furrowing. "Are you a nigger?"

Miss Frye let out a gasp of pure horror. "Ricky Welmers, you just earned yourself another trip to the principal's office!"

"Wait, it's okay," Des interjected.

"It is *not* okay!" she said firmly. "We have a zero-tolerance policy toward such language."

Ricky just sat there smirking. He wanted attention, and he was getting it.

"Ricky, what's the worst thing anyone's ever called you?" Des asked, strolling down the aisle toward him.

He stuck his chin out at her in defiant silence.

"C'mon, you can tell us," Des prodded him. "What was it—Fatso, Lardo, Piggy, *Miss* Piggy . . . ?" This drew snickers from the other kids, which Ricky did not like. "Words *hurt*, Ricky. If you hurt someone, they're liable to hurt you back. Is that what you want?"

"I can take it," he snarled at her.

"And if the other guy's got a gun? Then what do you do?"

Ricky stared up her, his eyes cold with hate. It wasn't racially specific, she felt. It was authority in general he was angry at. She wondered why.

Now the classroom door opened and a high school girl came in to tell Des she was needed in the superintendent's office.

Something in the girl's voice caused Miss Frye to say,

"I'll show Trooper Mitry the way, Ashley. Will you please stay here with the class until I return?"

They started down the school hallway together, moving briskly. Des, who had learned never to waste an opportunity, immediately went to work: "Ever think about adopting a kitten for your classroom, Miss Frye? It makes a wonderful science project."

"I'm afraid that's not possible. I've got several students with allergies."

"How about you yourself?" Des pressed her. When it came to placing a healthy neutered kitten she was ruthless. "Do you have a cat?"

"We have a dog."

"They get along fine. Don't believe the cartoons. I've got some Polaroids right here if you'd care to—"

"No, don't!" Miss Frye pleaded. "Don't show them to me. I'm a terrible soft touch."

"Oh, good, we'll get along just fine." Des smiled at her as they strode down the corridor, the teacher matching her stride for stride, which most women couldn't do. "Do you always keep the windows in your room open?"

"I do," she responded. "We've got a mold problem in the ductwork, and the old wiring is inadequate for air conditioners. They were supposed to upgrade it over the summer, but if they end up tearing the school down, then that would just be a waste of money—and so they did nothing."

"It's a sweet old school," Des said. "Seems a shame to level it."

"I couldn't agree more. It has its problems, but nothing that can't be fixed. Superintendent Falconer has *tried* to tell Mrs. Leanse—she's our school board president."

"Ben's mother?"

"That's right. But you know it's very hard to argue with a parent who feels his or her child's health is endangered. They want to do the best they can for their children. They've spent hundreds of hours working the phones, licking envelopes, packing the school board meetings. They even raised twenty-five thousand dollars of private funds to produce a ten-minute video that went out to every voter in town. All I keep thinking is, if you really care that much about the school, twenty-five thousand would buy us a lot of plumbing repairs. Or computers. Or a security system. Besides, the reality is that it's not the size of the building that matters. It's the size of the class and the caliber of the teacher and . . ." She glanced at Des apologetically. "I'll shut up now. You asked me a perfectly innocent question about mold and you're getting an entire lecture."

"I'm getting insight. I need that."

They pushed open the double doors at the end of the hall and started out onto the playground behind the school. The superintendent's office was in the middle school, a twenty-year-old flat-roofed brick building that was located across an expanse of blacktop.

"You handled the children very well," Miss Frye said, leading Des past the swings and monkey bars.

"I was thinking I could have been a little less confrontational with Ricky."

"Not at all. You were straight with him. He needs to be talked to that way. They all do. I'm sorry about his language. His older brother, Ronnie, was a handful, too. He's over at the high school now. Ronnie was just incredibly disruptive. Him they put on Ritalin, and he did better, but the mother was around then. Jay's raising the boys alone now, and he has his own problems. It's a real shame, because they're both very bright. Ronnie's probably the brightest student in our entire system. His IQ tested exceptionally high. But he's bored and he's angry, so he self-medicates."

"He's a garbagehead?"

"They caught him inhaling a computer keyboard cleaner out behind the Science Building last year."

"What was it, Duster Two?"

"That's it. He and two other boys. All three of them were suspended."

"Is there a lot of huffing in this town?"

"You wouldn't think so, but Dorset isn't Oz."

"Even Oz wasn't Oz," Des pointed out as they passed

through the door into the middle school. "What happened to Ricky's eye?"

"He gets in a lot of fights."

"This I can well imagine. Are you sure it didn't happen in the home?"

Miss Frye puffed out her cheeks. "Trooper, I'm not sure of anything."

When they arrived at Superintendent Falconer's outer office, Des encountered a harried, frantic secretary and a short, big-chested woman with bushy hair who was about to explode.

"Okay, what seems to be the problem?" Des asked them calmly.

"The *problem* is that I have been waiting out here like a piece of garbage for *thirty* minutes!" the short woman retorted angrily. "The superintendent is *supposed* to meet with me. Colin is *in* there. I *saw* him go in there. I have never encountered such *rudeness*, such-such—"

"Trooper Mitry, this is Babette Leanse, president of our school board," Miss Frye said quietly.

"You must be Ben's mom," Des said, smiling at her.

"I have an *appointment!*" she blustered, unswerving in her rage. She was an intensely focused, hard-charging little human blowtorch in a cashmere cardigan sweater and finely tailored wool slacks. Des made her for about forty. Her shock of black hair was streaked with silver. "That man *knows* I'm out here!"

"I see," Des said patiently. "And the problem is . . . ?"

"I've buzzed him repeatedly," spoke up Colin's frazzled secretary, whose desk nameplate identified her as Melanie Zide. She was a dumpy, moon-faced young woman with a pug nose, limp henna hair, eyes that looked sneaky behind clunky black-framed glasses. "I called out his name. I knocked. H-He just won't answer. And his door is locked from the inside and I don't have a key. I've got the custodian searching for one, but . . ."

Des jiggled the knob. It was locked all right. "Is there a window in there?"

"There is," Melanie said, chewing nervously on the inside of her mouth. "But it has security bars over it. And his venetian blinds are closed. You can't see anything."

Des tried rapping on the door. "Superintendent Falconer!? Colin!?" Then she put a shoulder to it. It didn't give. The frame was solid. There was a transom over it, of frosted glass. She pulled a sturdy chair over in front of the door and climbed up on it, placing her at eye level with the transom. She tried to pry it open with her pocket knife, only it was latched shut from the inside. She pursed her lips, frowning. "You're sure he's in there?"

"Positive," said Babette Leanse.

"For at least a half hour," Melanie added, her voice strained.

Des asked the others to get away from the door and used the butt end of her Sig on the frosted glass, smashing a jagged hole that she could see through.

What she saw was Colin Falconer slumped face-down at his desk, unconscious. On the desk, next to his left hand, there was an empty prescription pill bottle.

"Call nine-one-one," she ordered Melanie Zide sharply. "Tell them we need EMS *now*. We've got a possible overdose."

Miss Frye let out a gasp as Melanie lunged for the phone.

Babette Leanse just stood there with her mouth open, speechless.

The custodian still could not find a key to the superintendent's door. Des asked him for a pry bar instead. He returned with a foot-long crowbar that she applied to the lock while he threw his weight against the door. The frame gave with a sharp crack and they went in, the broken transom glass crunching underfoot.

Colin was breathing. His respiration was shallow, his pulse rapid, skin pale and cool. "He's in shock," Des said, checking the pill bottle. It was diazepam, the generic name for Valium. The bottle, if full, would have held fifty tablets, ten milligrams each. "We'll need blankets."

The custodian ran to get some from the nurse's office.

"Colin, you *fool*," Miss Frye said from the doorway, her voice heavy with sadness. "You stupid, stupid fool."

The ambulance got there in less than five minutes, pulling right up onto the playground next to the building, its siren silent so as not to alarm the children. Margie and Mary Jewett, who headed Dorset's volunteer ambulance corps, were no-nonsense sisters in their late fifties. Des had already encountered them at a couple of fender benders and found them to be well-trained and unflappable.

Margie checked Colin Falconer's blood pressure while Mary hooked him up to a cardiac monitor, the two of them barking shorthand at each other. They did the Roto-Rooter thing on his stomach, then gave him oxygen and administered two hundred milliliters of saline solution through a large-bore intravenous catheter while they continued to monitor his vital signs. He was now semiconscious, murmuring incoherently under his breath.

"He's still a bit shocky," Margie told Des. "But he's healthy and strong and it's pretty hard to kill yourself on Valium."

"Unless you're blind drunk to boot," Mary added.

When they had him stabilized Margie wheeled in the stretcher and they loaded him onto it. "Let's move!" she called out.

"Moving!" Mary affirmed.

And they hustled Colin Falconer out the door and off to the Middlesex Clinic in Essex, leaving Des to notify his next of kin.

"I guess that would be his wife, Greta," Melanie Zide spoke up. "She should be at the gallery by now."

Des thanked Melanie for the information, and Miss Frye for her help. The young teacher smiled at her tightly before she returned to her classroom, leaving Des with Babette Leanse. And the distinct impression that Dorset's school superintendent had tried to take his own life rather than face this woman.

"Mrs. Leanse, exactly what was this meeting between you two about?"

"Trooper, this is hardly the time to discuss it," Babette answered sharply, managing to look down her nose at Des even though Des towered over her by perhaps a foot. This was a woman who was trying very hard to command respect. If there was one thing Des had learned at West Point, it was this: The ones who had to work at it were seldom the ones who received it.

"So when would be a good time?" Des asked her, as Melanie watched the two of them intently from behind her desk.

"I suppose you could swing by my house this afternoon," Babette allowed. "But I don't understand why you're pressing me on this."

"Because my job is to see that things like this don't happen. That's rule number one in the resident trooper's unofficial handbook."

"And is there a rule number two?" Babette demanded.

"Oh, absolutely," Des said, smiling at her broadly. "Rule number two is to make absolutely sure that they don't ever happen again."

The Patterson Gallery was located right down Dorset Street from the old Gill House, home to the Dorset Academy of Fine Arts. The gallery was in a bright-yellow converted barn that had previously been a grain-and-feed store. The gnarly oak tree out front had a red ribbon tied around it, indicating where Colin Falconer's wife stood on the school-bond issue. Whatever was wrong between the two of them, Des reflected, it wasn't local politics.

Inside, Des found a clean, brightly lit space with sparkling white walls and polished fir floors. A fire crackled in the fireplace. Downstairs, the gallery featured an array of luminous early-twentieth-century landscape paintings from noteworthy shoreline impressionists such as Childe Hassam, Henry Ward Ranger, Carleton Wiggins and Elbert Frye, Wendell's grandfather. Prices ranged anywhere between one and five times what Des took home in a year. On the second floor Greta Patterson offered more modestly priced works by contemporary artists, many of them recent graduates of the Dorset Academy. She served on its board, as had her father and grandfather, who had operated the Patterson Gallery before her.

A discreet sign on the wall behind her massive oak partner's desk noted that the Patterson Gallery was the exclusive agent and legal representative of Wendell Frye, although there was no evidence of the great man's work to be found anywhere—no catalogs, no photographs. It was very low-key, considering the amount of hype that generally went on in the art world.

Greta was talking on the phone, but she quickly got off, bustled to her feet and offered Des a seat in one of the cozy armchairs set before the fire. Des declined an offer of coffee and sat, trying not to stare at the woman. Greta Patterson was a good deal older than she'd been expecting. At least sixty, possibly sixty-five. Plenty old enough to be Colin's mother. She was a wide-bodied, square-faced woman with close-cropped silver hair and a red blotchy complexion that suggested many years of serious drinking. She wore a hand-knit cream-colored vest over a burgundy silk blouse, roomy wool slacks and a good deal of bright-red lipstick, some of which was stuck to her front teeth.

"I know why you're here, trooper," Greta said to her in a booming, forthright voice. "Colin's already phoned me from the ambulance. He's assured me he's fine, totally fine." She did not seem the least bit fazed by her husband's suicide attempt. Or even surprised. "We've been living apart lately, as I'm sure you must know, but I'll bring him home just as soon as the clinic releases him." Greta settled in the other armchair, clutching a Dorset Academy coffee mug tightly in her blunt-fingered hands. "Naturally, I'll try to see that he behaves himself in the future. But I can't guarantee anything."

"Has this happened before?" Des asked, crossing her long legs.

Greta let out a guffaw. "What is this, his fifth try? Sixth? I've lost count. Colin is a deeply, deeply unhappy man. He's been undergoing treatment for depression for a number of years, and lately—" She broke off, weighing just exactly how forthcoming she wished to be. "Let's just say he wanted to work things out on his own. A lot of men undergo a change when they hit forty. I've seen it with countless artists—even the real swashbucklers. Their self-assurance is suddenly overtaken by doubt, anxiety, even panic. Some rush right out and nail the first female who's willing. Some buy themselves a convertible. And some, like Colin, fall into a deep, deep funk. Call it hormones. Call it male menopause. Call it whatever you want. But it's real. And for Colin, who was a brooder to begin with, it's been pure hell." Greta took a sip of her coffee and stared fretfully into the fire. "Up until now, we've managed to keep it between us. But now I suppose the poor boy will have to take a medical leave."

"Babette Leanse was waiting outside his office to see him," Des said. "Could this particular suicide try be related to that?"

"I have no doubt that it is," Greta answered emphatically. "Babette has been making his life pure hell ever since this mold issue came up at Center School. Attila the Hen, he's taken to calling her. Babette's a driven, determined woman, and God help anyone who gets in her way. Sadly, that *anyone* has been Colin." Greta shifted her bulk in her chair, sighing regretfully. "Dorset used to be a special place. Everyone got along with everyone else. There was an aura of true contentment—artists made it their home. Now we're living in a war zone. Sometimes the war is fought over whether to put in a sewer system. Sometimes it's about condos. And *sometimes* it's about building a new school. But it's always the same war. And it's always the same outcome— the future *always* wins. I know that as well as I know the difference between the genuine artist and the fraud. But I don't have to like it."

A piece of wood collapsed in the fireplace, setting off a shower of sparks.

Greta stared at it in heavy, angry silence for a moment. "Besides, this one leaves a bad taste in my mouth. Our school board president, a woman who has turned that new school into a holy crusade, *happens* to be married to a real estate developer who *happens* to be building new houses all over town. Please! She's his puppet, and little Brucie is busy pulling the strings and lining his own pockets. But don't get me started on them." Greta got up and put a fresh log on the fire, then stood there warming her broad backside as it crackled. "I honestly will try to get Colin to come home. But he's a very stubborn boy."

That was the second time she'd called him a boy, Des noticed.

"I'm sorry that the children had to be exposed to this. They must have found it alarming."

"It was handled very quietly," Des said. "Just Mrs. Leanse, his secretary and the custodian were there. And one teacher, Miss Frye."

Greta's face lit up. "Moose is Wendell's oldest girl. Isn't she wonderful?"

"I liked her quite a bit."

"Very fine girl," Greta said, nodding. "Considerate, kind. Steady as a rock. His other daughter, Takai, has that realty office right across the street from me." Des noticed that Greta did not say that Takai was a fine girl. What she did say was: "Takai was the first realtor in Dorset to hire fluffers."

"Hire what?"

"They're like set decorators," she explained dryly. "They dress up the houses to make them look like they're straight out of *House Beautiful,* thereby jacking up the selling price. They truck in family heirlooms, antique furniture, dishes, silver. Totally faux, but that's Takai. With her, it's always about making a style statement. She was a runway model in New York when she was still in her teens. And, to this day she remains totally image-oriented. Which I guess is her way of rebelling against her father. Wendell, you see, has a visceral loathing for anything that he perceives as manipulative or fake—such as, say, the entire concept of business. Not that I'm complaining, mind you," Greta pointed out quickly. "It's a great, great privilege to be his dealer. Ordinarily, an artist of his stature would be represented by a big outfit in New York, not a funky local gallery such as mine. But Wendell's magnificently quirky that way. The Pattersons were good enough for his grandfather and his father and that was all he needed to know. And this way more of the money stays right here in Dorset to nourish local artists. Thanks to Wendell, I'm able to provide scholarships to the academy, student loans, rent money, even money for canvases and paints." Greta smiled at her, her eyes glittering. "Tell me, trooper, are you a fan of his work?"

"I'm a tremendous fan," Des said. "But please don't ask me to explain why, because I don't believe I can."

"You're not alone, my dear," Greta said reassuringly. "The closest anyone's ever come to describing a Frye statue was a French critic in the early seventies who wrote that it was like a mirror into one's soul—when you try to understand it, you end up trying to understand yourself. Hell, I've known the man for the better part of fifty years, and I've never really known him at all. You just missed him, actually. He left not five minutes before you got here, full of my good Irish whiskey. Stopped by to discuss a legal matter—doesn't call, just shows up. That's Wendell. Mostly, I'm his gatekeeper. If someone wishes to commission him, they go through me. And either he says yes or no—usually no, because he won't take money from any corporation or individual whose ethical standards he doesn't approve of. He can really be quite maddening sometimes. The Museum of Modern Art approached us a few months back about marketing a line of candlesticks and jewelry made from his designs. The museums do a huge business nowadays through their gift shops and catalogs. It's really quite lucrative."

"He said no?"

Greta nodded. "Not only won't he be a party to hawking knickknacks, as he calls them, but he insisted that I rewrite his will so that no one can ever license his name for the sale of anything. That man simply does not care about making money. He owns no stocks or bonds. All of his wealth is in his farm and his art. That's how he wants it. So that's how it is."

Des nodded, wondering just how frustrated Greta Patterson was by a client who chose to leave so much money on the table. If she weren't frustrated, she wouldn't have brought it up. That was one of the most important things Des had learned about interviewing people: *What* they talk about can often be more revealing than the words they say.

"The Pattersons believe in artists," Greta explained. "And we always have. When I was young I honestly thought I wanted to get away from this. I studied law at Duke. But before I went in with a firm I put in a year in London at Christie's, another two years in New York, and before I knew it I was right back here working in the family business. I suppose, deep down, I always knew that I would be. I've run it on my own since my dad died." She narrowed her eyes at Des appraisingly. "I understand you're quite the artist yourself, my dear. Don't look so surprised. Talent can't hide. Especially in Dorset. I'd love to see your portfolio of murder victims. Perhaps we can do something with them, you and I."

Des swallowed, taken aback. "I'm really not ready to show them yet."

"Now you're being unduly modest," Greta scolded her. "You're a beautiful, take-charge woman of color. Your art is highly political. Wake up and smell the turpentine fumes, my dear. Your timing could not be better."

"But I don't even know how to paint yet," pointed out Des, who wasn't expecting such interest so soon even in her wildest dreams. "I'm still learning."

"Picasso was still learning until the day he died," Greta scoffed. "That doesn't mean you can't find a home for your work. Besides, raw immediacy can be very, very commercially viable. Especially coming from someone like yourself. Do you understand what I mean?"

Des understood perfectly. Greta was saying that because she was a woman of color, people's expectations would be considerably reduced . . . *Step right up, folks, and see the barefoot colored girl. She draws!!!* . . . Des sat there in silence for a moment, seething. Not that she was a stranger to this kind of prejudice. She'd lived with it her whole life. Had she honestly thought the art world would be any different? Of course not. That would have been deluding herself. "I still need a lot of work," she finally said in a muted voice.

"Good, I admire that. But please keep me in mind. I can get you wonderful critical attention in New York and Boston. Possibly even turn Oprah's head. Trust me on this," Greta said, eyeing her up and down. "You are *very* promotable."

Something about the way the older woman's eyes were gleaming at her now was giving Des a prickling sensation on the back of her neck. Or was that just her imagination? Greta Patterson was a married woman, after all. Albeit to a man at least twenty years her junior. What kind of a marriage did she and Colin have? Des didn't know. All she knew was that when you really got to know the private lives of people, especially the wealthy upstanding bluebloods in Dorset, one truth always won out:

No one was who they appeared to be. Everyone was hiding something.

So what was Greta Patterson hiding?

The Leanses lived on a twenty-acre mountaintop high above Lord's Cove from which they could see all the way down the Connecticut River to Long Island Sound. In days of yore, a fortified castle would have been built there.

Bruce and Babette Leanse had erected a post-modern jumble of cubes, rhomboids and scalene triangles that seemed to be tumbling right down the hillside, rather like a large child's toy made of rough-cut timbers, granite and glass. Gazing at it through her windshield in the late-afternoon sunlight, Des initially thought that it was a total folly. But the more she looked, the more she liked its spareness, and the way it didn't impose itself on the mountain so much as become a part of it.

She left her cruiser in the driveway next to a Chevy Blazer with Ohio plates. It was a vehicle she recognized. She'd seen it in the parking lot of the inn for a number of days. She rang the front bell.

"Trooper, glad you could make it!" exclaimed Bruce Leanse as he came charging out the door with his hand stuck out, all five feet six of him. "I've really been wanting to meet you. Babette's still on the phone with the school board's attorney about Colin. Poor guy."

He closed the heavy oak door behind him and walked Des around the house and then across a meadow of knee-high wildflowers and native grasses. The sun was low, the trees casting long shadows across the meadow. Overhead, there were thin wisps of white clouds. A turkey vulture wafted on an air current, searching for prey.

"I'm hearing such good things about you from everyone," Bruce said, glancing at her as they walked. He had a faint, knowing smile on his lips that Des didn't care for. It bordered on a smirk. "In a lot of ways, I feel we're *so* alike."

"Really? How so?" asked Des, who could not summon up one single thing they had in common.

"I'm an outsider, too," he responded earnestly. "And I feel like I'm constantly being watched and judged by the entrenched old guard, same as you are. Me, I wouldn't have it any other way. How about you?"

"Me, I can't have it any other way," Des responded coolly.

He let out a delighted whoop of laughter. "Well said."

Bruce Leanse may have been short but he was movie-star handsome, and he knew it. He had sparkling blue eyes, a rock-solid jaw, long, thin nose and lots of white teeth. His hair, which was flecked with gray, was short and spiky. He carried himself erect, the sleeves of his flannel shirt rolled back to reveal powerful, hairy forearms. He wore a fisherman's vest over his flannel shirt, jeans and work boots. Des had read a lot about him over the years. His life was one long-running tabloid story. He was a billionaire's son, a Rhodes scholar out of Princeton whose prowess on the downhill ski slopes had landed him a spot on the U.S. Olympic team. He was also someone who was not above crowing about his latest conquest. That was why the tabloids had taken to calling him the Brat. By the time he took control of the family real estate empire, he had climbed Everest, sailed solo around the world, hosted his own daredevil show on MTV, launched a magazine, a restaurant and a brewery, run for mayor of New York and dated a string of towering, glamorous supermodels. Lately, his private life had quieted down. And now here he was in Dorset.

Across the meadow, beyond a stand of cedars, Des could hear an occasional metallic *plink,* followed by shouts of husky male encouragement. "This is a very interesting place you have here," she observed, as they made their way past a wall of solar panels.

"God, don't let Babette hear you say that."

"Why not?"

"Because she designed it, and in the world of architecture *interesting* is synonymous with *bad.* People call something *interesting* when they truly hate it."

"Well, I meant that I liked it."

"Thank you," he said, gratefully lapping up her praise. He struck her as rather needy. People who craved attention generally were. "We wanted it to blend in with the landscape, unlike those gargantuan trophy palaces that everyone else seems to want these days."

"But you do build those, too, don't you?"

"That doesn't mean I like them," Bruce said defensively. "I'm in business. If you don't give people what they want, then you don't stay in business. This is a universal truth," he pointed out, as if this were a pearl of wisdom she might wish to jot down in her diary. "If someone is sinking two million into a house, then they want what *they* want, not what you think they should want. *We* wanted to be as green as humanly possible. We use less than a third of the energy of a normal house here. We installed geothermal heating and cooling, solar panels, waterless composting toilets. The lumber is native or reprocessed. I try to be eco-friendly, believe me. I'm someone who's active in the Sierra Club. And if you ask me, the suburb is the worst thing that happened to this country in the twentieth century. That probably sounds odd to you coming from a developer, but I believe it."

Des said nothing to that. The man was carrying on both sides of the argument all by himself. Hell, it was an argument *with* himself.

"But I also think it's foolhardy to believe that the future can be stopped," he went on as they made their way across the meadow, the *pings* growing steadily louder. "There are twice as many people living in the U.S. right now as there were when the baby boomers were born. We have to put them somewhere, don't we? Unlike a lot of people, I don't believe in standing on the sidelines complaining. Wherever we've worked—Seattle, San Francisco, Denver, Boston— we've devised revolutionary, low-impact development for the future. I *believe* in the future. I believe in cities that live in harmony with mass transit. And I believe in villages. That's why we've put down roots in Dorset. What we have here is a rare and endangered thing—a genuine community. And we have to fight to hold on to that."

Des nodded, thinking just how baffled the old-timers must be by this high-profile human dynamo with his deep pockets and his bulldozers.

"You're probably thinking that I'm nothing more than a kinder, gentler asshole. But I *believe* in what we're doing. I'm *excited*. Is there anything wrong with that?"

Des shrugged her shoulders, wondering why Bruce Leanse felt he needed to justify himself to her. Was he just naturally defensive about his chosen, politically incorrect career? Or was this an advanced case of Soul Man Syndrome—a liberal who was desperate for a black person's approval?

"Do you rock-climb, trooper?"

"Uh, no, I never have."

"Oh, you've absolutely got to. It's outrageous. A total high. Greatest physical rush there is." Bruce paused, grinning at her wolfishly. "Aside from you-know-what . . ."

Ah, so that was it—the Brat wanted him some of her form.

"Tell you what—I'll take you out some Saturday morning and we'll—"

"I'm afraid my sked's pretty crowded right now."

"Sure, sure. How about a run? Do you run? God, you must. Nobody's got a butt like yours without doing roadwork."

Des came to a stop and said, "Okay, I have to tell you that I'm not real comfortable with the direction this conversation is taking, Mr. Leanse."

"I'm just looking for a workout partner," he gulped, retreating hastily. "That's all I meant. I'm not looking for trouble. Really, I'm not."

"Good. Neither am I."

The breeze coming off of the river was getting chillier. The weatherman had predicted the first frost of the season that night. Des resumed walking, shivering slightly. Beyond the cedars there was a mown stretch of lawn where a baseball diamond had been marked off, complete with bases, a pitcher's mound and a batting cage. On the mound a pitching machine was disgorging fastballs. And at the plate, little Ben Leanse, her DARE essay winner, was flailing away at them with an aluminum bat that seemed as big as he was. With the oversized batting helmet that was planted on his huge head, the little fellow looked like one of those bobble-headed dolls they sold at ballparks.

A muscular, sunburned man in a short-sleeved polo shirt stood behind the cage with his big arms crossed watching him swing. . . . *Ping*. . . . As Ben feebly fouled off one pitch. . . . *Ping*. . . . As he popped up another behind first base, barely getting around on it. . . . *Ping*. . . . Des recognized this man at once—it was her third-floor mattress king from the Frederick House. A video camera was set up next to him on a tripod, filming the boy.

"Step into it, Big Ben!" he called out encouragingly. "Atta boy! Good job!"

"We've hired a batting tutor to help Ben up his game a notch," Bruce explained. "He's desperate to make the Little League team next spring." Bruce clapped his hands together and called out, "Way to go, guy!"

"I stink, Dad," Ben gurgled at him glumly. He had on a

fleece jersey with the words DOUGHTY'S ALL-STARS emblazoned across his chest. "I totally suck."

"No way—you're making real progress." Bruce seemed ill at ease around his boy, his manner forced. "Am I right, Dirk?"

At first, Dirk had nothing but a cold glare for Bruce Leanse. Des immediately wondered what that was about. Then Dirk ran a big hand over his weathered face and said, "We're doing real good. Just got to strengthen those wrists of yours over the winter, Big Ben. Right now, they're like cooked spaghetti."

"Okay, Coach," the little boy responded solemnly.

"I'll go see if I can hurry Babette along," Bruce said to Des. Clearly, the Brat was not anxious to stick around. In fact, he couldn't hurry back to the house fast enough.

Des stayed put. "Nice to see you again, Ben," she said to him warmly.

"Hello, trooper. Coach Doughty, this is Trooper Mitry."

"Make it Dirk," he said to her. "Pleased to meet you. Let's take some more cuts, Ben."

Des joined him behind the cage as the boy flailed away at more mechanical pitches . . . *Plink* . . . Des guessed that Dirk was in his early thirties. He was a solid six feet tall with broad, hulking shoulders and a massive chest. He held himself with the physical ease of an athlete in prime condition . . . *Plink* . . . Still, she noticed, his eyes had a defeated, beaten-down cast to them.

"We're both at the Frederick House, if I'm not mistaken," she said to him.

"That's right." His eyes stayed on the boy at the plate. "The Leanses have been nice enough to put me up there while I'm working with Ben. I'm all over the Northeast right now. Just spent two weeks in Nashua, New Hampshire. Soon as it turns a little colder, I'll follow the sun down to Florida for the baseball camps. . . . *Move* those hips, Big Ben! *Pull* 'em through the strike zone! . . . . Actually, I grew up around here. I'm headquartered in Toledo, Ohio now.

Married a Toledo girl." And yet, he wore no wedding ring. Some people didn't like to wear rings. Still, it made her wonder. "Ever been there?"

"No, I haven't," she said.

"It's not a bad place. Not as nice as Dorset, but not bad. And, hey, I'm still getting paid to do what I love."

"Dirk played in the show!" Ben exclaimed proudly.

"I'm impressed," Des said.

Dirk grimaced slightly. "All I had was a cup of coffee with the Detroit Tigers. But around here, that makes me a hometown hero. . . . Less top hand, Ben! . . . . I still hold all the hitting records at Dorset High and American Legion Post 103. Fun to be back, actually. It gives me a chance to catch up with old friends."

And possibly hump one of them night after night, Des reflected. It sounded as if Dirk was on the road a lot. If there was one thing she'd learned from her experience with Brandon, it was this: Men who spend a lot of time away from home do not wish to be home.

"The Tigers paid me a seven-figure signing bonus right out of high school," Dirk recalled in a tight, controlled voice. "I was going to be their catcher of the future. I was the complete package. I could hit for average. Hit for power. Had a gun for an arm. Ran the hundred in ten flat." . . . *Plink* . . . "Well, the bonus disappeared right away—my first wife cleaned me out but good."

"And the dream?" Des asked. "What happened to the dream?"

He showed her the two ugly surgical scars on the inside of his right elbow. "My first winter home from rookie ball I was in a car that hit a patch of black ice and rolled into a ditch. Couldn't throw a baseball for two years. And that was just the beginning. I had two procedures on my right knee, another on my left. Spent half of my career on the disabled list and the other half on the waiver wire." . . . *Plink* . . . "I also had me a bit of a nightlife problem. No longer. I've been clean and sober for four years . . . Good one, Ben! Now you're in the zone!" He fell silent, breathing slowly in and out. "I finished up with a hundred twenty-seven Major League at bats, trooper. My lifetime average is two forty-four, with four dingers. You can look it up. I also played two seasons in Japan for the Yokohama Bay Stars before the Tigers took me back and shipped me down to Toledo. Spent three more seasons there until they released me. That's when I knew it was over. Knew it in my heart. But what the hell, I chased the dream for twelve years. And now I'm actually doing some good. I had a high school girl down in Vero Beach last winter who was real close to getting herself a college softball scholarship. Working with me for two weeks put her over the top. That's a satisfying feeling, helping a kid who can't afford college earn herself a four-year ride."

Maybe so, Des reflected, but clearly he felt cheated by what had happened to him. It wasn't in the words he spoke. Dirk Doughty was saying all of the right things. It was in the way he bit off his words. It was in those defeated eyes of his.

"Mostly, I get kids like Ben," he confessed. "Their parents are looking for an esteem booster. What the hell, I don't mind. It's what I know . . . Okay, Ben! Let's call it a day!"

"Right, Coach!" The boy promptly laid down his bat and got busy gathering up the balls he'd popped feebly around the diamond, stretching out the belly of his fleece jersey to form a crude sack for them.

"Some of these yuppie parents can really get in my face," Dirk said, watching him. "They put so much pressure on their kids to succeed that they turn something that's supposed to be fun into something utterly joyless."

"Are the Leanses like that?"

Dirk considered this a moment. "Actually, I have to hand it to them—they're okay. Plenty involved in their own lives. And Ben's a real nice kid. Super-bright. He'll end up being a brilliant scientist or something."

Babette came tromping briskly across the grass toward them now, clutching a cell phone tightly in one hand. "Trooper Mitry, so sorry to keep you waiting. How is our ballplayer doing, Dirk?"

"Doing good," Dirk responded pleasantly as Ben dumped

a shirtload of baseballs into a duffel bag. "C'mon, guy, let's hit the kitchen for a protein shake." They headed off toward the house together, Dirk placing a big arm protectively around the boy's narrow shoulders.

Babette watched them go. There was a fixed brightness to her eyes, an intense sureness that Des found alarming. "We don't harbor any illusions about Ben's athletic ability," she said. "We know he'll never be another Mike McGuire."

"I think you mean Mark McGuire," Des said, observing once again just how imposing this woman seemed in spite of her height. Attila the Hen indeed.

"But he needs to be good at *something* so he'll be able to play with the other boys," she went on. "His teacher, Miss Frye, is in complete accord. It was she who recommended Dirk. There's a bench out on the rocks overlooking the river. Shall we sit there?"

The bench was sheltered by a rustic gazebo of rough, bark-covered posts and beams. They strolled across the field to it and sat, Babette pulling the shawl collar of her sweater up tighter around her neck. The breeze was really picking up. A sailboat was making impressive speed as it knifed its way toward the old iron bridge up at East Haddam.

"Needless to say," Babette commented, "the athletic facilities at Center School are as deplorable as everything else is. My God, every time I walk in that place and see those kids wearing their coats in class, I want to cry. This is Connecticut, not Kosovo! My friends in the city keep asking me why we don't just pull Ben out of there and put him in a private school."

"And how do you answer them?"

"I believe in our public schools," she replied firmly. "If people like us abandon them we will create a society of haves and have-nots. That's just not acceptable. But neither is Center School—over the summer, a state building inspector found over two *hundred* safety- and fire-code violations. I know the old guard in town thinks it can be fixed. Well, it can't. I'm telling you it can't, okay? I'm an architect. I *know* buildings."

Des nodded, well aware that this was the lady bragging on herself some. Because if architects really did know buildings, then there would be no need for engineers.

"Plus we need more classrooms," she went on. "There are new homes going up all over town. More people. People with kids. Where are we going to put them? We must build this new school."

"The support of the school superintendent wouldn't hurt, I imagine."

Babette shifted uncomfortably on the bench, her face tightening. "Look, I am very sorry about what happened this morning. I don't enjoy seeing anyone suffering. But this is simply another illustration of why it's time for Colin to go." She hesitated, her tongue flicking across her lower lip. "As to why I was there to see him . . . It's an extremely delicate matter. I can only share this with you in the strictest professional confidence. Because if word were to leak out . . ."

"It won't," Des promised her. "At least, not from me it won't."

Babette took a deep breath, as if to gather herself. "An allegation of gross personal misconduct has been leveled against Colin. I was there to urge him, for everyone's sake, to offer to resign quietly, thereby avoiding a public airing before the entire school board of his . . . behavior."

"Exactly what kind of misconduct are we talking about?"

"It seems he was using his office computer to conduct an online affair."

"Cyber romance is pretty common these days, isn't it?"

"It was a homosexual romance, trooper," she said tightly. "Male-on-male sadomasochism, as I understand it. Very explicit. Very pornographic. And he left it there on his screen while he was away from his desk. Melanie Zide, his secretary, happened upon it during the normal course of her duties. She has informed the school board that she was made to feel very uncomfortable."

"Sounds like she's hired herself a lawyer."

"That she has," Babette affirmed unhappily. "He's informed us that she intends to file sexual harassment charges against the Dorset school district unless we remove him. Our own lawyer says she's well within her rights—by leaving that material on his screen Colin created a hostile work environment. If we don't remove him we will be condoning inappropriate sexual conduct by a school official. That girl will nail us but good unless we take action. Even if Colin gets the boot she *still* may have grounds for a financial settlement." Again, Babette Leanse took a deep breath. "Obviously, you can see why we wish to handle this quietly."

"I absolutely can," Des said, her mind racing. Greta Patterson had called this school-bond squabble a war. And she'd said something else: "God help anyone who gets in Babette Leanse's way." Colin Falconer had done just that, and now he looked to be a battlefield casualty. Was all of this just his own stupid fault? Or was there something vastly more wicked going on here? "And I appreciate you filling me in. I like to know what's happening."

"A real mess is what's happening," Babette said sharply. "And I really, really don't appreciate getting caught in the middle of it. But, damn it, how can we let a man who's incapable of managing himself be responsible for the well-being of our children? The short answer is we can't. Colin's behavior is absolutely shameful. Intolerable. He *must* resign. I can't imagine he'd choose to fight us—it would end up in the newspapers that way, and that would not be in anyone's best interest. Trooper, I hope and pray he will go quietly. Because if he doesn't, if he decides to stand and fight, well . . ." Babette Leanse trailed off, shaking her head.

"Well what, Mrs. Leanse?"

"It will tear Dorset into little pieces," she warned in a voice that was frighteningly cold and quiet. "And no one, but no one, will ever be able to put them back together again."

CHAPTER 5

Wendell Frye did not have a doorbell, just a giant wolf's-head knocker that resonated like a clap of thunder when Mitch used it. The door itself creaked ominously as the old man swung it open to greet him.

Mitch had half-expected that the great sculptor would have forgotten all about inviting him to dinner. But he couldn't have been more wrong. Hangtown seemed genuinely pleased to see him, cheerful and bright-eyed. His flowing white hair and beard were neatly combed. He had red suspenders on over a navy-blue wool shirt, green mole-skin trousers that were tucked into a well-worn but polished pair of riding boots. Sam, his German shepherd, followed him, tail wagging, as he led Mitch into the living room, a damp, gloomy room that smelled of mold and genteel decay. There was no wheezing organ, but there may as well have been. Mice skittered in the walls.

"I'll get us a couple of beers," Hangtown offered. "Shall I do that?"

"That'll be great."

He lumbered slowly off with the dog, leaving Mitch there alone. Upstairs, he could hear Takai shouting into her cell phone about closing dates and engineering inspections, her sharp voice piercing the house's silence like a boning knife.

There were no lights on in the living room. What little il-lumination there was came from candles and the fire in the big stone fireplace, which did next to nothing against the chill. A chesterfield sofa and two battered leather wing-backed chairs were set before the fireplace, which was flanked by floor-to-ceiling bookcases. An antique rolltop desk was parked before the windows, an old Underwood manual typewriter set upon it.

But by far the most striking thing about Wendell Frye's living room was the pair of virtually complete suits of armor standing on pedestals in the center of the room.

"My proudest possessions, Big Mitch," Hangtown declared, returning with two large pewter mugs filled with dark beer, one of which he handed to Mitch. "Late fifteenth century. You want to talk about mm-rr-honest metal work, by God, they made these *by hand*. Hammered each part from a goddamned lump of metal. Missaglia family of Milan made 'em. No bogus fluting or scalloping either. Their beauty comes strictly from the form itself. And wait until you get a load of this . . ." A look of childlike glee lit up his creased old face as he raised the visor of one of the suits.

Mitch heard a click and the entire wall of bookcases to the left of the fireplace rotated slowly open to reveal a secret passageway laced with cobwebs. It was like something right out of an old haunted-house movie.

"Leads straight down to the dungeon," Hangtown explained, cackling. "Now get a load of this . . ." He went over to the rolltop desk and pushed a button under its middle drawer. Now a section of the bookcase on the other side of the fireplace popped open to reveal a secret wall safe with a combination lock. "Perfect place for storing secret documents, am I right?"

"Or maybe counterfeit plates," said Mitch, who found himself wondering what, if anything, the old recluse did keep in there.

Hangtown moseyed his way back over to the suits of armor now, a sly expression on his face. "How would you like to help me choose a wine for dinner?"

"Why, sure. I'd be happy to."

"Father, no!!" cried out Moose, who had just joined

them. She wore the same homemade outfit she'd had on that morning, her sleeves turned back to reveal forearms that were uncommonly muscular. "Mitch, move three steps to your left this instant," she commanded him urgently.

"But we're having *fun,* Moose," Hangtown protested. "Besides, he's a healthy young buck and he's—"

"Just do it, Mitch!"

"Tell her it's okay, Big Mitch," Hangtown pleaded. "Tell her you *want* to see what Jim and I have done."

"Well, sure I do," Mitch said uncertainly.

"Okay, fine," Moose said to him with weary resignation. "Hand me your beer. Give it to me."

Mitch gave her his mug just as he noticed Hangtown raising the right gauntlet of one of his suits of armor . . .

And suddenly the floor was gone under Mitch's feet.

He'd been standing on a trapdoor.

And with a *whoosh* he was gone. Falling feet-first down a fun-house slide, an involuntary roar coming out of him . . . Faster and faster he fell—unable to see, unable to stop, out of control . . . Faster and faster . . . All of the blood rushing to his head . . .

Until suddenly he landed with an *oof* on a cushioned surface of some kind, gasping for breath. Somewhere, he could hear Hangtown cackling with maniacal laughter—either it was Hangtown or Vincent Price. But Mitch could see nothing. Everything was pitch-black. He lay there like a lump as heavy footsteps slowly descended a creaky wooden staircase. Then he saw a faint light. A pair of lights, actually. Kerosene lanterns. Hangtown was clutching them as he made his way toward him down the basement corridor, still cackling with delight.

"How did you like it, Big Mitch?"

"This is the coolest house I've ever been in," he replied, taking in his surroundings in the lantern light. He was lying at the bottom of a chute in a bin that was filled with pillows.

"See? I told Moose she didn't have to worry about you."

Mitch got gingerly to his feet. His sweater and khakis seemed to have rearranged themselves and his feet felt numb. But once he'd stamped them on the concrete floor a few times they were fine. The narrow basement corridor they were in seemed to be part of a network of corridors. The walls were damp and slimy. It was like being in a catacomb. He accepted one of the lanterns from his host and said, "I'm half-expecting to run into The Creeper down here."

"Sure, I remember him," Hangtown exclaimed, wheezing as he led Mitch down the corridor. "What was that poor fellow's name who played him?"

"Rondo Hatton. He suffered from acromegaly."

"By God, you're a useful man to have around."

"I'm a waddling encyclopedia, all right."

Now they passed through an arched doorway and Hangtown flicked on a light to reveal an extensive wine cellar. The old man was quite a connoisseur. Hundreds of bottles were stored there in row upon row of wine racks. Three of the walls were of fieldstone and mortar. The fourth, a load-bearing wall from the oldest part of the house, was made of rough oak planks that were at least eighteen inches wide and were buttressed by hand-hewn chestnut posts.

"What's your pleasure, Big Mitch? A nice Medoc?"

"Sounds terrific."

Hangtown slid two bottles under his arm. "Oh, hey, get a load of this," he said, hobbling over toward the oak-plank wall. "Can't claim I did this one. Been here since Prohibition . . ." He lifted a dusty bottle of port from the top shelf of the wine rack. A section of the oak wall immediately popped open. It was actually a dummy wall that had been artfully built out from the original one so as to conceal a hidden cupboard. "They used to store their hooch in here," he said proudly, opening the cupboard doors wide for Mitch to see.

Not that there was anything in there to see. Just empty shelves coated with cobwebs and dust. Although it did appear, on closer look, that something had recently been stored on the lowest shelf—a distinct outline marked its place in the dust. It was the outline of something like a rolled-up rug, maybe eight inches wide and four feet long.

Hangtown was staring at it. He seemed startled. Almost transfixed.

"What is it?" Mitch asked him.

"Nothing." He swung the cupboard doors quickly shut, anxious to change the subject. "Something I've been meaning to ask you, Big Mitch. We were joking about it this morning, but this is serious . . ."

"Okay . . ."

"You really wouldn't mind if I came over to watch *Celebrity Deathmatch*?"

Mitch gazed at the great artist with openmouthed surprise. He couldn't believe how unassuming he was. "Are you kidding me? Come. *Any* time."

"Great," Hangtown exulted. "Just great." Now he led them out of the wine cellar and down a clammy stone passageway, halting at a recess in the stone wall where there was a narrow wooden spiral staircase. "This goes all the way up to the second floor—there's a secret chamber behind the master bedroom where they used to hide the slaves. A whole secret corridor runs along behind the upstairs bedrooms. In the back wall of each closet there's a way in. The girls keep theirs bolted shut, so don't get any sneaky ideas, heh-heh-heh. On the other side of the house it connects up with the old service stairs. You go that way. Take the wine. I'll close up down here, okay?"

"Wait, this is another trick, am I right?" Mitch asked, as the old man started to hobble off.

"No, no. Trust me, it's not, Big Mitch. Otherwise, I wouldn't be giving you the wine, would I?"

Mitch supposed not. Clutching the bottles carefully under one arm, he slowly climbed the steep, narrow spiral staircase, his lantern held out before him to ward off evil spirits and vampires. Up and up he climbed, up and around, up and around, until he finally arrived at a narrow, airless wooden corridor. It was barely as wide as his shoulders, and the ceiling was so low he had to duck or he'd get a mouthful of cobwebs. There were many spiders. A million spiders.

Every ten feet or so he passed a closed door with no knob—the secret doors to the bedrooms. Each had a peephole in it. Mitch tried looking through one, half-expecting to find another eye staring right back at him. There was nothing. Only blackness.

It was, he realized, very much like something out of a childhood dream. Or, more specifically, a nightmare.

When he had staggered his way down this wooden corridor to the other end of the house, he arrived at another staircase. This one was narrow and quite steep, almost like a ship's ladder. Descending it carefully, Mitch found himself confronting another closed door with no knob. Frowning, he gave it a push, activating the touch latch that popped it open.

He was standing in a big, modern farm kitchen. Or at least it would have been modern in 1952. It had a vintage GE fridge and freezer chest, an ancient gas stove, a deep, scarred farmhouse sink. In the middle of the room Moose was tossing salad greens at a cluttered trestle table.

"Well, hello there," she said to him pleasantly. "You survived Father's little fun-house ride, I see."

"God, this must have been a great house to be a kid in." Mitch set the wine and the lantern down on the table, catching a wonderful whiff of meat roasting in the oven.

"Actually, you never stop being a kid if you live in this house. Witness father."

"Anything I can do to help?"

"You can help me feed the pig," she replied, hefting the metal bucket filled with food scraps at her feet. "Unless that sounds too unglamorous for you."

"No, it sounds right up my alley."

He followed her out to the mudroom, where there were several pairs of men's and women's boots and garden clogs, all of them muddy. Also a second overflowing slop bucket. Mitch grabbed that one as Moose stepped into a pair of clogs, and they headed out the back door in the direction of the pigsty. It was a cold, clear night. There were stars overhead, and a full hunter's moon that cast a low-wattage light over the entire barnyard.

"Suppertime, Elrod!" Moose called out, dumping the slop over a low wire fence into the pig's aromatic home. "Sup-sup-suppertime!"

Mitch followed suit with his bucket, the pig ambling slowly over to check it all out. Snorking and slurping noises ensued. "I can certainly see why you've stayed," he said to Moose.

"Stayed?" She seemed puzzled.

"Why you haven't gotten your own place, I mean."

"This is my home, Mitch," she said simply.

"Does your sister feel the same way about it?"

"Well, *that* didn't take long, did it?"

"What didn't?"

"For us to start talking about Takai."

"We're not," Mitch insisted. "I was asking you about the farm."

"Sorry, my mistake," Moose said hastily, shooting an uncertain glance at him in the moonlight. "You shop for Sheila Enman, is that right?"

"Yes, I do. How did you . . . ?"

"We're old, old friends. It was Sheila who got me interested in teaching. It's very kind of you to do that for her, Mitch. It says a lot about you."

"I don't do it out of the goodness of my heart. I get amazing chocolate chip cookies out of it."

"Do you know her secret?" Moose asked him eagerly.

"Her secret to what?"

"Her chocolate chip cookies, you silly. I've been trying to get that darned recipe out of her for over ten years. And I just can't. She won't let me have it. You know how those old ladies are. They won't tell *anyone*. She makes her own chips out of the chocolate bars. I know that. But I also know she has a secret ingredient. If you do her marketing, you must have some idea what it is. Exactly what's on her shopping list? Try to remember. Try very, very hard."

Mitch found himself smiling at her. Because this was so *Dorset*. All of this intrigue over an old lady's cookie recipe. And him caught right in the middle, his lips sealed. Because he did know Sheila's secret ingredient. The sour cream. Had to be. Nobody *ate* as much sour cream as she went through in a week. Standing there, watching Elrod scarf up his supper in the moonlight, Mitch realized that here it was—the perfect hook to his Cookie Commerce story. Moose and her quest for Sheila's recipe. But how could he write about Moose without mentioning her famous, reclusive father? The answer was he couldn't. And that made it off-limits. He would not take unfair advantage of a private man who had invited him into his home. "If Sheila won't tell you," he finally said, "then you can't expect me to. That would be a betrayal of confidence, wouldn't it?"

"You're someone who can be trusted, aren't you," she said, kicking at the mud with her clog. "Father has amazing instincts." She lingered there watching Elrod, who didn't seem to mind. He was not in the least bit self-conscious. "Takai mentioned that you're in a relationship."

"I thought we weren't going to talk about Takai," Mitch chided her.

"We're not. We're talking about you."

"It's true, I am involved. And it's a big step for me. I . . . I lost my wife to cancer last year."

"And you still think about her."

"All the time," he said, his voice growing husky.

"I'm sure she'd be very proud of you, Mitch."

"That was a very kind thing to say," he said, glancing at Moose in the moonlight. "But I'm still not going to tell you what's in Sheila's cookies."

She let out an unexpectedly huge, full-throated whoop of a laugh. "Okay, you win. And in answer to your previous question, Takai *doesn't* feel the same way I do about this place. She isn't the least bit attached to it. In fact, if you get to know her better—and for your sake, I sincerely hope you do not—you'll discover that she doesn't care about anything or anyone."

Mitch wondered if he had ever heard someone deliver such a sweeping denunciation of another human being.

"We should really tell Jim that dinner's ready," she said

now, glancing over in the direction of his little wood-framed cottage, where lights were on. "He can seem a little scary, but he's been a good, good friend to Father."

Mitch began to hear music as they made their way to Jim's cottage—an old sixties San Francisco band, Quicksilver Messenger Service. Mitch had always admired the soaring, quivering licks of Quicksilver's lead guitarist, John Cipollina. He'd never been able to duplicate the sound on his Stratocaster.

"How come Jim was in prison?" he asked Moose.

She rapped on the crusty Vietnam vet's door with her knuckles. Inside, the music went silent. "You can ask him. He doesn't mind talking about it."

"Talking about what, girl?" Jim wondered as he pulled open the door, wearing an aged Pendleton plaid wool shirt over a tie-dyed T-shirt. A strong scent of marijuana came wafting out of the cottage along with him.

"Mitch wondered why they sent you to prison," Moose said to him.

"Son, I'm a big bad drug trafficker," Jim answered as the three of them started toward the house together. "Or so the law says. I say otherwise. Had me my own place over on the other side of those trees. Sixty good acres that had been in my family since forever. I was working that land and minding my own business."

"Jim raised organic produce for the local health-food stores," Moose said. "Lettuce, spinach, strawberries . . . All of it wonderful."

"So why did they come after you?"

"I raised me another crop, too," Jim replied. "The demon weed, son. Not for profit. Nothing like that. I grew it for my friends with cancer who were on chemo and sick to their stomachs night and day. I grew it for the older people who've got the arthritis so bad they can't get out of bed in the morning. It was medicine for them. I gave it to 'em for free."

"Some might even say he was an angel of mercy," Moose said.

"Don't know if I'd go that far," Jim said. "I did smoke me a lot of it, too. But, hell, I *was* doing some good. And it's legal to use it for medical purposes in this state. Just ain't legal to grow it. Someone ratted me out to the law. Got me a pretty fair idea who, too. And they said my farm was being used in the commission of a drug crime and therefore could be seized. They took my family's land away from me, son. Put me on the shelf for three years. I'm still on parole. And if Hangtown hadn't given me a place to stay, I'd be living out of a cardboard box under an overpass."

"What's happened to your farm?" Mitch asked.

"Some Canadian real estate syndicate bought it," he replied hoarsely. "Tore the house right down. Been in my family a hundred sixty years and they level it like a paper cup. Now the land's just sitting there waiting for something bad to happen. And Bruce Leanse's fingerprints are all over it."

"You can't prove that, Jim," Moose pointed out. From her tone, Mitch gathered that Jim had voiced his theory before.

"I know what I know," Jim said stubbornly. "He was the one making me all of those offers. He wanted my place, and he got it."

"What do you think he intends to do with it?" Mitch asked.

"Ask Takai," Jim said harshly.

"She's the Brat's realtor?"

Jim let out a laugh. " 'Enabler' is more like it. She's as slick as owl poop, too. But I *know* it was her ratted me out to the law. And if the day ever comes when I can prove it . . . Trust me, son, blood will get shed."

"Jim, I wish you wouldn't talk that way," Moose said to him crossly.

"It's the truth, girl. Can't help it if it ain't pretty."

They went back inside the house through the mudroom door. After exchanging her mud clogs for wool ones, Moose returned to the kitchen.

Jim tugged off his own muddy work boots and changed into Indian moccasins. Then he set to work washing his veiny hands in the mudroom's work sink. "Meantime, son," he said, a malevolent grin creasing his leathery face, "I know how to get even with Brucie."

"How?" asked Mitch, wondering if this particular swamp Yankee had smoked a bit too much of his own medicine.

"Next spring, soon as it gets good and warm, I'll plant me some dope plants on his place up on the hill. Deep in the woods, where he can't find 'em. Serve that bastard right." Jim reached for a towel to dry his hands, his expression turning serious. "Whatever you do, son, stay away from Takai. She's pure evil."

She was in the kitchen now, sipping a glass of wine and looking exceptionally gorgeous in an artfully unbuttoned cashmere cardigan, skintight leather miniskirt and spiked heels. Takai's legs were long, shapely and golden. She smelled of a musky perfume that was positively intoxicating.

"It's like I found out a long time ago," Jim added in a low voice. "Nothing that looks like that can possibly be good for you."

"What's that you're saying, Jim?" Takai demanded.

"Just saying how good you look, baby."

"Nice to see you again, Mitch," she said, her eyes gleaming at him. "I have this damned business meeting to go to tonight, so I won't be able to stick around for long. I apologize in advance."

"Absolutely no need to," said Mitch, who was starting to feel a bit light-headed. It was that perfume of hers.

Dinner was a roasted leg of lamb studded with garlic and rosemary, mashed potatoes and sautéed greens that Moose had harvested from the garden. All of it was superb. They ate in the low-ceilinged dining room, a very old room with exposed chestnut beams and a walk-in fireplace with a beehive oven and cast-iron crane. A big fire of massive oak logs roared in the fireplace, bathing the room in warmth and golden light. A highly precious handful of landscape paintings by Hangtown's father and grandfather adorned the walls, all of them paintings of this very farm. Hangtown sat at one end of the scarred oak dining table, his back to the fire and Sam at his feet. Mitch, the guest of honor, faced the fire.

"Used to do all of their cooking in that fireplace," Hangtown informed Mitch as they ate. "There was a spit with a clock-jack to turn it. House belonged to a clergyman then. There mm-rr-were a whole lot of clergymen in Grandmother's family. Distinguished theologians and scholars." He paused to sip his wine. "Obsessive foot fetishists, one and all. Inveterate toe suckers."

"Father!" objected Moose. "What has gotten into you tonight?"

"It's Big Mitch," Hangtown responded, his blue eyes twinkling devilishly. "He's a baad influence."

"Mitch is behaving like a perfect gentleman," Takai sniffed, gazing at him invitingly. Her eyes promised him unimaginable erotic riches. Strictly an act. Mitch knew a performance when he saw one. "Too perfect, if you ask me."

"Well, he cheers me up," Hangtown declared. "Nice to have a healthy young goat around here for a change." He pointed a wavering finger at Moose. "What's this I hear about Colin Falconer swallowing a bottle of pills today?"

"I was there," she affirmed somberly. "He would have died if the resident trooper hadn't gotten to him in time. Poor Colin's just *caught* in this awful school-bond snare. For his sake, I hope he resigns. He's a good, kind man."

"He's a wimp," Hangtown shot back. "Never punish yourself—punish the other guy."

"Besides, pills are the coward's way out," Jim added, nodding.

"I suppose if he were a manly man he would have blown his head off," Moose said sharply.

"What Colin needs to accept," Takai interjected, "is that there are a lot of people in Dorset who simply won't rest until he's out. They want their new school. And they want a superintendent who recognizes that we need it."

"Like hell we do, princess," Hangtown grumbled. "Fix the old one if it needs fixing. Fit it and shut up about it."

"A fine new school will be a credit to our community," Takai said.

"It will kill our community," he argued. "Our property

taxes will be doubled. The old folks on fixed incomes will be driven out. The working folks will be driven out. The only people who'll be able to afford to live in Dorset anymore are the yuppie scum with their fat six-figure incomes and their fat, snot-nosed brats!"

Takai drained her wine, patting her lips with her napkin. "Nonsense, Father. It's a very good deal for the town. Bruce is offering to donate that land on Old Ferry Road. And Babette's waiving her fee. She'll design it for nothing."

"In exchange for what?" Jim demanded. "People like them don't do anything for nothing."

"Bruce Leanse is a man of integrity," she responded, tossing her head. Her glossy black hair gleamed in the firelight, as if she were lit from within. "And he's bending over backward to do the right thing. I think he should be given credit for it, not vilified."

Jim lit a Lucky Strike and passed the pack over to Hangtown, who did the same despite Moose's disapproving look. "And when the dust settles," Jim said, drawing the smoke deep into his lungs, "he'll have brung a town road, power and phone lines into what used to be nothing but farmland and old-growth forest. That school's his damned Trojan horse, can't you see that, girl? We'll have sewers here before we know it. And town-house condos. And then this won't be Dorset no more."

"Jim, you're a paranoid lunatic," Takai said flatly.

"I know what I know," Jim insisted, glowering across the table at her. "Too many places in this valley are getting gobbled up all of a sudden. Big chunks of acreage, too."

"Not this chunk," Hangtown roared, pounding the table with his fist. "That bastard will never get his hands on my place."

"Look at a map sometime," Jim said. "Connect the dots—the school site, my place, them others . . . You'll see just how nuts I am." He turned his squinty gaze on Mitch. "You're the journalist, son. Ought to write about it. Tell the people what's going on here."

Mitch shot a glance over at Hangtown, whose face had

immediately turned to stone, his bright-blue eyes icy and un-yielding. "I'm not that kind of a journalist," Mitch said care-fully. "Besides, I'm not even sure I see a story here."

"Then maybe you ought to try opening your eyes," Jim growled at him.

"Leave him alone, Jim," said Moose, rushing to Mitch's defense.

"Well, I think we should be *flattered* that Bruce Leanse has taken an interest in Dorset," Takai said, glancing at the Rolex on her slim wrist. "He believes in environmentally sensitive growth. He believes in preserving an area's tradi-tion. Whether you know it or not, he's our best hope for the future."

"Our best hope for the future is that he gets cancer," Hangtown snarled.

"You're wrong about him, Father," she said, angry red splotches forming on her chiseled cheeks. "He's not Satan."

"He'll do," cackled Hangtown, who clearly relished these sparring sessions with his younger daughter.

His older daughter did not seem to be enjoying it at all. Moose's eyes were cast down at her empty plate, her hands folded in her lap.

"This is the price you pay for living in paradise," Takai said emphatically. "Other people want in, too."

"In which case it's not paradise anymore," Hangtown said. "We never learn. We destroyed southern California. We destroyed Florida. We destroyed Long Island—"

"Wait, I have to take issue with you there," Mitch inter-rupted. "Long Island was never nice."

"It's enough to make one wish for a nationwide economic calamity," Hangtown argued. "People need to simplify their lives. Spend less. Consume less. We are *pigs*."

"I'm going to have to take issue with you again—on be-half of Elrod," Mitch said. "He seems like a very efficient fellow who's doing no harm to anyone."

"I like this man," Hangtown said to Moose, as Jim refilled the wineglasses. "You ought to marry him."

"*You* are the pig, Father," Takai spoke up angrily. "*You* get to live here in luxuriant splendor but no one else can. That's not a community—that's a country club with a ceiling on its membership."

"I just want to be left in peace. Don't I have that right?"

"Not if it means denying other people *their* rights!"

Hangtown sat there in heavy silence for a moment, the fire crackling behind him. "You've been blinded by your own greed, princess. You think Bruce Leanse will line your pockets with gold, and you don't care who or what gets destroyed."

"You're wrong, Father. He's a good, good man."

He leered at her. "Well, you ought to know just how good he is."

"What's *that* supposed to mean?"

"Father, please," Moose interjected, glancing uncomfortably at Mitch, who was sitting there wondering if Hangtown was always so hard on Takai. "This is getting a little out of hand."

The old man ignored her, glaring across the table at Takai. "Shall I tell you what your problem is?"

"What is it?" she demanded hotly, glowering right back at him. "I'd really *love* to know."

"You inherited the Frye artistic vision but none of our talent. So you have to feed on real people in order to express yourself. You're a leech, my dear. A lovely, silken parasite."

"Th-that . . ." Takai was practically speechless, nothing but bottled-up fury. "That was an *awful* thing to say to anyone." She got up suddenly, toppling her chair over behind her, and threw her wine in her father's face. Then she stormed out, her spiked heels clacking, her hips swinging.

The dinner table fell silent as Mitch heard the front door slam, then the roar of the Porsche's engine. It pulled away in a splatter of gravel.

"Hot damn!" the great Wendell Frye exclaimed happily, using his napkin to dab at the wine that was streaming down his face and neck. "Another quiet evening at the Ponderosa. More lamb, Big Mitch?"

. . .

"I thought I'd make dinner for Bella here on Friday," Des said drowsily as she kneaded his chest with her bare toes. The two of them were lolling in Mitch's claw-footed bathtub together, still aglow from the atomic passion they'd just detonated upstairs in the sleeping loft. "I had hoped to be in my new place by now, but . . ."

"Not a problem," Mitch murmured contentedly, stroking her smooth, taut calf. "That's fine. Wonderful . . ."

With the bathroom door open they could see the fire in the fireplace and hear the vintage Doug Sahm on the stereo—Sir Doug's old San Antonio recordings with The Pharaohs. Both Clemmie and Quirt were balanced precariously on the edge of the tub, transfixed by the plopping, shifting water below. Quirt even dangled a paw down toward it, only to yank it back when Des playfully flicked water at him. It was strange how Quirt would only hang around in the house when Des was there, Mitch reflected. Even Clemmie seemed happier.

"There's somebody else I'd like to invite," she told him. "One of my . . . that is to say, a certain individual with whom I'm related is having a personal occasion."

Mitch eyed her curiously. Whenever she retreated into police-speak it meant she was ill at ease. "What kind of a personal occasion?"

"A birthday."

"And which particular relative would we be discussing, Master Sergeant?"

"Um, it's my father. And we have this tradition where I make Hoppin' John for him every year on his birthday. That's black-eyed peas and ham and—"

"Whoa . . ."

"Rice, with lots and lots of Tabasco sauce. I usually make cornbread to sop it all up and—"

"Whoa! Pull over a second, girlfriend. We're not exactly talking about what we're talking about, are we?"

Des frowned at him. "Which is what?"

"That you just said you want me to meet your father."

She fell silent a moment, shifting uneasily in the tub. "Well, yeah. Unless you don't want to, which I would certainly . . . Man, why are you grinning at me that way?"

"I'm *kvelling*."

"What does that mean—*kvelling*?"

"It's what your Jewish people do in lieu of an end-zone celebration. It means I'm tremendously pleased. But tell me, who am I supposed to be? A friend? An acquaintance? A portly, somewhat pink person you bumped into at the supermarket?"

"Okay, that's a fair question."

"And . . . ?"

"And it's none of his damned business."

"Hey, this sounds promising."

"Anyway, it doesn't matter. He'll know what's going on between us the second he walks through the door."

"How?"

"He's the Deacon, that's how. You think *you* can read me. Compared to you, he's Evelyn Wood. Besides which, I'm not a very good actress."

"I can't tell you how glad I am to hear that," Mitch said.

"Why's that?"

"Because it means you weren't faking just now when we were upstairs."

"Boyfriend, *nobody's* that good an actress," she said softly, her eyes shining at him.

Mitch had not known whether to expect Des when he got home from Hangtown's or not. Happily, he'd found her cruiser parked outside his cottage. And the lady herself parked on a stool at her easel, glasses sliding down her nose as she pondered an arrangement of empty bottles that she'd positioned on the floor at her feet. She'd stripped down to a halter top and gym shorts. And for Mitch there was something about the sight of her peerless caboose perched there on that stool that . . . well, within sixty seconds they were out of their clothes and up in his sleeping loft together.

It was so different than it had been like with Maisie. Within two weeks, he and Maisie had moved in together. Des was much more guarded and careful. In many ways, she was exactly like one of her feral cats. One moment she would inch toward his outstretched hand, purring. The next moment she would hiss and dart away. She was the most skittish woman he had ever known. Also the most alluring. Sometimes, he felt he knew exactly what she was thinking. Other times she totally befuddled him. For sure, she was not the sort of woman who he ever thought he'd find himself involved with. It was not the racial thing—which was not a thing at all as far as he was concerned. It was that she was a goddamned state trooper. And big into rules. She refused to keep any of her clothes at his place—always carting them to and fro in a gym bag. Refused to stay in his New York apartment, which she felt was Maisie's place. More than anything, Mitch felt, she was afraid of getting in too deep. Possibly this was the baggage she'd brought along from her divorce. Possibly this was because the two of them were so different. He didn't know. He only knew that she was beautiful and smart and honest, and the thought of her got him through each day.

"How was your drawing class tonight?"

"Way frustrating. He's trying to teach us three-point perspective. That's where you're looking directly *down* at the objects . . ."

"Hence the bottles on the floor?"

"Hence the bottles on the floor," she affirmed. "And it *looks* easy, but there's this killer foreshortening and I am *so* not getting it."

"On the plus side, I understand you saved Colin Falconer's life this morning."

"Man's a total mess," she acknowledged. "You would not believe what he's gotten himself into. But, word, you can't tell anyone one syllable of this. . . ."

"Not even Lacy?" Mitch usually told his editor everything.

"Okay, no one *local*. Promise?"

On his sworn oath she told Mitch about Colin's online romance with another man, his secretary's sexual-harassment lawsuit and Babette Leanse's insistence that he resign. "Either he goes quietly or he'll be outed," Des said, shaking her head. "It's amazing to me that somebody smart would mess up his whole life over cyber sex. Damn, it's not even *real*."

"What *is* real anymore?" Mitch countered. "Folks go to theme parks instead of actual places. They watch people do daring things on television instead of doing them themselves. Hell, *The Lord of the Flies* is now a prime-time game show. Can *real* get any weirder than that?" Mitch reached for a washcloth and mopped at his face with it. "While we're on the subject of a man messing up his life—would you bust a small farmer for growing pot on his land?"

"I have to," she responded. "It's against the law."

"Even if he wasn't selling it?"

"And I'm supposed to care because . . . ?"

"He was giving it away for free to cancer patients."

"It's still against the law."

"His name is Jim Bolan. He thinks a developer wanted his land and used the law to pry it away from him."

"Which developer?"

"Bruce Leanse."

Des fell silent, her body tensing slightly next to his in the water. "That man sure does think a lot of himself."

"He's what is known as a pub slut."

"Promoting himself is part of his business, isn't it?"

"Nope. It violates one of Hopalong Cassidy's most important rules in his Ten-Point Creed for American Boys and Girls: *Don't boast or be a show-off.*"

Des smiled at him, the mega-wattage smile that did strange, wonderful things to the lower half of his body. "Will you kindly explain something to me . . . ?"

"You're wondering how you ended up with someone like me."

"*How* did you know that?"

"Dunno. I just did."

"Well, how did I . . . ?"

"You got lucky, that's all. Don't question it. Just be thankful. I know I am." He sat up in the tub and kissed her gently. "Guess who else I met today," he said, his face very close to hers.

"I can't imagine," she said softly, gazing deep into his eyes. "Howdy Doody? The Lone Ranger? Lassie?"

A loud buzzing noise interrupted them. Someone was at the security gate that closed off Big Sister's causeway to the public. It took a key to raise it. Either a key or someone to buzz you in.

"Now who would that be?" Mitch threw on his robe and padded wetly to the kitchen window for a look. Across the water he could make out a single headlight at the gate, and faintly hear the phlegmy *putt-putt-putt* of a vintage engine. He immediately hit the buzzer, raising the security gate, and dashed to his closet for some clothes.

"Who is it?" Des called to him from the tub.

"Girlfriend, you are in for a real treat," Mitch assured her, flinging open the front door to the frosty night air just as Hangtown came roaring up to the cottage on his Indian Chief.

"Took you at your word, Big Mitch," he called out to him, yanking off his leather helmet and goggles. "Tonight's family night—it's Jerry and Ben Stiller versus Bob and Jakob Dylan." He was referring to *Celebrity Deathmatch*.

"Well, sure . . . Come on in." Mitch flicked on the television while his new friend came thumping heavily into the room. The old master seemed to fill the entire house with his massive size and aura. "Have a seat, Hangtown. Can I get you a whiskey?"

"Naw, I'm cool . . . Oh, damn!"

Johnny Gomez and Nick Diamond, *Deathmatch*'s commentators, were delivering their patented sign-off: "Good fight, good night." The Claymation wrestling show was already over. He'd missed it.

"Next time I'll tape it," Mitch vowed, as Des came striding in. She'd toweled off and thrown on one of Mitch's old flannel shirts, which just did manage to cover the essentials. "Hangtown, say hello to Desiree Mitry. Des, this is Wendell Frye."

Des was speechless. She could not believe she was face-to-face with such a famous and reclusive man.

"You're the new resident trooper," Hangtown exclaimed, feasting on her with his bright-blue eyes. "I was told that you mm-rr-draw beautifully. But I was not told you are an utter goddess. By God, if I were fifty years younger I'd fall right to my knees and kiss your dainty pink toes."

"*Dainty?* Man, you must be looking through the wrong end of a telescope."

"In fact, I just may have to anyway," he said valiantly. "Although I won't be able to get back up without assistance."

"You, sir, are an old goat," Des observed.

"Third generation. I come by it honestly."

"Well, if you don't behave yourself I'll have to get my handcuffs."

"Hey, you promised you'd only play that game with me," Mitch objected.

Now Hangtown was peering at the still-life display on the floor next to her easel. "God, you're in three-point perspective hell, aren't you."

"Totally," she answered glumly.

"You're frustrated. Don't be. I can help you with this. But you have to make me a promise."

"What is it?"

"I want you to think of yourself as growing one day *younger* each and every day for the rest of your life," Hangtown said to her, his voice soaring. "Growing more open to new ideas, more excited, more *alive*. Will you do that?"

Des considered this, her brow furrowing. "Okay . . ."

"Now, take this drawing—it's wrong, all wrong." He hobbled over to the easel and flipped her sketch pad to a fresh page, gripping the stub of graphite stick she'd left there. "Your problem is your damned adult brain," he said, squinting down at the arrangement of bottles at his feet. "It's telling you that the wine bottle is twelve inches high, the same way it tells you the curb you're about to step off of is twelve inches high, even though your eyes are *trying* to tell your brain it's only *four* inches high—that's the foreshortening. But if your brain believed your eyes, you'd fall in the street and scrape your beautiful knees, am I right?"

Des shook her head at him, mystified. "I guess, but—"

"A child *does* accept that the curb is four inches high, and *does* trip and fall. I say this to you, Desiree, because children in pre-school art classes can do three-point perspective without a hitch. They ace it. It's only we adults who have trouble with it. You must break free of your adult mind. See as a child sees. Accept as a child accepts. Here, I'll show you . . ."

Now Hangtown began to draw, working swiftly and lightly from top to bottom, first finding the proportions of his bottles, then his shapes. Then he began to apply more pressure, deftly using the side of the stick to add shading and weight until the bottles were suddenly *there* on the page, each in exact proportion to the other. The old man drew with passion and vitality, wielding the graphite stick like a sword. He seemed forty years younger. He reminded Mitch of Zorro.

And in less than three minutes he had created a still-life drawing that was not only incredibly accurate but bursting with vitality.

"I had no idea you could draw," Des whispered, awestruck.

"Of course I can draw," he said indignantly. "I'm an artist, girl. And you, Big Mitch, you're a lucky man. To think I was trying to press Moose on you."

"Moose doesn't have to be pressed on anyone," Mitch said, feeling Des's eyes on him.

"And now I shall leave you healthy young lovers. You've *much* better things to do. But before I go . . ." Hangtown hurriedly scrawled his name on the lower right-hand corner of his drawing, then dropped the graphite stub in Des's hand. "From me to you, Trooper Mitry. Welcome to Dorset."

Des stared at him, gape-jawed. By signing his drawing he had just presented her with a gift that was worth thousands of dollars.

"You know why I did that, don't you?" he said, cackling at her with glee. "Because I can't make love to you tonight. I'm too damned old, and you're my friend's girl. But I still fell in love tonight. Madly and truly." He leaned forward and kissed Des on the cheek. "Greta can authenticate it in case you ever need to sell it. Stuff happens. Believe me, I know."

"I-I can't accept this," she sputtered.

"Of course you can."

"But, Mr. Frye, you can't just *give* me this. This is insane!"

"Beautiful, and stubborn, too." Hangtown held a gnarled hand out, palm up. "Twenty bucks."

"Deal." She promptly went up to the sleeping loft to get her wallet, leaving Mitch alone in the living room with him.

"I wanted to assure you of something," Mitch said. "We were talking about it at dinner and it's been on my mind . . ."

"What is it, Big Mitch?"

"I'd never write about you. I'd never do that."

"Hell, I know that," he said, clapping him on the back. "But I also know that you may have to." Hangtown fell silent, a troubled look crossing his face. "Some things can't be avoided."

"What makes you say that?" Mitch asked, studying him.

"You get a feeling about things at my age," he replied darkly. "About people and what they might do. Whatever happens, Big Mitch, whatever needs doing . . . it's okay by me. Better you than some effete bed wetter who can't stand Bud and Lou."

Des came back down the stairs now, money in hand.

Hangtown snatched it from her and stuffed it in his jacket pocket. "Easiest double-sawbuck I ever made," he exclaimed happily. "Beer and smokes money for a week." He started toward the door now, waving an arm at them. "Good fight, good night."

"Are you okay to drive?" Mitch asked, heading outside with him. "I can run you home in my truck."

"Nonsense, I'm not drunk," he replied, climbing slowly back onto his bike. "Just crazy." And with that the great Wendell Frye kick-started his engine, donned his helmet and goggles and headed off into the night.

Mitch threw another log on the fire, and he and Des curled up together in front of it, snuggling under the afghan that Mitch kept there for that very purpose. Clemmie and Quirt, who had disappeared with such a big, loud stranger in the house, ventured back out, Quirt rolling around on his back while Clemmie determinedly pad-pad-padded at Mitch's tummy with her front paws. Clemmie did this with great regularity. Mitch chose to take it as a sign of affection, rather than a commentary on his weight.

"Well, well, he's still got him some funk in his trunks, hasn't he?"

"Quite the lady's man," Mitch agreed. "In fact, I'd be willing to bet there are beautiful women scattered all over the world with his signed drawings."

"Um, okay, did you just say what I think you said?"

"I don't know. What do you think I said?"

She batted her eyelashes at him. "That you think I'm beautiful."

"Why, do you have a problem with that?"

"Shoot no. I just like to know where I stand—especially when I find out someone's been pressing his daughter on you."

Mitch raised an eyebrow at her. "You're not jealous, are you?"

"I don't get jealous. Don't have to. I carry a loaded semi-automatic weapon, remember?"

"Believe me, that's not something I ever forget."

"See that you don't," she said, rubbing her cheek gently against his to let him know she was kidding. They were still new with each other's feelings, and still careful with them. "I met Moose myself today. I liked her."

"Well, you won't like Takai, believe me."

"She was bitchy to Bella on the phone. Really arrogant."

"That's Takai. She's hooked up with Bruce Leanse—in more ways than one, I gather." Mitch tipped her face up toward his, kissing her lightly on the forehead. "He hit on you today, am I right?"

Her eyes widened. "Damn, you scare me sometimes."

"Hey, I have a really crazy idea . . ."

"What is it?" she demanded, instantly tensing.

"Whoa, why are you suddenly on red alert?"

"Because the last time I heard those words from a man's mouth it was Brandon wanting to get us into a threesome with a paralegal named Amber."

"And did you?" asked Mitch. "Ow, that hurt!"

"So stop talking trash at me."

"I was *going* to suggest you spend the night," he grumbled, rubbing his arm where she'd slugged him.

"Mitch, we have been over this up, down and sideways. I am brand-new on this job. And appearances matter. And until the people get a chance to know me I don't want them getting any wrong ideas."

"They know all about us, girlfriend," he informed her. "Takai did."

"But how?"

"There are no secrets in Dorset, that's how. Gossip is their lifeblood. Face up to it—they are going to talk about us, and there's not a thing we can do about it except enjoy doing exactly what they say we're doing." He kissed her gently. Or at least it started out gently. If possible, they wanted each other more than they had an hour ago. "Although I can't imagine they have *any* idea just how good it is."

"None," she whispered, stroking his face, bathing him in the glow of her smile. "Um, okay, I'm thinking maybe I can make an exception tonight . . ."

"You won't be sorry," he vowed.

"I haven't been sorry yet."

"Des, I have a serious confession to make . . ."

"Now what?" she wondered, her voice filling with dread.

"At this very moment, in this very spot, I am the happiest man on earth."

She let out a faint whimper, which was something she did when he said something unexpectedly nice to her. Like that afternoon in Woodbridge when he brought her those flowers and they ended up together on the kitchen floor of her old house. Right now, she threw off the flannel shirt she had on and melted right into his arms, her caramel-toned skin warm and smooth and satiny.

They stayed right there in front of the fire, making slow, tender love deep into the night. Eventually, they stumbled upstairs to bed and slept, both cats curled trustingly around them.

Mitch dreamed he was in a dungeon. Rondo Hattan was there. And so was Des. The Creeper had her stretched out on a rack, naked, just as in one of those lurid comic-book illustrations of the early fifties. And he was mashing her dainty pink toes with a pair of pliers, one by one. And she was screaming. And Mitch tried to cry out, but he could not make a sound. Except for a beeping noise . . .

Until with a start Mitch realized he was awake and the beeping was coming from Des's pager. She was out of bed and reaching for the phone on his nightstand. He looked at the alarm clock, yawning. It was only five thirty. Barely light out.

"It's Mitry," Des barked into the phone. "Go." She listened to the calm, detached voice on the other end of the phone, her face revealing nothing. "I'll be there in ten minutes," she said, when it fell silent. Then she went dashing outside in Mitch's robe for the clean uniform that was in her cruiser.

Mitch padded downstairs after her, fuzzy-headed. He felt as if they'd slept for less than ten minutes. Quirt was meowing fiercely to be let out. Mitch complied, and was putting the coffee on when Des came back with her uniform inside a dry cleaner's bag. "Trouble?" he asked her.

"Got me a major-league hot one," she responded, starting toward the bathroom to change. "A car's exploded on Route 156 up by Winston Farms. I've got dead cows, bales of hay on fire. A real mess." She paused in the bathroom doorway, a troubled expression on her face. "Plus there's the remains of a victim inside the car. We can't be positive yet, but . . ."

"Who is it, Des?"

She took a deep breath and said, "Mitch, it's Takai Frye's Porsche."

"Oh my God . . ."

CHAPTER 6

It was the smell that got to her.

Des could smell the grilled meat from a half mile away. And what she found when she got to that rural crossroads at Winston Farms was uncommonly grisly. An explosion had flipped the red Porsche directly onto its back over by the feed troughs, where it ignited the poor animals and the bales of feed into a gas-powered fireball that she later learned could be seen twenty miles away in New London.

She was the first officer on the scene. Members of Dorset's volunteer fire department, with support from volunteer crews from East Haddam and Moodus, were still hosing down the smoldering wreckage with foam. As she got out of her cruiser in the dawn's gray light, Des could make out bits of charred, twisted auto debris scattered for hundreds of feet around. A dozen or more cows were dead, their body parts mingling with those of the Porsche. It had to be one of the ugliest crime scenes Des had ever seen. But it was the smell of that meat that bothered her more than anything else.

It would be a while before she'd find herself cutting into a steak again.

It was a calm, crisp morning. Glistening frost blanketed the fields, and steam rose off the man-made pond out behind the Winston's feed trough, where a collection of family members stood in saucer-eyed disbelief. A few horrified neighbors were out watching from across the road as well.

The volunteer firefighters seemed pretty shaken themselves. They were competently trained, but they were still civilians. Many of them were barely out of high school. They'd never seen anything like this.

Des's contractor, Tim Keefe, was the man in charge. Dorset's assistant fire chief was a husky, red-faced fellow with a walrus mustache. He was barely thirty, but very steady and mature. In the big city, a lot of men Tim's age still seemed like boys to her. Here in Dorset, they were middle-aged family men.

"Morning, trooper," he said to her grimly as he stood there in his firefighter's gear, clutching a license plate in one hand.

She motioned toward the car. "Is the victim still . . . ?

"What's left of Takai is still in there," he affirmed hoarsely. "Poor woman. No one deserves to die like that. I found this across the road." He held it out to her—it was a personalized plate that read: MYTOY. "It's hers, all right. I'd know it anywhere. Only new turbo in town. Damned car probably cost her more than my whole house did. We, uh, didn't attempt to move her yet. Didn't know what we were dealing with—whether it was a crime scene or whatever."

"You did right, Tim. What I need you to do now is keep everyone away from this scene until the Emergency Services team gets here. They have to check for undetonated explosives before we attempt to do a thing, okay?"

"Sure thing. I'll pass it along."

Des immediately got on her radio and reached out to the Westbrook barracks for Emergency Services, the Bomb Squad and Major Crimes. She also ran a check on the MYTOY license plate. It was Takai's, all right.

Then she slogged her way through the foam and crouched down for a firsthand look inside the Porsche, her stomach muscles tightening involuntarily. The internal temperature of a vehicle in a gas explosion was generally between eighteen hundred and two thousand degrees. A human being didn't stay pretty for long in that kind of heat. Takai Frye certainly hadn't. Not that what was in there even looked like a person now. Her body was nothing more than charred remains. It appeared to be intact, although some of the thinner bones, such as her hands, had turned to ash.

Des stared at it, thinking: *I will need crime scene photos. I will need to draw this.*

A pair of uniformed troopers pulled up now, the sirens on their cruisers blaring. They immediately got to work cordoning off the area and closing the road to all non-emergency vehicles.

Des strode out into the road to look for skid marks, Tim Keefe tagging along beside her. He seemed to have something more he wanted to tell her. She didn't see any skids— Takai hadn't swerved, hadn't hit her brakes. Whatever happened, it happened without warning. "Was it the farmer who phoned it in?" she asked him.

"No, that was me, actually," he replied, removing his big yellow firefighter's hat. He was losing his hair on top, and with his hat off he looked a lot older. "I live just up the road. I was up early, with the new baby and all. Soon as I heard the explosions I jumped in my truck and came flying down here."

"How many explosions did you hear, Tim?"

"Three. Two real quick ones, followed by a much louder one. I'm guessing the last one was the gas tank. As far as those first two, I never actually heard a car bomb go off. So I wouldn't know how it would sound . . ."

"How did *these* sound?"

"Like shots, to be honest."

Des raised her eyebrows at him. "A shotgun?"

He nodded. "That was my first thought. The sound sure carried like shotgun fire. It's duck-hunting season now, so I've been hearing it a lot—especially early in the morning." Tim trailed off, rubbing his high dome of forehead with the palm of his hand. "Except if it *was* a shotgun, man, it was a real boomer. The mother of all shotguns."

"Did you know Takai?"

"Everyone knew Takai," he replied with a shrug of his shoulders.

"I wonder why she was heading out so early."

"Heading home is more like it," he suggested, leaving the rest unsaid. "The Fryes live right down Old Ferry Road from here. She'd have made a sharp left here at the crossroads, then taken Old Ferry to Lord's Cove." Tim hesitated, clearing his throat. "This may not be the time or the place, but I've been meaning to call you about your roof."

She winced inwardly. "Now what . . . ?"

"Well, when they stripped the shingles off yesterday, they discovered that those old skylights were leaking. Whoever installed them didn't properly flash or caulk 'em . . ." Always, it was a previous workman's fault, she was discovering. "So there's water damage underneath. Your studs and sheathing are rotted out. That's all got to be replaced before the new roof goes on."

"How long will it take, Tim?"

"Another day or two. But there's no getting around it, I'm afraid. Your roof's not something you want to fool around with."

"Agreed, but let me ask you something straight up, Tim. Am I going to be in before Christmas?"

"Heck, yeah," he said reassuringly. "It's all coming together now."

Which was precisely what he'd told her two weeks ago. But Des didn't bother to point this fact out to him. She merely thanked him for the update.

Maybe Bella was on to something. Maybe she *was* a wuss.

The Emergency Services cube vans began arriving now, accompanied by a half dozen more cruisers. As resident trooper, Des's role was to fill them in and provide backup, if requested. The ES lieutenant, Roger Brunson, was someone she'd worked with often when she was with Major Crimes. He was smart and careful and good. After Des brought him up to speed he asked her to notify the next of kin. Then he and his men got busy looking for explosives.

Des climbed into her cruiser and took Old Ferry Road down to Lord's Cove Lane, a private bumpy dirt road that snaked its way deep into the woods. The sun's early-morning rays were just beginning to ignite the reds and oranges of the leaves on the maple trees all around her. When she spotted the totem poles and the giant grasshopper standing guard over the largest private junkyard she'd ever seen, she knew she had arrived.

The house itself was straight out of a postcard for rural New England, aside from its color, which was a shocking shade of pink. Hangtown's vintage motorcycle with its sidecar was parked out front, alongside an old Land Rover and a pickup truck. Lights were on in several windows.

Des got out, Takai's license tucked under her arm, and used the big knocker on the front door.

It was Hangtown himself who pulled it slowly open. The old artist was wearing a red flannel nightshirt, wool long johns and moccasins. His hair was uncombed, his gaze somewhat unfocused. He seemed dazed. "My God, girl, I just had a dream about you!" he cried out, peering at Des in astonishment. "You were wearing that very uniform. And I was being very naughty. And now here you are on my doorstep. Come in, come in . . . !"

She entered the house just as another man, a lean, leathery hard case wearing a moth-eaten Pendleton shirt and rumpled jeans, appeared from the kitchen holding a coffeepot. This one had ex-con written all over him—he immediately froze at the sight of Des's uniform, his jaw tightening.

"Say hey to Jim Bolan, trooper," Hangtown said warmly. Mitch's marijuana grower. That explained it. "Grab her a cup, Big Jim. We'll have us some coffee by the fire."

"None for me, thanks." Des stood there uncomfortably, her big hat in her hands. "I have to talk to you about an official matter, Hangtown . . ."

"Don't tell me I've pissed off another neighbor with my junk. Want to know what's wrong with these people, girl? They care more about their resale value than they do about their souls. Come on in and get warm. Jim's got us a fine fire going."

She followed them into the living room, noticing the suits of armor and the way that Jim Bolan seemed to hang back in the shadows. There were plenty of shadows. It was a gloomy room, and as cold as the inside of a tomb.

"Don't ever get old, Des," Hangtown grumbled as he limped toward one of the two leather chairs that were set before the roaring fire. A big German shepherd lay there on the bare wood floor, dozing. "Mornings are the mm-rr-worst— especially chilly ones." He eased himself slowly down into the chair, groaning. "Now tell me what I can do for you, girl."

Des removed the license plate from under her arm and said, "Does your daughter Takai own a red Porsche with the license plate M-Y-T-O-Y?"

"Yes, I do," a curt female voice answered. "Is there a problem?"

Des whirled, stunned, to find a tall, slender young Asian woman standing in the doorway. She wore a silk dressing gown, mules and a highly perturbed expression on her face.

"Why are you asking about my car, officer?" Takai Frye was extremely abrupt. Also haughty, condescending and beautiful. She was everything Des had expected her to be.

Everything except for dead.

Des stared at Takai in dumb silence, her wheels spinning. "I'm sorry to tell you that your Porsche, or what's left of it, is lying by the feed trough at Winston Farms. It exploded there at about five-twenty this morning." Des held the license plate out to her.

Takai stared at the plate but didn't reach for it. "I heard some explosions just before my alarm went off," she said in a cool, clipped voice. "Thought maybe they were dynamiting ledge up on Sterling City Road for another house."

"Did you hear anything?" Des asked Hangtown.

The old man shook his huge white head. "Not a thing. But Jim was lighting our fire right about then, weren't you,

Big Jim? The kindling pops and crackles and makes one hel-luva racket."

"We heard sirens," Jim spoke from the shadows in a thin, reedy voice. "Thought maybe there was an accident. Re-member, boss?"

Hangtown nodded, his piercing blue eyes never leaving Des's face. "You have more to tell us, don't you?"

"I'm afraid so," Des acknowledged. "The remains of one unidentified individual were found behind the wheel. Frankly, Miss Frye, I came here to prepare your father for the likelihood that it was you. Do you have *any* idea who was using your car this morning? Was it stolen? Is that what happened?"

The skin seemed to pull tighter across Takai's exquisite cheekbones. "Moose," she said softly. "It's my sister."

"Not a chance," Hangtown protested hoarsely, the color draining from his face. "Moose went to bed right after Mitch left, didn't she, Big Jim?"

"She did, boss," Jim Bolan said, fumbling for a cigarette. "Said she was going to take her a hot bath and turn in."

"She's still asleep," Hangtown insisted, his voice quaver-ing. "She's upstairs in her room."

"She's not up there, Father," Takai said, her eyes fastened on the floor.

"She is *so!*" Wendell Frye cried out.

"She . . . she went out after you'd gone to bed," Takai informed him in a strained, halting voice. "I loaned her my car because her damned Rover wouldn't start. She knocked on my door and asked me if she could borrow it. I'd just gotten home from a meeting with a client," she explained to Des.

"What time was this?"

"Twelve. Maybe twelve-thirty."

"No, she's upstairs in bed!" Hangtown erupted, his big gnarled fists clenching. "I *know* she is! Her alarm clock is going to go off any minute now. And she'll come right down those stairs to make us breakfast. She's *up* there!"

"Perhaps you should go take a look," Des said to him gently.

Jim helped the old man up out of his chair and the two of them went upstairs to find out.

Des stayed behind in the living room with Takai, who was fighting back tears. "I can't believe this," she whispered, biting down hard on her lower lip. "I just can't."

"Any idea where your sister was going at that time of night?"

"She'd been seeing a man lately. For the past two or three weeks. Always late at night. She'd get home before dawn."

"Any idea . . . ?"

"Don't ask me who he is, trooper, because I don't know. She's never confided in me that way. Not that there's ever been much to confide. She's always been the Frye family good girl. I'm the one who's the slut. Ask anyone in town. They'll be happy to tell you all about me. They just *love* to talk about me . . ." Takai was starting to run off at the mouth a little. It was her grief pouring out. "I was thrilled for her that she'd found someone. And if she didn't want to tell me who he was, okay by me. She deserves to be happy. She deserves to—"

An animal roar of pain came from upstairs now.

Des immediately dashed up there, Takai one step behind her, to find Hangtown sobbing uncontrollably in a bedroom doorway, his arms thrown around Jim Bolan.

"No, Jim, no . . . !" he moaned, tears streaming down his lined face. "No . . . !"

"C'mon, boss, let's have you a lie-down in your room," Jim said, steering the shattered old man slowly down the hall toward his bedroom. "You just take it a step at a time. Big Jim's right here."

"She was his little pet," Takai said to Des in a quiet, bitter voice. "He's going to have a really, really hard time handling this."

Moose Frye's bedroom was small and tidy. There was an old brass bed with a patchwork quilt on it. The bed was still made—it had not been slept in. There was a writing table with schoolbooks and lesson folders stacked neatly upon it. Over the dresser was a bulletin board where she'd pinned some of her students' artwork—watercolors of bunny rabbits and birds. Also a snapshot of a handsome young man and two little girls standing on a beach.

Takai noticed Des looking at it. "Moose was their au pair one summer, back when she was still in college. She had a mad crush on the father—not that she ever acted on it, of course."

Des backed slowly out of the room, touching nothing. "I'll have to ask all of you to stay out of here for the time being."

"Whatever you say."

"Any idea why her Land Rover wouldn't start?"

"Damned thing always gets moody when the weather turns cold. Key's in the ignition if you want to check it out."

"Someone from Major Crimes may wish to later on, so please avoid touching the vehicle as well."

Takai shook her pretty head at Des. "I don't understand why you're laying down all of these rules."

"Miss Frye, we don't know what we're dealing with yet," Des explained. "It may turn out that your sister hit a deer in the road. Or could be there was a gas-line leak." If so, the medical examiner would find accelerant in her lung tissue. "Could be she lit a cigarette and the car blew."

"She didn't smoke," Takai said. "That's not what happened."

"Okay, but until we figure out what *did* happen we don't want to compromise anything that might be evidence."

"You think this is a murder investigation, is that it?"

"I don't think anything of the sort," Des responded as they started back downstairs, Takai's mules clacking on the steps. "I'm just following procedure."

"Trooper, I really think you are missing the point here."

"Which is . . . ?"

"It was *my* goddamned car," Takai said, her voice rising shrilly. "Whoever killed Moose was after *me. I'm* the one who everyone hates. *I'm* the biggest bitch in Dorset. Don't you get it? They were after *me!*"

"You don't know that, Miss Frye," Des said to her in a calm, steady voice. "You're upset, which you have every reason to be. But what you need to do right now is stay cool." Des made her way toward the front door. "A top team is on its way down from Meriden. I promise you they'll get to the bottom of this. And if there's any reason to believe your life is in danger, they will protect you, okay?"

"Is there any chance it's *not* her?" Takai wondered, following Des outside in her dressing gown. In her grief, the woman was clinging to her.

"There's always a chance. But we should be realistic."

"How can you tell for sure?"

"By taking a DNA sample of the remains. We'll match it against a blood sample from a member of your family."

And if Moose's internal body parts were not totally incinerated they might also be able to get a DNA sample out of the semen residue within her vaginal cavity—leading them to the man she'd been having sex with in the night.

"I was just thinking I may know who he is," Takai said, as Des opened the door to her cruiser. "The man who Moose was seeing—it could be this guy who lives out on Big Sister named Mitch Berger."

Des immediately drew back from her, stiffening.

"The two of them *really* hit it off at dinner," Takai went on, a mean little glint in her eyes. "Maybe because they'd been seeing each other, and were just keeping it a secret from everyone. Maybe it was him she was with last night. What do you think?"

"I think not," Des growled at her balefully. Neither of them were women now. They were taut, predatory cats sizing up each other's underbellies, their ears pinned back, hackles up.

"Well, you would know," Takai said tartly. She'd done exactly what she'd set out to do—drawn blood. "There is one other thing you could do, trooper . . ."

"Yes, what is it, Miss Frye?" Des was angry at herself for letting this woman rile her.

"My father hates the media. This is just about his worst nightmare. Can you post someone at the road to keep them away?"

Des promised her she'd get right on it. Then she started up her cruiser and headed back toward the crime scene, watching Takai Frye in the rearview mirror as she sashayed back inside in the house, hips swinging in her slinky dressing gown. Even in her grief she'd had her claws out. Inflicting pain was what she thrived on.

Inflicting pain was Takai Frye's oxygen.

The Hartford and New Haven television news choppers were circling overhead now as the Emergency Services people combed the scene in their navy-blue windbreakers and baby-blue latex gloves. The Bomb Squad crime scene technicians were on hand, too. There were so many cube vans clustered together out there in the field beyond the feed trough that it looked as if the traveling circus were in town.

As Des pulled her cruiser alongside them, an unmarked slicktop with two plainclothesmen in it drew up next to her—and out popped the absolute last person in the world she wanted to see right now.

Back when she was a lieutenant on the Major Crime Squad, Des had been saddled with a petulant, muscle-bound little weasel of a sergeant named Rico "Soave" Tedone. He'd picked up his nickname from a Latino rap song by Gerardo that had briefly been a hit back when he was in the academy. Soave belonged to the so-called Waterbury Mafia, a tight-knit clan of Italian-American males from the Brass City who formed an elite inner circle within the state police. Most of them were related to one another—Soave was their deputy commander's kid brother, in fact. And he was, she'd come quickly to realize, someone who was trying desperately to outgrow being that kid brother. He pumped so much iron he looked positively reptilian. Grew a scraggly, see-through mustache that he thought made him look more mature. Dressed in sober black suits to lend himself an air of gravity. But none of it worked. He was a twerp. And their partnership had not been a success. He wasn't bad at his job, but he was immature and insensitive, not to mention extremely prickly about criticism. He had never reported to a woman before, and he couldn't deal with it. But he belonged to the Waterbury crew, and Des did not, and when things had gotten tight, he had stabbed her in the front. Now she was here, wearing a uni, and he was the lieutenant in charge of this investigation. And Des was not looking forward to this. No, not at all.

"Morning, Des," he said to her, sniffing at the air. "Smells like the parking lot at the Sizzler's out on the Newington Turnpike, am I right, Tommy?"

His sergeant promptly let out a reflexive hunh-hunh-hunh of a laugh. "Dead on, Soave."

"Nice to see you again, Rico," Des said politely.

"Back at you," Soave said, flexing his bulked-up shoulders, which was something he did when he was ill at ease. "Sergeant Tommy Salcineto, give it up for Master Sergeant Des Mitry. Tommy's my little cousin." Another Waterbury boy. "Known him since he was, like, three."

"Glad to know you," said Tommy, eyeballing her up and down. Clearly, Soave had bragged on her frame in the car on the way down. Tommy was younger, taller and decidedly dimmer than Soave. His eyes, which were just a bit too close together, seemed permanently set in a confused squint. He dressed just like Soave, wore his hair just like Soave and hung on Soave's every word.

All of which sent the little man off on an ego trip that he clearly relished. Christ, if the kid had breasts, Soave would have married him.

"So what have we got here, Des?" Soave asked her as they made their way across the field toward the wreckage of the Porsche. The all-clear had been issued—there was no evidence of any undetonated devices.

She told him that the victim was very likely one Mary

Susan Frye, age thirty-two. That the car belonged to her sister, Takai. That she had just been to the house and discovered Takai was home and her sister, who had borrowed the car, had been out all night.

"Out where?" Soave demanded gruffly. This was him acting take charge for Tommy's benefit. He even had his chin stuck out.

"She was visiting a man. Identity unknown."

"Maybe she ran into one of these cows in the dark," Tommy said. "You think?"

Soave went around to the front of the car for a look. "I don't think so, T-man. The front end isn't crunched. Any skid marks, Des?"

"None," Des responded. "Assuming the victim was on her way home, she would have come to a stop at the crossroads, then made a left and gone down that road toward the river. The assistant fire chief heard three explosions. He *thought* the first two might have been gunshots."

"Tommy, better have some uniforms canvass the neighbors," Soave ordered him. "Find out what they heard."

Tommy headed off to take care of it. Up above, the choppers were still circling.

"Anything else I ought to know?" Soave asked her.

"The victim's father is Wendell Frye, probably the greatest living sculptor in America. Also a major-league recluse."

Soave considered this, stroking his see-through mustache. "He got deep pockets?"

"I imagine so, yes."

"Any chance this is a money-related thing? A kidnapping gone bad, say?"

"Nothing should be ruled out at this point."

"Gee, thanks, I'll remember that," Soave said, bristling. Clearly, he felt she was lecturing him.

Des let it slide. "I've told the family a DNA test may be necessary to confirm Moose's identity—that's what they called her, by the way. If there's any way I can assist you from the local level, just let me know."

A photographer was snapping pictures of the remains

from as many angles as possible. Until he was done, Moose could not be removed to the medical examiner's office in Farmington. Des noticed that there was a strange, uncharacteristic hush among the technicians as they worked. It was the smell. It was all of the innocent animals that had died.

Soave was studying her curiously. "You're not enjoying this, are you?"

"I never enjoy a death, Rico."

"No, I mean the fact that I'm in charge now."

She let that slide, too.

"You know what I keep saying to myself?"

"Rico, I honestly can't imagine."

"I keep thinking you're the smartest woman I ever met. But tell me this: If you're so smart, how come you ended up back in a Smokey hat?"

"Priorities change," she answered.

He shook his head at her. "I don't get it."

"Not many people do."

"Are you telling me you're *happy* here?"

"I am."

He started flexing his shoulders again. Something was still on his mind. "Look, maybe we better stake out some ground rules—any information you gather on this case I want funneled through me. Are we clear on that?"

"Of course we are, Rico," responded Des, who knew exactly what was going on. He felt threatened by her presence here. He was, after all, a man. "Whatever you want me to do, I'll do. You want community liaison help, it's yours. You want a command center at town hall, it's yours. Otherwise, I'm in my ride and out of here. It's your case. I'm not looking to climb you."

He peered at her doubtfully. "You're not looking to get back in?"

"Not a chance."

"You're being incredibly mature about this whole thing, you know that?"

"Yeah, I'm all grown up." Des glanced at her watch. She

was due at Center School for traffic detail. "I'm going to take off now if you don't need me."

"Did you check out her gas tank?" he asked offhandedly, stopping her.

"No, I didn't."

"Want to have a look?"

She frowned at him. One minute he was creased, the next he was fishing for help. "Do you want me to?"

"Sure, if you'd like." Again, very offhanded. "I'm just saying I've got no problem with that. Unless you've got somewhere else you have to be . . ."

"Okay, let's have a look," she said, because the truth was that she was very interested in the condition of the Porsche's gas tank.

Lab tests would confirm if there had been a bomb—the device would leave nitrate or chlorate residue behind. But Des could tell it with her own two eyes—by the fracture pattern on the gas tank. A bomb explodes outside the tank, setting off a second explosion inside the tank. If, on the other hand, an explosion has been caused by a bullet piercing the gas tank, then it's the other way around—the tank explodes from the inside out. Entirely different distortion and bending of the metal.

As Des knelt there, examining the Porsche's gas tank, she had no doubt about what had happened.

Neither did Soave. "I got me a shooter, Des," he declared, as Tommy rejoined them.

"That you do, Rico," she agreed, shoving her horn-rimmed glasses back up her nose.

He had Tommy round up a dozen men to undertake a search for the spent bullet by fanning out in five-foot intervals around the wreckage. It was slow, painstaking work, but that was how you did things. And they might find it. Not that they'd be able to match it to a specific weapon—it would be too distorted from the explosion to do them much good in terms of ballistics. But maybe they could determine the class of weapon.

"Could be somebody was tailing her, Des," Soave said. "Got off a couple of pops when she came to a stop here at the crossroads, then hightailed it out of here. You think?"

Des found herself gazing around at the surrounding countryside in search of a shooter's blind, Soave's eyes following hers. From the open field where they stood she could make out a spot of high ground in the woods across the road, in the general direction of Wendell Frye's farm. There was a natural rise there, with an outcropping of bare rock that was partly shielded from the road by trees. "Unless he was waiting up there for her to come home," she countered. "Less risk that way. If he tailed her, somebody might spot him."

"Yo, Tom-meeee!" Rico hollered to his cousin, who was helping the uniforms search for the bullet. "Take a couple of men up to that outcropping across the road! See if you find any fresh shoe prints or anything like that. Be ultra careful, okay? The ground's damp."

"You got it!" Tommy obediently grabbed two troopers and started off with them across the road.

"What a big doofus," Soave grumbled sourly. "I have to tell him *everything*. And then I have to give him a cookie when he does good. He's not a man, he's dog. Was I ever that dumb? Wait, don't answer that . . . You don't mind sticking around for a little while, do you?"

"I don't mind." Des radioed the barracks to request an available trooper to handle the school traffic. Then she rejoined Soave, who was watching the medical examiner's men bag and tag Moose's remains.

Pictures. I will definitely need pictures of this.

"How's the jungle, Rico?"

"Same."

"And your girl—what's her name, Tammy?"

"Close, it's Tawny." She was a manicurist in New Britain. Enjoyed an IQ roughly equal to that of a muskmelon. "What about her?"

"How long have you two been seeing each other now?"

"Uh, since high school."

"Which makes it *how* many years?"

"Nine, I guess. So what?"

"Damn, Rico, you belong on 'Jerry Springer' or something." One thing hadn't changed—with Soave, Des grabbed her pleasure where she could. "What is *wrong* with that girl? Is she a doormat or is she just plain comatose?"

"I don't know what you mean," he said irritably. "What's the big deal?"

"You ought to be marrying her, that's what. Settle down and have yourself some little Tedones."

He made a face. "No offense, Des, but I liked you a whole lot better when you were just trying to stick me with a cat."

"No offense taken. But, hey, if you're really in the market for another kitten—"

"I'm not," he snapped. "Believe me, I'm not."

"Yo, Swa-vayyyy!" Tommy was calling to him now from the woods across the road, waving both arms excitedly in the air. "Yo! Yo!"

They started across the road toward him, crashing through the fallen leaves as they hiked over the rugged terrain. What they found when they reached the rock outcropping was Tommy and the two uniforms crouched in a semicircle around a spent cartridge. It lay on the ground underneath a mountain laurel.

"Looks like you figured right again, Soave," Tommy said eagerly. At least Des knew what to get the kid for Christmas now—a nice set of knee pads. "Must be he couldn't find it in the dark."

"Didn't want to risk hanging around," Soave concurred.

"We've got shoe prints, too," Tommy added. "Also a cigarette butt—the old-fashioned kind, without a filter."

"Nice going, T-man," Soave said to him warmly. Cookie time.

As for Des, she found herself puzzled. Because you did not leave a butt behind. Not if you were the least bit careful. She knelt down for a closer look at the cartridge. It was no ordinary one. It was a good six inches long. "Damn, I haven't seen one of these puppies since Kuwait," she said,

Tommy's eyes widening at her in surprise. Evidently Soave had neglected to mention that she had game. "This explains what Tim Keefe said to me."

"Which was what?" Soave growled. Now he was irritated by her presence.

She should just go. So why didn't she? "That it sounded like the mother of all shotguns," she replied. "What he heard was a Fifty-Cal Pal." Formally known as a Barrett .50-caliber long-range semiautomatic sniper rifle. The Barrett had been designed by the military for taking out enemy tanks and bunkers. It only weighed about thirty pounds, but had staggering power and range—its armor-piercing bullet could go through a manhole cover from a half mile away. "Pretty much weapon of choice among your wackos," she added, getting up out of her crouch. "Tim McVeigh owned him a pair."

And someone in bucolic Dorset had one, too. Not that Soave would have an easy time finding out who. It was easier to buy a Barrett at a gun show than it was a handgun. All you had to prove was that you were eighteen and had no felony convictions. There was no waiting period, and nothing to stop you from passing it on to someone else. The ammunition was a bit harder to come by, but not much. All of which was crazy, in her opinion. But this was Soave's crime scene, and she was not there to offer her opinions. So she kept them to herself as she stood there, inhaling the crisp morning air. It didn't smell of grilled meat up here.

"He was waiting here for her, Tommy," Soave said, gazing down at the road from their rocky perch. The view from up here was unobstructed. Also panoramic—the shooter could have seen the red Porsche coming from a mile away. "He planned this whole thing out in advance. Man knows how to shoot, too. What are we talking from here, two hundred yards?"

"Easy," Tommy said.

"Des, you'd better set up that command center for me at town hall, okay?"

"Be happy to."

"And I want you with us when we meet the family. Is there any kind of local angle you can give us? Any idea who might have wanted Moose Frye dead?"

"All I can tell you is how her sister Takai reads it," Des replied. "That someone was after *her* and got Moose by mistake—just Moose's bad luck that she picked last night to borrow her sister's car. Takai's afraid for her life, Rico. She thinks somebody still wants her dead."

Soave stood there smoothing his see-through mustache. He did that a lot. Tawny must have told him it made him look serious. "Any idea who?"

"Offhand, I'd have to say just about anyone who's ever met her."

"Okay, now I'm not following you," he said, scowling.

Des flashed a mega-wattage smile at him. "Not to worry, wow man. You will."

Des thought Soave was going to flex himself right into a coma when he got his first look at Takai Frye.

The little man huffed and he puffed as he strutted around the Fryes's living room, his chest stuck out and his muscles bulging. He was positively desperate to show Takai how in command he was. Takai was exactly the sort of tall, cool rich girl he was always trying to impress. She had put on a pale-green silk dress and high-heeled sandals. Her manner was subdued as she stood before the windows, her slender arms folded before her. She appeared to be in control of her emotions now. She also appeared to be oblivious to Soave and his preening.

The living room remained cold and gloomy, despite the fire roaring in the fireplace. Hangtown, who still wore his nightshirt and long johns, sat slumped in a leather wingback chair, staring with heavy sadness at the flames. The old man seemed to have aged five years in the hour since Des had been there. His eyes were hollow and bloodshot. His vital, madman's energy seemed to have been snuffed out. Des could not be sure that he even knew they were there.

Jim Bolan sat in the other leather chair, chain-smoking

Lucky Strikes and acting very much like someone who needed to find a drink. Or an AA meeting. His hands shook.

Soave had left Tommy behind at the crime scene. The uniformed trooper whom he'd brought along stood there in the living room doorway in stolid silence, hands on his hips, as the little man held forth.

Right now, it was the cartridge that Soave was talking about. "Somebody fired on that Porsche with a Barrett fifty-caliber rifle," he declared, keeping his voice deep and authoritative. "That's no Saturday Night Special, folks. Whoever used it knows his way around serious military hardware. If you know of *anyone* who fits that description—"

"You can pull over right there, boss." Jim spoke up in a hoarse, quavering voice. "I do. I was a sniper in 'Nam."

Soave stuck his chin out at him. "You own a gun like that, Jim?"

"I don't have no use for guns anymore," Jim replied, tossing his cigarette butt in the fire. "I already did enough killing to last me a lifetime."

"I see that you're a smoker, Jim."

Jim shook another Lucky out of his crumpled pack and lit it. "You going to run me in for that?"

Soave flashed a quick look at Takai to see if she'd reacted to Jim's crack. She hadn't. "Smart-mouthing doesn't go over so good with me, Jim," he said, moving closer to him. "Somebody comes at me with an attitude, I immediately think he's hiding something. If I ask you a question, I have a reason for it. Do we understand each other?"

"You're the man," Jim said sullenly. "Whatever you say."

"You got that right," Soave agreed. "And I say we found an unfiltered butt near that cartridge. Sure looked to me like it could have been a Lucky. What do you think, Des?"

"Could have been," Des said evenly.

"That's your brand, am I right, Jim?"

Jim ran a hand through his stringy gray hair. "So what?"

"So things suddenly don't look so good for you, Jim. We test the saliva on that butt and the DNA matches yours, then I've got you at the scene."

"You've got my cigarette, man. Not me."

Soave went over to inspect one of the suits of armor in the middle of the room. Hangtown stirred slightly when he did that, glancing at the floor under Soave's feet. Des didn't know why.

"You've been taken down before, am I right, Jim?" Soave demanded gruffly. Des had told him about Jim's record on the way over.

"I ain't no drug trafficker," Jim responded bitterly. "That was all a lie. But it cost me my family's land, and I sure do regret that." Jim was looking right at Takai when he said this, Des noticed. Now he turned his gaze back on Soave. "You want to polygraph me, go ahead. You want to test me for gun residue, go ahead. You're looking at the wrong man. No way I'd do anything to hurt Moose. She was like a sister to me."

"Are you sure that's all she was to you?"

Jim started up out of his chair, seething with anger. "You got some nerve, mister, talking like that in front of the old man!"

"Now just relax, Jim," Des cautioned, stepping between the two of them. Hangtown just continued to sit there, staring into the fire. "The lieutenant's only trying to get answers."

"You tell him to watch his mouth," Jim warned her between gritted teeth.

"I hear she was visiting some guy, Jim," Soave went on, undeterred. "Maybe you didn't like her stepping out on you. Maybe you waited at the crossroads for her to come home, shot her and hightailed on foot back here through the woods before anyone was the wiser."

"Lieutenant, you could not be more wrong," Takai spoke up in a measured voice. "There was absolutely, positively nothing between my sister and Jim."

"I appreciate your input, Miss Frye," Soave said to her, all but tugging at his forelock. "But it's looking real bad for you, Jim. Worse and worse, you want to know the truth."

Des knew exactly where her ex-sergeant's mind was going. He was thinking: *I am going to have this buttoned up by lunchtime*. She could see him liking Jim for it. There was definitely a circumstantial thread. But if Jim *had* shot Moose, why was he still hanging around? He'd be halfway across Canada by now, wouldn't he? Not sitting here in front of the old man's fire, waiting to get nailed.

"You're the man," Jim said to him once again. "You'll throw down if you want to, and there ain't nothing I can say or do will change that."

"You're going to the School House, Jim," Soave informed him coldly. The Central District Major Crime Squad headquarters in Meriden had previously been a state-run reform school for boys. Everyone on the job called it the School House. "There'll be more questions, and a blood test. Have him held until I get there," he ordered the uniformed trooper.

Hangtown sat up in his chair for the first time since they'd arrived. "Must you take him away, Lieutenant? Must you take my friend?"

"It's strictly routine questioning, Hangtown," Des said to him gently.

"Yes, but can't you do that sort of thing mm-rr-here?" Hangtown pleaded. "Jim is my hands. I can't work without him. And if I can't work right now, I-I'll just . . . I won't get through this agony, this . . ."

Soave softened in the face of the great artist's pain. Plus he was anxious to show Takai his caring side. "Give me a good reason why I should trust you, Jim."

"I'll never leave the property, sir," Jim vowed. "Not with all of them reporters trying to jump our fence. I got to watch out for the boss. That's what I do. So you got no cause to worry. Word of honor."

"I don't want to have to come looking for you," Soave warned him.

"He just gave you his word, Lieutenant," Hangtown said balefully. "That may not mean much to you, but around here it means everything."

Soave struck his thoughtful, smoothing-the-mustache pose. "Okay, Mr. Frye. We'll do it your way. As for *you*,

Miss Frye, rest assured that a state trooper will be on the front gate twenty-four hours a day. Also a man stationed right here in the house. You have no reason to be frightened. But if anything does bother you, anything at all . . ." He handed her his card. "You can reach me day or night. Don't hesitate to call."

Takai accepted the card, but said nothing in response, which left Soave thrown for words. Hastily, he turned to Des and said, "Did you try starting the victim's car?"

"No, I didn't," Des replied. "Key's in the ignition."

"You ever drive that Land Rover, Jim?" Soave asked him.

"We all drive it. Only car we got that can make it down to the plowed road when it snows." Jim's eyes narrowed at him. "My prints are all over it, if that's what you're wondering."

Soave told the uniformed trooper to give it a go. The trooper fetched a pair of protective latex gloves from the trunk of his cruiser and hopped in, Des and Soave watching him from the front doorway of the house.

Moose's Land Rover kicked over and started without a hitch, clouds of exhaust billowing from its tailpipe.

"I thought she told her sister it was dead," Soave said, astonished.

"She did," Des said, the trooper getting out to raise the hood for a look.

"So what do you make of that?"

"I take it you've never owned a vintage British automobile, Lieutenant," Takai said rather archly from the entry hall behind them.

Soave drew back slightly, sensing he was being dissed. "No, I never have, miss. Why does that matter?"

"I'm terrible at jokes, but there's an old one about the reason why the Brits drink their beer warm. The punch line is that the same outfit that does the wiring on their cars also makes refrigerators. They're famously unreliable, in other words. Especially when the weather turns cold. You say a prayer that it will start. You tap the dashboard three times for luck. You stroke it. And, above all, you make sure you park it where the morning sunlight will hit its hood."

Which Moose had done. The Land Rover was sitting directly in the morning sun.

"Doesn't appear to have been tampered with," the trooper called to Soave, slamming the hood shut.

"May I drive it, Lieutenant?" Takai asked him. "I've lost my own car."

"I don't see why not. But you ought to get yourself something you can really count on. If I lived around here I'd buy me a Grand Cherokee."

"Yes, but you don't live around here, do you," she pointed out.

Soave stiffened. Now he *knew* he was being dissed.

The phone rang in the kitchen. Takai went to answer it.

"Yo, I'm beginning to see what you meant about her," he muttered at Des.

"Rico, I had me a feeling you would."

Takai wasn't gone long. She looked somewhat pale on her return.

"Who was it, girl?" Hangtown asked her, limping his way heavily from the living room toward them.

"No one, Father," she answered shortly.

"Don't be coy, damn it!" he thundered at her. "Who was it?"

"It was just the school calling," Takai said, her voice fading. "About why Moose didn't come to work this morning. They . . . they wanted to know whether she'd be back tomorrow."

The old man let out a sob of pure anguish. "I'm not going to make it," he cried out. "I will die. Oh, Lord, I will die!"

CHAPTER 7

Scareeee . . . reeee . . . yeeeeowww . . .

Mitch was working his way through the chord changes in Hendrix's lead-in to "Hey, Joe," an achievement that for him ranked right up there with scaling Everest's south summit, when the bad news came down.

Scareeee . . . dee-dowwww . . .

Playing his Stratocaster had been Mitch's third choice for how to keep sane after Des went tearing off toward Winston Farms in the pre-dawn darkness. First, he had tried going back to sleep. An entirely logical thing to do. Clemmie certainly had no problem. But Clemmie also had a brain the size of a garbanzo bean. So Mitch got up and tried to channel his nervous energy into his reference book on Westerns—a sidebar on Quirt's namesake, Quirt Evans, the wounded gunfighter played by John Wayne in *The Angel and the Badman*, a tidy little 1947 release with Gail Russell and Harry Carey that *Witness* ripped off some forty years later. But Mitch found he had about as much luck working as he did sleeping. The words on his computer screen were just meaningless squiggles. So he played.

Skchsssschaheee . . . chaheeee . . .

Mitch had no ear for music. He knew this. But he had the love and he had the power. And, in the immortal words of Meat Loaf, two out of three ain't bad. So he played, his pair of Fender twin reverb amps cranked up high, one set of toes curled around his wa-wa pedal, the other around his Ibanez tube screamer. He played, his eyes shut, tongue stuck out of the side of his mouth.

Scareeeeeee . . . reeee . . .

Until Des finally phoned to tell him it wasn't Takai who was dead.

"It's Moose, baby," she reported grimly. "At least we think it is. Her body's burned beyond recognition."

Mitch was so stunned he could barely speak. "Any chance it's *not* her?"

"Slim to none." Des explained to him how Moose had borrowed Takai's Porsche to go see a beau and never returned. "She'd have to be pulling one of the most elaborate disappearing acts in history. Look, I don't know if I'll be able to see you tonight. My time may not be my own for a while."

"I understand," he said, hearing the dread in her voice. "Are you okay?"

She fell silent a moment. "I'm interfacing with my old crew from Major Crimes—first time since I put the uni back on. It's weirder than weird."

"You're doing what you want to be doing," he told her. "That makes you way smarter than they are. Not to mention ten times hotter."

"Guess I just needed to hear the words," she said faintly. "Thanks, baby."

"That's the second time you've called me baby. You never did that before."

"Do you mind it?"

"The next time we see each other, I'll show you just how much I mind," he said to her with tender affection.

But as soon as he hung up the phone Mitch was overcome by feelings of confusion and helplessness. Twelve hours ago he and Moose were feeding Elrod together. And now, through no apparent fault of her own, she was gone. Why? He stood there for a long moment gazing out his windows at a lobsterman in a Boston Whaler as he chugged his way slowly out onto the Sound. Mitch wondered what it would be like to be that man. He wondered what was on his mind right now, at this very second. Then he shook himself and called Lacy.

His editor answered on the first ring. She had just gotten in, but she already sounded alert and sharp as a razor. That was Lacy. "To what do I owe this honor, young Mr. Berger?"

"I had a nice hook on that Cookie Commerce story," he told her glumly. "Emphasis on the word *had*."

"You're talking about Mary Susan Frye, am I right?"

"Now how on earth did you know that?"

"The first report just came in over the wire," Lacy answered. "They passed it on to me because of who her father is. What's going on out there? Talk to me."

He talked to her. Told her how he had befriended the reclusive Wendell Frye, hearing the immediate uptick of excitement in her voice. Told her about Takai and how she was hooked up with the Brat, who was building houses all over Dorset and offering to donate the land for a big new elementary school. And how his wife, Babette, president of the school board, was the one pushing hardest for it. He told her about how Babette was squared off against the school superintendent, Colin Falconer—the hush-hush cyber-sex scandal, his suicide attempt. He told her about how this battle over Center School wasn't about a school at all, but over the very soul of a quaint, rural New England village.

As he talked, Mitch began to realize that he was pitching Lacy a story. He hadn't planned to, but deep down inside he must have wanted to. Why else had he felt the urge to call her?

"Mitch, how does the death of Wendell Frye's daughter fit into all of this?" she asked when he'd finished filling her in. "How do the pieces fit together? *Do* they fit together?"

"Lacy, I honestly don't know. But I'd like to look into it."

"Go for it. I'll talk to the magazine and call you back."

Mitch hung up and reached for a fresh notepad and started jotting down questions that needed answering. Questions like . . . How much of Dorset had Bruce Leanse actually bought up? What were his real plans? How did the school figure into them? How did Takai?

Now his phone was ringing. He picked it up, thinking it would be Lacy.

"I'm going to kill the son of a bitch who did this to my Moose!" Hangtown roared at him. "You hear me, Big Mitch? With my own two hands!"

"Hangtown, I'm so incredibly sorry—"

"He's a dead man! Dead!"

"That's no answer. You've got to let the law handle this."

"But that lieutenant's a muscle-bound cretin—he's actually trying to pin it on Jim!"

"Des will keep an eye on things," Mitch assured him. "Believe me, nothing gets by her. And if there's anything I can do . . ."

The old master was silent a moment. "Are you my friend, Big Mitch?"

"You bet."

"You'll help me?"

"Just tell me how."

"Jim and me, we were smoking ourselves some home-grown when Moose was killed. Understand what I'm saying?"

"You were getting stoned together."

"It helps me with my arthritis pain. Mornings are the worst. I can barely get out of bed. But I can't tell them we were getting high because it's a violation of Jim's parole. They'll send him back to jail. And, wait, there's more—Jim still keeps his hand in. Had some dynamite plants growing out behind the cottages this summer. I've got *pounds* of the stuff stashed in my dungeon, Big Mitch, and a state trooper camped on my doorstep at this very minute—" Hangtown broke off, wheezing. "Will you tell Des for me?"

"Tell her what, Hangtown?"

"The *truth*—that I can vouch for Jim's whereabouts. That he's innocent. Only, you've got to whisper it in her ear, or they'll set the dogs loose on him. Can you do that for me?"

"I can. But I can't guarantee how she'll respond."

"She'll do what's right," the old man said with total certainty.

"Hangtown, there's something else we need to talk about. I just spoke to my editor at the paper—"

"You're going to write a story about this. Of course you are. I understand."

"How did you know last night? That I might have to write about you. How did you know?"

"I told you—you get a sense of things when you get to be my age. You lose your friends. The people who you love . . . they get taken from you. But you do gain that."

"I won't quote you. Not unless you want me to."

"I don't care, Big Mitch. Don't care about that stuff anymore. My Moose is gone. My Moose is . . ." Wendell Frye let out a strangled cry. "Someone just cut my *heart* out." Sobbing, he hung up the phone.

Mitch's own chest felt heavy with grief. Moose's death was causing him to revisit emotions he hadn't gone near since he lost Maisie. He didn't want to go through this. He didn't want to go to another funeral. He didn't want to ask himself those awful, painful questions that had no answers, such as: Why does someone vibrant and good get snuffed out before her time while the cruel, the dishonest and the horrible just keep right on using up air and skin until a ripe old age? When he was on the job in a darkened screening room, alone with his notepad, Mitch never had to ponder such unanswerable questions. Hollywood movies steered carefully around them. Hollywood movies steered carefully around anything that made audiences unhappy. But out here in the sunlight, he did have to think about such things. Because if you got involved with people, things happened to those people, and not all of those things were good.

In fact, sometimes it seemed that none of them were.

And so he hopped in his old truck and went rattling over the wooden causeway toward town, where he could begin to deal with it.

First he had to stop at Sheila Enman's mill house in front

of the waterfall on Eight Mile River. She needed to be told. It would be better if she heard it in person.

The old schoolteacher was seated on a plain wooden chair by her kitchen window, her stooped, big-boned body clad in a ragged yellow cardigan and dark green slacks. Her walker—Sheila called it her giddy-up—was parked near at hand.

Mitch enjoyed Sheila Enman immensely. She was a feisty old Yankee who'd lived in her wonderful mill house all of her life. She had great stories to tell, and age hadn't slowed her mind one bit.

Except today it seemed to have ground to a halt entirely. Gazing out of her window at the waterfall, Sheila was almost like a different person—vacant, remote and despondent. "Selectman Paffin just stopped by," she said to Mitch in a muted, hollow voice. "Is it true, Mr. Berger? Is she really gone?"

Mitch dropped into the chair next to hers. "I'm afraid so, Mrs. Enman."

"She had every reason in the world to be stuck-up. Her father's position and all—Lord knows, Takai is. But not Moose. Never Moose. She was so sweet, so giving . . ." Sheila pulled a wadded tissue from the rolled-back sleeve of her sweater and dabbed at her eyes. "I must apologize, but I didn't bake anything for you this morning. I just couldn't bring myself to."

"Don't be sorry about that, Mrs. Enman. Don't even think about it."

"But I have such a favor to ask. That is, if you don't mind . . ."

"Of course not. Anything."

"Will you take me with you when you go to her funeral?"

Mitch sighed inwardly and said, "Absolutely. I'll be happy to."

Dorset's town hall was a sober two-story brick building with dignified white columns, a flagpole and a squat bronze monument out front honoring the village's Civil War dead.

Inside, it smelled of musty carpeting, mothballs and Ben

Gay. The office of First Selectman Paffin was just inside the front door. He kept his door open at all times—if anyone had something to say to him, they could simply walk right in. One of those quaint small-town New England customs that Dorset cherished.

Ordinarily, Mitch found town hall to be about as lively as a wax museum. Today, its corridors were buzzing. People dashing in and out of one another's offices, gathering in doorways for urgent conversations about Moose's death, their voices animated, eyes shiny. Today, the natural order of things had been knocked utterly off-kilter.

The town clerk's office, where property deeds were recorded and kept, was all the way down at the end of the hall. Connect the dots, Jim Bolan had urged Mitch. Here were the dots.

The town clerk was a chubby, pink-cheeked grandmother named Jessie Moffit. "Do the troopers have any idea what happened yet, Mr. Berger?" she asked Mitch eagerly.

Which Mitch thought was a bit odd, since he and Jessie had never actually met before. He drew two conclusions from this, just in case he'd harbored any doubts. One was that everyone in Dorset knew him when they saw him, and two was that the new resident trooper was wasting her hard-earned money at the Frederick House. They *all* knew.

"Not yet," Mitch replied. "But I'm sure they will."

The property deeds were kept in a walk-in fireproof vault that looked as if it belonged in Dodge City, stuffed full of gold. Hanging from an inside wall was a U.S. Geological Survey map of Dorset's wetlands and estuaries. The plot plans were kept in an oversized map book. Jessie found him the map for the area of Connecticut River frontage where Hangtown lived, also the map encompassing Jim Bolan's old farm and the proposed site for the new elementary school. The deeds were recorded and filed by an index number. To find out a property's index number he had to look it up in the index book under the deed holder's name. Which presented a problem since he was trying to *learn* the deed holder's name.

Not to worry, clucked Jessie, who sent him down the hall to the assessor's office to dig up who had been paying taxes on the properties in question. After spending two hours there, combing through surveyer's map books and grand lists, and another hour back in the vault, Mitch was able to piece together not only who owned the major parcels of undeveloped land surrounding the proposed school site but when they had taken title to them.

Jim Bolan had not exaggerated. Huge chunks of land had changed hands in the past twenty-four months, just under three thousand acres of pasturage and forest in all—a vast amount of land for the precious Connecticut shoreline. The parcels formed a half-mile-wide ribbon between Route 156 and the river, bordered on the north by Uncas Pond and on the south by state forest. The ribbon was a continuous one, with the notable exception of Hangtown's farm, which was situated right smack-dab in the middle and enjoyed the choicest river frontage.

Jim Bolan's old farm was now owned by an outfit called Great North Holdings of Toronto, Ontario. Great North also owned two other parcels, 88 acres and 232 acres apiece. Bruce Leanse owned some 400 acres in all. Twenty that he lived on. Ten that were earmarked for the new school. The rest were presently under development as housing sites. Pilgrim Properties of Boston, Massachusetts, had bought three parcels numbering 40 acres, 22 acres and 410 acres. Two more chunks of land, totaling 860 acres, were owned by Lowenthal and Partners of New York City. The remaining 600 acres belonged to Big Sky Development Corporation of Bozeman, Montana.

A good start, Mitch reflected as he emerged, bleary-eyed, from the vault, feeling every inch like Erin Brockovich, minus the push-up bra. Now he'd have to find out who was behind all of these different companies, and what, if anything, they had in common. A journalism school buddy of his was a real estate reporter on the newspaper. In exchange for two seats to the premiere of the new Tom Cruise, she would tell Mitch how to track these people down.

He ran into Dorset's resident trooper on his way out. She was standing in the doorway of the conference room with her hands on her narrow hips, looking tall, trim and very lovely. "What's up, Master Sergeant?" he asked, smiling at her.

"Setting up a command center. What are *you* doing here?"

"I spoke with Lacy this morning. I'm writing a story about this."

Des's green eyes widened with surprise. "About Moose?"

"That's right," he affirmed, nodding.

She motioned for Mitch to join her in her office. It wasn't an Emergency Services facility—just a community outreach cubbyhole where she tried to make herself available to the public for an hour every day. The walls were papered with public service posters for handgun safety, spousal abuse and drug prevention. There was a desk and a phone. Otherwise, the office was impersonal and bare.

She sat down at the desk, shaking her head at Mitch when he started to close the door behind them.

He pushed it back open and said, "Her death is just my jumping-off point. It's really going to be about the changing face of a small New England town. The Leanse invasion, the battle over Center School, the Colin Falconer mess. What I'm searching for is how it all fits together."

"So you think it does?" she asked, glancing uneasily out at the hall every time someone walked by her door. An awful lot of people did, it seemed.

"Oh, definitely," Mitch responded. "I don't believe things like this happen by coincidence. That's the hallmark of mediocre screenwriting."

"Um, okay, this is the part where I remind you that we're talking about real life, not a movie."

"I may need to interview you. Being the resident trooper and all. Oh, and I've got something for you from Hangtown . . ." Mitch told her what Wendell Frye had said he and Jim were doing when the red Porsche was blown off the road. "He's hoping you'll know how to handle it. He seems to feel you will."

Des sat back in her chair, making a steeple of her long fingers. She never painted her nails. Considered nail polish a frivolous affectation. "I'll see what I can do. That's the best I can give you."

"Is Jim really a suspect?"

"Soave likes him."

"Soave?" Mitch frowned. "Wasn't he your sergeant?"

"Man's got his own sergeant now."

"Hangtown thinks he's an oaf. Muscle-bound cretin, to be exact."

"He's a competent officer," Des insisted, refusing to bad-mouth Soave to an outsider even though the guy had ratted her out to further his own career. She was strangely loyal that way.

"Do you think he'll arrest Jim?"

"Too soon to say. They're still collecting crime scene evidence." Des filled him in on what she knew about the Barrett. "They'll run a statewide search to see if anyone around here's got one. Hit the gun dealers and shows, one by one," she added, looking up again at the sound of footsteps.

These belonged to Bob Paffin, the red-nosed, snowy-haired first selectman, who stood there in her doorway with a jovial grin on his long, horsey face. "Trooper Mitry, I'm sorry to interrupt if you're having a personal conversation—"

"I'm not," she said crisply. "Mr. Berger is working on a story for his New York newspaper."

"Sure, Miss Enman says very nice things about you," Bob Paffin said, shaking Mitch's hand. "Awful business, this. Can put a real stain on a place. I hope you'll be kind to our little town in your story. You're one of us now."

"It's nice of you to say so," said Mitch, who was well aware that he would never, ever be *one of them,* not if he lived in Dorset for the next fifty years and served on every board and commission that existed. He was a Jew from New York and he always would be.

"What can I do for you, Bob?" Des asked the first select-man politely.

"I got another call from a merchant this morning about

those *boys,*" Paffin told her. "They spray-painted more of
their obscene graffiti last night."

"Where was it this time?" asked Des, sighing.

"Tyler Brandt's fish market. I can't even begin to describe
the anatomical filth they drew on that poor fellow's window . . ." Paffin shuffled his feet uneasily. "I'd really like to
assure the local merchants that you're making some genuine
progress on this. May I tell them that the Mod Squad's days
are numbered? Would that be an appropriate thing to say?"

Des narrowed her eyes at him. "I'm working on it."

"I'm sure you are," he said soothingly. "No criticism intended. Everyone is *thrilled* with the job you're doing. But it
would go a long, long way toward cementing folks' comfort
level with you if you were able to bring these boys to heel—
and soon."

"I am well aware of that," Des said, raising her voice
slightly. Des did not like to be pressured. Mitch had learned
this about her. "And I am working on it."

"Good, good. Well . . . keep it up." And with that,
Dorset's first selectman skedaddled back down the hall to
his own office.

The two of them sat there in tight silence for a moment.
More than anything, Mitch wanted to take her hand and
squeeze it, to touch her, feel her. But she had an iron-clad
rule against Public Displays of Affection. "You're having a
real problem with Moose's murder, aren't you?" he asked
her. "Sitting on the sidelines is not exactly your style."

"That's something I'll just have to work through," she
conceded, looking through her eyelashes at him. "How
about you? Not like you to seek out a story this raw, is it? I
know you wrote about your landlady, but that was different.
That happened to you. This didn't."

"Yes, it did," Mitch countered. "That's what it means to
live here—if something happens to one person, it happens to
you. You're involved, whether you want to be or not. I
learned a very valuable lesson today, Des."

"Which is . . . ?"

"When you live in Dorset, everything is personal."

Someone was waiting for Mitch at the security gate that blocked public access out to Big Sister Island.

That someone was Takai Frye, who was standing there next to Moose's old Land Rover trying in vain to buzz his house. A brisk, chilly wind was blowing off the Sound, and Takai wore nothing more than a green silk dress and teetery high-heeled sandals. No jacket or sweater. Not so much as a stitch under her dress, either. Her nipples, hardened by the cold, poked indecently right on through the flimsy silk.

"I was j-just t-trying to buzz you," she said to him, her teeth chattering.

"Where's your jacket?" Mitch asked, remembering the beautiful shearling she'd had on yesterday.

"I left it somewhere," she answered vaguely, shivering. "You're p-probably wondering what I-I'm doing here."

"You mean, aside from freezing to death?"

"I'm afraid to be at home, Mitch. Out here, it's safe."

"Aren't the police watching your house?"

She nodded. "But they can't watch the woods. Or all of father's secret goddamned passageways. C-can we talk?"

"Absolutely. Hop in."

Takai grabbed her suede shoulder bag from the front seat of the Land Rover and got in the truck with him. He drove across the causeway and led her inside the cottage. She stood in the center of the living room, gazing somewhat dumbly out at his view. He went and got a pair of heavy wool socks as well as a fisherman's knit sweater that Des was known to borrow from time to time. He brought these to her and lifted her bag off her shoulder so she could throw the sweater on over her head.

Her bag was surprisingly heavy, and it landed with a metallic *thunk* when Mitch set it down on the table. He drew back from it, frowning.

Takai showed him what was inside. It was a gun. A small, trim Smith & Wesson model called a Ladysmith.

"Is that thing loaded?" he asked her, gulping. He was not comfortable around guns. Guns went off.

"Always," she said determinedly. "In my job, I sometimes have to be alone in some pretty isolated houses with
some pretty strange characters."

"By characters you mean men."

"And they get ideas."

"And you discourage them."

"No one is going to hurt *me*." Takai sat now in his one
good chair, kicked off her sandals and crossed her bare legs
so she could put on Mitch's heavy wool socks, thereby affording him a fine view. Her legs were exceptionally long
and shapely and smooth. "Not that I've ever had to use it,
mind you."

"Do you know how to?"

"What's to know? You point and click, just like Ameri-
trade."

"Are you hungry? Can I get you anything to eat?"

"Not for me, thanks."

Mitch put coffee on and rummaged around in the fridge
for his pot of leftover American chop suey, wondering what
it was that she wanted from him. Takai Frye was someone
who would always want something. He grabbed a fork and
returned to the living room, shoveling hungrily from the
pot. "I didn't have any lunch," he explained between mouth-
fuls. "Plus I eat when I'm nervous, which accounts for my
appearance."

She watched him hoover down his cold concoction,
frowning prettily. "I'm making you nervous?"

"I would think that you make just about everyone nervous."

"Now I don't know whether to be flattered or insulted."

"I'm not trying to insult you, believe me."

Takai got up out of the chair, all woolly and warm, and
padded over toward the windows. "This is a darling cottage.
I can see why you'd never want to leave. And the *views*.
God, if a developer ever got his hands on this island . . ."

Mitch took some kindling out of Hangtown's old copper
bucket and started building a fire in the fireplace. "That can't
happen. It's been declared a historic landmark, thanks to the
lighthouse."

"How did you manage to get title to it?"

"Friend of the family."

"It helps to have friends."

"It sure does."

"I admire you, Mitch," Takai said suddenly, smiling at him. "You don't lead a conventional life. I've tried to do that, too, in my own way. I never wanted to be ordinary like . . . like Moose was. Not that there's anything wrong with being a teacher. I just . . . I don't ever want to be *average*."

"You're not," Mitch said, watching her carefully. She seemed to be starting the slow, painful process of dealing with her sister's death. He laid a couple of logs in and lit a match. The fire caught right away, snapping and crackling and lighting up the room with its golden glow. "How do you take your coffee?"

"Black."

He went in the kitchen and filled two cups, dumping a generous slug of chocolate milk into his. Takai was back in the chair when he returned with them. She took a grateful sip and set hers down on his coffee table, which he'd made by bolting a storm window onto an old rowboat. Clemmie moseyed over for a sniff, thought about testing out Takai's lap, but opted for the kibble bowl instead.

Takai watched the cat disappear into the kitchen. "I don't have any friends. All I had was Moose. And now she's gone and I—" She broke off, her voice choking with emotion. "Whoever did that to her was after *me,* Mitch. It's my fault!"

"You didn't pull the trigger. You're not responsible for what someone else did."

"Yes, I am," she said, her eyes welling up with tears.

Mitch stared at the fire in silence for a moment, wondering once again why she was here. "Any idea who it was?"

"God, take your pick," she answered bitterly. "Everyone in Dorset despises me. I'm an aggressive, independent woman. I know what I want and I go after it. They don't like that. They don't like it at all."

She wasn't totally off-base, Mitch considered, remembering the old Bette Davis adage about Hollywood: If a man puts his foot down they call him a strong-willed professional who cares. If a woman does it, they call her a bitch.

"But there *is* one person in particular . . ." Takai admitted, reaching for her coffee. "I did something a while back that I'm not very proud of, Mitch. I told the state police that Jim Bolan was growing marijuana on his farm. I did it anonymously. Called them from a pay phone. But ever since it happened, well, Jim's *convinced* I'm the one who did it."

"Why did you?"

Takai shrugged her narrow shoulders inside the chunky sweater. "I knew someone who wanted the property, and I delivered it. Strictly business."

"Was that someone Bruce Leanse?"

She didn't respond, just sipped her coffee, clutching the mug tightly in both hands.

Mitch watched her, the purpose of her visit clear to him now. "You want me to pass this information on to the resident trooper, is that it?"

"I'm *afraid*, Mitch!" she cried out. "What if he was trying to pay me back? What if he comes after me again?"

"It wasn't Jim," Mitch assured her. "Your father told me that the two of them were getting high together when it happened."

"Father's lying," Takai said with sudden savagery.

"Why would he do that?"

"Jim's his hands, that's why. If they put him away, Father won't be able to work. And that's all that matters to him. When it comes to people, forget it. He is beyond cruel. He drove my poor mother to a nervous breakdown with his abusiveness. And when he drank he used to beat her up. She was a sweet, gentle soul. A great beauty. And she ended up all alone out in California, working as a cashier in a Rexall drugstore in Laguna Beach. He wouldn't give her one cent. What little money she had she got from me. I even had to pay for her funeral."

"He said her death was very sudden."

"It doesn't get any more sudden—she hanged herself," Takai shot back, her smooth, finely planed cheeks mottling.

"And he did everything but kick the chair out from under her feet. As for me . . ."

"What about you?"

"He's never wanted my love, and he's never given me any in return." She was fighting back tears now, her chest heaving. "Don't be taken in by him, Mitch. He's a monster. He *destroys* people."

Mitch went over to the fire and poked at it for a moment. "I'll pass your information on to Resident Trooper Mitry, if you want. Only, do you honestly think your father would falsely alibi Jim for the murder of his own daughter?"

"Mitch, I don't know *what* to think." Takai got up out of the chair and came over next to him. She wasn't nearly as tall with her heels off, and looked rather frail in his sweater. "I'm not thinking too clearly right now."

"Because you're a little upset," he said, smelling her musky perfume.

A puddle of tears started forming in her eyes. Mitch was just about to offer her a tissue when she let go—hurled herself right into his arms and began sobbing uncontrollably. He held on to her tightly as she sobbed and she sobbed, her face buried wetly in his flannel shirt. Compared to Des, there wasn't much to her. She was as delicate as a bird.

"God, I am so sorry," she snuffled when she was finally cried out.

"Don't be. It's good for you."

"I never do that. I never, ever . . ." She raised her face to his, startled. "My God, you're doing it, too."

"I'm actually famous for my somewhat free-flowing tear ducts," he confessed, wiping his eyes. "The other New York critics call me the Town Cryer. I even sobbed through the end of *The Blair Witch Project*."

She let out a laugh of relief as he fetched a box of Kleenex. When the two of them were done honking like Canada geese, she went over to the window and gazed out at the barn swallows that were swooping down into the cedars beyond the lighthouse. "Moose was my moral compass. Without her, I'll be lost."

"No, you won't."

She glanced at him, her eyes red and swollen. "You sound so sure."

"I felt the same way when my wife died—lost. But I got through it. Not over it, but through it. And you will, too. In a lot of ways, it makes you a much richer person."

"You're a very sweet man, you know that?"

Mitch winced in pain. "That's what girls used to say to me in college when they didn't want to have sex with me."

"All I meant was I thought you were a bit of a smart aleck when I first met you. Now I realize you're not. And I really love this sweater," she added, snuggling inside it.

"Go ahead and wear it home. Consider it a loan."

"Thank you, I will. In fact, thank you for everything." She finished the last of her coffee and said, "If there's ever anything I can do for you . . ."

"Actually, I *could* use some help with my story." Mitch lunged for the heap of plot plans he'd just copied at town hall and hurriedly began spreading the pages out on the floor to form a large map.

"What's all this?" Takai asked, looking down at them guardedly.

"In the past two years several different development companies have bought up the land surrounding the proposed site of the new school. I was wondering two things," Mitch said, settling back on his ample haunches. "One, if you brokered any of these sales. And two, if you know anything about these companies."

"Yes and yes," she answered promptly.

"Excellent. We've got a Pilgrim Properties of Boston, Big Sky Development of Bozeman, Lowenthal and Partners of New York and Great North Holdings of Toronto. What I'm anxious to find out is who actually owns them."

"Bruce Leanse does. He's the principal owner of all four companies."

Mitch stared at her with his mouth open. "What, they're dummy fronts?"

"No, no, it's all perfectly aboveboard. Pilgrim's his New

England operation, Big Sky's his Western subsidiary. Lowenthal is Babette's maiden name. Great North is a Canadian holding company that gives Bruce a foot in the development door for Prince Edward Island, which he thinks is about to get really hot. For that one, he has a Canadian partner. Has to."

Mitch peered at the maps intently, scratching his head. "So Bruce Leanse owns all three thousand acres?"

"He does. It's the single largest tract of undeveloped land in New London County. He bought the parcels under different names because he was afraid the sellers would get wise to him and jack up their asking prices. Common strategy when big developers move into an area. Disney does it all the time."

"I understand," said Mitch, who did not understand why Takai was being so candid with him about Bruce Leanse's plans. After all, the Brat had gone to a great deal of trouble to cover his tracks. Was she so grief-stricken over Moose's death that she was telling him more than she should? Or was there no longer any need for secrecy?

"What do you get out of this?" he asked her, remembering that Jim had called her Leanse's "enabler." "Besides a commission, I mean."

"Bruce has *huge* plans. I'm talking about something that will literally reinvent how we live. He's a visionary, Mitch," she declared, growing more animated and flushed the more she spoke about Bruce Leanse. "He sees things no one else sees. And he knows how to make them a reality. There will be zoning hurdles, no question. That's why Babette is running for the zoning commission in February. There will be foot-dragging about the wetlands, the additional traffic—"

"Wait, how *much* additional traffic?" Mitch broke in.

"But he is totally sensitive to these concerns, and totally sure that this is something Dorset will want to embrace. So am I. It's our best hope for the future. And I want to be a part of it. I want to be a part of *him*. That's what I 'get' out of this, Mitch. But if you really want to understand what he's doing, you should go see him."

"He'd talk to me about this?"

"Absolutely."

"What about your family's land?" Mitch asked her, pointing down to the eight-hundred-acre chunk of prime river frontage that sat smack-dab in the center of Bruce Leanse's holdings. "What will happen to it?"

"Father's not stupid. And neither is Greta. She'll convince him to sell. He'll have to sell. It's inevitable."

"I kind of got the impression he thought Bruce Leanse was Satan."

"He's not Satan," Takai argued. "And nothing is that black or white. You're a smart man. You should know that."

"Moose certainly didn't want to sell."

"No one *wants* to sell, Mitch. God, I sure don't. I wish Dorset could stay exactly the way it is. But it can't. It's a living organism. If it doesn't grow it will *die*. Look, just talk to Bruce, will you? If you don't come away convinced, then I've misjudged both of you. And I almost never misjudge men . . ." Now Takai tilted her head at him coquettishly, wetting her pillowy lips. "That wasn't what I was hoping you'd say. When I asked you if there was anything I could do for you . . . Tell me, just how tight are you and that trooper?"

"Why do you want to know?"

"I was wondering if you could be pried apart."

"Not even by the Jaws of Life," he informed her. "You must be very upset or you wouldn't say something like that."

"No, I would, Mitch," she confessed with a regretful sigh. "I'm a consummate bitch—whenever I see a man who someone else has I immediately want him for myself. Especially if the woman's pretty, which I suppose Trooper Mitry is, in her way." Takai went and fetched her bag, complete with loaded handgun, and slung it over her shoulder. "I've taken up enough of your time. You must have better things to do than play host to a hysterical female."

"Can I ask you one more thing before you go? And if it's none of my business just say so."

"We shared a good, honest cry together. You can ask me anything."

"Who was Moose's boyfriend?"

"I have no idea. She never told me."

"Weren't you the least bit curious?"

"Not at all. And this will sound horrible, but it's the truth—I didn't care who he was because I knew I wouldn't be the least bit interested in him. We always had different tastes in men, she and I. Except for one time. Just once . . ." Takai trailed off, a fond, faraway look crossing her lovely face. "But that was a long, long time ago, Mitch. And I was much younger then. We were all much younger then."

Bruce Leanse ran his Dorset operation out of *The Brat*, an antique wood-hulled cabin cruiser that he kept tied up at Dunn's Cove Marina, a deepwater mooring in the Eight Mile River that had access to the Connecticut River and Long Island Sound. The marina was off Route 156 at the end of an unmarked dirt road less than a mile south of the cross-roads where Moose Frye had been killed.

It was a small, shabbily exclusive boatyard that catered to the gentlemen farmers who owned the nearby country estates. Here, the boys kept their toys. Yachts, as a rule. Big ones, though none as big as *The Brat*, which looked like something FDR might have toodled around in. The boatyard was deserted on this weekday afternoon in late October. There was only one car in the gravel parking lot, Bruce Leanse's shiny black Toyota Land Cruiser.

The developer heard Mitch pull in and came bounding out on deck to greet him, his handshake hard and dry. He had not sounded surprised when Mitch phoned him for an interview. Clearly, he'd already been alerted by Takai. He was dressed in a canary-yellow Patagonia fleece vest over a denim shirt, corduroy trousers and Topsiders. Mitch had seen photographs of Bruce Leanse in the New York tabloids many times over the years, but the pictures did not convey just how robust and self-assured the man was—or how short. Mitch was shocked to discover he towered over him.

"She's a one-of-a-kind, Mitch," he responded proudly

when Mitch asked him about the boat. "She was built in 1931 for the Connecticut state shellfish commissioner. She's got a sixty-eight-foot hull made of long-leaf yellow pine on white oak frames. I've had her for three years," he added, Mitch thinking that there was something faintly self-conscious about his dogged used of the nautically correct *she*.

There was an enclosed wheelhouse. A circular staircase wound its way down to the main saloon, which had interior cupboards of polished Philippine mahogany and banquettes of burgundy leather. A good deal of natural light came from the portholes on either side of the saloon. A built-in teak table served as Bruce's desk. He had a Power Book, laser printer and fax machine set up there. Papers were heaped everywhere. A fine old Van Morrison recording, *Astral Weeks,* played softly on his built-in sound system, which Mitch resented. He did not want Bruce Leanse to have good taste in music. He wanted him to be listening to Mariah Carey.

There were three staterooms aft, crew quarters forward. Steam heat, stall showers, all the creature comforts. The galley had a four-burner gas stove, a full oven and refrigerator.

"She runs on a pair of Fairbanks-Morris diesel engines," Bruce explained, showing Mitch around. "There's a three-hundred-gallon main tank, a seventy-five-gallon day tank. I can take her to Maine, the Cape, anywhere, except that Babette and Ben both get seasick on her—they can't stand the diesel fumes. So she's mostly my floating office. I'm going to hate pulling her for the winter. I always like having a place where I can kick back with my business associates."

Business associates like Takai Frye, observed Mitch, who could not help but notice her beautiful shearling jacket wrapped around a chair in the main stateroom.

"Can I offer you a beer, Mitch? Or how about some Juniors cheesecake? I had it sent out from the city this morning."

Mitch's stomach immediately started rumbling. "You might talk me into that."

Bruce disappeared into the galley while Mitch poked

around in the saloon, the big cruiser rocking gently under his feet. One entire mahogany wall was lined with photos of Bruce Leanse testing life's limits. There were shots of him rocketing down Alpine ski slopes, scaling remote Tibetan mountaintops, kayaking white-water rapids, shooting big game in Africa.

There were no pictures anywhere on the wall of his wife or son.

He returned now with a slab of cheesecake for Mitch and a frosty Sam Adams for himself. He cleared space for them on the teak table. They sat across from each other.

Mitch dug into the cheesecake, which was excellent. "Do you mind if I tape our conversation?"

"Not at all. I'm going to do the same thing myself." Bruce flicked off the music and set his own microcassette recorder right next to Mitch's. "I've had some trouble with journalists in the past, Mitch. They decide from the get-go that I'm a rich asshole and then they just go ahead and make up the quotes to prove their point." He took a sip of his beer, studying Mitch from across the table. "I hope you're coming to this with an open mind. Because as far as I'm concerned there's absolutely no reason for us to be adversaries. You and I really have a lot in common, when you stop and think about it."

Mitch did stop and think about it. Bruce Leanse's grandfather had been a reviled Lower East Side slumlord, his father a Park Avenue real estate baron who'd spent most of his career and his political capital trying to eliminate rent-stabilized housing in New York City. Mitch was one of those grubby little people who had been raised in a a rent-stabilized apartment. For thirty-six grueling years, his father taught algebra to ghetto kids at Boys and Girls High in the Bedford-Stuyvesant section of Brooklyn. His mother was school librarian at the predominately Latino Eleanor Roosevelt Middle School in Washington Heights. A lot in common? Not a chance.

In fact, it didn't even bear thinking about.

"Why do you think reporters have such a negative opinion of you?" he asked Bruce Leanse.

"Because I'm a happy person," Bruce spoke up boldly. "The press only likes rich, famous people who are in drug rehab or divorce court or jail. But if you have a wonderful wife and family, work that you love, friends whose company you enjoy, then they go after you. Human nature, I guess. They absolutely cannot accept the fact that someone who has it all *enjoys* having it all."

Mitch had himself another bite of cheesecake, wondering if the kids at school ever stole Bruce's lunch money or threw him in the shower with his clothes on. He doubted it. Bruce Leanse was still very much the Brat—a spoiled prince who'd always gotten his way.

Right now, Bruce was reaching for a set of blueprints and unrolling them on the polished teak table, pinning down the corners with leather-bound paperweights. "I am thrilled to have this opportunity to talk to you about my plans for Dorset, Mitch. What we're doing here is just incredibly exciting. Let's have a peek, shall we . . . ?"

What Mitch seemed to be looking at was the plot plan for an entire town, each area marked by an oddly understated designation: The Homes, The Stores, The Farm, The Water, The Woods . . . It seemed to Mitch like something vaguely out of Orwell.

"I want you to do two things for me, Mitch," Bruce said, launching into a well-grooved sales pitch. "First, I want you to look at the calendar. Can you see what it says? The entire baby boom generation is turning fifty-five. Second, I want you to forget everything you ever knew about continuous living choices."

"You're building a retirement village?" Mitch asked him in astonishment.

Bruce shook his head. "Not a chance. I am talking about something entirely new. Let's face it, the boomers will *not* want condo colonies. They will *not* want shuffleboard. Can you see them lining up for the Early Bird dinner special in their lime-green slacks and white shoes? They sure can't. And neither can I. What I'm looking to do here in Dorset is create a new concept in rural living that they *can* see—a vibrant, supportive community that revolves around nature. Mitch, I call it The Aerie," he intoned somewhat grandly, "because it's a place where eagles nest."

Now Bruce paused so that Mitch might pay some form of awed tribute to his genius. Mitch did so with a polite smile and nod. He wanted Bruce Leanse to keep talking, not that he thought for one second the man could be stopped.

"The Aerie will be a self-sustaining collective enterprise," he continued, his eyes growing bright. "A commune, in plain language. Just like back in the sixties, only this time with a Web site and a business plan and a full-time staff of paid professionals who know what the hell they're doing. When you buy your individual solar-heated cottage in the woods, you're also buying a share in the collective. There'll be a bakery, an organic-produce market, a butcher—all selling products raised and processed in The Aerie by retired professionals from all walks of life. Imagine making your own cheese from your own goats, Mitch. Wool clothing made from your very own sheep. Imagine a grist mill. An art studio where you can paint and draw. A spa so you can stay in shape. A full-time medical staff for when you can't. It will be like the Woodstock fantasy all over again, except this time it's *real*."

Mitch had to admit that Bruce Leanse was one terrific salesman, his enthusiasm both genuine and contagious. From his lips, The Aerie sounded not only possible but downright inevitable. It was as if by *wanting* his dream to happen, he could *make* it happen. All you had to do was click the heels of your red shoes together three times and *believe*.

"And what's going to happen here?" he asked, pointing to an area of the map labeled The Lodge.

"That's our profit hub," Bruce answered quickly, tapping the blueprint with his finger several times for emphasis. "A spa-type luxury retreat, complete with a world-class restaurant featuring our own organically grown foods. Think

Canyon Ranch, except you can actually *live* on the grounds year-round. Think of the millions of baby boomers who are nearing retirement age." Now he was back into his spiel. "We have to find a place for them. We have to find a new philosophy. The Aerie is it. I see dozens and dozens of Aeries springing up in desirable rural areas all across America, each one of them a sustainable communal enterprise. It's the future, Mitch, and it starts right here in Dorset. This is my pilot project."

Mitch peered more closely at the blueprint, trying to get his bearings vis-à-vis the river. "It seems to me that the proposed site of The Lodge is right where Wendell Frye's farm is."

"That's absolutely correct. And your point is . . . ?"

"Well, how significant is his property to the successful completion of your project?"

"Okay, sure. Good question. I'd like to have it. I absolutely would, since much of what surrounds his place is wetlands, which I can't disturb. That farm of his is a prime building site. However. . . ."

"It's not for sale," Mitch pointed out.

"Which I totally and completely respect. I don't run people off of their land, Mitch. I adjust. If there's one thing I've learned in my business, it's that you have to be flexible. Wendell Frye is one of the major artists of this past century. A true giant. You don't screw around with a guy like that—especially in a small town like this. Worst thing you can possibly do is move into a new place and piss off its leading citizen. That's bone-headed. Totally suicidal." Bruce sat back with his hands folded behind his head, grinning at Mitch. "Next question. You must be full of them."

"How many residents will The Aerie accommodate?"

"Four hundred full-time residents. The spa's projected to handle a hundred and fifty guests at a time."

Plus staff. Plus deliveries. That meant a whole lot of cars and trucks coming in and out of what was now a remote area. There was no way narrow little Route 156 could handle that kind of volume, Mitch realized. And no way this wouldn't completely transform Dorset. Building The Aerie would be like plopping a big factory down right in the middle of the village. Which had to be the real reason why Bruce Leanse had been so careful about buying up the parcels under different names. He hadn't wanted the townspeople to get wise to what he was doing.

Until now. Now he was suddenly choosing to reveal his plans to Mitch's newspaper. Why? Because he needed some favorable ink? Or was Moose's death a factor? Did he hope to gain something from her murder? *Had* he gained something from her murder?

Actually, Mitch knew a bit about Bruce's business affairs—he'd spoken to his friend from the real estate section before the interview. From her he had learned that the Brat was leveraged to his eyeballs. Exceedingly cash-poor. Which meant he needed smooth sailing here in Dorset or his financial backers could, and would, break him into small pieces.

Bruce was watching him carefully from across the table, trying to size him up. "I'll be up-front with you, Mitch," he said in a confidential voice. "A project of this magnitude is not an easy thing to pull off. Particularly in a wealthy area. Wealth breeds a sense of entitlement. People think they've *earned* the right to keep Dorset the same as it was a hundred years ago. As a result, there are a lot of Bananas around here—that's developer-speak for Build Absolutely Nothing Anywhere Near Anyone. I've faced these people before in the Pacific Northwest. The mobbed zoning-board meetings. The petition drives. The lawsuits. With all due respect, they're less in tune with the real world than my eight-year-old, Ben. They're just not being practical."

Mitch said nothing in response. He actively disliked people who thought that clinging to values and ideals was something to be outgrown, like acne. This was how they slept nights, Mitch supposed. They told themselves: *I am a grown-up. Anyone who disagrees with me is a child.*

"Please don't get me wrong," Bruce added hastily, sensing the chill coming from Mitch's side of the table. "I do understand their concerns. I live here, too. And if you showed up here looking to put in a toxic-waste dump down the road from me, I'd fight you with everything I've got. But that's something that would have a negative environmental impact. The Aerie won't."

"But it *will* have an impact."

"It absolutely will," Leanse agreed, draining the last of his Sam Adams. "But in a positive way—by protecting from development more acres of green space than cul-de-sacs and strip malls would. Long-term, this is *better* for Dorset than traditional development. People need to realize this. They need to be educated. They need to understand that I truly care about Dorset. I've tried to reach out to them . . ."

"By offering to donate the land for the new school?"

"Exactly. I'm a new face in town. I'm trying to make friends."

"Otherwise, you don't get your building permits for The Aerie, right?"

Bruce scowled at Mitch. "You said that, I didn't. And you'd better not try to put those words in my mouth, guy, because I've got what I said on tape, word for word. And I said nothing about any quid pro quo. Not to you, and not to them. The parents want a new school. The community needs it. I simply said, 'Here, take this land.' "

"Your wife is head of the school board. How does that factor in?"

"It doesn't," he answered sincerely. "Beyond the fact that we're the kind of people who don't believe in taking. When we become part of a community, we get involved."

"Is she an active participant in your business?"

"No, she's not."

"What about Takai Frye?"

Bruce stiffened slightly, his nostrils flaring. "Takai Frye has expedited a number of local transactions for me. I've often found it helpful to take on a well-connected local individual as my point person." Now he paused, searching Mitch's face carefully. "Why do you ask about her?" he wondered.

"Well, for starters, she told me that she's the one who ratted out Jim Bolan to the state police—so you could snatch up his farm from the bank."

Bruce grew pale. "She *told* you that?"

"She thinks it was Jim who tried to kill her this morning. She's more than a little bit upset, as you can imagine."

Bruce jumped up out of his seat and began to pace restlessly back and forth, much the way Quirt did when he wanted to be let out to pee. "Look, I'd really rather not discuss Takai any more, Mitch," he said, running his hands through his short, bristly hair. "Let's just drop her, okay?" He continued to pace, his jaw muscles clenching. He seemed profoundly agitated. "Unless . . . That is to say, if you'd be willing to turn off your tape recorder." He lunged for his own and shut it off. "I'd talk to you about her then, strictly man-to-man. Christ, I've got to talk to *someone* or I-I swear I'll go postal!"

Mitch immediately shut off his microcassette recorder and sat back in his chair, arms folded across his ample tummy.

"Great . . ." Leanse heaved the hugest of sighs. "Thanks, guy. I mean that." He sat back down, taking several slow, deep breaths to calm himself. "The truth is, Takai's a bit of a problem in my life right now. See, the two of us had a-a romantic relationship. I quickly realized it was a major, major mistake, and I tried to break it off. But she won't let go of me. I can't get rid of her. I just can't!" He fell into miserable silence for a moment before he added, "And now I don't know what the hell to do."

Mostly, Mitch found himself wondering why Bruce Leanse was confiding in him this way. Had he no one else to spill his guts to? Someone like, say, a friend? Maybe not.

"How did you know about us, Mitch? You *did* know, right?"

"That's her shearling jacket in your stateroom, isn't it?"

"Dead on," Bruce affirmed. "She was here with me last evening. Left in a bit of a huff. We . . . we quarreled. I haven't always been a good boy, Mitch, and that's the sad truth. But I wasn't looking for this. All I wanted when we moved out here was a nice quiet family life. No more tabloid photographers. No more hassles. And, above all, no more sneaking around on Babette. I was really, really trying to turn over a new leaf, okay?"

Mitch nodded, thoroughly aware that he was talking to someone who'd busted a move on Des less than twenty-four hours ago, and was therefore a total snake. But he was not there aboard *The Brat* to point this out. He was there to listen.

"But then I met Takai. And, Mitch, I've never wanted a woman as badly as I want her. I'm talking about *ever*." Bruce shot a hungry glance up at the spiral staircase. "I hear the rustle of her nylons on those stairs and I can barely get my pants down fast enough. Half the time we don't even make it into the stateroom. I've torn her dress right off her back, just like some crazed animal. Five minutes later, I want her all over again. And then, in the night, when I'm lying in bed next to my dear wife, I start wanting her all over again. My heart pounds, the sweat pours off me. I-I've had to start sleeping in the guest room." He glanced at Mitch uncomfortably. "You're probably asking yourself why I don't just roll over and give Babette a jab . . ."

"Well, maybe something like that."

"It's not the same," he insisted. "Babette is a genuinely classy person, a distinguished architect, my soul mate. She went to *Harvard*, for God's sake. Do you honestly think I can do to her some of the things I do to Takai?"

"I really wouldn't know, Bruce." Nor did he want to.

"Believe me, Mitch, it's a bad thing to be so out of control. Especially because I can't even *stand* the woman. Takai Frye is an astonishingly not nice person. She's mean, calculating, greedy. I need to break it off. I need my sanity back. Only, she won't go quietly. I'm her ticket to the big dance, or so she believes. She wants a cushy, high-profile job in my company—or else."

"She's threatened you?"

Bruce nodded reluctantly. "Either I give her what she wants or she'll tell Babette about us. Not only Babette but everyone in town. She'll trash me with the old guard, Mitch. Turn the zoning and planning people against me. Tie up The Aerie for years and years. And she'd do it, too. She's *that* vindictive. I don't know what to do. I really don't.''

"Would Babette be surprised?"

"Not in the least," he answered bitterly. "That's precisely my problem. The last time this happened, in Boulder two years ago, she told me flat-out she'd leave me if I ever slept around again. And take Ben with her. I cherish what Babette and I have together. I love my son. I don't want him to spend his whole life thinking his father's some horny louse. I want him to respect me. I don't want . . ." Bruce's voice cracked with strain. "I don't want to lose my family, Mitch."

Nor that comforting illusion that he was a decent human being, Mitch reflected. Bruce needed this illusion about himself. True or not, it kept him going.

"I'm not the one who tried to kill her," he said to Mitch quietly from across the table. "If that's what you're thinking."

"I'm not," said Mitch, which wasn't entirely true. He was thinking that Bruce Leanse was a desperate man whose dream family and dream project were both about to go up in smoke, thanks to Takai Frye. That gave him more than enough reason for wanting her dead. Or maybe Babette had taken matters into her own hands—tried to save her marriage by eliminating the competition. This, too, was possible. Assuming she knew how to fire the humongous Barrett that Des had told him about.

And Mitch was thinking something else. That Takai wasn't wrong.

She still had every reason in the world to be afraid.

CHAPTER 8

"If you don't come here with passion, then don't come at all!" Paul Weiss barked as he paced along behind them, glancing over their shoulders at their drawing pads. They were at the easels, warming up with one-minute gesture drawings of that evening's model. "Stroke like you mean business!"

There were ten students in Figure Drawing. Half of them were college-aged kids enrolled full-time at the Dorset Academy, supremely gifted and dedicated young artists who dressed in torn, paint-smeared clothes and sported numerous body piercings. On breaks, they clustered together over cigarettes to murmur to each other in their own language. It being an evening class, the others were part-timers. Retired blue bloods who were there for fun, middle-aged divorcées who had too much free time and money.

And then there was Des. No one else in the studio was quite like her. But she was used to this particular fact of life. She wore a black T-shirt and jeans, and kept a fresh uniform in her cruiser in case she got beeped. So far this semester, she hadn't been.

"Leave it on the page!"

The model stood nude atop a wooden platform, bathed in the glow of a spotlight as she worked her way through a succession of quick poses. Her breasts were heavy and pendulous, her hips wide, thighs and buttocks exceedingly abundant. *Rubenesque* was the way to describe her. The notion that artists' models resembled swimsuit babes was strictly a male fantasy. In fact, the Dorset Academy preferred their models on the plump side—generous curves were vastly more expressive. Furthermore, many of these overweight nude models were in fact *men*.

"Don't tighten up yet! Stay loose!"

Paul always tried to loosen them up at the start with gesture drawings. Sometimes he had them draw with their wrong hand. Or even with their eyes closed. For the first hour he wanted them to open up, stroke boldly, *feel* the strength and movement of the pose. Only after they had moved on to longer poses would he start to get demanding about skeletal proportions, musculature and shadows—subjects about which he knew virtually everything there was to know. This stooped, slightly built man in his sixties was one of the foremost animal illustrators in America. He was exacting and tough but passionate. Des liked him quite a bit. And found herself soaking up his wisdom like a sponge.

"Draw with your whole arm!"

She drew with her whole arm, giving herself over fully to the lines and the shapes. Shutting down her intellect. Loving it. She cherished her time here in the paint-splattered studio with its huge glass skylights. It was a sanctuary. Every time she walked in here she felt privileged. And had no doubt whatsoever that she had made the right move. None.

"You've come with a lot of passion tonight, Desiree," he said approvingly when he paused at her drawing pad. "Your lines are much more expressive. You're not just pushing the lead around the page. Good, good."

She knew why, of course. It was seeing Moose Frye dead. It was the horror. That was what got her started drawing in the first place. And although she hadn't realized it until this very second, her *need* to draw had diminished since she'd parted company with Major Crimes. Now that the action had found her once again, she could feel her juices flowing, roiling, *demanding*.

As the model reached for the heavens with both arms raised, her face exuding unbridled sensual rapture, Des flipped to a new page and kept on stroking, well aware that this was another reason why she was bringing something extra:

Their pleasingly plump model this evening was none other than Melanie Zide.

No mistake about it—Colin Falconer's dumpy, henna-haired secretary, a young woman who was preparing to sue the school board for sexual harassment, was a nude model after-hours at the Dorset Academy of Fine Arts. And *what* a model! Freed of her drab clothes and thick glasses, Melanie was a woman transformed—graceful, uninhibited and positively charged with voluptuous female sexuality.

None of which added up. And Melanie knew it. Between poses, she kept shooting uncertain, myopic glances in Des's direction.

Every twenty minutes, the model got a rest break. When her timer went off, Melanie immediately stepped down from the platform and slipped on her robe and glasses. Most of the models brought a book to read on their breaks. Melanie buried her nose in *The Journals of Sylvia Plath* while the students streamed out of the studio for some fresh air. It tended to get quite warm in there with the door closed. But it had to stay closed when there was a model, just as there had to be a sign on the door that read: MODEL POSING—DO NOT ENTER.

"I almost didn't recognize you, Melanie," Des said to her, flexing the cramped muscles in her drawing hand. "We met in Superintendent Falconer's office yesterday, remember?"

"You probably think me being here is really weird," Melanie blurted out. Clearly, she'd been expecting Des to come at her.

"No weirder than me being here myself," Des responded, smiling at her.

"It takes me to another place," Melanie offered as explanation. "It's very Zen, very in the moment. I enjoy expressing myself this way."

"I hear you."

"Besides, they pay me in cash, and I need it," she said defensively. "Dorset's an expensive place to live and I've got a mother who's in a nursing home and a brother who can't deal with it."

"I'm sorry to hear that. Where did you learn to pose?"

"I took modern dance when I was in college."

"It shows, girl. What school did you go to?"

"Why are you asking me so many questions?" Melanie demanded, her round face scrunching tightly.

Des backed right off, taking a long drink from her bottle of mineral water. "I'm an admirer, that's all."

"Look, they know all about this at school, okay? And it's perfectly okay with them."

"I'm sure it is."

Now Melanie shoved her book into the pocket of her robe, peering at Des warily. "You *know,* don't you. That Colin's a cyber creep. Mrs. Leanse told you."

"Yes, she did."

"It was awful. The stuff he left on his screen. I mean, you would not believe the things those two men said to each other. I'm *glad* Colin's on medical leave, because he is one sick individual. You work alongside someone every day, and you think you know him and then . . . Wow, it's just *so* weird." Melanie was starting to blither now. She seemed anxious and frazzled, as if she had a special reason to be concerned about Des. Des wondered what it was. "I work in a small-town school, you know? Nothing *ever* happens. And suddenly there's this thing with Colin. And Moose Frye getting killed. And, I mean, there was even a television news crew from Hartford in the office this afternoon. That is just so *weird*." Melanie paused, chewing on the inside of her mouth. "Do you think they'll catch her killer?"

"I'm sure they will," Des said. "They have a top man on the case."

She had passed along to Soave the information Mitch had picked up from the Frye family. That Takai had been the one who'd informed on Jim, costing him his farm and thereby giving him a reason for wanting her dead. That Hangtown could alibi him for the time of the murder—the two of them were getting high together, which violated Jim's parole but surely ranked as the least of his worries right now. Des couldn't help wondering how it all hung together. Were Takai's fears of Jim warranted? Was Hangtown lying to protect him? *Had* Jim been the one perched up on that granite outcropping with the Barrett? Why the Barrett? Why such devastating firepower?

Melanie's timer went off now, ending their rest break. Des returned to her easel as the others trickled back in. As soon as Paul Weiss had shut the door behind him, Melanie discreetly disrobed and returned to the platform, where she stretched out on her side, one arm outreached, the other folded beneath her neck. Her back was arched, her chubby toes pointed. It was a languorous, provocative pose that emphasized the generous curves of her hips and buttocks.

Des was just getting her placed on the page when somebody pushed open the studio door without knocking and barged right in. It was Soave, who stood frozen there in the doorway with his eyeballs bulging. He simply could not believe that he was in a public place staring at a naked woman.

Paul Weiss immediately demanded to know what he wanted.

Des, who had left word where she'd be if Soave needed her, flung her stick down and led him out into the corridor, closing the door behind them.

"Wow, I could get into art big-time," he said to her eagerly.

"Grow up, Rico," she snapped. "That is *so* not mature."

"What's her name, anyway? Could I meet her?"

"What you could do is shut up. You're embarrassing yourself."

Soave held up both hands in a gesture of surrender. "My bad. Sorry."

"Is there something wrong with your setup over at town hall?" she demanded irritably.

"No, it's perfect. Got everything I need."

"Then what in the hell do you want?"

"To touch base," he explained, shrugging his muscle-bound shoulders.

"Does it have to be right this minute?"

"I'm afraid so. You don't mind, do you?"

They went in the lounge, where Soave flopped down on one of the sofas. There were tables to eat at, vending machines filled with junk food and truly awful coffee. The walls were crowded with drawings and watercolors that students had pinned up. Most were classroom exercises, a number of them astonishingly good. A young couple was slouched on one of the other sofas, eating take-out pizza. Otherwise, Des and Soave were alone in there.

"I've been fighting off the media all day," he complained wearily. "The TV people just nailed me at town hall. Wanted to know what we knew."

"How much did you give them?" Des asked, standing before him with her arms folded. She generally didn't care for the way Soave handled himself under the bright lights. Rather than keeping his comments terse and specific, he was prone to making vague, empty promises that made him sound like a politician who was running for something.

"I told them Jim Bolan is presently under house arrest," he answered. "Pending the results of further investigation."

"You *gave* them Jim?" she asked, aghast. It qualified as a total rush to judgment, in her opinion. It would be several days before the forensics lab would know whether the DNA from the saliva on the cigarette butt matched Jim's blood sample. "He tested positive for gunshot residue, is that it?"

"So he wore gloves," Soave growled at her. Translation: The residue test had turned up negative. "I still like him for it, Des. I like him large. He has motive, opportunity. He was a sniper in 'Nam. He's done time."

"What about Wendell Frye's alibi?"

"It can be shaken," Soave said confidently. "Who's to say the old guy didn't nod off for twenty, thirty minutes? He *admits* he was stoned. Maybe Jim even slipped a little something extra into his coffee. If that's the case, we'll find traces of it in the blood sample we took." They'd taken it so they could test Hangtown's DNA against the victims. "Besides which, we bagged us a pair of Jim's boots in the mudroom, okay? The soles look like a dead-nuts match for the shoe impression we found up at the shooter's roost. If we can make that stick, we're in."

"Not without the gun, Rico. Without the gun you're still a dollar short."

"We'll *find* the gun," he insisted. "You ask me, it's still around there somewhere. Trouble is, that old man's house has a million *way* creepy secret passageways. *Plus* he has that studio out in the barn, full of blowtorches, welders, saws—Jim could have broken the Barrett down into bits."

"You still have to find them." Des tapped her foot impatiently, anxious to get back to class. "Otherwise, the state's attorney will kick it right back at you."

"Maybe so," admitted Soave, who didn't seem anxious to go anywhere. Just sat there, smoothing his mustache. "I sent Tommy out for some dinner. He's my cousin, and I love him, but I sure do wish I had a partner with a useful, functioning brain. Somebody I could riff with like you and me used to. Know what I mean?"

Perfectly. The little man wanted her help on this, but he couldn't ask her for it without swallowing his pride. Des, for her part, had no intention of making this easy for him. She didn't exactly want him to beg but, well—*yes, she did*.

"The thing is, Des, I can't request a new partner or it'll be a knock on me. That stuff matters—your ability to inspire loyalty from your subordinates."

"Yes, I remember how that works," Des snarled at him between gritted teeth.

Soave recoiled as if she'd slapped him. The man was totally taken aback by the sharpness of her tone.

Des almost felt guilty for zinging him so hard. Almost, but not quite.

Now her damned beeper went off. She went out to her cruiser to radio in, convinced that she would never be permitted to draw again. After she hung up she cleared her things out of the studio and changed into her uni in the ladies' room. On her way out she stopped by the lounge. Soave was still flopped there on the sofa, his knees spread wide apart. He looked like a frog on steroids.

"Want some backup?" he offered rather forlornly.

"Not your kind of deal, Rico. Just routine community work."

"Hey, I don't mind. We could go someplace and de-freak afterward. Get us a brewski and talk."

She paused, furrowing her brow at him. He seemed genuinely down. This was new for him. "Why don't you go see Tammy?"

"I told you—it's Tawny."

"So why don't you?"

"We don't talk," he complained. "Not about serious things. We're not real close that way."

"Well, you've got to work at it. Find common interests."

"Like what?"

Des did consider telling him about that helpful new Web site: *getalife.com*. But she remained gracious. "Find something besides The Big Sweaty that you both like to do together."

He thought this over carefully. "Okay, sure. But tell me one thing before you go: What's he got that I haven't got?"

"Who?"

"Berger," he replied. "The Jew."

Now it was Des who was taken aback. Although Soave *had* made a play for her after she and Brandon split up—he and every other so-called player on Major Crimes. Not a one got so much as a single soul kiss out of her. Just a healthy, neutered stray kitten for their trouble—Little Eva in Soave's case, now known as Bridget. "Are you sure you want to go there?"

"I really do," Soave insisted. "I want to take something positive from the experience. I want to know where I come up short."

"Well, okay . . . Mitch Berger has brains, ethics, talent. And, let's see, maturity, tenderness, warmth, sensitivity, taste, humor . . . Oh, and he's hung like a horse, too," she added sweetly.

Soave looked hurt. "You can be real cruel sometimes, you know that?"

"Don't get sensitive on me, Rico," she shot back. "You'll mess up your portrait, and I don't want to have to do you all over again."

Then she strode out of the lounge with her sketch pad and charcoals, leaving him slumped there on the sofa with his mouth open.

The call came in from a woman named Felicity Beddoe, who lived in Somerset Ridge, a new development made up of a dozen elegant McMansions that had been carved out of the forest about a mile up the Old Post Road from Uncas Lake.

Somerset Ridge was the sort of upscale cul-de-sac that Des was used to seeing in places like Fairfield and Stamford, which were within commuting range of New York. But the Internet was changing how people went about their business. More and more white-collar professionals telecommuted out of the house, and could live anywhere they wanted. They wanted to live in a place like Dorset.

There was nothing casual about Somerset Ridge. Each majestic colonial was set back from the gently curving road behind lavish new fieldstone walls, artfully positioned young dogwoods and three or more acres of Chemlawn. The dogwoods out in front of the Beddoe house, she noticed, had green WE CARE ribbons tied to them.

A long gravel driveway lined with carriage lanterns twisted its way up to a circular turnaround in front of the house, where Des parked and got out. One door in the three-car garage was open. Inside, there was a gold Lexus. She could hear the whine of a leaf blower coming from a neighbor's place—someone trying to keep up with the fallen maple leaves. The Beddoes's front walk was ankle-deep in them. Resisting a powerful girlish urge to go skipping through them, kicking them high in the air, Des plowed her way to the front door, which was flanked by decorative urns filled with assorted seasonal squashes and pumpkins. Most Martha Stewarty. She rang the bell.

She was invited in by a slender whippet of a career woman in her early forties. The gray flannel business suit Felicity Beddoe had on was tailored perfectly. Her ash-blond hair, which was cropped stylishly short, shimmered in the light from the entryway chandelier. Felicity was quite attractive in a toothy, Saran-Wrap-tight sort of way, although right now she seemed tremendously frazzled. "I'm *so* sorry to drag you away from your dinner, trooper," she apologized, leading Des quickly in the direction of the kitchen, her low Ferragamo heels clacking on the quarry-tile floor.

"Not a problem," said Des, following her. The living room and dining room had been furnished by an interior decorator. Everything was *just so*. "This is my job."

"Still, you *must* have better things to do than listen to some hysterical mother rant and rave," Felicity said, her voice soaring with strain. This woman was more than frazzled, Des realized. She was truly terrified. Trembling with fear.

She led Des into a cavernous gourmet kitchen. There was a sit-down center island topped with granite counters. A stew bubbled on the stove, and on the television *The News-Hour with Jim Lehrer* was busy dissecting North Korea. Felicity immediately flicked that off and turned down the stew. From a nearby room Des could hear the tentative, trembly trills of someone practicing the flute.

She removed her hat and leaned a flank against the granite counter. "Now what can I do for you, Mrs. Beddoe?"

Felicity said, "It's just that Richard, my husband, is away on business. And this *always* seems to happen when he's . . . And *I* just got home from work myself. And . . ."

"Where is it you work?" Des asked pleasantly, trying to slow the poor woman down. She was sooo hyper. On a good day she probably got by on two hours of sleep and 240 calories. Today was clearly not a good day.

"I'm with Pfizer," she answered, swiping nervously at a loose strand of hair in her eyes. The pharmaceuticals giant had recently built a big research and development facility thirty miles away in Groton.

"So you're a chemist?" Des asked, twirling her hat in her fingers.

"Who, me? God, no." Felicity let loose a jagged, painful laugh. "I'm chief marketing weasel. Vice president of, to be exact. We haven't been here long. Just moved here from Brussels. Richard's an economist with the World Bank. He's in London right now and I'm . . ." She trailed off, wringing her hands.

"What happened this evening, Mrs. Beddoe?"

"I had just gotten home," she answered, her mouth tightening. "I was putting our dinner on. It's just Phoebe and me. She's our girl. She's . . . Phoebe's fourteen."

Des nodded, thinking how much house this was for three people. How many empty bedrooms did they have? Three? Four? What did they *do* with so many empty bedrooms?

"Please believe me, trooper, I'm not looking to make trouble. But we have talked to him and talked to him and it has done *no* good. So I-I felt it was time to contact you. I honestly didn't know how else to proceed. I've no experience in these matters. None. Zero."

"Exactly who are we talking about here, Mrs. Beddoe?" asked Des, shoving her horn-rimmed glasses back up her nose.

"Jay Welmers," she answered, her cheeks mottling. "Our neighbor."

Why did the name Welmers sound familiar? Des couldn't place it offhand. "And what is it that he's . . . ?"

"He's a peeper," Felicity blurted out. "I don't know what else to call him—is 'pervert' more apt? He *watches* Phoebe through her bedroom window. Tonight, I-I caught him in our yard. There's a granite ledge out behind the house. Phoebe was upstairs in her room doing her homework when she heard footsteps in the leaves back there. She called out to me. I flicked on the floodlights, thinking, *hoping* it might be deer. It was Jay, perched back there with a pair of binoculars. It was *him*. I know it was him."

"I see," Des said, not liking where this was going at all. "Let's talk to Phoebe, shall we?"

Felicity called to her, and she appeared in the doorway to the study, clutching a flute in her small, soft hands. Phoebe Beddoe was no lubricious tartlet. She was a slender, serious little teenaged girl with large, moist brown eyes and smooth, shiny blond hair—the kind of hair that the sisters up in Hartford's Frog Hollow section would kill for. She wore a baggy fleece sweater, sweatpants and fuzzy bedroom slippers. And Des had no doubt whatsoever that *something* had happened to her—the girl was pie-eyed with fear.

Des smiled at her reassuringly. "Nice to meet you, Phoebe. I'm Resident Trooper Mitry, and I have to ask you something a little personal about this evening, okay?"

Phoebe nodded at her, swallowing.

"Did Mr. Welmers show you anything?"

"Show me anything?" she repeated in a quavering voice.

"Trooper, is this absolutely necessary?" Felicity cut in.

"I have to know what I'm dealing with, Mrs. Beddoe," Des explained. "Otherwise, I can't help you. And I want to help you. You're old enough to understand what I'm talking about, aren't you, Phoebe?"

The girl hesitated, then gave a short nod. "I guess."

"Well, did he?"

"I don't think so," she replied, ducking her head. "No."

"Okay, thank you," Des said. "That's all I needed to know."

"Phoebe, will you please excuse us now?"

The girl darted back into the study, her slippered feet barely making a sound.

Felicity yanked a half-empty bottle of Sancerre out of the refrigerator and filled a goblet. She took a sip, her hand shaking. "I'm sorry, that . . . was not something I was emotionally prepared for."

"Why did you call me, Mrs. Beddoe?" Des asked, watching her closely.

"Because I want something to be done about that man."

"You've had trouble with Mr. Welmers before, I take it."

Reluctantly, she nodded. "He always waits until Richard is out of town. And then he starts in again—watching Phoebe, *saying* things to her in the driveway."

"What kind of things?"

"Things that he'd like to *do* to her," Felicity said angrily. "She's just a *child*. It's obscene. *He's* obscene. And those two boys of his are absolute monsters!"

Of course. Now Des knew why the name sounded familiar. "Have you told your husband what goes on when he's away?"

Felicity's eyes widened. "Absolutely not."

"Why not?"

She didn't respond, aside from a brief shake of her head.

"Are he and Jay friends?"

"Not at all. That man's been nothing but hostile toward us both since the day we moved in."

"Does Richard keep a handgun in the home?"

"Yes."

"You're afraid he might try to use it on him, is that it?"

"Yes," she said once again, fainter this time.

"If that's the case, why don't you let me hold on to it for a while?"

"I can't go behind Richard's back that way. He would take it as a lack of trust on my part."

"I understand," said Des. "Look, I'll go have a talk with Mr. Welmers, okay? See if we can't smooth this out. We're all reasonable people here, right?"

"Right," Felicity said, lunging for her wine. "Absolutely. But please don't . . ."

"Don't what, Mrs. Beddoe?"

"I just . . ." Her face tightened into a mask of fear. "Never mind. Thank you."

Des showed herself out and went next door on foot, the whine of the leaf blower growing steadily louder as she made her way up Jay Welmers's lantern-lined driveway. His own dogwoods, she noticed, were tied with red SAVE OUR

SCHOOL ribbons. And his expanse of floodlit lawn had been blown completely free of leaves. It looked as spotless as a freshly vacuumed living room rug. Des had never quite understood the leaf-blower compulsion. It was one of those Man versus Nature hang-ups that baffled her. Plus the sound of the damned thing bore in at the base of her skull like an ice pick.

She found a middle-aged man busily blowing the leaves from his circular turnaround toward a swale at the base of the trees edging the property. His leaf blower was a hi-tech backpack unit that resembled a personal jet pack. He worked intently, wearing protective goggles over his eyes and earmuffs against the horrible racket he was producing.

The rottweiler that was chained to a post on the front porch started barking furiously at Des as she approached. None of which the man heard. She had to tap him on the arm to get his attention.

His gaze immediately hardened at the sight of her uniform. He shut down the unit and stripped off his earmuffs. "What is that woman complaining about now?" Jay Welmers demanded, instantly on the offensive. "Is it the noise? Is little *Phoebe* trying to practice her *flute*? I swear, some people you can't please . . . Shut *up*, Dino!" he hollered at the barking dog.

The dog did not stop barking.

"Can we go inside, Mr. Welmers? We need to talk about a certain matter."

"I can't *believe* she called you. I'm just trying to spruce things up."

"I understand, sir. Can we go inside?"

He grabbed hold of the dog so Des could get in the front door without having her ankle torn off. A bag of golf clubs was propped against the entry-hall closet door. Otherwise, the huge house was bare to the point of vacant. There was no furniture in the living room. No pictures on the wall. Not even any curtains.

Jay Welmers was in his fifties. He was a big man, at least six feet three, with a flabby gut and a red, choleric face. His wavy rust-colored hair was streaked with white. His eyes were blue, his hands freckly. He wore a yellow crew-neck sweater and a pair of those wool tartan plaid slacks that no black man on the face of the earth would ever be caught wearing. Jay looked as if he was fresh off the eighteenth hole at the country club. Or make that the nineteenth hole— he reeked of alcohol.

He led her back toward the den, their footsteps echoing in the empty house. There was a set of cheap plastic patio furniture in there, and a big-screen TV inside a home entertainment unit. Nothing else. Two boys were sprawled out on the rug, watching a movie.

One boy Des recognized right off. It was Ricky, the little no-necked bully with the black eye. The one who'd asked her if she was a nigger.

The other one was about fifteen, with a long, wiry build. His peach-fuzz goatee and furry, overgrown burr cut gave him the look of a wolf cub. This would be brother Ronnie, the garbagehead Moose Frye had told her about. Ronnie Welmers dressed in thug chic: baggy prison jeans that were falling off him, sleeveless black T-shirt, red bandanna knotted around his throat, Timberland work boots. He was trying to look like a gangbanger, but sprawled here on the floor of his Dorset McMansion, he looked about as street as Britney Spears.

Des smiled at the younger boy and said, "Nice to see you again, Ricky."

Ricky mumbled something in response that sounded vaguely like hello.

"How you know my boy, trooper?" Jay Welmers asked her.

"I was at his school for a presentation," Des replied, noting that big brother's eyes never left the television. Ronnie would not make eye contact with her. "Sorry to hear about your teacher, Ricky. She seemed like a nice lady." To Jay she said, "Your neighbor, Felicity Beddoe, reported a prowler in her yard this evening. I wondered if you saw or heard anything."

Jay considered his reply for a long moment, his red face revealing nothing. "Do you boys want to excuse us?"

"But, Dad, this is the best part," protested Ricky.

"What are you guys watching?" Des asked him.

"It's called *Westworld*," Ricky answered. Ronnie still wasn't giving up anything. "Yul Brynner plays a really cool robot."

"You can watch it later," Jay said brusquely. "Go take Dino for a walk."

Ronnie flicked off the TV, sighing, and the two of them shuffled slowly out of the room. A moment later she heard eruptions of boyish laughter.

"I was just going to fix myself a Scotch and soda," Jay said. "Can I offer you anything? Coffee?"

"No, thanks."

He went into the kitchen for a moment, returned with his drink and sat in one of his patio chairs, his movements measured and careful. He'd already had him a few, and was trying not to show it.

"What is it that you do for a living, Mr. Welmers?"

"I'm a financial planner."

"Is that right? I'm in the market for one of those—who are you with?"

"I *was* with Fleet Bank for twenty-two years," he answered. "Got downsized right out the door last year. So I've set up on my own. Much better that way, really. Don't have to worry about corporate politics anymore. I can focus on what I do best, which is helping people plan for the future. It *does* come, you know . . ." He took a business card out of his wallet and offered it to her.

"Great. Thank you." She pocketed it, glancing around at the decor, or total lack thereof. "Are you refurnishing?"

Jay let out a short laugh. "I guess you could call it that. My wife took the furniture when she left me—the furniture and everything else, except our two boys." He sipped his drink, shifting uncomfortably in his chair. It was too small for him. "Exactly what did Felicity tell you?"

"That she saw *you* over there, Mr. Welmers."

"I was looking for one of my golf balls a little while ago," he conceded, very casually. "Ricky knocked it into their yard. He fancies himself a golfer now."

"You were looking for your golf ball," Des said back to him.

"That's right."

"In the dark?"

"There's no law against that, is there?"

"Not at all. But there *is* a law against peeping through bedroom windows. And making verbal suggestions to a fourteen-year-old girl her in her driveway."

"Felicity said *that*?" Jay Welmers shook his big red head at her disgustedly. "Nothing like that has ever happened, believe me."

"You're saying Mrs. Beddoe is mistaken?"

"I'm saying she's new in town and she's frightened to death of everybody. Especially when her husband's away. And that girl of hers, that Phoebe, is so terrified of men she runs away screaming if I so much as say hello. That's how we are in Dorset—friendly. We say, 'Good morning, don't you look pretty today?' I've lived here my entire life, trooper, so maybe I haven't heard the news. . . . Is that a crime now?"

"No, of course not."

"And is it sane behavior to *call the police* if a neighbor sets foot on your property?"

"She seemed like a pretty decent lady to me."

"She's a hostile, uptight bitch," Jay snarled. "And you *know* how teenaged girls are."

"No, how are they?"

"They overdramatize," he said, peering over his glass at Des. The color had risen in his face. He looked as if he had a real temper. "She's just looking for attention, that's all."

Des raised her chin at him. "And what are *you* looking for, Mr. Welmers?"

"Believe me," he said in a low voice, "I'm not casting around for trouble."

"I'm sure you're not," Des said soothingly. "But could

you do me a huge favor? Next time you need to go over there looking for your golf ball, could you call her up first and tell her you're coming? Because she *is* new here. And she's ill at ease. Maybe she's overreacting. Hey, maybe there's no maybe about it." Des flashed a smile at him. "But it seems like an easy enough thing to do if it would smooth things over. Mr. Welmers, you seem like a good neighbor to me—a responsible homeowner, a father. I don't want to have to come back here. It's within your power to make sure that I don't. The ball's in your court. Do you understand what I'm saying to you?"

"Of course I do," he responded coldly. "I'm not an idiot."

"Good. Then I won't take any more of your time."

As Jay led her out, Des asked him about Ricky's black eye.

He waved a freckled hand in disgust. "He got in another fight at school. He's a got a mouth on him, that one. Inherited it from his mother."

"I see," Des said, leaving it there even though she was positive the man was lying to her. About Ricky's eye. About Phoebe Beddoe. About it all. Trouble was, she had nothing to go on. Just her instincts, which were telling her loud and clear that Jay Welmers was a bum. She could smell it all over him. Same way she could smell that Felicity Beddoe was no hostile bitch and her daughter was not delusional. But she had to play this call straight down the middle. No taking sides. She'd done all she could for now.

She crossed the lawn back to the Beddoes's house in the darkness, hearing footsteps crashing through the fallen leaves, playful barking, youthful laughter. The Welmers boys and Dino.

Felicity answered her doorbell at once.

Des filled her in on her conversation with Jay Welmers. "He says he's not looking for trouble, Mrs. Beddoe."

"And what do you say?" Felicity asked, her eyes searching Des's face.

"I say that he's been put on notice. If anything else happens, there are avenues you can pursue. This is not a free country. Not if grown men are acting inappropriately toward young girls."

"Do you mean some form of restraining order?"

"My hope is that it won't come to that," Des said carefully, not wanting to throw fuel on the fire. "For now, I want you to call me if there's anything else I can do. Just pick up the phone, day or night. That's why I am here."

"Thank you, trooper. You've been very understanding."

Des tipped her hat and strode back to her cruiser—only to discover that her windshield had been liberally smeared with mud. Absolute monsters, Felicity Beddoe had called those boys. Shaking her head, Des got some paper towels out of her trunk and started to wipe it off. It was only when she got a good, strong whiff of it that she realized it wasn't mud.

It was fresh dog poop.

Seething, she uncoiled the Beddoes's garden hose and washed her windshield off with their power sprayer. If Felicity wondered what she was doing out there, she didn't ask. There was a work sink in the garage, where Des was able to wash up. As she was drying off her hands on a fresh paper towel she heard a faint crunching of leaves nearby. They had a small enclosure attached to the garage for their trash cans. Someone was crouched behind it, watching her. Des sidled over and stuffed her used paper towels in one of the cans.

Then swiftly grabbed little Ricky Welmers by the scruff of the neck and yanked him to his feet. "Got something you want to tell me, Ricky?" she demanded angrily.

"N-no . . . !" he cried out, bug-eyed with fear. "N-nothing, I swear!"

"You're a real comedian, aren't you? Had yourself a good laugh."

"No way!"

"How would you like me to run you in for defacing public property? You could spend the night at the youth detention lockup in New London with the gangbangers and drug addicts. Would you think that's funny, too?"

"M-my brother made me do it. Please don't . . . Please!"

Des stood there a moment, scowling at him and thinking: *Here is the job. This is where it officially starts*. She released her hold on Ricky, softening. "You know I'm on your side, don't you?"

He peered up at her, tugging at the neck of his T-shirt. "How so?"

"I kept you out of the principal's office yesterday, didn't I?"

"So what?"

"I'm not running you in for trashing my ride, am I?"

"Not yet . . ."

"Right," she affirmed, nodding. "Because I'm your friend. Now it's *your* turn to show *me* the love. That's how it works with friends."

"Like what?" he demanded suspiciously.

"Take a spin with me in my cruiser."

His jut-jawed young face lit up. *"Really?!"*

"Did you eat dinner yet?"

"We were maybe going to order a pizza."

"Well, I have to get me some dinner, and I hate to eat alone. Sound okay?"

"Okay!" he replied eagerly.

Des got her briefcase out of the front seat and dug around in it for a Citizen Ride Along release form. She filled in Ricky's name and address. "This is a permission slip. Have your dad sign this and we'll hit the road."

Ricky went dashing off through the trees to his house, form in hand. While she waited for him to return she spotted Ronnie watching her from under the trees, the lit end of his cigarette growing brighter as he pulled on it.

"Why don't you ease up on him, Ronnie? He's just a little kid."

"I don't know what you mean, lady." Ronnie still had a reedy, adolescent voice. He sounded like a boy, not a man.

"Sure you do. You put him up to trashing my ride, didn't you?"

"He *told* you that?" Now Ronnie stepped out of the shadows into the floodlights, his smoke stuck between his teeth.

His hands were buried deep in the pockets of an oversized silver-colored ski parka. His red bandanna was tied over his head. Dressed that way on the wrong block in Hartford, he'd be shot on sight.

"He didn't have to tell me. I've got two eyes of my own."

Ronnie stood there hipshot, his head cocked at her defiantly, body language straight out of a rap video. Des remembered Moose Frye saying that he was probably the brightest kid in the entire school system. "My old man cheesed off Mrs. Beddoe again, didn't he?" he demanded.

"He'll have to be the one to tell you about that."

"They want the new school, he doesn't. I heard him arguing with them about it in the driveway the other day." Ronnie took one last pull on his cigarette and flicked it off toward the Beddoes's gravel turnaround, where it continued to burn among the fallen leaves. He smirked at her, daring her to give him a fire safety lecture. She kept silent. She was more interested in keeping him talking. "The old people are always arguing," he went on. "But they never *do* anything. They're, like, total lying hypocrites. Like with the new school—they *say* they want it because they care about us. But that's bullshit. They just want another trophy to feed their egos. It's all about trophies. *We're* trophies. If we do well, it makes them look good."

"Your dad wants to save Center School, doesn't he?"

"Only because he's afraid his taxes will go up. If his career wasn't in the toilet he'd be flying a green ribbon, too. Anything to make himself look good."

"Maybe he wants you to do well because he wants good things for you. Maybe he loves you. Ever think of that?"

"You know dick about it, lady," Ronnie shot back, sneering.

She nodded her head slowly. She'd had feral strays living out of Dumpsters who were exactly like this one. Always, their first impulse was to rake you across the face. "Understand you're a major film freak."

"So what?" he demanded.

"I'm friends with a film critic who lives here in Dorset. He works for one of the New York papers."

"Mitchell Berger, sure," he said. "Me and my friends read his reviews out loud and laugh at them."

"He loves to talk about movies. Sometimes I can hardly shut him up. Maybe you'd like to meet him sometime."

"What for? He's an officially sanctioned bore."

Not only bright but a smarty-pants, too. An off-putting combination, to be sure. The question was: Did it add up to the Mod Squad?

Ricky came scampering back through the trees now, signed form in hand. She started to invite Ronnie to join them, but the older boy had already vanished into the darkness without a sound.

It was as if he'd never been there at all.

Ricky hopped in next to her in the front seat. She adjusted his seat belt for him while his eyes took in her crime girl stuff, especially her new three-thousand-dollar digital hand-held radio on the seat between them. It was something to behold. Looked as if it belonged on the space shuttle.

She circled back down the driveway and headed down the cul-de-sac toward the Old Post Road, Ricky riding with his jaw stuck out and his beefy arms crossed. His feet swung back and forth in the air, heels striking the seat again and again.

She took him to McGee's Diner, a shabby and much-beloved local greasy spoon down on the Shore Road. During the summer McGee's had been packed with sunburned, boisterous beachgoers who stopped there to munch on lobster rolls and gaze out the windows at the sun setting beyond the Big Sister lighthouse. Tonight, the parking lot was deserted except for a landscaper's pickup truck and an ancient Peugeot wagon. Some of this was attributable to the time of year, but much of it had to do with the red SAVE OUR SCHOOL colors Dick McGee was proudly flying out front for all to see. Most of Dorset's business owners had stayed neutral, not wanting to lose precious customers. Not so Dick, and he was feeling it—the WE CARE crowd were definitely boy-cotting him.

Inside, not a newcomer was to be found. Just an old geezer having pie and coffee in a booth and a pair of twenty-ish swamp Yankees hunched over bowls of chili at the counter. They hunched even lower when they caught sight of Des in her uni. An older-than-oldies radio station was play-ing Perry Como out in the kitchen. Dick McGee clung stub-bornly to the prehistoric when it came to music.

She and Ricky slid into one of the booths and Sandy, Dick's waitress, came sauntering over. Sandy was about forty, stubby, and frizzy-haired. Highly sour, but a ripe prospect if ever Des had seen one. She'd been working on her for the past couple of weeks.

"Hey, Sandy, have you talked to your boyfriend about adopting one of my kittens?" she asked her warmly.

"Not possible," Sandy answered. "Chuckie hates cats. If I take her, he'll never spend a single night at my place."

"So you can stay at his place."

"No, I can't. His place is a dump."

"Girl, you folks *need* a cat. Your lives aren't complete yet."

"You going to order anything, or or are you just going to tell me how to live?"

Des ordered them hamburgers, spiral fries and chocolate shakes, and Sandy headed off to the kitchen, grumbling un-der her breath.

"Talk to me about your brother," Des said to Ricky. "He give you that eye?"

Ricky frowned at her. "Why you asking me that?"

"Because if he did, that's one thing. But if your dad did, then it's different."

"Why?"

"Because your dad's supposed to know better, that's why."

The little boy fell silent. "Ronnie gets nasty when he drinks."

"Does he drink a lot?"

"Ronnie does everything a lot."

"He smokes, too, I noticed. Does he ever smoke unfiltered cigarettes?"

"You mean like Joe Camels? Sure."

"How about Luckies? Does he smoke those?"

"Ronnie smokes whatever. He doesn't care."

"Does he smoke dope?"

Ricky started to squirm in his seat. "Do I have to answer that?"

"Not if you don't want to."

Sandy returned with their food. Ricky dumped a half bottle of ketchup on his fries and attacked them first. He ate like a starved animal.

"Okay, now you can ask me something," Des offered, biting into her burger.

"I can?"

"You bet. That's how it works with friends."

"Um, you got a boyfriend?"

"Yes, I do."

"He a black man or a white man?"

She took a sip of her milk shake, staring over her glass at him. "He's white."

"How come?"

"You don't choose the people who you get involved with. It's not like you order them out of a catalog or something. Stuff just . . . it *happens*."

Ricky nodded, frowning. "Do you suck on his dick?"

"Boy, what is wrong with you?" Des erupted angrily. "Here I am, sitting down with you, treating you like a person, and you talk trash at me like I'm some gutter whore! Why are you disrespecting me this way, huh? Answer me!"

Ricky didn't answer. Just sat there with his eyes downcast, greasy hands in his lap.

"You don't belong with people," she huffed at him. "You should be in a cage. Feed you peanuts, hose you down once a day. Have you got *anything* to say to me?"

"I-I'm sorry," he murmured, wiping his mouth on his sleeve.

"And you've got the table manners of a coyote—use your napkin! Sit up straight! Where's your mother anyway?"

He wiped his mouth with his napkin and said, "She lives in Pennsylvania somewhere."

"Do you miss her?"

"She's been gone since I was a baby. I don't know her at all, except from pictures."

Des popped a spiral fry in her mouth, mulling this over. Jay Welmers had definitely tried to spin it that she'd left him very recently, thereby explaining the lack of furniture. Clearly, the man was in deep financial trouble, his spanking-new McMansion merely a shell. How long did he have before he'd lose it? "What about Ronnie? Does he miss your mom?"

"He doesn't say much about her. Dad gets pissed off if we mention her."

"Does your dad have a girlfriend?"

Ricky shook his head.

"How about Ronnie?"

"He's in love with Claire Danes," he answered, snickering. "The movie star."

"Who does he hang with?"

"Lots of people."

"Boys mostly?"

Rocky chomped on his burger, nodding.

"What about Phoebe Beddoe? Does he ever hang with her?"

"Nah, she's real stuck-up. Won't have anything to do with him."

"Why did Ronnie do that to your eye?"

Ricky dropped his gaze, his eyes avoiding hers. "I wanted to hang with him and his friends. He didn't want me to. So he punked me."

"Hang with them where?"

"Antics," he answered, shrugging. "Y'know, stuff they do

for fun. This can be a real boring place. There's not a whole lot going on."

"Hmm . . . I may have to start keeping a closer eye on Ronnie and his boys."

"No, you can't do that!"

"Why not?"

"Because he'll *know* I told you something and then he'll . . ."

"He'll what, Ricky?"

Ricky stuck his jaw out. "Nothing. I ain't no snitch."

"I'm going to tell you something straight up. Strictly because you and I are friends, okay?"

He looked at her guardedly. "Okay . . ."

"I think Ronnie might be getting into something that he'll be real sorry about when he's old enough to know better."

"You don't have to worry about Ronnie—he's way smart."

"I know he is. I'm just trying to help. That's my job."

"I thought your job was to bust people."

"That's only when I fail. I'm just like a fireman, okay? Sure, I know how to put out fires. But what I really want to do is *prevent* those fires from ever getting lit. Understand what I'm saying?"

He shook his head at her. "You're still the law."

"I'm somebody who you can talk to about things," Des persisted, handing him one of her cards. "You have a problem, call me anytime, twenty-four seven."

He pocketed it without comment. "My dad gave me money for dinner."

"Your money's no good here. When I ask a man to dinner, I pick up the tab." After she'd paid it and said good night to Sandy, they headed back outside together. "Yeah, I think I'd better go have myself a talk with Ronnie."

"No, don't!" Ricky pleaded. "He'll pound me."

It was a crisp, starlit evening. Des stood there by her cruiser, inhaling the fresh sea air and waiting the little tough guy out.

"What if I tell you a secret?" he finally offered. "Will you stay away from him then?"

"Depends on what it is."

"Something he told me. But you have to promise not to tell anyone else."

"I can't do that, Ricky. I'd be lying to you if I said I could. What I *can* do is promise not to tell anyone where I heard it. And I'll do my best to keep Ronnie's name free of it. But I have to know what it is."

Ricky thought this over carefully as they got back in the car. Then he took a deep breath and told her Ronnie's secret.

Town hall was buzzing that evening. Lights blazing all over the building. The WE CARE leaders were holding a strategy session in the upstairs meeting room. The Planning Commission was having its monthly meeting in the main conference room. And the Major Crimes Squad was working the Moose Frye murder in the spare conference room.

Soave had not been happy when Des phoned him with her news. He wanted to see her right away. Tommy was out following up on it when she got there.

He was alone in the makeshift office, sipping take-out coffee and fuming. "I thought you weren't going to butt into my case, Des."

"Don't be a chump, Rico," she responded coolly. "I came into information pertinent to your investigation and I reported it directly to you. If I were trying to butt in, I would have run with it on my own."

"Okay, that's true," he admitted grudgingly. "But, damn it, I've already got Jim Bolan all sewn up."

"Maybe so. Then again, maybe you ought to be keeping your mind open."

"Stop lecturing me, will ya?"

"I can't help it. I changed your diapers—once a mother, always a mother."

Tommy came walking in now with Dirk Doughty in tow. Ben Leanse's baseball tutor seemed composed and calm.

"Thanks for coming by, Mr. Doughty," Soave said to him.

"Not a problem. Your sergeant said it was important."

Bringing Dirk to town hall had been Des's idea, actually. Soave had been all for bracing him in the lounge of the Frederick House. But people would talk about it, and she didn't feel that would be fair to him. In a place like Dorset, it was important to tread lightly on someone's reputation.

Dirk was wearing a sweatshirt and jeans. On his head was a bright-blue DOUGHTY'S ALL-STARS baseball cap. He turned a wooden desk chair around backward and sat, his big arms folded imposingly before him. Dirk still possessed the effortless physical confidence of a professional athlete. It was the kind of animal self-assurance that Soave sought to achieve with all his weight lifting. And failed at.

"I'll get right to the point, Mr. Doughty," he began, pacing back and forth in front of him. Tommy remained in the doorway, watching impassively. "We came into some information this evening from a local individual who likes to scope out the Frederick House's parking lot in the middle of the night. If any of the guests leave their cars unlocked, he takes whatever he can find."

"I haven't had anything stolen, Lieutenant," Dirk said.

"This individual spotted Takai Frye's red Porsche parked halfway down the block from the inn late last night," Soave went on. "What's more, Trooper Mitry claims she's been hearing a couple going at it up on the third floor in the wee hours. According to the inn's registry, Mr. Doughty, your room is on the third floor."

Dirk looked at Des curiously. "You figured that was me?"

She didn't respond. It was Rico's interrogation.

Dirk took a stick of sugarless gum out of the back pocket of his jeans, slowly unwrapped it and popped it in his mouth. "I only wish it was," he said, his jaw muscles going to work on it. "I've been hearing them myself, and they sound like they're having themselves one hell of a time. But I'm a married man, Lieutenant. My wife Laurie is in Toledo—"

"And you're here," Soave said roughly. "Cards on the table, Mr. Doughty—were you seeing Moose Frye romantically?"

"No, I was not," he answered forthrightly. "And that's the truth."

"What about her sister, Takai? Are you mixed up with her?"

"Not hardly." Dirk's weathered face tightened. "Not anymore."

Soave frowned at him. "Are you telling me you used to be?"

Dirk let out a laugh. "I used to be *married* to her. Takai was my first wife."

Des drew her breath in, stunned. Wheels within wheels—that was life in Dorset. How long would she have to live in this place before she'd comprehend its tricky little ins and outs? Ten years, twenty years, *ever*?

"I'm talking ancient history here," Dirk added as explanation. "We were just kids. I was twenty. She was barely out of high school. Mind you, Moose was the one who I dated when we were growing up, not Takai. Moose was my high school sweetheart, I guess you could say."

"Well, was she or wasn't she?" Soave asked him irritably.

"We were friends," he answered carefully. "Good, close friends. But we didn't . . . she wasn't ready for anything more than that."

"And Takai was?"

"Takai was a runway model in New York when she was sixteen. That girl slept with whoever she wanted. Not that she ever wanted Dirk Doughty, star of the Dorset High Fighting Pilgrims. Not until I was a bonus baby with money in my pocket. Suddenly, I intrigued her. So she decided to steal me away from her big sister. That's the kind of person she is. And I let her steal me away. That's the kind of person I was. Not that I was very proud of myself. But, believe me, it's hard to be a healthy young male and have a gorgeous creature like that coming after you." Dirk trailed off into regretful silence, his jaw working on the gum. "Moose never forgave me. I couldn't blame her. I treated her badly, and I was never man enough to apologize to her. I wish I had, because now I'll never get the chance."

Des cleared her throat. "Lieutenant, if I may . . . ?"

"Yeah, go ahead," he growled, smoothing his see-through mustache.

She remained seated. She'd never been a pacer. "It was Moose Frye who recommended you to the Leanses for tutoring Ben. Did you know that?"

Dirk's eyes widened with surprise. "No, I didn't."

"You didn't see her when you got back to town?"

Dirk shook his head. "Babette just said she got my name from a-a friend." He broke off, swallowing. He seemed genuinely moved. "Thank you for telling me that. It's nice to know."

"How would you describe your relationship with Takai these days?"

"That's easy," he replied. "We don't have one."

Nonetheless, someone might have *thought* they did— seen her car parked near the inn, figured she was visiting Dirk and went after her in a jealous rage, taking out Moose by mistake. It certainly played. And Takai certainly had a way of stirring men up. "You mentioned an ex-wife when we spoke yesterday," she went on. "You said she cleaned you out of your signing bonus when you divorced. That was Takai?"

"Yes."

"Why didn't you share that with me?"

"I don't air my dirty laundry."

"What happened to your marriage?"

"The accident happened," he said quietly. "She was behind the wheel when I blew out my elbow. We were coming home from a New Year's Eve party here in town. It was a cold, cold night. There was ice on the road, and she was driving too fast. She always drove too fast. Flipped us into a ditch up on Route 156. She didn't have a scratch on her. I needed two operations to put my elbow back together. She got tired of me sitting around the house with my arm in a sling. We lasted eighteen months."

"Sounds to me like she ruined your career," Soave spoke up pointedly.

"I might have been a star if it hadn't been for that," Dirk admitted. "Then again, I might not have. I don't let myself go there. Nothing good comes from that woulda-coulda stuff. Pain is mandatory. Suffering is optional. You have to move on. Takai sure did. Soon as she realized I wasn't going to make it to the show, I was of zero use to her. I soon discovered she was no longer being faithful to me. Had herself a string of men, some of them married men. And we were history."

"And it's been eating away at your guts for years, hasn't it?" demanded Soave, moving in on him. "She ruined your baseball career, slept around on you, made a fool out of you . . ."

Dirk refused to be baited. "Look, man, I know where you're trying to go with this. But I didn't try to kill her. And that's the truth."

Des said, "Dirk, you told me that being back here was giving you a chance to catch up with some old friends. Who did you mean exactly?"

"Well, Timmy Keefe," Dirk responded, as Soave resumed pacing. "He was my best friend growing up. We're like brothers. And his wife, Debbie, is my cousin. She's the only real family I have left around here. I've been up to their place for dinner a few times since I've been here. Timmy and me took out his Boston Whaler Sunday. He's got a few lobster pots. We cleaned them out. Had ourselves one mean feast when we got home."

"Tim's been fixing up my house," Des said.

"Yeah, he told me. You'll be real pleased with how it turns out. Timmy never cuts corners. He may take a little longer than some of the others, but it'll be worth it."

"I'm sure it will." Des knew no such thing, although she sure did know about the taking longer part.

"He's been trying to get me to come in with him for years," Dirk said. "Buying places and fixing them up together. Plenty of money to be made, if you're good with a hammer and have some capital. Laurie and me have talked about it, too. But her family's in Toledo. She's got a real support network there. And a good job with a regional bank. Still, I'm not getting any younger," he added wistfully. "And I'm away from home an awful lot. That gets old fast."

"Can anyone vouch for your whereabouts at five-twenty this morning?" Soave asked him.

Dirk shook his head. "I was asleep in bed—alone. I don't fool around on Laurie. I had me a lot of seasons on the circuit. And a whole lot of girls. But I made a promise to myself that when I settled down with the right one I'd give all of that up. I haven't touched a drop of alcohol in four years either. A lot of peace of mind comes with that. I sleep soundly at night."

"Yet you don't wear a wedding ring," Des observed, her eyes falling on his meaty ex-catcher's hands. "Why is that?"

Dirk's face broke into a broad grin. "Can't grip a bat—especially an aluminum one." He reached inside the collar of his sweatshirt and pulled out the gold chain he wore around his neck. His wedding ring was suspended from it. "I keep it right here."

"Let's talk about Bruce Leanse," she suggested, shifting gears on him.

Dirk immediately chilled. "What about him?"

"You gave him a decidedly nasty look when I was there yesterday. What was that about?"

"I'd rather not say," he replied, lowering his eyes.

"We have zero time for crap, Doughty," Soave said harshly, his chest puffing out. "Give it up right now or you're on your way to Meriden for formal questioning."

Dirk remained stubbornly silent.

"Does it have anything to do with him and Takai being romantically involved?" Des asked him.

Dirk drew back, narrowing his eyes at her. "No way to keep a secret in Dorset, is there?"

"I wouldn't say that," she responded. "Moose sure managed."

"Takai's up to her old tricks," he disclosed reluctantly. "I don't like it. Don't like to see her messing up another marriage. Ben's a nice, nice boy. And Babette's one tough lady, but she's a good mom and she genuinely cares about that lying bastard. Those two deserve better than what he and Takai are doing to them."

Soave moved in on Dirk again. "You didn't try to *rescue* that family, did you?"

"I didn't shoot anyone," Dirk said patiently.

"Any chance that Bruce was seeing *both* sisters?" Soave pressed.

"Moose was no home-wrecker."

"And yet, she was visiting *someone* on the third floor of the Frederick House just prior to her death, correct?"

Dirk shrugged his broad shoulders. "Certainly sounds that way."

"And you're trying to tell us it wasn't you?"

Dirk looked Soave right in the eye, his gaze steady and unwavering. "I am."

"Do you actually expect us to *believe* you?"

"I do," Dirk said, refusing to be shaken from his story.

Des found herself believing him. Even though it absolutely did not add up. Not at all. Because, damn it, they'd *checked* the inn's registry. And they *knew* who else besides Dirk had been staying up on the third floor. And if it wasn't Dirk who Moose was mixed up with, then, well, this case was getting more whacked by the minute.

In fact, it made absolutely no sense at all.

"Yo, this is just like old times," Soave remarked as Des steered her cruiser down the Old Shore Road toward Smith Neck Cove. He rode shotgun. Tommy was running Dirk back to the inn. "You and me going out on a call together, huh?"

"Don't let Tommy hear you say that. He'll think you miss me."

"I *do* miss you, Des. Geez, I thought I made that awful clear . . ." Now the man sounded hurt. He was still pouting over her stinging rebuke in the art academy lounge. "We worked good together. Our minds meshed. Plus you notice things quicker than I do."

"Only because I'm a woman."

"What's that got to do with it?"

"Women *listen*. Men are too busy strutting around, trying to impress people."

"I miss working with you, Des."

"Rico, you're a day late and a dollar short," she said to him coldly.

He fell into troubled silence for a moment. "The thing is, I had my whole future to think of."

"Yeah, you made that pretty clear at the time."

"No, you don't understand! Hear me out, will ya? I was under a ton of pressure from up above to stick with my boys." He was referring to the Brass City crew—his brother, his uncle, the whole lot of them. "They watch out for me, Des. I need that. I need *them*. I'm nowhere on my own. And you . . ."

"I was a lone wolf. Say no more."

"If I had it to do all over again, I would have protected you better. I owed you that. I realize it now."

Des kept her eyes on the road. "We all do what we have to do," she said grudgingly.

"I realize that, too. But tell me this—why do I still feel so lousy about it?"

"You're picking at your own scabs, Rico. I can't help you."

He peered at her intently from across the seat. "You're a hard woman, Des."

"I have to be. If you want soft, call Tammy."

"It's *Tawny!*"

Along with her family's thriving art gallery, Greta Patterson had inherited a sprawling Cape Cod–style cottage out at the end of Smith Neck Cove. Its half-mile-long private driveway was flanked by vineyards. Going into the entry hall, where Greta greeted them, was practically like walking in the front door of an art museum. Paintings lined the walls from floor to ceiling. Landscapes, mostly, many of them by Wendell Frye's father and grandfather. One of Hangtown's own sculptures was featured prominently in the entryway, a tower comprised of old beauty-salon hair dryers, toasters, television sets and the front end of a 1957 T-Bird.

Greta's wide-bodied frame was covered in a caftan of purple silk lined with gold brocade. She wore a pair of black velvet lounging slippers on her feet and an extremely guarded expression on her square, blotchy face. Her mouth was freshly painted a garish red. In one hand she was clutching a long-stemmed goblet of red wine. She was drinking alone—her husband was nowhere to be seen. "May I offer you folks a taste of mine own merlot?" she asked them.

"You folks produce your own wine here?" Soave asked her, awestruck, after they'd politely declined her offer.

"Well, I'm getting there," she replied huskily. "The vines are starting to yield grapes of genuine depth and subtlety." She held her goblet up to the light, the better to admire its color. "There's a cooperative winery in operation in Stonington that I belong to, although I am by no means a winemaker myself. I wouldn't even know where to begin."

"Nothing to it," Soave said, grinning at her. "You just got to be Italian—my grandfather used to make it in his bathtub."

Des, for her part, was thinking about how many times Greta had used the word *I* instead of *we*.

She led them into the living room, where there were more paintings, a well-stocked bar, a roaring fire. Also a gold-inlaid Browning twelve-gauge shotgun in an ornate glass case. Des's eyes fell right on that.

So did Soave's. "Who's the shooter?" he asked Greta.

"I am. Colin hates guns."

"You hunt?"

"No, never. I shoot for sport. Targets . . ."

"Ever fire a Barrett fifty-caliber?"

"That's not sport. That's a weapon of mass destruction."

"How is Colin feeling?" Des asked her.

"Defiant, that's how," Greta replied. "He is *not* going to be railroaded out of his job by that woman. I say this not only as his wife but as his attorney—Colin Falconer is Dorset's superintendent of schools and he intends to remain so."

"May we speak with him?"

Greta padded over to the fireplace and poked at the fire. "What's this all about? You were maddeningly vague on the phone."

"We need to speak with him, ma'am," Soave said, his voice firm.

"Well, he's having a lie-down. Poor thing's exhausted. But I'll see if—" She broke off, glancing up at the doorway.

Colin stood there in a red silk dressing gown, looking pale and unsteady. There were purple smudges under his eyes, and his hair was disheveled.

"There's my boy now," Greta spoke up with motherly good cheer. "How are you, darling?"

"I feel . . . like I'm dreaming," Colin replied in a hollow, shaky voice. "I keep thinking I'll . . . wake up and everything will be . . ." He let out a sudden strangled sob and slumped into an armchair, his head in his hands.

Soave shuffled his feet uncomfortably. He did not deal well with emotionally overwrought men. This one also happened to be married to a woman who was easily twenty years his senior. Ozzie and Harriet they were not.

"We're sorry to bother you right now, Colin," Des said. "But there are some questions we absolutely must ask you."

"Oh, God . . ." Colin moaned, his long bare legs stretched out before him. He had the skinniest, whitest legs Des had ever seen. She doubted that they had ever been exposed to sunlight. "I'm so confused."

"We're all confused," Greta said to him gently. "The whole damned world is full of confused people."

"We're only concerned with the ones who kill other people," Soave said.

"Of course," Colin said. "A-and you have a job to do. I understand."

Greta said, "I want you officers to understand that I am acting here as my husband's attorney. If I feel any of your questions are inappropriate, I will step in . . . How about a brandy, darling? It might put some color back in your cheeks."

She poured Colin a generous slug from a decanter and

brought it to him. He drank it down in one gulp, making a face at the taste. Clearly, he was no drinker.

Des and Soave took seats on the sofa. Greta sat in the armchair next to Colin's, watching him protectively.

"Colin, how long were you and Moose Frye lovers?" Des asked.

Colin immediately glanced over at his wife, whose face registered no surprise. Either Greta knew all about them or she was a very good actress.

"It's . . . out in the open then?" he asked Des uncertainly.

"We know it was you who she was visiting every night on the third floor of the Frederick House," Soave said.

"We'd been together for several months." Colin's eyes drifted over toward the fire. "I've just lost someone who was very dear to me, you see. Mary Susan was my everything. And she always will be."

Again, Greta didn't react—no outward emotional response at all to her husband's declaration of undying love for another woman. A very cool customer, Des observed, turning her attention back to Colin. "At breakfast yesterday you complained to me about all the noise 'they' were making up there. How come?"

"I was afraid you thought it might be me," he answered guiltily. "I was just trying to be discreet."

"Not to mention clever," Des pointed out.

"We had to keep it a secret," Colin explained. "I'm a married man. She was an employee of the school district. The board couldn't find out. An 'inappropriate' relationship such as ours could have cost us our jobs."

"Not that it should," Greta spoke up angrily in his defense. "Colin and I had separated, Moose was single. Why can't two adults have a consensual sexual relationship anymore? What country are we living in?"

"She called me a madman last night," Colin said suddenly. "She was so worried about me."

"Because you'd swallowed the Valium?" Des asked him.

He ducked his head, nodding. "My life's totally out of control. I couldn't *take* it anymore. And by ending it all—

this was something I *could* control." He smiled at Des faintly. "Strangely enough, after you rescued me I felt much better. I seem to be more in control of my emotional responses ever since I swallowed those pills. Greta wanted me to spend last night here . . ."

"But he refused," Greta spoke up.

"I needed to be with Mary Susan."

"What did you two talk about last night?" Soave asked him.

"Sheryl Crow," Colin answered tonelessly.

Soave frowned. "The singer? What for?"

Colin fell back weakly against the seat cushion. "We talked about what we always talked about—ending it."

"And what did you decide?"

"Not a thing. Except that we couldn't live without each other."

"And she left your room at approximately five A.M.?"

"Yes, that's right. I dozed for a while, then showered and dressed and went down to breakfast. That's when I first heard the news about Takai's Porsche. But it wasn't until I dropped by my office to clear out some personal effects that I found out Mary Susan h-hadn't come to work."

"You knew about their affair?" Soave asked Greta.

She reached for her wine, gripping the glass tightly. "I did."

"How did that go down with you?"

"It hurt," Greta replied, her eyes glittering at Soave. "I am a human being, after all. But I'm also an adult. I accepted it."

Des said, "Colin, I understand Babette Leanse has an issue with you involving *another* of your romances."

"I would hardly call that a romance," Colin said, shifting uneasily.

"Okay, what would you call it?"

"Sick, filthy porn," he said bitterly. "Vile, sadomasochistic perversion. It was . . ." Colin halted a moment to grab hold of himself. "It was curiosity more than anything else, at first. Someone to talk to. Then it became much, much more intense than that. In fact, there was such a ferocity to my relationship with Mary Susan that I began to fear I was using her to push away my growing feelings for my cyber partner."

"I realize I'm being personal here," Des said, "but would you characterize yourself as bisexual?"

Colin glanced over at Greta, who gave him a slight nod. "My wife and I have not had a conventional marriage by most people's standards. Both in terms of our respective ages and our . . . inclinations. We have each gone our separate ways from time to time. Wherever those ways took us."

So maybe it hadn't been her imagination, Des realized. Maybe Greta *had* been coming on to her yesterday at the gallery. "What can you tell us about your cyber partner, Colin?"

"Why is that important?" Greta demanded, padding over to the bar to pour herself more wine.

"Because we say it is," Soave said. "Let us do our job, okay, counselor?"

"It's okay, I don't mind. His online name is Cutter," Colin revealed, and proceeded to provide them with the name of the Internet service he'd met him on. It was a brand-name-commercial provider, one of those that allow members to employ a half dozen or more different online identities.

"And his real name?" Des asked him.

"We've never exchanged names," Colin said. "I know him only as Cutter."

"The two of you have never met face-to-face?"

"That's correct, trooper."

"Time-out here," Soave broke in. "Are you telling us you're sexually involved with some guy, and it may cost you your job, and you have no idea who the hell he is?"

"I never wanted to know," Colin explained, coloring slightly. "The not-knowing part is what makes it so liberating. You're totally free to be yourself."

"Exactly what has he told you about himself?" Des asked.

Colin shrugged his bony shoulders, sniffling. "He's a long-haul trucker. Owns his own rig. Spends a lot of time on the road alone."

"And how did you two hook up?"

"We met in a gay men's chat group. One thing led to another."

"Which one of you initiated it?"

"We both wanted it to happen. Each of us felt *something* was missing from our lives . . ." Colin trailed off into troubled silence. "We haven't communicated since Attila the Hen found out about us. I haven't dared."

"You used the word 'ferocity' to describe your relationship with the victim," Soave said to him. "Had things changed between you two in recent days?"

"I'm afraid I don't know what you mean," Colin replied.

"Was she putting any pressure on you? Making any demands?"

Colin shook his head at Soave, bewildered. "Such as . . . ?"

"Did you get her pregnant?" Soave wanted to know. "And don't lie to me—the medical examiner will know the truth soon enough."

"I wasn't going to lie to you," Colin said indignantly. "And I resent your supposition that I would."

"As do I, Lieutenant," Greta said to him coldly from the fireplace, where she was poking at the logs. "Colin is being candid and cooperative. You have no cause to speak to him that way."

"You haven't answered my question," Soave persisted, undeterred.

"Mary Susan said nothing to me about any pregnancy," Colin answered. "If she had, I would have been thrilled. Children are my life. I love children. I loved *her,* can't you understand that?"

"Had you two discussed marriage?" Des asked him.

Colin glanced furtively at his wife. "It was something we'd talked about."

"And . . . ?"

"That was never going to happen," Greta responded, with an edge of authority to her voice. "I will not be alone. Not now. Not after so many years." She sat back down and took a sip of her wine, smacking her bright-red lips. "If you don't mind my saying so, you officers are missing the big picture here when it comes to Colin."

"Which is what?" Soave wondered.

"That there is a calculated, willful effort by this school board president to oust him from his job," Greta replied. "It all comes down to this damned pissing match over Center School."

"We can renovate it for one-third the cost of a new school," Colin explained. "I have a good, sound plan."

"But Babette and her little hand-picked followers on the board won't hear of it," Greta said, her voice rising. "They *need* their new school. Hell, they've practically turned it into a holy crusade. And when they couldn't win Colin over to their side, Babette got down and dirty. This whole ugly business about Melanie suing the school district—that has Babette's fingerprints all over it."

"I believe she's put Melanie up to it," Colin said. "Because if Melanie truly did have a problem with my behavior, she would have *told* me. Okay, so it was inappropriate for me to use my office computer. An error in judgment on my part. I concede that. But do you actually throw a person away for that?"

"The *real* error you made," Greta spoke angrily, "was giving Babette something she could use against you."

"What do you think the school board will do about you?" Des asked Colin.

"I am under a doctor's care," he replied softly, wringing his pale hands in his lap. "When the doctor feels I'm ready, I'll return to work. It is my hope that they'll let me."

"And if they don't?"

"Then we intend to sue them for violating Colin's civil rights," Greta said. "His doctor will certify that Colin is suffering from clinical depression, which happens to qualify as a disability, thereby entitling him to legal protection from just exactly this type of callous, discriminatory firing. Trust me, the board will not want to open up this can of worms—not unless they're prepared to face a drawn-out court battle *and* a multimillion-dollar settlement. But if that's how they choose to proceed, so be it. We will make them very, very sorry."

Des looked at Colin and said, "Is that what you want?"

The superintendent let out a long, pained sigh. "I want my life back. I love those kids."

"And they love you," Greta said. "And they *don't* need any new thirty-four-million-dollar school."

Soave studied Greta in thoughtful silence for a moment, smoothing his see-through mustache. "Your husband claims he was alone in his room at the Frederick House after the victim left. Where were *you* at the time of the murder?"

Des glanced over at him, smiling faintly. His mind was working the same way as hers. She'd trained him well.

"I was here," Greta answered. "Asleep in bed."

"Alone?" Soave asked.

"Quite alone," Greta said, nodding her silver head. "There's not a big market out there for sixty-three-year-old bull dykes who look like they just rolled in from the Roller Derby circuit."

"Please don't talk about yourself that way," Colin objected.

"Tell us a little more about Melanie Zide," Soave went on. "What's her situation? What's she like?"

"You've seen her," Des mentioned to him.

"I have?" Soave looked at her blankly. "When?"

"Tonight. She was the model at the art academy."

Soave's eyes widened in surprise. "Time-out here . . . Are you telling me that a woman who poses buck-naked in front of total strangers is suing the school district because this guy left some dirty words on his computer screen?"

"That's exactly what we're telling you," Greta said.

"Yo, this is totally wiggy," said Soave, scratching his head. "What the hell kind of a place is this anyway?"

"A quaint little village that positively oozes with historic New Englandy charm," Greta responded dryly. "Me, I call it home."

Melanie Zide lived on Griswold Avenue, a dimly lit dead-end street of bungalows near Uncas Lake. Des had walked by it several times on her way up to her new place from the inn. Some of the little bungalows were well-tended and freshly painted, their lawns mowed and raked. Others showed signs of serious, long-term neglect—knee-high weeds out front, broken windowpanes, peeling paint. Melanie's place was one of these.

Her lights were on inside the house, though no car was parked in her short gravel driveway. There was no garage. Des pulled her cruiser into the driveway and they got out, Soave waiting by the car. She climbed the two steps to the broad, sagging front porch, where an old sprung sofa sat on concrete blocks, and tapped on the door. There was no sound of footsteps inside. No response at all. Just a dog barking down the street somewhere.

Soave automatically went around to the back, just like when they'd worked together. He returned in a moment, shaking his head. "Don't see anybody in there."

Across the street, a man came out onto his own sagging porch to watch them. Des noticed him standing there under his porch light, arms folded before his chest. He was still standing there as she and Soave started back toward her ride.

"Be right back, Rico." She moseyed on over there and tipped her hat at him. "Good evening, sir. I'm Resident Trooper Mitry."

He was a big, suety man in his forties with thinning black hair, a slovenly beard and the sly, crafty eyes of a man who thought he was smart even if no one else did. He wore a blaze orange hunter's vest over a frayed white T-shirt, jeans and work boots. What she noticed most about him was the message he had tattooed on his knuckles, one letter to a knuckle. On his right hand the tattoos spelled out *J-E-S-U-S*, on his left hand *S-A-V-E-S*. Behind him, through his open front door, she could see a living room cluttered with dirty dishes, pizza boxes and beer cans. On a card table in the middle of the room sat a personal computer, its screen illuminated. There was a stack of printouts next to it.

"We just wanted to ask your neighbor some questions," Des explained. "Your name is . . . ?"

"Gilliam," he answered, sullen and suspicious. Des wondered if it was her uniform or her pigment. Both, possibly. "Chuckie Gilliam."

"Hey, you wouldn't be Sandy's Chuckie, would you?" Des asked brightly.

"Yeah, I am. And, lady, I don't want no cat."

"Are you *sure?* I've got Polaroids. Want to see Polaroids?"

"No!"

"Okay, we'll come back to that . . . Chuckie, have you seen Melanie this evening?"

"I saw her go out maybe six o'clock," he said. "Come home about nine."

Des nodded. This would square with Melanie's modeling gig. "Did she stay home long?"

"Left again right away, then came back again a while later."

"How much later?"

"Lady, I dunno," he said, his voice a low growl.

"Could you take a guess, please? It's important."

"Half hour. Maybe an hour. She popped her trunk, loaded some stuff into her car. She was in a real hurry."

"What kind of stuff?"

"Suitcases. She made a couple of trips in and out, then she split."

"What does she drive?"

"A Dodge Neon, blue. Is Melanie in some kind of trouble?"

"She have any men in her life?" Des asked, wondering if Chuckie was one of them. Or perhaps wanted to be. He kept mighty close tabs on her.

"I haven't noticed nobody. It's been pretty quiet over there lately. Her brother used to be around, but he split."

"When was this?"

"Last year. Her mother used to live there, too. Old lady was gonzo in the head. Alzheimer's. Every once in a while she'd fall. I'd help Melanie hoist her back into bed. But Mrs.

Zide's not around no more. Melanie put her in a nursing home."

"Any idea where that would be?"

"Norwich, maybe."

Des glanced inside again at the computer on the card table. "What do you do for a living, Chuckie?"

"Why do you need to know?" he demanded.

"It's just for my paperwork. I have to fill in those dumb blanks."

"I'm a carpenter here in town."

"Is that right? Who are you working for?"

"I'm between jobs right now."

That was saying something, the way new houses were going up around Dorset. The contractors were so starved for manpower, they'd take anyone who knew which end of a nail gun to use. This had to be one real-live nowhere man, Des reflected. Poor Sandy would be so much better off with a nice pair of cats. "You and Sandy don't live together, am I right?"

"What's that got to do with anything?"

"I'm just wondering if you live here by yourself," said Des, who was also wondering if Chuckie Gilliam had a sheet. He smelled like he did.

"I'm here by myself," he said grudgingly. "Anything wrong with that?"

"No, not at all. Some of the smartest people I know live alone, myself included." She thanked him for his help and crossed the street to fill in Soave.

"It's unlocked," he mentioned idly, as the two of them stood leaning against her cruiser. "Her back door. If we want to go in and take a look."

"Do we?"

Soave shifted his bulky shoulders. "What do you say?"

"I say that it's your case, wow man."

"Let's go for it," he declared, heading around back once again.

He let Des in through the front door. Melanie's living

room was small and it was dingy. There was a moth-eaten purple love seat and a harvest-gold Naugahyde lounge chair that had been patched together with silver duct tape. Both pieces looked as if they had come from the dump.

The wall phone in the kitchen was off the hook, the receiver dangling in mid-air. Des immediately felt a small uptick in her pulse.

There were two bedrooms. In the smaller one there was an old iron bed, stripped down to its stained mattress. There was no dresser in there. No other furniture, period. The narrow closet was empty except for a few wire hangers.

There was a double bed in the other room. Its covers were rumpled, the linen gray and sour-smelling. Everything in this closet was gone, too, including the hangers. All that remained was an unsigned nude drawing of Melanie thumbtacked to the inside of the closet door. The proportions were way off, Des observed critically. Melanie's torso was too long, her calves too short. Clearly the work of an unaccomplished art student.

Soave knelt and looked under the bed. Nothing. He pulled open the dresser drawers. Empty. So were the drawers of the cheap pine student's desk set before the bedroom window.

Same story in the bathroom—the medicine chest had been cleaned out.

All Melanie had left behind were a few clean dishes in the kitchen cupboards. And some food in the refrigerator. Not much—a half-eaten take-out pizza, a plastic liter bottle of Diet Coke, a quart of low-fat milk. There was a pull-down hatchway ladder in the kitchen ceiling that led up to the attic. Soave gave it a pull. Des handed him her flashlight. He went up and poked his head around. Nothing.

There was nothing in the shallow crawl space under the house either.

Des stood there looking around at the vacated house and remembering the anxiousness in Melanie's voice when they'd talked that evening in the studio. Melanie had seemed frightened. Of whom? Of what? Was it about Babette

Leanse's case against Colin? Had Melanie been coerced into fingering her boss? Had she been bought? Or did she know something about Moose's murder? Did the two cases connect up with each other? If so, how? Why had Melanie been in such a huge hurry to clear out of town? What was she so afraid of? What did she know?

Des didn't know. Didn't know a damned thing.

Except that Melanie Zide, the one person who might be able to help them make some sense of this whole mess, was way gone.

CHAPTER 9

"So we're here to catch strays?" Mitch asked her, yawning, as he sat there slumped behind the wheel of his Studebaker pickup.

"In a manner of speaking," Des responded from next to him in the darkness.

"How come we didn't bring your have-a-heart traps and those yummy little jars of strained turkey?"

"Different kind of strays."

"Gotcha," Mitch said, nodding. "Okay, I'm thinking any minute now you're going to tell me what the hell we're doing here."

"Here" was the parking lot of Dorset's A & P, which was mostly deserted since it was presently two o'clock in the morning and they closed at eleven. The market's interior night-lights were on, casting a faint, ghostly glow out into the lot. But it was still quite dark. And they were quite alone. The delivery van from the florist next door was parked there for the night. A couple of rusted-out beaters with FOR SALE signs in their windshields were on display—the A & P's parking lot doubled as an unofficial low-end used-car emporium. And there were Des and Mitch, a thermos of coffee and a box of Entenmann's chocolate chip cookies for Mitch on the seat between them.

"We're hanging," she said curtly, her hands folded in her lap.

She had shown up at his cottage around midnight, taut as a tuning fork. He was asleep in bed when she got there, exhausted by his day of fact-finding but very happy to see her. And ready and willing to show her just how happy. But instead of stripping off her uniform and sliding her sleek frame under the nice warm covers with him, she'd barked, "Get dressed. And bring a warm jacket." Sounding much more like a drill instructor than the new, babe-a-licious love of his life. "I need your truck."

"Take the keys," he'd offered, groaning.

"I need *you*. I'm about ready to chew my own hands off. And if I don't talk to somebody, namely you, I will."

So he got dressed while she made the coffee and they piloted his Studey over the causeway to the market and parked it there. And now they sat, growing chillier by the minute, which Mitch didn't mind. He was amply dressed, not to mention padded. What he minded was that she wasn't talking.

"Are we on a stakeout?" he pressed her.

"We're doing some surveillance, cool?"

"Cool. Does this make us a crime-fighting team?"

She raised an eyebrow at him. "What, like Starsky and Hatch?"

"It's Hutch. Actually, I was thinking more along the lines of Salt and Pepper, a vastly underrated—"

"Man, don't even go there," Des growled.

"Okay, what's upsetting you?" he asked, munching on a cookie. "Is it Soave?" Her ex-partner was not someone Mitch had been impressed with. In truth, he thought the guy was a pinhead. And not exactly Mr. Sensitivity. Mitch had seen him smiling for the cameras on the six-o'clock news. When someone asked him why anyone would want to shoot Mary Susan Frye he'd replied, "People may have thought they knew the victim, but maybe they didn't." A smarmy bit of innuendo that made it sound as if Moose had been asking for what she got. Des would never have left something that tactless hanging in the wind. She would have shown more consideration.

But Des was not running the case.

"I think he's got blinders on," she said tightly. "He's so in love with Jim Bolan that he's not seeing Colin. No matter which path you take, you end up right back at that man. And now Melanie has cleared out and I'm with you—it all fits together. I just can't figure out *how*." She paused, glancing at him uncertainly. "You didn't know he and Moose were a couple, did you?"

"No, I didn't. And I'm positive Hangtown didn't. But it shouldn't come as a surprise to us." Mitch reached for her hand and gripped it. "In case you haven't noticed, lonely people have a way of finding each other."

"Is that what *we* are?" she asked, caressing the back of his hand with her thumb. "Two lonely people?"

"Not anymore." He leaned over and kissed her softly on the mouth. "What else can you tell me?"

"Wait, is this for your article?" she asked, her eyes narrowing at him.

"I'll take whatever you can give me. But if this is awkward, just say no."

"The medical examiner just confirmed that Moose had sex shortly before she was murdered. And she was not pregnant."

"Did you think she was?"

"Not really, but she was involved with a married man. It's something you have to consider."

"But that would mean you think *she* was the intended victim, not Takai."

"I don't know what to think. The more I find out, the less I know."

"How about the gun dealers—have you gotten anything from them?"

"Not yet. Not a single reported Barrett sale ties in to anyone involved in this case." Nor had a trace on Melanie Zide's credit cards yielded anything yet. "She hasn't used a single card. Hasn't stopped at an ATM. She didn't even wait around after class to pick up her modeling fee. She just . . ."

Des stiffened, peering through the windshield at something across the deserted parking lot.

Mitch followed her gaze. He saw nothing out there but the darkness. "She just what?"

"Skipped town. That girl was scared."

"Of what?"

"When we figure that out we'll know who our shooter is."

Mitch glanced at her curiously. "Sure you're not upset about something else?"

"What else would there be?"

He didn't bother to answer. He knew what else. They both knew.

She turned her steady gaze on Mitch. "What about you—pick up any news I can use?"

"Well, Takai carries a loaded gun in her purse. Did you know that?"

"No, I didn't. But that's not so unusual anymore, I'm sorry to say. Anything else?"

He filled her in on The Aerie, Bruce Leanse's hugely ambitious dream project for Dorset. And about the man's overheated romantic entanglement with Takai, which could torpedo both the project and his marriage. "He has every motive in the world for wanting Takai gone. And so does Babette," Mitch said. "Although, personally, if I were in Babette's shoes, *he*'s the one I'd be going after."

"I'm down to that," Des agreed. "And I'd aim *low*." Now she leaned toward the windshield, drawing her breath in. "Lookie-lookie, I *thought* I saw them . . ."

There were five of them in all. Teenaged boys, as far as Mitch could tell. They were doing their best to avoid the floodlights as they crept their way out of the shadows from the loading zone behind the market. All of them wore dark clothing. All of them carried knapsacks. Briefly they paused, each reaching into another's sack to remove spray can after spray can of paint. Graffiti artists—that's what they were. Now they started their way toward the market's enticingly huge, pristine picture windows, brandishing their weapons.

"Start your engine, Mitch," Des said in a low voice. "Hit your lights."

"Don't you want to catch them in the act?"

"No, just go ahead and do it."

"But they'll run away."

"I want them to. Start it *now*."

He did, and at the sound of his engine kicking over they disappeared instantly back into the darkness—not scattering wildly like the cockroaches in Mitch's New York City kitchen but in a planned fashion, each in a different direction from the others. The choreography was straight out of *West Side Story*.

Mitch grinned at her admiringly. "That was *them*, wasn't it? That was the Mod Squad."

"The skinny one's named Ronnie Welmers. His kid brother called me just before I came over to your place. Told me they'd be hitting the market tonight."

"Why would he tip you off?"

"He's afraid. Ronnie told him they were about to pull something major."

"Like what?"

"Like something he could go to jail for."

"Where?"

"That part I don't know yet," she answered. "We're done here if you want to head home."

Mitch put the truck into gear and started back toward Peck Point in the darkness of the small-town night.

"Talk to me about an actress named Claire Danes," Des spoke up.

"She got hot a few years back in *My So-Called Life*, a teen-angst TV series. Played a sensitive, misunderstood high school girl."

"Has she got game?"

"She was very effective in that. Then she went on to the big screen, and the results have been decidedly mixed— *Romeo and Juliet* with Leonardo DiCaprio, followed by what is possibly the single worst film ever made, *The Mod*

Squad—" He broke off, glancing at her in surprise. "Okay, I'll bite—how does *she* connect up?"

"Ronnie's madly in love with her. Beyond that, I have no idea. Never saw the movie."

"It was based on the TV show from the sixties," he said, hitting the brakes as a deer darted across the Old Shore Road ten yards in front of them. That happened a lot late at night. "She played one of three bad kids who've gone good as undercover cops. The series was a big success at the time. Very 'heavy.' And they should have left it alone, same as they should have left *The Avengers* alone. It stank out loud. Gone and forgotten in a week."

"Not by everyone, apparently," she pointed out. "Ronnie's a serious movie buff. Knows your work well."

"Don't tell me he's a fan."

"Actually, he thinks you're a bore. I believe his exact words were 'officially sanctioned' bore."

"Sure, when I was his age I felt the same way about Pauline Kael and Vincent Canby. I didn't realize how good they were until I grew up."

"Wait, you grew up?" she said teasingly.

"That's pretty standard stuff for teenaged boys. So is the graffiti thing."

"Explain that to me, will you? Why are a bunch of middle-class white boys freakin' like this? They live in big houses, have money in their pockets, brains, every opportunity in the world . . . Why?"

"They want attention."

"From who?"

"Girls, silly. That's why we do everything. We pound on drum kits, slam into each other on the football field, paint dirty words on public buildings—anything so that girls will notice us. It's always about girls. And it never stops. When we get a little older we just find more permanent ways of saying *Look at me.* Which explains the Bruce Leanses of the world."

She thought about this for a moment. "That's totally pathetic."

"We're a pathetic lot, all right. Maybe now you can begin to appreciate just how fortunate you are that you found me."

"Um, okay, I'm thinking I liked you better when your self-esteem was a couple of dozen notches lower, boyfriend."

"You have no one to blame but yourself, Master Sergeant. I'm floating on a cloud, thanks to you."

"Mitch, I'm floating along right next to you," she said, suddenly serious. "And there's nothing underneath me. If you go down, I go with you."

He glanced over at her, startled and pleased. "That's the nicest thing you've ever said to me, you know that?"

She said nothing in response, just swiveled her head and stared out her window. He couldn't see her face. She didn't want him to see her face.

It was nearly three by the time they got back to his cottage. Mitch tromped straight up to bed. Des, who was still wired, set up her easel in the living room. She had some grisly crime scene photos of Moose's charred remains that she was anxious to depict in charcoal. It was her way of dealing.

Mitch didn't look at the photos. He didn't want to see them.

She was still down there working when Quirt started meowing outside the front door, shortly before dawn. She let him in, but Mitch padded downstairs anyway, yawning and blinking, to find a dozen or more haunting portraits torn from her pad and flung all over the room.

Everywhere he looked there was Moose Frye, or what was left of her.

Des's hands and face were smeared black with charcoal, her eyes bloodshot. She was so fried that she barely seemed to notice Mitch standing there. She was still inside of it. Still bothered. In spite of all of the years he had spent as a critic, Mitch had never truly understood what artists put themselves through until he met her. He had newfound respect for people who create things, thanks to Des. She was definitely rubbing off on him. Was he rubbing off on her? He wondered.

He went in the kitchen and put coffee on and said good morning to Quirt, who was hunched over the kibble bowl with single-minded intensity. He threw on rumpled khakis and a sweatshirt and ran his fingers through his hair. He poured two cups of coffee and carried them into the living room. Handed Des one. Put a jacket around her shoulders. Took her by the hand and led her out the door, stepping over that morning's fresh headless mouse, and on down to the beach. Des came willingly enough, and sat next to him when he patted the driftwood log where he liked to perch in the early morning with his coffee. There was a sliver of moon on this calm, frosty morning. Geese flew overhead in V-formation.

"Look, it's just something that we have to get through."

She gazed bleary-eyed out at the water, shivering. She seemed very far away from him at that moment. "What is?"

"You know perfectly well what." Tonight was the Deacon's birthday dinner. Her father and Mitch were going to set eyes on each other for the first time. "It'll be fine. We'll all be fine. You're my soul mate, he's your closest living relative. I *want* to meet him."

"I'm hearing it," she grunted. "But I'm disbelieving it."

"Believe it. Besides, this is not a totally new experience for me. I went through this with my own folks and Maisie. They thought she was from the planet Pluto—all because her people came over on the *Mayflower*."

"Now there's an eerie coincidence for you—mine came over on a boat hundreds of years ago, too. The only difference is they were in chains at the time."

"By the time Maisie died," Mitch plowed on, "they'd convinced themselves that she was actually half-Jewish."

"Then they'll just love me. According to Bella, I'm a member of the lost tribe."

Mitch sipped his coffee in guarded silence. "I'm not going to let you do this."

"Do *what?*"

"Pick a fight with me so you'll have to call off the dinner. That's not going to happen."

"Doughboy, you are *impossible,* you know that?! You just sit there acting nice to me when all I want to do is bite and scratch and get mean. Damn, what is *wrong* with you?"

"If you want to wrestle, we'll wrestle. That's fine by me. I not only outweigh you but I have a lower center of gravity. I'll whup your skinny ass. I am talking *pancake* here—your nose down in the sand."

"Has it ever occurred to you that we have no business being together?" she demanded. "That our lives are spiraling out of control? That we're completely insane?"

"Sure," he said easily.

"And . . . ?"

"And then I do this . . ." He leaned over and kissed her softly on the lips. "And I know everything I need to know."

She let out that little whimper of hers and flung her arms around him, hugging him tightly. They kissed. They kissed some more.

"How about we go back to the house and, like, I play 'Stairway to Heaven' for you on my Stratocaster?" he murmured in her ear.

"How about if we go back to the house and, like, you don't?"

Des never did get any sleep that night. In fact, she barely had enough time to shower and climb into her uniform before she was due at Center School for traffic control.

"I should buy him something today for his birthday, right?" Mitch said as she hurriedly dumped a bag of dried black-eyed peas into a pot of water to soak.

"No, don't. He doesn't like gifts. That's why I make him dinner."

"Well, can I at least get a bottle of wine?"

"The Deacon never touches it."

"Beer?"

"Don't bother," she said, kissing him good-bye. "I'll get it."

After she had sped away in her cruiser Mitch parked himself in front of his computer and logged on to that morning's New York tabloids. Moose Frye's murder had gone directly to page one. LOVE CRAZY, screamed the *Post*'s banner headline. OH, TEACHER, cried the *News*. Mitch was not surprised. She was a nice-looking small-town New England schoolteacher. She was the daughter of one of America's greatest living artists. And she'd been having a wild, clandestine affair with the married school superintendent—a man who was presently on medical leave because he'd recently tried to kill himself. Such juicy details were bound to surface quickly. It was impossible to keep them under wraps.

Yes, it was page one, all right. And the editor of the Sunday magazine had already e-mailed Mitch twice that morning to put his pedal to the metal and go.

So Mitch went.

Not that it was exactly easy to get in. A dozen news vans were crammed this way and that at the entrance to Lord Cove's Lane, where a stone-faced young trooper had set up a barricade to keep the press out. Mitch had to convince him to radio the trooper stationed inside the house, who had to check with Hangtown before Mitch could pass on through.

Hangtown was at work in the barn with Jim. A radio was blasting old Johnny Cash, and the woodstove was lit against the morning chill. Sam, the German shepherd, was curled up right next to it with one eye closed and the other on Jim's baby-sitter, who was parked on an old car seat with a copy of *Hemmings Motor News*.

The old artist had on a pair of glasses with magnifying lenses that made him look like Dr. Cyclops. He was drawing intently at his workbench, a foam-wrapped pencil clutched in his arthritic hand, an open bottle of Old Overholt rye whiskey within arm's length. He barely seemed to notice Mitch's arrival.

Jim was on his knees assembling an ungainly eight-foot-high stand made of one-inch copper tubing. It had four legs and looked something like a hat rack with elbow joints. Lengths of tubing and rolls of copper flashing were heaped around him everywhere on the dirt floor. Most of the flashing was aged and paint-splattered.

"What is this thing?" asked Mitch, crouching next to Jim.

"The inner workings, son," Jim replied, flipping on a pair of safety goggles. "Hold her steady for a sec, will you . . . ?" Jim reached for a portable oxyacetylene torch and ignited it. "We use a copper-compound braising rod. She melts at about two thousand degrees. You don't want your copper to get much hotter than that or it will burn." Almost immediately Mitch began to smell the smoldering phosphorous and copper compound as Jim started to weld the pieces of the four-legged creature together. "She may look a little unstable right now, but you got to remember that she'll be standing in a twenty-gallon tank of water. You won't see these here feet at all. Or the submersible pump, which'll push the water through that center pipe all the way to the top. It dribbles back down, then gets recirculated."

"Okay, so this will be a fountain, right?"

"You're looking inside the beast, son."

"And what will the beast look like?"

"You'll have to ask the mad doctor there. Me, I'm just Igor."

Hangtown was still at his workbench, padded pencil in hand. What he was drawing resembled an elongated ziggurat of cubes and rectangles heaped one atop the other. "Made one of these back when I had to quit smoking, Big Mitch," he mentioned to him, pausing to light a Lucky. He did not say hello. He acted as if Mitch had been around the house all morning. "Helped keep my mind off of things."

"But you didn't quit smoking."

"That part didn't work out," Hangtown admitted freely. "But the fountain was a major success. Really quite hypnotic, if I do say so myself."

Sam sat up suddenly now, a low growl coming from his throat. A moment later Mitch heard what the dog had heard—cars making their way up the gravel drive toward them. They pulled up right outside the barn with a splatter of gravel. Mitch heard voices and car doors slamming. Jim's baby-sitter got up and tromped over toward the barn door to see what was going on.

In barged Soave and his sergeant, Tommy Salcineto, followed by Des. She looked very ill at ease. She would not make eye contact with Mitch.

"Good morning, trooper," Hangtown called to her, pointedly snubbing Soave. The muscle-bound little lieutenant instantly bristled. "When may I have my girl back? When may I bury her?"

"I don't have a date yet, Mr. Frye," Des answered, pawing at the ground with her brogan. "They can't release her until they've run all of the tests they need to run. I'm sorry."

Hangtown reached for his bottle of rye whiskey and took a swig, swiping at his bearded mouth with the back of his hand. "Then why have you come?"

"Because the DNA on the cigarette butt we found up on the rocks matches Jim Bolan's blood sample," Soave said, turning a cold-eyed gaze on Jim. "Same goes for the shooter's shoe print. It's a dead-on match for your work boots, Bolan."

Jim sat back on his heels, a sick expression on his face. "I've hiked around up there a million times with Sam," he said dejectedly. "Sometimes, I have me a smoke. That's all there is to it. I didn't *do* it, man. You're making a mistake."

"What does all of this mean?" Hangtown asked.

"It means they need a bad guy and I'm it," Jim growled, flinging his safety goggles away in disgust.

"It *means*," Soave said forcefully, "that we'll have to bring him in for formal questioning."

"For how long? When will he be back?"

"I can't answer that, Mr. Frye," Soave said. "That's entirely up to him."

"Well, does he need a lawyer?" Hangtown demanded, his frustration mounting. "Are you arresting him?"

"We're taking him in for questioning, Mr. Frye. He'll be detained at the Major Crime Squad's Central District headquarters in Meriden, okay?"

"No, it is *not* okay!" the old man thundered. "You can't take Jim away from me! I *need* Jim!"

"Sir, I'm afraid I have no choice," Soave insisted.

Another car pulled up outside now. Mitch heard high heels clacking hurriedly on gravel—it was Takai, wearing a gray flannel business suit and looking quite rattled. "I—I came just as soon as Trooper Mitry phoned me, Father," she said, rushing across the barn toward him. "I am so sorry. Are you all right?"

"You get away from me!" Hangtown snarled at her. He was in no mood for her even in the best of times, and these were not the best of times.

Takai backed slowly away from him, stung, her eyes shining. The old man might just as well have cuffed her across the face with his hand. Mitch felt very bad for Takai Frye at that moment.

"Not to worry, Big Jim," Hangtown said to his friend with forced good cheer. "We'll have you home in no time."

"C'mon, Bolan, let's move out," Tommy Salcineto ordered him gruffly.

Jim started out the door, head hung in defeat, his babysitter on his heels. Soave followed, with Des bringing up the rear.

Mitch stopped her and said, "Do *you* think he did it?"

"It's possible," she answered quietly.

"Then again, this could all be for the benefit of those news vans out there, right?"

"Please don't ask me anything more, Mitch," Des pleaded. "I'm strictly a community liaison officer." She bit down on her lower lip, sighing. "Look, I'll see you tonight, okay?" And then she left with the others.

"Takai, do something for me, will you?" Hangtown said to her as they drove off.

"*Anything,* Father," she replied, brightening considerably. The woman was so starved for his love, so eager to be called upon that Mitch found it pathetic. "Just tell me what you want."

"Call Greta. Have her line up a top criminal lawyer for Jim. Money's no object."

Takai's eyes widened. "But he *murdered* Moose! How can you even think of helping him?"

"Because he didn't do it. Jim's my friend. He would never do anything to hurt me."

"Father, the state police have evidence!"

"The state police have *nothing*," he said with total certainty. "Now will you call her or won't you?"

"Of course I will. Whatever you want." Now Takai started for the door, motioning for Mitch to join her. He walked her out to the Land Rover, where she shook her head at him in weary resignation, "My God, he's totally deluding himself."

"It's pretty hard to believe that a friend could do something like that."

"Well, at least it's over," she said, yanking open a creaky door.

"Do you really think so?" Mitch asked her.

Takai raised an eyebrow at him curiously. "Don't you?"

"I honestly don't know."

"Here, I have something for you . . ." She reached across the seat, offering him a prized view of her behind, and pulled out the sweater he'd lent her, neatly folded. "I wore it to bed last night. I hope you don't mind."

It smelled strongly of her perfume, so strongly that he suddenly felt a bit dizzy. "Why . . . did you do that?"

"It made me feel all safe and snuggly," she replied, her eyes glittering at him seductively. "I even dreamed about you. I can't tell you what the dream was, though. I'll have to know you a *lot* better before I do that." And with that she climbed into her dead sister's Land Rover, started it up and sped off, waving at him over her shoulder.

Mitch watched her disappear around the bend, wondering what kind of game she was playing with him. And why she was playing it.

The barn seemed empty and silent now. Hangtown had shut off the radio and was slumped at the workbench smok-

ing a big, loosely rolled joint. "They won't let me be, Big
Mitch," he grumbled, running a misshapen hand through his
mane of white hair. "They never have. They never will. To
hell with all of 'em." He took a long toke on the joint and
held it out to Mitch, who shook his head. "Life ain't for
sissies, that's for damned sure. Just gets harder and harder—
until one day you can't take it anymore. That's when you
know it's time for your nice long dirt nap."

"Hangtown, if there's anything I can do . . ."

He immediately brightened. "As it happens, there is.
You'll have to be my hands today. There's no one else. So
grab yourself a pair of tin snips. Now's when the fun starts."

Mitch stared at him with his mouth open. Hangtown's
mind had already gotten past what had just happened—com-
partmentalized it and shut it away so that he could focus
completely on his work. Mitch had never before witnessed
such intense willpower.

"You *will* work with me, won't you?" Hangtown pleaded.

"Of course I will. But I'm still writing that article—okay
if I turn on my tape recorder while we work?"

Hangtown shrugged and said, "If it makes you happy."

Mitch set it on the workbench, grateful that he'd brought
along extra microcassettes, while Hangtown got busy showing him what he needed from him.

What he needed, first, was for Mitch to take the snips to
those sheets of copper flashing and make him dozens and
dozens of rectangles in an array of sizes ranging from as
small as six by eighteen inches to as large as four times that.
Next, Mitch had to turn those measured rectangles into a
vast assortment of copper boxes by folding them around different blocks of wood and pounding them into shape with a
rubber mallet. Once the boxes were completed, Hangtown
could arrange them one atop the other around the pipe skeleton that Jim had been making and—again, with Mitch's
assistance—weld them together to form his tower.

It was slow, painstaking physical work—donkey work.
Mitch had always heard that copper was soft, and maybe it
was as metals go. But this was nothing like trying to cut and

fold paper. The flashing was stiff and resistant and its fresh-cut edges were razor-sharp. If he hadn't put on a pair of Jim's work gloves his hands would have been cut to shreds. Still, it was work that the old master couldn't do anymore, and Mitch could, so he dived in, inspired by the heady realization that he was actually in Wendell Frye's studio helping the great artist create a work of art. This was something he would be able to tell his grandchildren about someday: *I once built a fountain with Wendell Frye.*

"What will you write, Big Mitch?" Hangtown asked as he fiddled with his plans at the workbench, deciding which blocks went where.

"I don't know yet," Mitch replied, grunting from his exertions. "I'll write the truth, as I see it."

"I was with him. I was with Jim when Moose died."

"There's no chance you might have drifted off for a few minutes?"

"Even if I had, it's a good fifteen-twenty-minute walk to those rocks from the house, and the same back. Plus he had to wait there for her, unless he knew exactly when she was coming home. Then he had to hide the gun when he was done with it—which they have *not* found . . ." Hangtown fell silent a moment, absorbed by his work. "Maybe I closed my eyes for a second. But I wasn't asleep in front of that fire for no forty-five minutes. I *know* that. And I ain't senile. And that so-called evidence of theirs means nothing—not if Jim has himself a good lawyer."

Mitch agreed. It wouldn't hold up for a second in court. Soave had to know that. So why had he taken Jim away? Did he think he might be able to squeeze a confession out of Jim once he had him in custody? "Jim did have a good reason for wanting to kill Takai," he pointed out.

"Plenty good," Hangtown admitted. "Only, why would he go to such elaborate lengths to do her in? Why not just go upstairs to her bedroom and slash the greedy bitch's throat while she sleeps? Think about that. It makes no sense."

The old man had a valid point, Mitch acknowledged, as he finished cutting out one of the pieces with the tin snips.

Already his fingers were starting to ache, and he still had hours of work ahead of him.

Hangtown's bomber had gone out in the ashtray at his elbow. He relit it and toked on it, coughing. It was a phlegmy, rumbling cough that sounded not at all healthy. Actually, the more Mitch looked at Wendell Frye, the more he realized that the artist did not look good. His cheeks seemed more hollow than they had two days ago, and his complexion was positively gray.

"Maybe . . . maybe this is my own sins catching up with me," he said to Mitch, wheezing. "Someone getting even for the evil *I*'ve done."

Mitch sat back on his haunches, peering at Hangtown curiously. "Like who? For what?"

"There's a reason why I live like this, Big Mitch," he said, his breathing growing more erratic. "Cut off from people. I'm *hiding,* don't you understand?"

"I'm afraid not," Mitch said. "But I'd like to."

Hangtown paused for a swig of rye, struggling to compose himself. "I took my fists to Takai's mother, Kiki, when I drank. Couldn't help it. I was so *angry* in those days. I married her too soon, you see. Wasn't ready. Was still grieving over Moose's mother, Gentle Kate. But I didn't know that then. How could I? Kate . . . Kate was the great love of my life. Big, strapping girl like Moose. Died when Moose was barely three. In 1972, it was."

Mitch went back to working the copper, wondering why Wendell Frye seemed to have such a sudden, powerful need to confess his sins. What was weighing on the old man's conscience?

"That was our summer of sunshine, Big Mitch," he recalled. "We had artists staying out in the cottages then. Some stayed for weeks on end, working the farm for their keep. We had picnics every afternoon in the meadows. We drank our wine and smoked our dope and screwed our blessed brains out. I was a lion in those days, with a huge appetite for the young lovelies. Kate was a good, loving woman. But I was bad to her. Because I wanted them all—

every single one of those tender young barefoot girls. And I *had* 'em all." Hangtown heaved a huge, pained sigh. "Selfish and cruel, I was. Thinking only of my own pleasures. Had me a Volkswagon bus in those days. I'd meet 'em at the academy, take 'em down to the beach in my bus—no conscience, no shame, no regrets. Not a one . . . Until one hot morning in August, middle of a heat wave it was, a slender little sculptress with shining black hair down to her bottom came drifting through. Crazy Daisy, we called her. I never even knew her real name, and that's the truth. She'd hitchhiked all the way from Winnipeg just to be here. She was a homeless waif, no family. Barely sixteen. But a tremendous talent, very gifted. And the prettiest little thing you ever saw in a pair of tight bell-bottoms, my friend." Hangtown fumbled for his Luckies and lit one, his hands trembling now. "Late one night Daisy asked me to pose for her. I obliged. It was a warm, humid night. Not a leaf was stirring. Naturally, I was nude. Naturally, we were soon in each others arms, right here in this barn, on a paint-splattered drop cloth, the sweat pouring off of us. And I roared like a lion. And then . . . then I heard another roar coming from that doorway right over there," he recalled, shuddering violently. "It was Gentle Kate. She had herself a temper, my Kate. You did *not* want to make her mad . . ."

"What happened here that night, Hangtown?" asked Mitch, his voice nearly a whisper.

"Moose had awakened in the night. Couldn't sleep. It was the heat. Kate gave her a cool sponge bath and got her back to bed. And then she came looking for me out here—thought I might want something to eat or drink. She found Crazy Daisy and me together in each other's arms on the drop cloth, humping away . . . Kate let out a roar and grabbed the nearest thing she could find—a mallet—and she hurled it right at me. I-I ducked. Crazy Daisy didn't. It hit her right between the eyes. Killed her dead on the spot."

Mitch had stopped working now. He was just sitting there, transfixed, his recorder taping the old man's every word.

"I murdered that girl!" Hangtown cried out, his voice choking with emotion. "Kate threw the mallet, but it was *my* doing. *My* pants I couldn't keep on. *My* marriage I was trashing. A-and there's more. Believe me, it gets even worse . . ."

"Hangtown, are you sure you want to tell me all of this? I'm here as a member of the press, remember?"

"There's no point in holding back anymore," he answered despondently. "Not with my Moose gone. What does it matter? What does any of it matter? Don't you see, my life is *over* now!" He broke off, his barrel chest heaving. Tears were beginning to stream down his deeply lined face. "We . . . rolled her up in the drop cloth with her knapsack and the few pieces of clothing she had. Dug a hole up on the hill and buried her up there. No one else was staying here that weekend. It was just Daisy and us. I erected a cairn to mark the spot. It's still there, not far from where they found the shotgun shell, in fact. It looks like something I did for a kick. But that's Crazy Daisy's marker . . . When folks asked us where she'd gone to, we told them she'd hitched a ride out of town early one morning, heading for New York. She'd been hoping to make her way down to Morocco on a freighter. She'd told a lot of people that. So no one doubted our story. And no one ever came looking for her. She had no one. And nothing—no driver's license, no credit cards, no permanent address. She was just a drifter passing through. A lot of people passed through in those days. Not so many anymore. The world is not as kindly a place now." Hangtown hung his head for a moment, his breathing ragged. It had to be Mitch's imagination, but he could have sworn that Wendell Frye was actually growing older by the minute. "Within a couple of weeks she was forgotten by everyone," he added hoarsely, stubbing out his cigarette. "Everyone except Gentle Kate and me."

"Whose idea was it to keep it from the police—yours or Kate's?"

"Mine, of course," he answered bitterly. "All mine. Because the guilt was all mine. My selfishness cost that poor girl her life. Yet Gentle Kate was her killer—or so the law would say. She was the mother of my child. I loved her. How could I make her pay for my sins? The answer is, I couldn't. So we buried Crazy Daisy and we tried to move on. Except she couldn't. The guilt weighed on her, heavier and heavier. She couldn't sleep. Barely touched her food. Big Mitch, that strong healthy woman just wasted away right before my eyes. Within a few weeks she was merely a shell of herself. I kept telling her: 'Yes, what we did was horrible. But you have to get on with your life. You have Moose to think of.' But it was too much for her. Four months later, she was dead. It's truly amazing just how quickly we can go when our will to live is g-gone." He let out a wrenching, painful sob. By the woodstove, Sam stirred slightly, but drifted back to sleep. "And I killed her, my friend. Just as surely as if I'd taken a knife and buried it in her chest. I killed her and I left poor Moose motherless." He paused now, swiping at his tears with the back of his gnarled hand. "Kiki *tried* to be a mother to her but those two never did hit it off."

"Where did you meet Kiki?"

"At Greta's gallery. By then, three years had gone by. All I'd done was work. I buried myself in it. Kiki had come up from New York for my new show. I was instantly smitten. She was gorgeous, very elegant and sophisticated. I married her and brought her home, but Moose was already a confirmed tomboy by then, and she had no use for this perfumed New Yorker in high heels. After we had Takai, I tried to change my wicked ways. No more artists in residence. No more picnics. No more tender lovelies. I even sold my VW bus. I tried, Mitch. God, how I tried. But all that did was bring out my anger, which I took out on poor Kiki until she could stand no more. Eventually, she left me."

"Takai holds you responsible for her suicide."

"I'm guilty," he conceded. "I killed them both—first Kate, then Kiki. And now . . . now I've killed Moose, too."

"What do you mean? *How* did you kill her?"

"This is a burial ground," the old man said in a hollow, faraway voice. "A curse hangs over this entire place. And over me. That's why I can't have people around. I'm not fit to be around them. So I smoke my smoke and drink my drink. I work and I work. But I never forget. Not ever." He turned his intense blue-eyed gaze on Mitch. "*That* is my curse, don't you see?"

"What did you mean when you said you killed Moose, too?"

"No, you *don't* see," growled Hangtown, ignoring Mitch's question once again. Barely hearing him at all. "You're too young. Your comprehension is limited by what you can understand. The real truth is what lies just beyond— it's what you *can't* grasp."

Mitch stared at the great artist, perplexed. "Hangtown, who else knows about Crazy Daisy?"

"Jim does. I told Jim because he could understand what it means—he doesn't belong around people either. Not since 'Nam. I've never told Greta. Never told the girls. My God, I *couldn't* tell Moose. That would have destroyed her love for me."

Still, Mitch found himself wondering: *What if*. What if Moose had found out? What if Jim told her? Could this have had something to do with her death?

Mitch's eyes fell on the little tape machine that was recording every word of Hangtown's gut-wrenching confession. He'd held this in for thirty years. Now the whole world was going to know. "Why are you telling me this?" he finally asked him. "Why now?"

"Because it's all over," the old man answered tonelessly.

"What is?"

Hangtown sat there slumped at the workbench, looking mournful and defeated. The spark of life seemed to have gone right out of him.

"Hangtown, who killed Moose?"

No answer.

Mitch tried it again, louder. "Hangtown, who killed Moose?!"

At last the old master shook himself and gazed down at Mitch. He seemed very distant from him now. He seemed to be somewhere else entirely. "Don't you get it, Big Mitch? The past did."

CHAPTER 10

She was on her way to Mitch's house to start dinner when the call came through from Felicity Beddoe—it seemed the lady was having trouble again with her next-door neighbor, Jay Welmers.

The late-afternoon sunlight was slanting low through the trees by the time she pulled into Somerset Ridge, its rays casting long shadows on the wide, leaf-blown Chemlawns. The folks at one place were busy putting up their Halloween decorations. The orange-and-black bunting had a rough time competing for attention with all of those red ribbons and green ribbons tied around every other tree. Personally, Des was tired of looking at them. Could not wait for the school bond vote to be over and done with.

Felicity Beddoe answered her door casually clad in slacks and a sweater. Her manner was no calmer than it had been before. The lady looked as if she'd snap like a breadstick if you laid a finger on her. Plus her face had broken out in hives. A pair of reading glasses was nestled in her short blond hair, and her kitchen table was heaped with folders and printouts.

"Thank you for coming, trooper," she said edgily. "I am so sorry to bother you again."

"I told you to bother me," Des reminded her. "Is this about Phoebe?"

Felicity gave her a brief nod. "I couldn't stay at the office after she phoned me with the news. She's at soccer practice right now. I felt it would be better if I spoke to you alone."

"Okay," Des said easily. "What did he do this time?"

"That man has cut a huge branch off one of the sycamores in between our houses. He's been out there with a chain saw all afternoon."

"Is it his tree, Mrs. Beddoe?"

"Technically, it is," Felicity conceded. "He's within his legal rights. I called over at town hall to find out."

"So . . . ?"

"So he can now see directly into Phoebe's bedroom window from the second floor of his place," she said angrily. "He no longer has to tiptoe around in the dark to spy on her—he can do so from the comfort of his own home!"

"You're sure about this?"

"Come look for yourself if you don't believe me," Felicity insisted, leading Des out the French doors onto the blue-stone terrace.

When the developers had cleared the land for Somerset Ridge they'd wisely left a stand of four gnarly old sycamores as a natural divider between the two houses. By hacking off a lower limb from the rearmost tree, Jay Welmers had cleared himself a bird's-eye view of the back of the Beddoes's house from several of his upstairs windows. Felicity was right, no question.

"Tell that girl to draw her curtains," Des said, as they stood there listening to the harsh whine of his chain saw. He was still busy over there somewhere cutting the branch up into pieces.

"Twenty-four hours a day?" Felicity demanded, her cheeks mottling. "Look, you may as well know this—I've contacted a realtor today. We're putting our place on the market. I can't take this anymore."

"If that's the case, why did you call me?"

"Because I-I . . ." She was unable to say the words aloud. All she could do was wave her hands helplessly in the air.

"What does your husband say about this?" Des asked gently.

"Richard still doesn't know about it," she confessed.

"And is that loaded gun still in his nightstand drawer?"

"Yes," Felicity said faintly. "What I thought I'd tell him was . . . I thought that I'd like to live closer to work. Mystic or Stonington."

"I wish you wouldn't do this, Mrs. Beddoe. You can't let fear rule your life."

"But I'm not *comfortable* here anymore," Felicity said, shooting a nervous glance over Des's shoulder at Jay Welmers's house. "You can understand that, can't you?"

"I totally can. But if you leave, he wins."

"Let him," she snapped. "I'll still have my husband in one piece."

"You need to stay. If you leave, it means that I've failed, and I don't handle failure well."

Felicity Beddoe said nothing in response. Just stood there wringing her hands, utterly distraught.

"Look, why don't you give me another chance before you pack up the moving van? Just one more chance, okay?"

"If you'd like," Felicity allowed, her voice lacking conviction. "Go ahead."

Des followed the sound of the chain saw. She found Jay Welmers out in front of his garage in the driveway, cutting the sycamore up into logs and loading them into a garden cart. The big, flabby financial planner—make that onetime financial planner—was not used to such demanding physical exertion. His red face was flushed a dangerous shade of purple, and he was positively drenched with sweat. His bulging gut stuck wetly to the front of his pink polo shirt, and his shirttail had worked itself loose from his tartan slacks, revealing a whole lot of fat white booty crack when he bent over. Most unappealing. His rottweiler, Dino, was chained to the post of the front porch just as before, barking at Des madly. The boys were nowhere to be seen.

"Good afternoon, Mr. Welmers," she said, tipping her hat at him politely.

"It's *my* tree," he declared without so much as looking at

her. "It's on *my* side of the property line. I can do what I please."

"I thought you wanted to be neighborly."

"I do," he grunted, heaving a heavy log into the cart.

"That being the case, it seems to me you could have mentioned something about this to Mrs. Beddoe before you did it."

Jay paused to swipe at his purple face with a sopping-wet hankerchief. "She won't speak to me. Hangs up as soon as she hears my voice. You call *that* neighborly? You call *that* fitting in? Besides, what business is it of hers if I want to prune one of my trees?"

"She thinks you did it so that you can see through Phoebe's bedroom window."

"She's *crazy!*" Jay erupted. "Why would I do that? I'd have to be some kind of a pervert!"

Des took off her hat and twirled it in her fingers for a moment. "Are you?"

Jay went back to loading the cart with logs. "You've got a lot of nerve asking me that."

"Okay, then I'll ask you something else: Why don't you pull this stuff when her husband's around?"

"How would I know when he is or isn't around?"

"You look through their windows, that's how."

"You know, I don't think this is fair at all," he protested angrily. "From the second you came over here you've made up your mind that I'm in the wrong. You don't care what I have to say."

Young Ricky came out the front door of the house now, dribbling a basketball. His black eye had faded to a sickly shade of yellow. "Hey, trooper," he called to her, waving.

"How's it going, Ricky?" she called back.

"Where do you think *you're* going?" Jay demanded as the boy started down the driveway.

"Nowhere," Ricky replied, sticking out his pugnacious, bully-boy chin. Clearly, it was a defensive pose that came from dealing with his father. "Just over to Trevor's."

"Well, don't you stay there for dinner," Jay ordered, jabbing at the air with his finger. "She's always feeding you, and I don't like it. Understand?"

Ricky said he did, and kept on going down the driveway. Jay grabbed up his chain saw and headed into his vast three-car garage with it. Des followed him. There was one car parked in there, a Ford Explorer. A tractor mower sat in the space next to it, alongside the boys' bicycles. The rest of the garage was used for storing trash barrels and tools and empty beer cans. Lots and lots of beer cans. As Jay hung the chain saw up on a hook on the wall, Des hit the button that lowered the automatic garage doors behind them.

"What do you think you're doing?" he demanded.

"Giving you some free advice," Des replied pleasantly, as the doors slammed tightly shut. The overhead light stayed on. Otherwise, they would have been standing in the dark. "For your own good—I think you should let this thing go. You're heading down a slippery slope."

"So are you, honey," he warned her, his eyes flicking over to the closed doors.

"I'm telling you straight up, Mr. Welmers. No good is going to come out of this."

"And *I'm* telling *you*—mind your own damned business."

"Sir, this *is* my business. You're driving good people out of Dorset."

"That's not my problem," he said with a shrug. "I have my rights."

"So do other people," Des countered. "Your son Ricky, for instance."

"What *about* Ricky?"

"Where did he get that black eye, Mr. Welmers?"

"He gets in fights. I *told* you."

"I know you did. I just didn't happen to believe you."

"That's your problem, not mine."

"Okay, I'm schooled to you now," Des said, nodding her head at him. "In your choice little corner of the world, it's *never* your problem. You do whatever you feel like doing, and if somebody else objects, that's *their* problem. You're not going to cut Mrs. Beddoe any slack, are you? No matter how I put it to you, you just won't let her up. Does that about cover it?"

Jay raised his chin at her, his nostrils flaring. "Not totally, no. I'd be a lot happier with a resident trooper who isn't looking to stir up trouble. Maybe you don't fit in here yourself, young lady. Have you thought of that?"

"Not really," Des said, raising an eyebrow at him. "But I sure am standing here wishing you'd elaborate on it."

"Okay, now you're getting all touchy," he said, with a faint smirk on his face. "Right away, you think this is about race."

"Don't kid me, Mr. Welmers. I've been black all my life. And it's *always* about race." She moved in closer to him. "You think I'd be more at home in the projects, is that it?"

"I didn't say that."

"I wish you would," she said, shoving him in the chest with her hand.

"Hey, you can't lay hands on me that way!"

Des shoved him again, rougher this time. "What's the matter, don't you like colored folks touching you?"

"Cut that out, lady!"

"Say it, Mr. Welmers." She shoved him again, right up against the garage wall. Her face was only inches from his now. "Say what you really mean. Or aren't you *man* enough?"

"I'm man enough to tell you to leave people like us alone!" he roared back at her.

"People . . . like . . . us." Des smiled at him, her huge wraparound smile, the one that could light up Giants Stadium. "Thank you so much for that, Mr. Welmers. That was just lovely." Now she removed her hat, placing it carefully on the hood of the Explorer, whirled and punched Jay Welmers in the nose—a strong right that came all the way up from her hip. She could feel the cartilage crunch under her fist. He let out a strangled, high-pitched sob as the blood began to spurt out of his nostrils, but he stayed on his feet. Until she punched him in the stomach, putting her full weight behind it. Now he fell to his knees and threw up, instantly filling the garage with the smell of his sour, beery vomit.

"You can't do this," he groaned at her in feeble protest. "I'll file charges against you. I'll sue you."

"I can't wait," Des responded, putting her hat back on her head. "I'm just dying to tell my side to the newspapers. People will really want to entrust their life's savings to a man who peeps through windows at little girls."

"What . . . do you . . . want?" he gasped, breathing in and out through his mouth.

"I want you to leave the Beddoes alone. If I hear about you bothering them again, if you so much as blink at Phoebe, I swear I will break both of your legs."

"You *can't* threaten me this way. It's against the law."

"Understand something, Mr. Welmers. I *am* the law. This is *my* town. And you will live by *my* rules. Am I making myself clear?"

He nodded, ducking his head in defeat.

"Good answer."

She left him there on the garage floor in his own vomit and went back over to the Beddoes' to tell Felicity that Jay Welmers would not be bothering her anymore.

Then Des got back in her cruiser and headed out, taking no pleasure in what she'd just done. But it needed doing, so she'd done it. That was the job. It was not a pretty job. It was not a pretty world. She knew this. Nonetheless, she felt quite certain that she would never share the details of this particular incident with Mitch. He would not believe she was capable of such behavior. She adored that about him. And she wanted him to keep on believing it.

It was a lovely fantasy.

Ricky was waiting for her at the stone pillars that marked the entrance to Somerset Ridge, his basketball tucked under one arm. She pulled over and lowered her passenger side window. "Hey, Ricky, you got game?"

He had something on his mind, was what he had. He got in next to her and sat there squirming in anxious silence for a moment before he said, "Remember I told you how they were planning some serious antics?"

"Ronnie and his boys? Sure, I do."

"It's gonna happen real soon."

"Any idea where?"

Ricky knew where. And when he told her she was shaken—it was probably her single worst nightmare.

But she did not let her face show this. She merely nodded and said, "That's not antics. That's prime-time trouble."

"I *know* that. I—I'm scared."

"Don't be. You did the right thing, telling me. Everything will be okay, little man. You've got my word on that. Where are you headed now?"

"Home."

"Want a ride?"

"Naw, I can walk." He started to get out.

"Oh, hey, I'd take it slow with your dad for a while, if I were you."

Ricky frowned at her. "Why?"

Des smiled and said, "He just ate something that didn't agree with him."

CHAPTER 11

Bella Tillis's mud-splattered Jeep Wrangler, with its personalized CATS22 license plate, was parked outside his carriage house when Mitch got home, his head spinning and his limbs aching from exhaustion. Des's trooper mobile was there, too, snugged up next to an unmarked police cruiser.

Des was in his kitchen hard at work on her fragrant concoction of black-eyed peas, ham hocks and rice. A cornbread was cooling on the windowsill, and a mountain of freshly washed collard greens was draining in the sink. Des had on a black turtleneck and jeans. She looked exceedingly uptight and, when she laid eyes on Mitch, way pissed. Not only was he a half hour late but he was filthy and stank of oxyacetylene.

"I'm incredibly sorry," he apologized. "I just couldn't leave the old guy. He was all alone and his work is all he has." Mitch ran a grimy hand through his hair, still seeing copper rectangles before his eyes. "I'll hop right in the shower."

"Please do," she said tautly. "And hurry."

Before he could get there, little round Bella appeared in the kitchen doorway, blocking his path. "Hello, tattela!"

"Hi, Aunt Bella," he responded warmly, kissing her on the cheek.

"I didn't realize that you and Mr. Berger were related," a booming baritone voice spoke up from behind her.

"We're not, Buck," Bella explained. "We just feel like we ought to be."

Mitch was not prepared for just how huge Buck Mitry was. The deputy superintendent of the Connecticut State Police—the man whom Des and everyone in law enforcement called the Deacon—was at least six feet four, powerfully built and ramrod-straight. His hand, when Mitch shook it, was as big as a family-sized pizza. Mitch's own hand disappeared in it. The Deacon wore a somber dark gray suit and he had not gotten comfortable—he still had his jacket and tie on.

"I'm really sorry I'm late, sir," Mitch said, swallowing. *Sir? Where did that come from?* Mitch knew perfectly well where—Des's father instantly made him feel like a pimply, horny sixteen-year-old with a condom in his wallet and not a thing on his mind but how to get his precious daughter naked. "You must think I'm the rudest person in the world."

The Deacon towered there in the doorway, his gaze steely and intimidating. Clint Eastwood had nothing on this man. "It's perfectly understandable, Mr. Berger," he responded. "I've spent my entire career never being in charge of my own schedule. Take your shower. Take your time. We'll be here."

"Thanks for being so understanding," Mitch said, smiling at him. "I'll be right out."

He hopped in a steaming hot shower, his mind still reeling from everything that Hangtown had told him. What had the old man meant by "the past"? Had he been referring to Crazy Daisy? Was her death connected with Moose's? How? Should he be telling Des about this? Should he save it for his story? Or should he not even put it in his story at all? Because if Hangtown was, in fact, an accessory to a thirty-year-old murder, he could go to jail. And Mitch's story would be sending him there. Did he really want to do that? What was his responsibility here? What was right?

Dazed and confused, Mitch changed into clean khakis and a blue oxford-cloth button-down shirt. His guests were busy watching the local Connecticut news on television.

Mitch rejoined them just in time to see Soave holding forth for the cameras on his good strong case against Jim Bolan: "We have credible physical evidence that places him at the scene," the muscle-bound little lieutenant crowed. "This is an individual who has vast experience with long-range firearms, a revenge motive and no convincing way to account for his whereabouts at the time of the shooting."

Bella shook a blunt finger at the TV and blustered, "That little man has *bupkes*. If he really had anything on this Bolan, he would have charged him. I want you to know that the public sees right through this type of thing, Buck."

"Yes, ma'am," growled the Deacon, who seemed displeased by Soave's performance.

Mitch went foraging in the refrigerator for a beer. Couldn't find any.

"Did you leave it out in the truck?" Des asked him.

Mitch frowned at her. "I thought *you* were going to get the beer."

"No, no. I asked *you* to."

The Deacon was looming in the kitchen doorway now, watching them intently.

"Whatever," Mitch said easily, even though he was positive she'd said she would take care of it. "I'll go get some right now."

"Not on my account," the Deacon said. "I'm not a big drinker."

"Nor am I," Bella chimed in.

"Got to have a glass of beer with your Hoppin' John, Daddy," Des insisted. "I'll go get it. You guys hang. Take a ride with me, Bella."

"I'd rather hang with them," Bella said.

"And I'd rather look like Halle Berry," Des shot back. "Come on, girl."

And with that the two women were out the door, leaving Mitch certain that Des had purposely forgotten the beer so that he and the Deacon could spend some time alone together.

The Deacon immediately began to pace Mitch's small living room. He seemed caged and restless. Briefly, Mitch wondered if Des's towering, commanding father was as uncomfortable about this as he was. "I've been sitting at a desk all day, Mr. Berger," he said suddenly. "Mind if we stretch our legs?"

"Not at all," Mitch said. "Provided you start calling me Mitch."

"Very well . . . Mitch."

He left a note for Des on the kitchen counter, grabbed his flashlight and jacket and they headed out, the Deacon pausing to fetch his topcoat out of his car.

"I understand you used to be a baseball player," Mitch spoke up as he led them down the path to the beach. The man's stern silence was making him incredibly nervous.

"That's correct," the Deacon affirmed, striding along with his shoulders back, chin up. "I was in the Pirates' organization before I joined the state police."

"There's a former player mixed up in this murder case," Mitch said. "The victim's sister, Takai, used to be married to a catcher named Dirk Doughty."

"Sure, I remember Doughty from his American Legion days," the Deacon said. "Best young player to come out of this area since Jeff Bagwell. The Tigers thought he was going to be the next Johnny Bench. Never happened, though—just like it never happened for me," he added without regret.

"How do you deal with that?" Mitch asked. "The disappointment, I mean."

"You turn the page, Mitch. Same way you do when you bury a loved one, as Desiree told me you've had to do."

"You move on," Mitch acknowledged. He hadn't particularly wanted to talk about Maisie, but at least they were talking. "You must."

"Absolutely. What's Doughty doing with himself?"

"Teaching baseball to kids. He's a private coach."

"That's not moving on," the Deacon said with flinty disapproval.

They had reached the island's rocky little beach now. The tide was moving in. Rain was expected overnight, but right now the stars were out, a gibbous moon low over Fisher's Island. They started along the water's edge, heading east. The Deacon seemed terribly out of place in his topcoat and shiny dress shoes. Mitch found himself remembering the gang of topcoated young slackers striding the beach in Fellini's *I Vitelloni*, which inspired Barry Levinson's vastly inferior *Diner*.

"Lovely spot you picked here, Mitch."

"It picked me. And I feel very lucky."

"What are those lights out there?" he asked, gazing at a boat that was making its way back toward the mainland. "Lobstermen?"

"That's the Plum Island workboat. They take the workmen out every morning at seven-thirty. Bring them back home right around now." Mitch found he was starting to puff for air. The Deacon had the same long, tireless stride as his daughter. "I was going to get you a birthday gift, but Des said not to."

"My daughter knows me pretty well. And I thought I knew her. But lately, she's been thoroughly confounding me. Mind if I ask you your advice, Mitch?"

"Not at all."

"This art thing that she's pursuing . . . Do you think it's something she'll stay with?"

"I really don't know the answer to that. You can never tell with artists."

"So you believe she *is* an artist."

"Oh, definitely. She's very, very gifted, Mr. Mitry. She can go as far as she wants, if she has the desire and the dedication."

"Will that make her happy?"

"Well, artists aren't happy people, as a rule."

The Deacon walked along the rocks in thoughtful silence for a moment, considering this. "And why is that?"

Mitch glanced over at him, frowning. It was just beginning to dawn upon him how little the Deacon understood about his daughter's new life. Art was something totally outside the realm of his personal experience. "Artists are people who live up inside their own heads," Mitch answered slowly. "They're trying to make some sense out of this spiky little pinball that's careening around up there, driving them to that blank canvas. In other words, there's something inside of Des that's trying to come out, and she doesn't necessarily know what it is or even what it means, because she's not in control of it. She simply has to surrender herself to it, wherever it takes her. And that can be pretty scary. It would be safer and saner to *never* go there, but then she wouldn't be fulfilling her destiny."

"So you believe in destiny?"

"Why do you ask me that?"

"Trying to figure out what you believe in."

"I believe it's a sin to waste a gift. And she has one. Right now, she's trying to figure out how best to use it. Which she will—she's a very smart person, Mr. Mitry."

"From where I stand, resident trooper is the road to nowhere."

"I'm sure she has misgivings," Mitch conceded. "Like with this murder investigation—she wants to be in charge, and she isn't, and that's tearing her apart."

They had made their way to the lighthouse now. They stopped, gazing out at the moonlit water.

"Desiree is my only child," the Deacon said. "And she's always made me proud of what she's accomplished. She graduated from West Point with honors. Served her nation proudly. Rose through the ranks of the state police faster than any woman of color in history. Brandon was a fine young gentleman, a Yale Law School graduate. Yet, somehow, none of it quite worked out the way she planned. It occurs to me that what may be happening now is that Desiree is simply floundering a bit." He paused, clearing his throat. "What I mean to say, Mitch, is that you might be her walk on the wild side."

"No, no. That can't be. I own no motorcycle. I wear no goatee. I'm no one's walk on the wild side."

"Nonetheless, she's doing things she's never done before. Taking these art classes. Dating a white man—which is fine with me, by the way. I'm not troubled by that at all. We're *all* learning as we go along. Finding out new things about ourselves. My own wife, for instance, recently discovered that she was still in love with her high school sweetheart. And now I live alone, which I—"

"You aren't lonely? I'd be lonely."

"I'm quite all right," the Deacon answered crisply. "I'm fine. What I'm trying to say to you, Mitch, is that the life you two are building down here may simply be a phase Desiree is going through. She may want back on Major Crimes in another few months. You may not be in her plans. I wondered how you would feel about that."

"I'd be very unhappy," Mitch replied. "But you have to accept what the people you love want to do. Otherwise it's not love."

"Is that what it is?"

"Absolutely. I'm totally gaga over her."

"And how does she feel?"

"You'll have to ask her that."

"I already did."

"And what did she say?"

"She told me to mind my own damned business."

"Yeah, that sounds like her."

The Deacon let out a short laugh. "You don't worry about the differences?"

"When I'm with her, I don't worry about anything."

"And *your* folks. How do they feel about it?"

"They're just thrilled that I've met someone who makes me happy."

Mitch could hear Des calling them now from down the beach, see the beam of her flashlight. He waved his beam in return, and she caught up with them, clad in the same heavy sweater that Mitch had lent to Takai.

"Bella's cooking the greens," she announced. "Ready to head back?"

"I am," the Deacon said. "How about you, Mitch?"

"Absolutely."

They started back, Des sneaking quick, nervous glances at the two of them. "So, did you two have your man-to-man talk?"

"Well, we did talk," the Deacon replied solemnly. "And we're both men. So I guess the answer to your question is yes."

Delighted, she squeezed in between them, hooking one arm inside her father's and the other inside Mitch's. "Why does this ratty old sweater of yours reek of perfume?"

Mitch told her.

"What did that girl do, pour a whole bottle over herself and roll around in it naked?"

"Something like that."

"You are *so* lucky I'm not the suspicious type," Des said to him sweetly.

"Wait, you *are* the suspicious type."

"That's right, I am," she shot back, laughing wickedly. It was a laugh that Mitch had never heard come out of her before. Sheer relief—she'd been dreading this meeting with her father even more than she'd let on.

"What's that up there at the edge of the water, Mitch?" the Deacon spoke up, as his flashlight beam glanced over a large lumpy shape ahead of them.

"Another seal beached itself." Mitch aimed his light on it. "Usually it only happens in February, but—"

But it was not a seal. Not unless it was a seal wearing a soggy flannel shirt and waterlogged jeans.

The Deacon flipped the body over, ignoring the salt water foaming over his shiny shoes. It was a woman's body, and when Des got a good look at her she let out a startled gasp.

"Know her?" the Deacon asked.

"I do," Des said. "Her name was Melanie Zide."

CHAPTER 12

There were lights everywhere. Headlight beams from cruisers. Overhead beams from the Coast Guard choppers circling above them. The blob of cold, dead meat that had once been Melanie Zide lay on a tarp, her skin the color of wet clay.

Des could not get her mind around this. She kept seeing Melanie bathed in golden light up on that pedestal at the art academy, her naked flesh rosy and alive. Now she was just a floater covered with seaweed and sand. She had two bullet holes in her that Des could see—the size of the wounds indicative of a smaller caliber weapon than the Barrett. And there were people everywhere. And everyone was gazing at her. And no one was drawing her.

The medical examiner's people were there. Soave was there with Tommy Salcineto. The Deacon was there, Soave tiptoeing his way around him like a cowed little boy.

And Mitch was there, too, standing next to Bella with a stricken expression on his face. Not exactly the get-acquainted dinner that he'd had in mind.

Des went over to him and said, "Our Hoppin' John will have to wait, baby. I'm on the job for the rest of the night."

"I kind of figured that," he said. "Go ahead and do what you have to do."

"Mitch and I will be fine, Desiree," Bella added reassuringly.

"I think I was making a real good first impression," Mitch said. "Until we found the dead body in my front yard, I mean. I think he liked me."

"How could he not?" Bella said. "You're a nice, polite gentleman. You're steadily employed, a published author . . ."

"Don't puff the boy up, Bella," Des warned her. "He'll become a total pain."

"As if," Bella sniffed.

Now Des turned her gaze out at the Sound, her mind on the job. "When things wash up out here, where do they usually come from?" she asked Mitch.

"Off boats, mostly. I pick up all kinds of garbage. You wouldn't believe what pigs people are."

"Oh, yes, I would," Bella said with withering disapproval. "Who's still going out?"

"The yachters have pretty much packed it in for the season. I still see a few Boston Whalers—guys fishing or checking their lobster pots. That's about it." Mitch pointed westward to the tidal estuaries where the Connecticut River emptied into the Sound. "Upriver's also a good bet. The current brings stuff down. I've found dead animals beached out here lots of times."

"What kind of animals?"

"Deer, raccoons . . . I had a coyote a few weeks ago."

She glanced eastward in the direction of Dorset's rugged coastline. "Does stuff float out here from the town beaches?"

"The tide has to be going out," Mitch said. "And you need a north wind. But, yeah, it happens."

"What's the tide doing right now?"

"It's coming in."

"What about last night?"

"Same story."

Des considered this, her mind weighing the possibilities. So many possibilities. Could be that Melanie's body had been dumped upriver and drifted down on the current. Could be it washed out to sea from a town beach early that morning, when the tide was going out, and now had made its way back on the incoming tide. Could be her killer took her out on a boat last night and dumped her. The Coast Guard would be able to narrow it down somewhat by computing how far Melanie could have floated based on the tide and wind direction. Likewise the speed of the river's current. And the medical examiner could estimate how long she had been dead based on her body temperature, the water temperature, and state of decomposition. Sure, they'd be able to narrow it down. But as of right now, where and when Melanie Zide had been killed was wide open.

In fact, there was almost nothing that Des knew for sure—except that Melanie had been right to be afraid.

"Where are you at, Lieutenant?" the Deacon was asking Soave, his manner icy and exacting. There wasn't a young officer in the state who didn't quake under his questioning.

"Sir, she was dead when she hit the water," Soave answered miserably. Melanie's death blew a huge hole in the scenario he'd been working. "I'm guessing she's been dead since—"

"I don't want your guesses, son," the Deacon said sharply. "I have no use for guesses. I'm only interested in what you *know*."

Soave cleared his throat, chastened. "Okay, what I know is . . ." One knee started to jiggle nervously. "I know we've been holding a man for questioning on the Mary Susan Frye homicide and . . ."

And, despite Des's warnings not to commit himself too soon, Soave had boasted all about it on television and now his career was passing right before his eyes. Because his case against Jim was in shreds—Jim had had a twenty-four-hour baby-sitter on him for the past two days. He couldn't have shot Melanie. Not unless he'd somehow managed to slip out on his guard undetected, which was highly unlikely. Meaning that Jim was an innocent man. Unless, that is, these two small-town murders were completely unrelated. Which was even more unlikely.

"I repeat, Lieutenant," the Deacon said, scowling, "Where . . . are . . . you . . . at?"

"Back to square one," Soave conceded, smoothing his see-through mustache. "I'll reach out immediately to Captain Battaglio for more manpower. And I'd also like to employ Resident Trooper Mitry's services until we can clear this up. She knows the principals and, as you know, has Major Crimes experience."

"Mind you, I would not have suggested that to you," the Deacon said in response. "But since you've raised the idea, I would call it sound, mature thinking. What about this man you're holding, Bolan?"

"We'll have to take a good hard look at releasing him in the morning."

Right now, there were press vans waiting on the other end of the causeway and Soave had to deal with them. He had to give the cameras something, anything for the eleven-o'clock news. And he had nothing—not even Melanie's name. Tommy was still trying to locate a legally competent next of kin. Her mother's nursing home did have an address for Melanie's brother up in Portland, Maine, but until Tommy could track him down, they could not release her name.

Soave kept glancing hopefully at the Deacon as the three of them strode across the wooden causeway to the cameras. Des could tell he was praying that the Deacon, as senior officer on the scene, would want to step up to the mike—thereby letting him off the hook. But she knew better. Her father was never one to make an officer's job any easier. This was Soave's case, in good times and bad, and either he could deal or he couldn't.

So it was Soave who had to stand before those bright lights, blinking, and say, "At the present time we don't know how or if this death relates to the Mary Susan Frye murder investigation. We are presently gathering evidence, and we are extremely confident we will have a suspect in custody shortly."

Which was official police-speak for: *Help me, I've fallen and I can't get back up!*

Afterward, he sidled over to Des, ducking his head

glumly. "I guess you're feeling pretty good about things now."

"If you think that, Rico, then you don't know me at all."

"I *don't* think that," Soave insisted, sneaking a peek over at the Deacon, who stood at the railing looking out at the water, his broad back to them. "I really don't. I'm just . . . I just . . ." He broke off, his breathing becoming shallow and rapid. Soon, she thought he might need to stick his head in a paper bag. "Des, I sure could use your help on this."

"Just tell me what I can do."

"I want to get some unis canvassing right away. I thought I'd have them try the town beaches for starters. But if you have any other ideas . . ."

"I'd check out the Dorset Marina," she offered. "See who took their boat out last night. Based on the way the tides are running, her body might have been dumped at sea. Or it might have drifted downriver. Better check the river moorings—there's Dunn's Cove Marina, North Cove, the Essex Yacht Club, Millington Boat Basin. There's also a car ferry at Millington."

Soave was writing this down. "Okay, good. Anything else?"

"Did you nail down the identity of Colin Falconer's on-line lover yet?"

"Who, Cutter? Not yet." Soave peered at her, intrigued. "What's that got to do with this?"

"Maybe nothing. Maybe everything."

"Okay, sure. We'll call the Internet provider's security people right away."

"I'd like to re-canvass a couple of people on my own," Des added. "I might be able to eliminate some things."

"*What* things?" Soave demanded.

"I'll keep you informed," she assured him.

"See that you do," he growled officiously. Then he started back across the causeway to the crime scene, arms held stiffly out from his sides in the classic bodybuilder's strut.

She stayed behind with the Deacon. "Sorry about your party, Daddy."

"Not to worry, girl. We'll do it another night."

She lingered there, waiting for him to say something else, anything else. Nothing. Not a word. "Well, I guess I'll be seeing you," she said finally.

"That you will, Desiree. Oh, by the way . . ." He flashed her a quick smile. "Your friend is all right."

Your friend is all right?

Just exactly what in the hell did he mean by that? Des dissected it, fuming, as she steered her cruiser toward Griswold Avenue. By "friend," did he mean Mitch was a trivial, unsubstantial plaything, a toy, as opposed to a substantial individual suitable for a serious relationship? Or had he just not known what else to call him? And what did he mean by "all right"? All right as in so-so, fair to middling, better than a poke in the eye with a sharp stick? Or all right as in totally, one-hundred percent . . . righteous? God, that man could be so cryptic sometimes, so vague, so . . .

Impossible. That was the word to describe her father.

Chuckie Gilliam, the unemployed carpenter with the faith-based advertising tattooed on his knuckles, had him some company tonight. He and Sandy, the frizzy-haired waitress from McGee's, were sprawled in front of the television watching a college football game and drinking beer when Des knocked on his door. Otherwise, not much had changed around there. Chuckie's computer was still parked on the card table in the middle of the room, and it was still turned on. And Chuckie was still wearing his orange hunter's vest over a soiled white T-shirt.

"Hey, it's the cat lady!" Sandy exclaimed when she spotted Des there in the doorway. Sandy's voice was cheerful, but her eyes were wary pinpoints. "What are you doing, trooper, making house calls now?"

"I need to talk to you some more, Mr. Gilliam," Des said to him quietly.

"Yeah, sure," grumbled Chuckie. To Sandy he said, "It's okay, I know what this is about." He grabbed his beer and stepped out onto the porch with Des, closing the door behind him. Clearly, he did not want Sandy to hear their conversation.

And Sandy didn't like it. Through the front window, Des could see her stomp off into the kitchen, where she started slamming cupboard doors. Des wasn't happy about doing this. She didn't want to complicate Sandy's life for her. But there was really no way around it. She needed answers.

"Melanie's body washed up on Big Sister tonight, Mr. Gilliam. Somebody shot her. Just wanted to let you know."

"Jeez, that's too bad," he said heavily, gazing across the road at her house. "If you want me to keep an eye on her place or something, I'll be happy to. Anything I can do."

"Well, now that you mention it, I've been asked to eliminate certain peripheral parties such as yourself. Strictly routine stuff."

Chuckie's semi-smart eyes narrowed warily. "Yeah . . . ?"

"I noticed your computer is on—do you spend a lot of time online?"

"I guess," he grunted, taking a swig from his beer.

"Which Internet provider do you use?"

He gave her the name. It was the same service on which Colin claimed he had met Cutter. This didn't necessarily mean anything—millions of people used it. Still, it was certainly worth knowing.

"What's this got to do with Melanie?" Chuckie asked.

"Mr. Gilliam, have you ever been in trouble with the law?"

He scratched at his unkempt beard, his eyes avoiding hers. "Maybe," he admitted.

"Um, okay, this is really a yes-or-no kind of a deal, Mr. Gilliam," Des told him. "I can check it myself, but it's better if I hear it from you."

"Look, I had a run-in with a contractor I was working for, okay?" he muttered, his manner turning decidedly surly now. "Tim Keefe accused me of taking some roofing materials off of a job. I lost my temper and popped him one. The piss-ant bastard filed assault charges against me. I ended up serving six months county time."

"Did you do it?"

"Do what, lady?"

"Steal the roofing materials."

"Stuff happens," he grumbled, scratching impatiently at the J-E-S-U-S on his right knuckles. "What else do you want to know?"

"The real deal about you and Melanie."

Chuckie glanced nervously over his shoulder at the door. "Okay, so we went out a few times," he admitted, lowering his voice. "But she wouldn't have nothing to do with me after the thing with Tim."

"Why was that?"

"She didn't want to be some guy's mother, was how she put it."

"How did you feel about her modeling at the art academy?"

Chuckie made a face. "If she wanted to show off her body to a lot of old ladies and fags, that was her business."

"Okay, let's talk about last night," Des said. "You told me you saw her car leave the house about nine, then come back again a half hour later, right?"

"Right . . ."

"Then you saw her load up her car and clear out again, this time for good. Mr. Gilliam, are you absolutely sure that's what you saw?"

Chuckie took a long time draining his beer before he said, "Lady, why are you climbing me?"

"Believe me, I'm not. I'm just thinking about something I learned myself at the art academy—it's not strictly old ladies and gays, by the way. They get all kinds. And one thing they tell you is to draw what you *see* as opposed to what you *know*. Did you really *see* what you saw? Or do you just *know* you did? Are you with me?"

"Not even close," he said, running a hand through his thinning hair.

"How good a look did you get at her? Try to be as specific as possible. Believe me, it'll be worth your while—if you can help me, I'm in a position to help you."

"Uh-huh, I get it now," Chuckie said sourly. "If I don't

help you, you'll be all over me for every little thing, right? My taillight's out on my pickup. My dog's disturbing the neighbors. Sure, I know how it goes. Well, let me tell you something, lady. I don't got no dog!"

"And that's not how I go about my business."

"Bullshit," he shot back. "You got the law on your side and I got nothing."

"Here's the deal, straight up," Des said evenly. "If you help me I can tell the big bad lieutenant to steer his investigation right around Chuckie Gilliam. Chuckie Gilliam is a cooperative, fully rehabilitated citizen who did everything he could to be of assistance. If you don't, given your record chances are excellent he'll be stuffing your frame in a cruiser and taking you up to Meriden. Days and nights will go by. Sandy will have to come get you, if she still wants you. And there won't be a single thing I can do to help you. Now let's try it one more time, shall we? Tell me what you *saw*."

"Okay, okay," he said hotly. "What I *saw* was Melanie getting out of her car and running inside."

"Describe her."

"Well, she was kind of hunched over. And she was wearing this big red ski parka like I seen Melanie wear a million times. It has a hood that's lined with coyote fur or something."

Des nodded. Melanie was not wearing a coat when she washed up. "Okay, good," she said encouragingly. "Did she have her hood up?"

"Uh . . . yeah."

"And so you assumed it was Melanie. Anyone would, right?"

Chuckie frowned at her, perplexed. "Huh?"

"Think about this for a second: Is it possible that the person who you saw *wasn't* her?"

"You're saying, like, what if some other woman was driving her car and wearing her jacket?"

"Yes."

"I guess it's possible," Chuckie admitted.

"And is it possible it wasn't even a woman at all?"

"What?"

"You saw a hunched-over figure in a big, hooded jacket. You and I both know that Melanie was a good-sized girl, solidly built. This street's dimly lit. You were standing all the way over here. So I'm asking you: Is it possible that the person you saw was a man? Think hard, please. It's important."

"I guess . . ." he allowed. "But why would someone do that?"

"To make it look like Melanie was skipping town, when in reality she was already dead. I think you saw her killer, Mr. Gilliam. The hooded parka was strictly in case a neighbor such as yourself might be watching." And it might have played, too, if Melanie's body hadn't washed up so soon. That couldn't have been part of the plan. A mistake. Had to be. Des lingered there on the porch, sensing that Chuckie was still holding on to something. He had a semi-foxy look on his mega-dumb face. "You told me that Melanie had no man in her life lately," she mentioned, taking a stab.

"That I know of," he acknowledged, scratching at his beard. "None dropped by is all I know."

"Did anyone else drop by?"

"Like who?"

Des raised her chin at him. "Like anyone else."

He cleared his throat uncomfortably. "Well, she did get visits from Greta Patterson. Melanie used to do clerical work for her over at the gallery."

"You mean before she went to work for Superintendent Falconer?"

"Yeah, three, four years back. I recognized Greta on account of I've done work for her myself on her house—siding, sill work."

"How often?"

"How often have I worked for her?"

"How often did she stop by to see Melanie?"

"Pretty often," Chuckie admitted.

"What, once a week?"

"Twice a week, maybe."

Des took off her big hat and stood there twirling it in her fingers. "You say Melanie used to work for Greta. Is that all she was to her?"

"I don't know what you mean," he answered sharply.

"Yes, you do." Des stared at him intently. "You know exactly what I mean."

He looked away, swallowing. "Okay, maybe I do. But I don't know the answer."

"You didn't wonder?"

Chuckie heaved a pained sigh and said, "Sure, I did. I wonder about a lot of stuff, lady. That don't mean I get it."

"Now you're living on my side of the street." She put her hat back on, flashing a smile at him. "Don't take it so hard, Mr. Gilliam. We're not supposed to know all the answers. In fact, we're lucky if we even figure out what the questions are. Please be sure to tell Sandy that I said good night, will you?"

There were lights on inside the Patterson Gallery. And when Des slowed up her cruiser out front she could see Greta seated in there at her oak partner's desk, pecking away at a computer in the soft glow cast by her desk lamp's old-fashioned green glass shade.

Des got out and rapped her knuckles on the glass front door. Greta squinted at her over her reading glasses, then waved and came over to let her in.

"I hope I'm not interrupting you," Des said, as Greta unlocked the door.

"Not at all, trooper," she said cheerfully. "I was just trying to catch up on some of my gallery work. I'm afraid that Wendell has hogged most of my time lately. First he had me handling some estate-related matters. Then I had to find a criminal attorney for Jim Bolan. Do have a seat," she said, filing the work she had on her computer screen.

Des sat in the wooden chair next to Greta's desk, crossing her long legs. "This estate work you were doing—it wouldn't have any bearing on Moose's death, would it?"

"You know I can't talk about that," Greta responded with a grin.

"Never hurts to ask," Des said easily. "What *can* you talk to me about?"

Greta sat back in her swivel chair, studying her. "Try me."

"How about Melanie Zide?"

She let out a harsh laugh. "What about that little cow?"

"Somebody shot her. Her body just washed up on Big Sister."

Greta froze for a second, stunned. Then her squarish, blotchy face seemed to scrunch inward upon itself, like a beer can being crushed in a strongman's fist.

Des had wondered if she'd get a reaction. She got one. She got pain. Definitely pain. "I'm told that Melanie used to do clerical work for you."

"That's true," Greta said hoarsely. "She's . . . she was a good little worker. But she needed more hours than I could give her, so I helped her get that job with the school district."

"You two were close?"

"If by that you're wondering whether we were mixed up in some form of unwholesome, incorrect, same-sex physical relationship, the answer is yes," Greta said bluntly. "And in answer to your next question: Yes, I did care about her. What else do you want to know?"

"Did Colin know about you two?"

"We have no secrets from each other." Greta's voice suddenly sounded very tired and old. "I told you that already."

"And I didn't believe you. Everyone has secrets."

Greta got up out of her chair and went over to a landscape painting by Hangtown's grandfather that hung over the fireplace. It depicted the tidal marshes near Lord's Cove at dawn, with the steam rising off the water and the early-morning sunlight slanting low. "I love the light in this painting. Every time I look at it I feel as if I've never truly *seen* the dawn before." She gazed at it a moment longer, then shook herself and turned back to Des. "I was devastated when Colin moved out. It made me realize that you really can't count on anyone else in this world. We'd had our ups and downs, naturally. But I'd still expected that he'd be there by my side when I got old and decrepit. Now . . ." Greta trailed off, shaking her head. "Now I'm not so sure. *He*'s not sure. And so I find myself living these days in a constant state of paralyzing fear, I'm ashamed to say."

"Fear's nothing to be ashamed of."

"I'm one of the reasons why the school board wants Colin out, you know," Greta pointed out bitterly. "I didn't want to say anything to you about this last night, in front of him, but *they* don't approve of me—the concerned young mothers. They don't think I am a suitable school superintendent's wife. It's the Salem witch hunt all over again, you know. The intolerant and self-righteous are taking over, and they're imposing their mean, narrow vision of *correct* behavior on everyone else. If you're not one of them, then you are someone to be shunned, someone *evil*. The new school building is just a smoke screen. The real reason they want Colin out is that he's a bisexual depressive with an aging bull dyke for a wife. They don't want him or me anywhere near their dear, precious kids, twisting their dear, precious minds. These are scary times, trooper. These are not the enlightened sixties and seventies of my youth. I was fooled. I thought we had become more open-minded, more accepting of other people's differences. We didn't. The pendulum has swung back the other way, and now we are hurtling back to the dark ages all over again, fighting the same old battles. Only now we're *losing*." She came back to her desk and sat down again, her eyes beginning to puddle with tears. "Poor Melanie . . . Poor cow."

"Where did you go last evening after the lieutenant and I spoke with you at your house?"

"I was home with Colin all evening," she answered, cocking her head at Des curiously.

"You didn't leave?"

"No, I didn't leave. I was concerned about him. So we threw another log on the fire and we worked on a jigsaw puzzle together—Fountain Head. We do that one every year.

We went to Hawaii on our honeymoon, you know. Doesn't that just *quaint* you to death?" Greta broke off, her chest rising and falling. "Now if you'll please excuse me, trooper, I-I have a lot of work to do."

Des thanked her for her time and started for the door. By the time she had closed it behind her she could hear Greta Patterson sobbing.

"Can I buy you a round, trooper?"

Dirk Doughty was drinking hot cider all alone at a tavern table in front of the fire in the Frederick House's wood-paneled pub. On the table before him was a copy of *The Sporting News,* opened to the waiver-wire page with its long columns of agate type detailing which teams have signed or cut which players. In the world of journeymen ballplayers, old habits apparently died hard.

"I think I'd like that," said Des, taking a seat across from him. An older couple was sipping brandy at one of the other tables. Otherwise, they were alone in the pub. "But let's put it on my tab, because I never did get my dinner tonight." She ordered a roast turkey sandwich to go along with the cider, then said, "I'm real sorry to bother you again, but there are some other things I need to ask you."

"That's okay by me," he said, squaring his broad shoulders. "I'm always better off when I'm talking to other people. I don't do well if I sit by myself for too long. I think too much."

"I guess we can all do that."

Dirk sat back in his chair, folding his arms in front of his chest. He wore a navy-blue fleece top emblazoned with the logo of a sneaker maker. "How can I help you?"

"By telling me what you know about Melanie Zide."

Dirk reddened slightly. "Melanie? Well, sure. We went to high school together. In fact, I ran into her just the other day over at Doug's Texaco. We stopped and got caught up. She was real glad to hear I've remarried and I'm staying sober and all."

The pink-cheeked barmaid returned now with Des's sandwich and cider.

Des dived in hungrily. "Were you ever involved with Melanie?"

"Why are you so interested in her?"

Des told him why. "Naturally, the lieutenant's asked me to find out as much background about her as I can," she explained.

Dirk sat there staring grimly into the fire for a moment, a thumb absently stroking his square jaw. "I can help you out, I guess. But I want you to know this is not something I would talk to you about under normal circumstances, and I take no pleasure in doing so now. I always liked Melanie, understand?"

"I do."

Dirk shot a furtive glance over his shoulder at the other couple in the pub, then leaned across the table toward Des, lowering his voice. "The real deal is that *everyone* was involved with Melanie—me, Timmy Keefe, Timmy's brother, Will . . . Back when we were fifteen years old, Melanie was a rite of passage, I guess, you'd call her. Everybody's first. You got yourself a couple of joints, a six-pack, and you hit the beach after dark with Melanie Zide. It wasn't like she'd do just anybody. If she thought you were stuck-up or phony, she wouldn't let you anywhere near her. But if she thought you were okay then, well, you were in." He trailed off, shifting uncomfortably in his chair. "I can't believe somebody *shot* her. You say her body washed up on Big Sister?"

"It's possible that someone took her out on their boat and dumped her." Des took another bite of her sandwich, dabbing at her mouth with her napkin. "You mentioned you've been out on Tim's Boston Whaler."

"That's right. He and I . . ." Dirk's eyes suddenly widened in alarm, his body tensing. "Wait, you don't think *I* did it, do you? I swear I didn't. You've got to believe me."

"It's not my job to believe or disbelieve you, Mr. Doughty," Des said, calmly sipping at her cider. "I'm simply recanvassing, that's all. Since I'm the lowly resident trooper,

I've been given the longest of the long shots. But I have to do my job, understand?"

"I guess." Dirk relaxed a bit, although his big calloused hand was still gripping his cider mug so tightly that his knuckles were white. "As long as you understand I had no reason to kill Melanie. I mean, hell, why would I?"

"In theory? Because she knew something that could hurt you."

"Like what?"

"Like, say, the identity of Colin Falconer's male cyber lover, Cutter."

"Why the hell would I care about that?"

"Because you're Cutter."

Dirk gaped at her in shock. "Now look, I *know* I use a laptop, but that's to keep track of my billing, not to carry on some . . . some . . . Hey, we *are* still talking theory here, right?"

"All we're doing is spitballing," Des assured him.

"That's good," he said, pausing to sip his cider. "Because I honestly can't think of a single reason why I'd want to carry on with Falconer that way."

"I can—to ruin his career."

"Why would I want to do *that?*"

"Because he was having an affair with Moose Frye, and you still loved her. You never stopped loving her. That's why you came back to Dorset—to try to win her back."

"Whoa, I'm calling time-out here . . ." Dirk furrowed his brow at her, bewildered. "Are we *still* spitballing?"

Of course they were. But there was no reason he had to know that. So Des said, "You tell me. She got you that job with the Leanses, didn't she?"

"Well, yeah," he admitted. "But what does that mean?"

"That you were still in touch with her, maybe."

"She was like a sister to me," Dirk insisted, his voice catching slightly. "We all grew up together—me, Moose, Takai, Timmy, Melanie—all of us."

"And your wife, Laurie?"

"What *about* Laurie?"

"Is your life together back in Toledo as solid as you've been portraying it?"

"It's rock-solid," Dirk said, his face a tight, angry mask.

"Would she echo that if I called her up on the phone?"

"Okay, so we have some issues," he said defensively. "Name one couple that doesn't. I want kids. A whole bunch of kids. She wants to keep working full-time. My work takes me on the road a lot. She hates the road. She loves Toledo. I *hate* Toledo. But the important thing is I'm staying focused and sober. We can work this stuff out. We can work it all out."

"When was the last time you spoke to Laurie?"

"Three weeks ago," he admitted, ducking his head. "How did you know about us anyway? Have you already called her?"

"No, but *you* should. The more you talk, the better."

"You sound awful sure about that," Dirk observed.

"Only because I've been through it. He was in Washington. I was in New Haven. Our marriage died somewhere on the New Jersey Turnpike, just outside of Trenton. You have to stay each other's best friend, Mr. Doughty. The day the friendship stops, the marriage stops. So call her. Call her to say good morning. Call her to say good night. Damn it, just call her, will you?"

The charred remains of the feed troughs and livestock had been cleared away from the ditch out in front of Winston Farms. But a foul stench still lingered in the air, just to serve as a reminder of what had happened there—not that Des or anyone else in Dorset would ever be able to forget.

She cruised another half mile past the crossroads before she turned at the fire station onto Mill Road. Tim Keefe's was the third house on the right, an old wood-shingled farmhouse with a sagging porch. His pretty blond wife, Debbie, was finishing the dinner dishes in the kitchen. Tim was out in his shop, she informed Des cheerfully.

It was a converted barn fully rigged up with a big band saw, lathe, drill press, router and workbenches. It smelled of linseed oil, glue and fresh-sawed lumber. Husky young Tim, with his ruddy face, walrus mustache and air of steady maturity, was brushing a coat of water-based polyurethane sealer onto some oak kitchen cupboards, ZZ Top providing background music on the radio.

"Come on in, Trooper Mitry," he called to her, turning down the music. "Just getting your cabinets ready for installation. How do you like 'em?"

"They look great, Tim." In fact, they were even nicer than she'd imagined. "Really great."

"I think so, too," he agreed. "Hey, we got those new roof joists in for you today."

"So the roofers can start tomorrow?" she asked hopefully.

"If the weather holds." Tim never, ever just said yes. Always, there was an if. "What brings you by—is it the Melanie thing?"

"You heard the news on the radio?"

"No, Dirk just called me," he answered, continuing to brush on the sealer, his strokes smooth and sure. "Why would someone want to do an awful thing like that to her?"

"That's what we're trying to find out. I understand you and Dirk knew her pretty well back in high school."

Tim immediately reddened, just as Dirk had, and shot a nervous glance through the open barn door at the house. "That was a long time ago," he pointed out delicately. "Before Debbie and me ever started going together."

"You went to school with Moose, too, am I right?"

"You bet," he agreed, eager to change the subject. "Absolutely."

"How did she feel about Dirk?"

"She loved the guy, no two ways about it. Would have married him, too, if Takai hadn't turned his head. Dirk, he liked Moose well enough, but he didn't appreciate her. Not when we were seventeen, eighteen years old. Let's face it— when guys are that age we're drawn to certain flashier qualities in women."

She smiled at him. "You mean you're *taken in* by certain flashier qualities, don't you?"

Tim let out a laugh. "Okay, you win. What Moose had going for her was intelligence and warmth and good, common sense. She would have made a fine wife and mother, a partner for life. Dirk would have come to realize that as time went on, but he never got the chance. Takai made sure of that," he added with obvious distaste.

"Why did she?"

"Because she could," he answered simply. "And because she never could stand Moose having anything that she didn't have. That's Takai. Hell, she never really *wanted* Dirk. But she got him. And she poisoned that well for all time. I've always felt bad about it, to be honest. If she'd just left him alone, cast her spell on some other poor slob, he and Moose might have had something solid together. Moose would have kept him level-headed, despite all of those ups and downs of his ball-playing career. He'd have a life there on that farm with her. He'd have been happy." Tim finished coating the cupboards and went over to the work sink in the corner to wash out the brush. He kept an old refrigerator next to the sink. He offered her a beer. She declined. He pulled out a cold bottle of Corona, popped the cap and took a long, thirsty gulp. "As it turned out, neither one of them ever got happy."

"And Takai?"

"I don't know how that nasty bitch lives with herself. But she'll get hers, and it won't take any shotgun, either. One of these days, not so many years from now, she'll be a wrinkled, dried-up old hag. No man will so much as look at her. And she'll totally freak. That's a day I'm looking forward to, trooper. I've got it circled on my calendar. And if that sounds small and mean of me, then I guess I'm small and mean."

"Dirk told me you two have been going out together on your Whaler."

"Yeah, we've gone out a few times since he's been back. For me, being out on the water is like going to church." Tim let out an easy laugh. "Actually, it's *instead* of church."

"I know I'm a landlubber, but it's getting a little late in the season, isn't it?"

"Not for lobstering. Best time to catch 'em is in January. Mind you, there's a real art to it—you need a strong back and a weak mind. Me, I'm strictly what the old Maine lobstermen call a ragpicker. An amateur with six measly pots."

"When's the last time you went out?"

"Sunday. Got us four fine lobsters."

"You haven't taken her out since then?"

"Nope."

"Could someone else? Without you knowing about it, I mean?"

Tim stared at her stonily. "Someone like Dirk?"

"Yes."

"There's no chance of that, trooper. None."

"How can you be so sure?"

"She's grounded, that's how. Her engine was misfiring on Sunday. I pulled it when we got back, and haven't fixed it yet. It's still sitting on a tarp in my garage. Go take a look," Tim challenged her, his temperature starting to rise. "Take a look if you don't believe me."

"Don't get sore on me, Tim. I'm just asking you the questions they told me to ask."

"Sure, okay," he said grudgingly. Clearly, Tim Keefe was being protective of his childhood friend. He was also not someone who liked having his word doubted. "I understand. Go ahead and ask away."

"Dirk's marriage is not so hot, I gather."

"Straight up, Dirk Doughty's a guy I feel sorry for," Tim said, taking another gulp of his beer. "You wouldn't think a carpenter like me could ever feel sorry for a big leaguer like Dirk, but I do. See, when he was a teenager they *told* him that he was going to win the lottery. Live a life that the rest of us can only dream about. That was dangled right in front of him, okay? And then—whiff—it was snatched away, and I don't think he's ever recovered. When you're a guy like me you *know* there are certain things you will never be. I will never be famous. I will never be rich. I will never sleep with a supermodel. I *know* these things. I know who I am and where I belong and who with. Dirk doesn't know any of those things. And he'll never be happy settling for anything less than what he thinks he deserves. That's how his drinking came about. He gets itchy."

"And what does Chuckie Gilliam get?" Des asked him.

"Chuckie?" Tim curled his lip at her. "Why do you want to know about that loser?"

"He lived across the street from Melanie, and was mixed up with her. Said he used to work for you."

"He did," Tim answered shortly. "Until I caught him loading some of my materials onto his truck. When I confronted him about it the stupid jerk popped me one in the nose. I'd have cut him some slack over it—he has his troubles. But that was over the line. I don't take that from any of my men."

"What kind of troubles?"

"Gambling. Chuckie's poison of choice is blackjack. He can blow his whole paycheck up at Foxwoods in ten minutes."

"Every time I'm at his place he's on the computer. What's up with that?"

"He's always trying to come up with some formula for how to beat the house. All he's come up with so far is a way to lose every dime he's ever made—and then some."

"And what about that *Jesus Saves* thing on his knuckles?"

"He saw God for a while," Tim answered dryly. "I don't think he sees him anymore. Or maybe he just didn't like the odds God was giving him. Hey, look, Chuckie's a swamp Yankee through and through, just like me. Most of us are good, hard-working people. Some of us aren't." He hesitated now, eyeing Des carefully. "You don't really think Dirk's a killer, do you?"

"Tim, I don't know what to think. But I had to ask, like I told you." Des swallowed, steeling herself for what she was about to do. "And there's something else I need to ask you . . ."

A wary expression crossed his ruddy face. "What is it?"

"Do you think you could finish my damned house by next week?"

"Oh, hey, we're getting there," he assured her cheerfully. "And if everything breaks right we'll—"

"No, sir. No more ifs," she said firmly. In her mind, Bella was cheering her on. "I hear that word *if* again and I will scream. I *know* that quality work takes time. I have *tried* to be patient. But the monster is out of her cage. I *need* my own space and I need it *now,* understand?"

Tim nodded his head vigorously. "I do. I absolutely do. And if . . . I-I mean, I sure will do my best to finish up as fast as I can. You've got my word on that. Ask anyone in town— my word's gold."

She knew that. She gave him her biggest smile and told him so.

But that still didn't stop Des from waving her flashlight around inside his garage as she was on her way back to her cruiser. And, yes, there was a blue tarp in there. And, yes, there was a greasy outboard motor sitting on it. But for how long? There was no guarantee that it had been sitting there since Sunday. None.

And she knew that, too.

She swung by the Dunn's Cove Marina on her way back down Route 156. Found it to be deserted. There were no cars parked in the gravel lot. No cabin lights coming from the yachts and cruisers moored there. The rich boys were all home for the night. Good. She killed her engine and got out, flashlight in hand. It was very nearly pitch-black out. The boatyard was not floodlit, and the moon had disappeared behind some low heavy clouds that had moved in, smelling of rain.

Bruce Leanse's boat, *The Brat*, was as huge and beautiful as Mitch had said it was. He had also mentioned that it was scrupulously maintained. Des took off her black brogans and hopped aboard in her stocking feet. Carefully, patiently, she checked over its deck from bow to stern, hunched low over her flashlight beam in search of scuff marks. She found none—the deck's surface was spotless. Perfect condition. Next she started in on the railings and brasswork, looking for any gouges or scratches, no matter how tiny. Anything that might indicate a struggle had taken place on board. But it was as if someone had just gone over the entire boat with Brasso and a toothbrush. Des found not one thing anywhere on deck to suggest that *The Brat* had been used to dispose of Melanie Zide.

As for the cabin, well, the cabin was locked. And she had no authority to bust in. No authority to be on board, period. Not unless she thought she'd heard a prowler. Which would be her story if anyone found her there.

And, damn, now she did see headlights. A car coming down the marina's gravel drive directly toward her. It pulled up right next to her cruiser and somebody got out. She heard footsteps crunching on the gravel. Footsteps coming directly toward her. Des bit down hard on her lower lip. She was in no mood to be found on board *The Brat* by Bruce Leanse. She really did not want to have to explain herself to that man. Hurriedly, she grabbed her shoes and hopped back onto the dock, where she immediately ran smack-dab into a short, stocky man who grabbed her by the arm, shining his light on himself so she could get a good look at him.

It was Soave. "I was just going to call you when I spotted your car in the lot. Find anything interesting?"

"Didn't find anything, period. And you can let go of my arm now." He released his grip on her and she stepped back into her shoes, bending over to tie them. "Why were you going to call me?"

"I got an ID on Cutter from the Internet service. Man, they do not make it easy. I've been jumping through flaming hoops for like the last two hours." He grinned at her. He was pumped. "Take a drive with me, Des."

"Where to, wow man?"

The Leanses. They took Soave's slicktop, Des riding shotgun.

"Your father hates me," Soave said to her as he drove. "Treats me like I'm some kind of a total yutz."

"Rico, he treats everyone that way."

Soave glanced across the seat at her. "Even you?"

"*Especially* me. He demands best effort, and he accepts

nothing less. Why do you think I gave you such a hard time when we partnered up? Because I've been getting hammered by that man since I was four years old."

"Are you just saying this to make me feel better? Because I have to tell you something—it's working."

"Rico, it's the real deal."

He furrowed his brow thoughtfully now. "Tawny thinks that you and me never got along because deep down inside I feel threatened by you."

"Smart girl, that Tawny. She's wasting a fine brain, sitting there all day in a beauty parlor with an emery board in her hand." Des paused, raising her chin at him. "Do you two talk about me a lot?"

"You've been on my mind a lot lately, Des," he confessed, suddenly sounding like a painfully earnest adolescent. "Some of the things you said to me about my future. I guess I've been doing a lot of thinking lately . . ."

"Careful, that can become habit-forming. Before you know it, you'll be doing it every day."

"You're never going to let me back up, are you?" he demanded, flaring. "There's no second chances in this perfect world you and your father live in, is that how it goes?"

"I don't live in that world anymore. I dropped out, remember?"

"Like hell you did. You're still the same ball-buster you always were."

Des smiled at him sweetly. "You really *do* miss me, don't you?"

"Aw, shut up."

All lit up at night, the Leanses's post-modern mountaintop home reminded Des of the Mount Rushmore house in that superb Hitchcock movie Mitch had shown her, *North by Northwest*. This was a brand-new phenomenon, it dawned on her. She never, ever used to compare real life to movies, not until she met that man. Mitch was rubbing off on her. Was she rubbing off on him? She doubted it.

"This house looks like a damned space station," Soave observed, gaping at it through his windshield.

"Just don't tell him you find the architecture interesting, or he'll bite your head clean off."

"Yo, I wasn't going to."

They got out and rang the bell to the big oak front door. It was the little pumpkin head, Ben, who answered.

"Good to see you again, Ben," Des said to him pleasantly. "Give it up for Lieutenant Tedone. Ben here was our DARE essay winner."

"No way!" Soave exclaimed, sticking out a hand. "Glad to know you, Ben."

"Glad to know you, too, sir," the boy responded in that gurgly voice of his. "My dad's on the phone in the den—whoa, what a surprise. My mom's down in the gym. Come on in."

The Leanses' living room was a cube-shaped lookout of stone and glass. The living room floor was polished concrete, as was the stairway that led down the hill to the rest of the house. There were no rugs. No adornments anywhere. Only bare walls and windows and clean surfaces. What furniture there was—a grouping of low leather banquettes, a table and chairs of polished blond wood—was spare to the point of sterile. It struck Des as something out of an architectural magazine, not a real place where real people lived.

"Ricky Welmers was bragging that he took a ride in your cruiser," little Ben said to her as he ushered them in, their footsteps resounding on the polished floor like rim shots on a snare drum. "Is that for real?"

"It is."

"How come you gave *him* a ride?"

"He needed one. I'll be happy to give you one, too. Anytime you want."

"She'll even handcuff you," Soave confided.

"Really!?"

Des heard a set of footsteps coming briskly up the stairs now and Bruce Leanse charged into the room with a broad, manly smile on his face. "Trooper Mitry," he said brightly, showing her thirty or more of his perfect white teeth. "Really good to see you again. And, hey, you must be Lieutenant

Tedone. Welcome to my home—both of you." Bruce was dressed casually in a gray turtleneck sweater and jeans, and he was working the chummy thing hard. Too hard. Underneath, he seemed edgy and preoccupied. "How may I help you?"

"The lieutenant and I just came from your boat . . ." Des responded.

"Please don't tell me somebody broke in. That can't be. This is Dorset."

"No, nothing like that, Mr. Leanse," Soave spoke up. "We wanted to talk to you is all. We tried you there first, but nobody was around."

"Because he's been working there *much* too late these past few weeks," Babette Leanse said pointedly as she came padding up the stairs to join them, perspiring freely from her workout. She had on a blue leotard and sneakers. A towel was around her neck, and her bushy hair was gathered up in a rubber band atop her head. "I insisted he stay home with his family this evening."

Des nodded, wondering if Attila the Hen was hip to his thing with Takai. Sounded like it. "The lieutenant and I would like to have a talk with you both."

"This sounds serious," Babette said, managing once again, somehow, to look down her nose at Des—who still could not figure out how the woman managed to perform such a physical impossibility. "Do we need a lawyer present?"

"Entirely up to you," Soave answered grimly.

Babette's mouth tightened. "Ben, would you please excuse us?"

"No way!" Ben exclaimed. "This is just starting to get good!"

"Ben . . ."

Glumly, the little boy headed downstairs.

Babette waited until he was gone before she turned to Des with a defiant expression on her face. "Well, do you recommend we phone our lawyer or not?"

"That's your decision," Des replied, offering nothing.

The Leanses exchanged a hopelessly bewildered look before Bruce shrugged his shoulders and said, "Come on, let's sit in the kitchen."

Their gleaming gourmet kitchen was down one flight of stairs from the living room. It was vast. It was to die for. Commercial Jenn-Air range with built-in grill and two ovens. Sub-zero refrigerator and freezer. Copper pots and pans galore. A center island with stools where the four of them sat. In comparison, Des realized, her own beautiful new kitchen would look like something belonging inside a trailer park in Homestead, Florida. But that was okay by her. Because she would never want to trade places with Babette Leanse.

Not now. Not ever.

"You made a play and you lost, Mrs. Leanse," Soave began, his voice chilly and authoritative. He played the blustering intimidator well. He loved to stick it to people. Especially rich people. "Your days as head of the Dorset school board are over. You are toast. That's a given. But if you're straight with us, we *may* be able to keep you out of jail."

Babette's eyes widened with alarm. *"Jail?"*

"Whoa, time-out here," Bruce broke in, staggered. "What are you *talking* about?"

"Melanie Zide is dead," Soave fired back. "Maybe you heard the news."

Babette sat there limply, the color draining from her face. "Dead?" Evidently, she hadn't.

"Someone shot her," Des said quietly. "And then tried to make it look like she left town."

"We now have a positive ID on Cutter," Soave continued, staying on the offensive. "What we don't have, Mrs. Leanse, is the real reason why Melanie was pursuing her sexual-harassment claim against the superintendent. What was in it for her? Who put her up to it?"

Babette said nothing in response. Just sat there in tight-lipped silence, her small hand wrapped around a plastic water bottle.

Her husband, however, flew into a panic. "Honey, if you

know *anything,* you'd better tell them!" he said in an agitated voice. "I am trying to build something *huge* here. If there's so much as a whiff hanging over me I am roadkill—no planning commission approval, no building permit, *nada.* They won't let me build a damned phone booth in this town, get it?"

Des was certainly trying to. Mostly, she found herself wondering if Bruce's little speech was scripted for their benefit. She found it doubtful that anything this elaborate had been undertaken without his knowledge.

Now he was getting up off his stool. "Do you want me to call Jack?" he asked his wife. "Maybe I'd better call him at home in New York. We'll put this on speakerphone so he can advise you what to say or what not to say or—"

"No, don't," Babette said faintly, putting a hand on his arm. "I want to tell them everything I know. I need to. I'm positively ill about this whole thing."

"Okay, if that's what you want . . ." Bruce settled back down on his stool.

Babette sat there for a long moment in silence, a deeply pained expression on her face. "But first I want you officers to understand that this was all *my* doing. My husband knew nothing about it. You must believe that. Everyone must believe that. If he had known, he most certainly would have told me not to do it."

"Fine, whatever," Soave said impatiently. He wasn't buying this either.

"A few months ago," Babette began slowly, "I discovered Melanie was mixed up in a kickback scheme involving our district's classroom supplies—she'd switched us to a new distributor in exchange for money under the table. I found out about it from our old supplier, who'd refused to ante up. It wasn't a lot of money—a few hundred here, a thousand there—and it *is* a fairly common practice among office managers who do institutional ordering. But it's highly unethical."

"Grounds for dismissal, too, I'd imagine," Des said.

"Absolutely," Babette concurred. "When I confronted

Melanie about it she was extremely contrite. And laid this whole sad story on me about her poor sick mother in the nursing home. And *then* she said, 'Isn't there any way we can work this out?' I said, 'Melanie, I can't imagine what you mean.' And she said, 'Well, what are our common interests?' Of course, I knew immediately what she meant. She was well aware that I'd prefer to have a superintendent who backs the new school. Then she said, 'I have this friend who's a secretary in the tax collector's office up in Hartford and she got rid of her boss, a real nasty jerk, by claiming he'd sexually harassed her.' I said to her, 'Melanie, has Colin been making improper advances to you?' Melanie said, 'No, but he doesn't even have to.' All her friend did was buy some gay porn magazines and leave them lying around her boss's office. Then she filed a complaint against him, claiming that she'd been made to feel sexually harassed by his conduct. The state, which was not anxious to have the story hit the news, immediately offered him a lucrative early retirement package if he'd go quietly. And he did, even though it was a complete fabrication, because he didn't want to put his wife and family through the embarrassment of having it go public." Babette paused to drink thirstily from her water bottle. "Melanie knew that Colin was partial to online chat groups," she continued, her voice low and strained. "Particularly the gay ones. She'd observed him participating in them during his lunch hour. She suggested we *find* someone to engage him in a male cyber romance. All she had to do was catch him at it in his office one time and she'd testify against him. Faced with public humiliation and shame, she felt sure Colin would fold his tent the same way her friend's boss had." Babette took a deep breath, swiping at the perspiration on her face with her towel. "And that's the whole dirty, rotten little plan—Melanie would keep her job, Colin would lose his, and Dorset would get its new school."

"Honey, I don't *believe* this!" Bruce protested, aghast.

Again Des found herself wondering whether his reaction was strictly for their benefit.

"This whole scheme was Melanie Zide's idea?" Soave demanded, glaring at Babette Leanse accusingly. "You had *nothing* to do with it?"

Babette lowered her eyes. "I—I had the power to tell her no. And I didn't."

"It means that much to you?" Des said to her.

Babette looked at her blankly. "What does, trooper?"

"The school. It's worth ruining a man's life just for the sake of a new building?"

"Nothing is more important than our children's well-being," Babette replied with total conviction. "Colin was too bound up in local tradition to see that."

"And so you flattened him," Des said.

"Yes," she admitted quietly.

"The new school's also pretty important to the future of The Aerie, am I right?"

"One's got nothing to do with the other," Bruce argued hastily. "Not a thing."

"Really? That's not what I'm hearing," Des said.

"Why, what are you hearing?" he demanded.

"That you'd like to build a New Age retirement village on three thousand acres of prime farmland and forest adjacent to the river," she replied. "That in order to lock up zoning and wetlands approval you've paid to play by donating the land and the design plans for this new school that you insist the town needs, even though a lot of people don't happen to agree with you. From where I sit, Mr. Leanse, *you're* the one who needs the new school."

"Our children need the new school," Babette insisted. "Center School is unhealthy."

"And there's *no* quid pro quo," Bruce said vehemently. "That's a lie. A vicious, evil lie. People repeat it often enough, they think it becomes the truth. It *doesn't*. It's still a damned lie!"

God, they were cagey, Des reflected. From their lips it was impossible to tell truth from spin. Perhaps the two were one and the same to people such as these. Perhaps the whole cyber-romance scheme had been Babette's idea, not Melanie's. It wasn't as if Melanie were around anymore to dispute her version of the facts.

"I-I didn't want Bruce to know about Colin," Babette spoke softly. "I wanted this to be my own contribution. To accomplish something on my own."

"You accomplished something, all right," Soave said to her coldly. "You placed yourself right in the middle of two murders."

"And a suicide attempt," Des added. "Let's not forget that."

"I shouldn't have let it happen." Babette's eyes were beginning to shimmer, as if she might cry. "It was sneaky and wrong, just wrong. And I am deeply ashamed. But Colin *did* willingly engage in that pornographic online relationship. And he *did* leave smutty material on his screen for Melanie to see. That was his own doing. No one held a gun to his head. If he had behaved appropriately, then he would have had nothing to fear. He'd—" She broke off, her voice quavering. "Or at least that's what I keep telling myself. But it was an awful thing to do to someone, and I know it. I could have stopped it from happening, and I didn't. And now I will have to accept the consequences."

Soave stared at her in disapproving silence. "Who shot Melanie Zide, Mrs. Leanse?"

"I have no idea who, Lieutenant," she replied. "Or why. Possibly Melanie got greedy. It was certainly like her to get greedy."

"Forgive me if I sound dense," Bruce cut in, running a hand through his short, spiky hair. "But there's one thing I'm still not getting . . ."

"Which is what, Mr. Leanse?" Soave asked him.

"This online lover of Colin's," he said slowly. "This Cutter fellow—just exactly who the hell is he?"

CHAPTER 13

There was so much sobbing coming from the other end of the phone that at first Mitch couldn't even tell who the caller was. When he finally recognized the voice he laid down his fork and said, "Slow down, Takai. What's wrong?"

"It's Father!" she cried out. "I-I don't know *what* to do or who to . . . I'm *so* sorry to bother you, but I—"

"It's okay, I'm not doing anything special." In truth, he was busy wolfing down a third helping of Des's remarkable Hoppin' John. Des was still on the job. Bella had headed back to the Frederick House for the night and the Deacon had gone home. So had the helicopters that had been circling overhead for the past two hours, making him feel as if he were living in a war zone. "Just tell me what's happened—is Hangtown all right?"

"No, he is *not* all right! He's in one of his drunken rages. *Totally* out of control. And they're not releasing Jim until the morning and I'm *all* by myself and—"

"Wait, isn't there still a trooper stationed there?"

"He's parked way down at the gate to keep the damned press out. There's no one *here* besides me. And I just can't *handle* him. H-he's really scaring me, Mitch. I've never seen him this bad. Could you . . . ?"

"Don't say another word. I'll be there in ten minutes."

He went right out the door into the darkness, jumped into his pickup and headed over the wooden causeway to Peck

Point. It had gotten windy out, and a cold drizzle was beginning to fall. A couple of TV news reporters from Hartford
were still huddled under bright lights at the gate, trying to
hold on to their hairdos as they filed their stories on Melanie
Zide's murder for the eleven-o'clock news. He steamed right
past them and got onto the Old Shore Road and floored it,
heading north with his brights and wipers on.

By the time he turned off of Route 156 onto Old Ferry
Road the drizzle had become a hard, steady rain. There was
no press corps clustered at the foot of Hangtown's private
drive at this hour. Only the one state police cruiser that Takai
had mentioned, which sat there blocking the entrance to the
drive, its lights on, its engine running, a lone trooper behind
the wheel. Mitch pulled up and waited but the trooper
wouldn't budge from his nice dry ride, so Mitch had to get
out and slog through the rain with his head down to tell him
that Takai was expecting him. The trooper didn't seem the
least bit interested. He didn't even roll down his window
when Mitch tapped on it. Asleep. The big oaf was asleep.

Annoyed, Mitch yanked open the guy's door and—

Out he tumbled, his weight bowling Mitch over onto the
wet ground underneath him, the trooper staring right down
at him with half of his head blown off and a look of blind
terror on what was left of his face.

Mitch let out a strangled cry and scrambled out from under him, shuddering with revulsion. Now he was seeing
blood and more blood in the light of his truck's beams.
Some of it had gotten on him. And there was broken glass all
over the dead man and the seat and the dashboard. Whoever
shot him had fired right through the passenger-side window.

Mitch stood frozen there, overcome by the shock and the
horror of it. Briefly, he thought he might pass out. Dazed, he
stumbled blindly away . . . And then . . . And then he started
running, slipping and sliding on the wet leaves, falling, getting back up. Up the long, twisting dirt drive he ran in the
black of night, hearing himself panting, his footsteps chunk-
ing heavily. Mitch ran and he ran. Past the totem poles made
of personal computers, alongside the meadow filled with car

parts, around the big bend toward Wendell Frye's hot pink house. The place was ablaze with lights. Every light in every window was on. Mitch ran and he ran, staggering to a halt only when he'd reached Moose's old Land Rover, which was parked right out front.

He fell against it, gulping for breath, his chest aching, when suddenly Sam came lunging furiously at him from the front seat, throwing himself against the rolled-up windows, barking and snarling.

Someone had locked Hangtown's dog in the car, and the normally mellow German shepherd was totally beside himself, a hundred and twenty savage pounds of fangs and muscles. Mitch didn't know why he'd been locked up. But he wasn't going to let him out. Not the way he was acting.

The front door to the house was wide open.

Mitch proceeded inside, calling out Takai's name, calling out Hangtown's name, listening, hearing nothing in response. No sound at all except for his own heart pounding in his chest. Dripping wet, he headed straight for the phone in the kitchen to call for help. Des. He would call Des. He picked up the phone and was starting to punch in the numbers when he realized it was dead. Nothing but stone-cold silence greeted his ear.

The line was out. Someone had made sure it was out.

Mitch did have a cell phone for emergencies, but in his mad haste he had left it in his truck. He was standing there in the big farm kitchen thinking seriously about going back for it when he heard the scream.

It was a woman's scream. A scream of absolute terror. No time for phone calls. Only time to *do* something. The scream had come from the direction of the living room. Mitch started that way . . . Only now he could hear footsteps running directly overhead. Doors slamming. A cackling of maniacal laughter. Another scream—this time it seemed to be coming from the basement.

The passageways. They were in Hangtown's secret passageways.

He grabbed a flashlight from the counter and dashed into

the living room, trying to remember which suit of armor activated which hidden door. And exactly *where* that damned trapdoor in the floor was. He was not anxious to take another wild funhouse ride down to the cellar. Bracing himself, Mitch took a deep breath and raised the right gauntlet of one of the suits . . . and the trapdoor immediately dropped open right next to his feet. Greatly relieved, he lifted the visor on the other suit, opening the bookcase next to the fireplace. He barged through it into the utter darkness of the narrow secret passageway, flashlight in hand, fingering his way along its damp, cobwebbed walls. His knees did not feel entirely normal. Rubbery was not normal. And the beam of the flashlight was beginning to flicker. The batteries were almost gone, and a horrified Mitch was suddenly realizing . . .

My God, I have seen this movie a million times. There's always a tight shot on the Amiable Boob who's just trying to help out. And as he stupidly gropes his way along, the Drooling Madman jumps out of the darkness behind him with an ax and the audience sees him and the Amiable Boob doesn't and . . . WHAM! Only I am NOT sitting safely in a darkened theater with a jumbo-sized tub of hot buttered popcorn in my lap. I am IN this. Moose and Melanie are really dead. That cop out at the gate is really dead. And, if I don't watch out, I am really dead.

Now the floor fell away before him. He'd reached the spiral staircase to the cellar. He went down slowly, the narrow wooden stairs creaking under his weight as small creatures skittered along the water pipes right near his head, squealing. Rats. They were rats. At the bottom of the stairs he reached a cement floor, the flashlight's dimming beam falling on the slick catacomb walls. He inched his way forward, hearing footsteps running above him, alongside him, *next* to him. And cackling. He heard a man cackling. And now a woman's voice was crying, "No, don't! No!" *Christ, where were they?* And now, yes, he was in the wine cellar. He'd found the wine cellar. Fumbling for the light switch, he flicked it on.

Nothing. No lights came on.

Mitch waved the flashlight's faltering beam around. The hidden cupboard in the wall, the one where they used to stash booze during Prohibition, was wide open. He searched the shelves in hopes of finding candles or matches. But he found nothing but dust. And now his flashlight was practically dead and he was going to be stranded down here in the blackness, blind and helpless, if he didn't come up with a plan, and fast . . .

The kitchen. There were kerosene lanterns in the kitchen. If he could just find that passageway that Hangtown had led him down . . . Yes, here it was. This one . . . Okay, good, and *here* was the other spiral staircase, the one that led up to that secret corridor behind the upstairs bedrooms. On the other end of that corridor was the old service staircase to the kitchen. It was a plan. He could do this.

Mitch felt his way up the winding stairs from the cellar to the second floor in almost total darkness. His flashlight was barely giving off a glow now. Groping the wall for balance, he heard a door slam. And then Hangtown's voice cry out, "You won't get away from me! You will never get away!" And Takai shriek, "Father, you don't know what you're doing!" Both of their voices seemed only inches away from him. But all he could see was blackness.

Where were they? *Where?*

Now he stumbled. There were no more stairs. He had reached that narrow second-floor corridor. He'd forgotten just how low the ceiling was. He ran headfirst into the cobwebs, his face covered with them. A spider moved across his cheek en route to his mouth. He swiped it away, his skin crawling, and felt his way blindly around one sharp corner, then another . . .

Until suddenly he came upon blessed, golden light. It was the secret doors in back of the bedroom closets. They'd been flung open, the bedroom lights flooding the passageway with illumination. Blinking, Mitch halted at the first room he came to and parted the clothing that hung there in the closet before him. The entire room had been trashed. Furniture was overturned, bedding strewn.

Now he heard a tremendous crash from the room next door, followed by a shriek.

And Takai was streaking down the narrow corridor toward him, her face stricken with terror. Takai's white silk blouse was ripped to shreds, her gray flannel slacks torn at the knees. And she was limping. One shoe was off, her bare foot bleeding. "Oh, thank God, thank God, thank God!" she cried as she ran smack into Mitch, hugging and kissing him madly, hysterically. She was absolutely out of control, her breath sour and hot as she clutched him, great sobs coming from her throat. "You're here! You're really here! Oh, thank God!"

Mitch could hear glass being smashed in the next bedroom, heavy footsteps thudding on the floor. "Where are you, princess?!" Hangtown roared. "I'll find you! I'll *kill* you!"

"What's happened?" Mitch demanded, shaking Takai by the shoulders. "Tell me!"

"Where's your gun?" she sobbed. "You must . . . you've *got* to shoot him!"

"I have *no* gun. Try to get a hold of yourself. *What's* going on?"

"He's gone c-completely mad!" Takai managed to get out. "First he shot the cop at the gate. Now he's trying to shoot me. He's been chasing me all over this crazy house. H-he has the Barrett, Mitch. That giant shotgun he used on Moose."

"I'll *kill* you!" Hangtown's footsteps were coming closer now. "You can't get away from me!"

Takai let out a scream. Mitch grabbed her by the hand and yanked her roughly back down the corridor into the darkness.

"Mitch, I can't *see*!" she protested breathlessly, stumbling against him as they descended the spiral staircase blindly.

"Just hold on to me," he whispered, Hangtown's footsteps growing fainter as they escaped farther back down into the blackness, Takai's slim hand cold and clammy in his. "*He* shot Moose, is that it?"

"Yes, Mitch. God knows why. He loved her. He *needed* her. He . . ." Takai's voice trailed off in the darkness, her breathing shallow and uneven. "He keeps mumbling something about his damned will, of all things."

"What about it?"

"I don't know. He's making no sense . . . *God!*"

"Do you know where he keeps it?"

"What difference does that make? We have *got* to get out of here before he kills us both!"

"My truck's down at the gate. So is my cell phone, I'm afraid. Your phone is out."

"I know—he cut the outside wires. And stole my cell phone out of my shoulder bag."

"Does he keep his will in that wall safe in the living room?"

"I think so," she replied, as they inched their way down the staircase, step by step. "But I don't know the combination. No one does, except for Father."

"Okay, that's not a problem."

"Are you saying he told *you* the combination?"

"He didn't have to—I know how his mind works."

"I've known that awful man my whole life and not once have I *known* him. How can you even say that?"

Because he was certain, that was how. In fact, Mitch had never been as certain of anything in his whole life.

They reached the passageway at the bottom of the staircase now, standing there in the blackness as Mitch tried to regain his bearings. "I don't suppose you can find your way back to the living room from here, can you?"

"With my eyes closed," she replied. "We used to play down here when we were kids."

Now she was the one leading Mitch. Slowly and surely, she led him back through the darkness of the catacombs toward the rickety wooden staircase. Up they climbed, back toward that secret doorway next to the fireplace, back into the living room. They stood there hand in hand, blinking from the lights. Listening for Hangtown. Hearing only silence. Takai suddenly becoming aware of how revealing her torn blouse was. She folded her arms primly in front of her exposed, taut left nipple, her bare shoulders scratched and bleeding, one cheek scraped raw. Her bare foot still oozed blood.

Mitch started toward the big rolltop desk over by the windows and pushed the button under the center drawer, triggering the panel of bookcases that hid the wall safe. "The combination will be taped underneath one of the other drawers," he told her.

"How do you know that?" Takai demanded, sticking close to him.

"Because that's where it is in every old movie I've ever seen—more important, *he*'s ever seen."

"Make it fast," she said urgently. "We've *got* to get out of here before he finds us."

Quickly, Mitch knelt before the desk and started yanking out its drawers, dumping their contents out onto the floor and flipping them over, one after another after another . . . until, sure enough, there it was, on the underside of the bottom left-hand drawer, scrawled in pencil on a piece of masking tape: *R16-L18-R26-L08*.

Mitch tore it off and headed for the wall safe with it, Takai gaping at him in amazement. After spinning the dial a couple of times he carefully entered the correct combination, paused and yanked the safe open.

The first thing he found inside was cash. Lots of cash. Stacks and stacks of hundred-dollar bills wrapped in rubber bands.

"My God," Takai gasped, piling them onto the desk. "That crazy old man must have a hundred thousand bucks in there."

"You didn't know about it?"

"Are you kidding me? If I had, I would have told him to put it in the damned bank."

Deeper inside the safe, Mitch found a metal strongbox. It

was unlocked. He found a fistful of stock certificates and legal papers inside. But it was the folded legal brief right on top that was of greatest interest, the one proclaiming itself "The Last Will and Testament of Wendell Frye."

It was not an old document. It was on crisp new paper that still smelled of fresh ink. In fact, it was dated only three days ago, Mitch noticed. "He must have changed his will," he mused aloud. "Sure, that must be what he meant."

"Here, let me see that . . ." Takai snatched it away from him, her eyes scanning it quickly. And growing narrower and narrower as she began to comprehend the details. "Oh, that bastard!" she hissed. "He will *never* get away with this!"

"Oh, yes, I will, princess," a heavy voice spoke up from the front hallway.

It was Hangtown, standing there in the doorway with the huge .50-caliber Barrett propped against his shoulder. It looked something Rambo might have used to shoot a chopper out of the sky. As for the aged artist, he seemed exhausted and disheveled, but calm.

Eerily calm.

"I took you out of my will and there's not a damned thing you can do about it," he said, his voice low and menacing. Now he propped the Barrett on a table, the weight of its long barrel steadied by its own built-in stand, and pointed it directly at his younger daughter. "Care to know why I did it, Big Mitch?"

"Whatever you say, Hangtown," Mitch replied, his eyes never leaving that big gun.

"He'll kill us both, Mitch!" Takai cried. "He's out of his mind."

"I've never been more sane in my life," Hangtown said. "That evil woman's trying to trick you, Mitch. It wasn't me who shot Moose. It was she. She killed Colin's secretary. And she killed that cop at the gate, too. She wanted you to think *I* did it so you'd come running to her rescue. She was hoping you'd shoot me down like a rabid dog."

"I could never do that to you," Mitch insisted. "Not in a million years."

"Then she would have done it herself," Hangtown told him. "With you serving as her sympathetic witness. But I stopped her. And now it's all over."

"Put down that gun, Father," Takai pleaded, her voice quavering. "You're sick. You need help."

Hangtown ignored her, staring down at the gun in his hands. "When I gave you that tour of my wine cellar the other night," he told Mitch, "I discovered that somebody had been using my secret hooch cupboard. Hiding something in there. Something wrapped up in a rug or a blanket."

"I noticed the outline in the dust," Mitch recalled. "I remember that you seemed bothered."

"Damned straight I was. Because there were only three other people on the face of the earth who knew that cupboard existed—Takai, Moose and Big Jim. And because I had no idea what was going on. None. Not until it was too late. Too damned—" He broke off, his voice choking, before he turned his penetrating blue-eyed gaze on his daughter.

Takai had begun to back slowly up against the fireplace, her own eyes wide with fear. She was trapped and she knew it.

"After you murdered your own sister with this thing," Hangtown said to her, "you stashed it back in the hooch cupboard, knowing the police would never find it there. But I found it in there. That's when I knew you'd done it, you evil bitch. But I kept quiet—I didn't want the law to have you. I wanted to take care of you myself, just as soon as the two of us were alone. I wanted the satisfaction of telling you that you were too late. I wanted to see the look on your lovely, twisted face when you realized that you killed Moose for *nothing*." He stood there grinning at her crookedly. "It may not be much, but it's the only satisfaction this old soul has left. That and seeing you die before I do."

"You bastard," she snarled at him, the skin stretching tight across the bones of her face. "You mean, sick bastard."

"Go on and tell him, princess," Hangtown thundered at her. "Tell Mitch how you killed your own sister."

"Screw you!"

He fired the Barrett, a colossal, deafening boom that took out a fist-sized hole over the mantel less than a foot from her head.

She shrank back against the fireplace, her teeth chattering.

Mitch stood there frozen, his ears ringing, realizing that there was only one way this could possibly turn out. Takai was going to die—right here, right now. There was no way he could stop it. The only question that remained unanswered was whether he himself was about to die, too.

If only Des knew he was here. If only he'd called her. If only . . .

"It's all about this farm," Hangtown explained to him, his gnarled, misshapen hands loosely cradling the huge gun. "That's why she killed her. My old will left it to both of them after I was gone. And my Moose would never, ever sell out her heritage to any pillager like Bruce Leanse. *Her* I raised right. So Takai took her out, ensuring that she'd come into the whole thing when it's time for me to take my own dirt nap—or so she thought. I was one step ahead of her, Big Mitch. The more involved she got with Leanse, the more positive I became that she'd try to destroy this place after I'm gone. And I couldn't let that happen. Not on my watch. I'm *responsible* for our land. So I've taken care of it. Left it to the art academy. They'll maintain it as a place where young artists will always be able to live and work. The Nature Conservancy will see to the wetlands. And you, my dear sweet princess, get *nothing*. Not one acre. Not one cent." The old man's finger tightened on the trigger once again. "Tell him, girl," he commanded her. "Tell Mitch how you killed your own sister. Tell him or I'll put this one right between your treacherous eyes!"

"Fine!" Takai spat at him defiantly. "I'm *happy* to tell him. I'm *proud* of what I did. I started planning it when I went out to Southern California this summer to visit the grave of my mother, a sweet, beautiful woman who you tormented until she killed herself, you sadistic bastard. I wanted to blow your head to pieces. I wanted the biggest gun money can buy. I wanted *that* gun. I bought it at a gun show in Gardena with a fake ID. I bought my Porsche out there, too. That's how I got the damned gun home. I drove back with it cross-country. Got in some target practice in the Mojave Desert, too, so I'd be good and ready. I bought it with the express purpose of killing you," Takai said to her father with cold, quiet savagery. "Until, slowly, it began to dawn on me that I'd be letting you off the hook that way—if you were dead, you wouldn't feel any pain. I *wanted* you to feel the pain, every day and every night. I wanted you to suffer like I had suffered. There was only one person on the face of the earth who you gave a damn about—Moose. So I killed *her*."

Now Mitch understood. Now he knew what Hangtown had meant when he said the past had killed Moose. Payback. It was payback.

"I killed her knowing that you'd spend the last days of your cruel, miserable life in torment," Takai went on, her eyes feverish. "I killed her knowing that when you *did* finally die I'd be your sole heir—and could do what I wished with this run-down, weedy old junkyard . . . I waited for the right opening. She handed it right to me when she started sneaking out every night to bang Colin. All I had to do was pull the ignition coil on her Land Rover." Now Takai let out a shrill, mocking laugh. "You taught us all about cars when we were little, remember, Father?"

"And how to hunt," Hangtown affirmed miserably. "I remember."

"I knew she wouldn't want to bother with jumper cables at that time of night. All of that raising and lowering of hoods might wake you or Jim up. Plus she was anxious to be with Colin. And my bedroom light was on. So she asked if she could borrow my car. I gave her my keys and reconnected her coil as soon as she took off. Easy. When the trooper tested it the next day, and it kicked right over, I passed it off as nothing more than quirky Lucas wiring. Totally believable."

"Just as it was totally believable that someone in Dorset would try to kill you," Mitch spoke up, the pieces beginning to fall into horrible place now. "You were the one with all the enemies. You were the one noted for her night moves. It was your car. Everyone assumed that you were the intended victim—and that poor Moose simply got caught in the wrong place at the wrong time. But that wasn't it at all. *She* was the target all along. Very clever."

"Not clever," Hangtown argued. "*Evil*—through and through."

Takai didn't respond, just stood there smirking at her father in ugly triumph.

"Yet you cried for Moose in my arms," Mitch said to her. "Genuine tears. How were you able to do that?"

"I was crying for my mother," she answered bitingly. "I've cried for her each and every night. But I got even. It took me years, but I got even."

"And you found yourself a fall guy in Jim Bolan," Mitch said.

"That part was even easier," she said, nodding. "Since he'd been a sniper in 'Nam, I chose a sniper's roost. And planted one of Jim's cigarette butts there that I stole from an ashtray. With three pairs of heavy socks on, I was able to wear his mudroom boots up there. By carrying the Barrett, my weight even approximated his. If they wanted to build a case against him, and they did, the shoe prints were his. I knew what time she'd be getting home. I waited for her there at the crossroads. When she came to a stop, I let her have it. It was perfect. And I would have gotten away with it, too, if that damned pig Melanie hadn't wrecked everything. She wanted twenty thousand to keep quiet. Twenty thousand or she'd talk. *Damn* that woman!"

"She found out?" Mitch asked.

"Not about *this*," Takai snapped contemptuously. "About the other thing."

Mitch shook his head at her, confused. "What other thing?"

"That I was Cutter," Takai explained. "Colin's male cyber lover. Or at least he thought I was male. It was a scam that Melanie and Babette cooked up. I agreed to help them out—because the new school is vital to my future, and because I know what men want. I know how to hook you, and how to keep you hooked. You are *so* easy . . . I created an online identity for myself and I went after Colin and I hooked him, but good. It worked like a charm—until Melanie got greedy. I was afraid she might wreck my whole plan. I just couldn't chance that. So I had her meet me upriver at the Millington Ferry parking lot late at night. Supposedly to pay her the money she wanted. Instead, I shot her with my Ladysmith. Then I dumped her body in the river and made it look like she'd left town."

"What you didn't plan on," Mitch said, "was her body washing up right away on Big Sister, correct?"

"I thought the river current would float it way out to sea," Takai admitted. "Maybe it would wash up on the north shore of Long Island in a month. I was wrong. But the law has nothing on me. I bought that gun with a fake ID, too. It's at the bottom of the river now. They'll never find it. They can't *prove* I killed her. They can't prove I killed anyone."

"They won't have to," Hangtown said ominously, his finger still on the Barrett's trigger. "You'll already be dead."

Takai said nothing to that, just glared at her father defiantly.

"You say the new school's vital to your future," Mitch said. "How so?"

"The Aerie," she replied. "Without the new school, it'll never happen. And without this farm, it'll never happen. Bruce promised me a future with his company if I can deliver it for him. The Aerie will *make* me. This is my one chance to put myself on the map. I *need* this to happen."

"Why?" Mitch asked her.

"What do you mean, *why?* Isn't it obvious?"

"Not to me," Mitch responded, shaking his head. "I can't imagine any personal goal that would enable me to justify murdering three human beings, one of them my own sister. No, I'm afraid not. No."

Takai gaped at him in amazement, as if she'd just discovered he was way beyond stupid. "Father understands why," she said, her eyes flicking back to Hangtown. "He told me so. I'm a Frye. I have this intense desire to create. It's in my blood. But I have *zero* talent. I can't draw. I can't paint. I can't do anything. And yet, I *need* to create."

"So do lots of people who don't commit murder," Mitch said coldly.

"Not people who are the great Wendell Frye's daughter. Do you have *any* idea how hard that is? I am supposed to *be* somebody. Instead, I spend my days and nights peddling ugly, overpriced houses to rich assholes with no taste. It's not *fair,* damn it!"

Mitch was aware of this happening to the children of film stars. The burden of carrying around a famous name brought many of them to their knees. Drug and alcohol abuse were common. Instead of trying to destroy herself, Takai had turned her anger outward. "Life *isn't* fair," he said to her. "You can't use that as an excuse. It doesn't justify what you did."

"Evil," Hangtown repeated, his voice barely more than a whisper now. "She was always evil."

"And Moose was always good," she jeered at him. "And look where it got her, Father. She's in a body bag at the morgue. And look where it got Mother—a lonely grave in Laguna Beach. Because of you. All because of you. You killed them both, you bastard. And now you're feeling the pain I felt. I *want* you to feel it. I hope you feel it for a long, long time. I hope you live for goddamned ever!" Takai broke off, glancing sidelong at Mitch. "My shoulder bag's right there on the sofa next to you," she murmured, her eyes flicking back at the Barrett.

"What about it?" Mitch's own eyes were on the Barrett, too.

"I have another gun. It's in there. He wouldn't let me near it before, but—"

"Don't try it, Big Mitch," warned Hangtown. "I genuinely don't want to hurt you."

"He'll never shoot *you*," Takai said, urging Mitch on. "He likes you. And so do I. We could build something together, Mitch. We could be terrific."

"Thanks, Takai, but somehow I don't think it would work out."

"I can't *tell* you how I felt when you came to my rescue just now," she went on, her voice getting throaty and seductive. "Everything fell right into place, Mitch. There's *nothing* I won't do to make you happy. And, believe me, I can do things to you that no one else has ever dreamed of—for sure not that uptight black girl. Get me that gun and I'll show you, Mitch. Get it for me, It's *right* there . . ."

"Don't try it, Big Mitch."

"I won't," Mitch promised, although he *was* thinking that if he had Takai's gun he might be able to persuade Hangtown to drop his. Maybe this could be settled without bloodshed. It was at least worth a try. Slowly, he inched a bit closer to the sofa, his arm beginning to reach out . . . out . . .

And Hangtown fired at him—blowing out the window right next to his head.

Mitch instantly froze, his ears ringing all over again. "Okay, okay, I'm not moving! But listen to me. Just listen . . . If Takai *did* do these things, don't you want her to suffer?"

"No, I want her to die," Hangtown said, turning the gun back on her. "And now she's going to."

Takai cowered against the wall in her torn clothing, her eyes darting wildly around the room for a means of escape, a shield, something, anything. There was nothing. Nowhere to run. Nowhere to hide.

"But you'll be letting her off the hook," Mitch argued, his voice rising in desperation. "If you kill her, she won't suffer. She wins. But *jail,* that's something else. Think about it, Hangtown. She'll have to live in a cage for years and years. She'll get fat and ugly. Now *that's* the ultimate revenge— not killing her."

Hangtown considered this for a moment, his finger easing slightly off of the trigger. "You make a good point," he conceded. The old master remained amazingly calm. "But she killed my Moose. And now I'm going to kill her."

"You *can't* kill your own daughter."

"You couldn't be more wrong. I'm the only one in the world who has that right."

"How do you figure?" Mitch asked.

"Because I gave her life," Hangtown answered simply. "I gave it to her, and now I'm going to take it away."

"I thought only God had the right to do that," Mitch said.

Hangtown let out a great big laugh. "Haven't you heard the news—there *is* no God." Then his creased face fell and he gazed at his daughter with nothing but profound sadness. "Good-bye, princess," he said huskily, his finger tightening on the trigger.

"No, Father. No . . . !"

"Drop your weapon, Hangtown!" a booming voice abruptly commanded him. "Drop it *now*." It was Des, blessed Des, standing there in the doorway with her Sig-Sauer aimed at Hangtown and every muscle in her body tensed.

Mitch had never been so happy to see anyone in his entire life. "Good evening, Trooper Mitry. We were just hashing out a family dispute here."

"So I see," she said, edging closer into the room, rain glistening on her slicker and big hat. "Drop your weapon, Hangtown."

"Drop your own weapon, Desiree," he growled. "This is a private matter. We have no need for any law."

"It was Takai who murdered Moose and Melanie," Mitch told Des. "And the trooper down at the gate."

"We just found Trooper Olsen. Soave's phoning it in." Des glared at Takai and said, "That man had a wife and two young children. But I don't suppose that matters to you very much."

"Of course it matters," Takai said indignantly. "Do you think I'm some kind of a psychopath?"

"I really don't know what you are, Miss Frye. I'm just here to arrest you."

A sudden sob of relief came from Takai's chest. "Well, thank you for that."

"Don't thank me," Des snapped at her. "Whatever you do, don't thank me."

"You can't have her," Hangtown objected. "She's *mine*."

"It's no use, Mr. Frye," Des said, moving in still closer. "Lieutenant Tedone is right outside. And this place will be swarming with cruisers any minute. You'll just end up getting yourself shot. Don't do it. Let us have her."

"Give me a reason," Hangtown insisted. "Give me one good reason."

Now Takai was starting to edge slowly away from the fireplace. She *did* have a means of escape, Mitch suddenly realized. The trapdoor. The open trapdoor on the other side of the sofa. True, she was a good ten feet from it. But if she could manage to dive through it without getting shot she might actually get away through the catacombs.

"Trooper, I'd like to call my lawyer," she said in a soft, trembly voice, inching her way closer and closer to the trapdoor. "Before we go, if I may."

"You just chill out, Miss Frye," Des said, her eyes riveted on Hangtown as Takai continued to edge closer to that gaping trapdoor. "And for God's sake, shut your pretty-girl hole, or I'll shoot you myself . . . *Please* put it down, Hangtown," she begged, her own gun still aimed right at him, clutched tightly in both hands. "I have great respect for you. I like you. But if you don't put it down, I'll have to shoot you. Don't make me do it. Don't make me shoot you. *Please*."

"Let the law take its course," Mitch urged him. "Think about Crazy Daisy. Think about how you and Gentle Kate felt."

"I am being punished for my sins," Hangtown muttered under his breath, his finger on the trigger, eyes on Takai.

"Who the hell's Crazy Daisy?" Des demanded, her finger on the trigger.

Mitch didn't respond. He was standing there thinking: *I am not in the living room of a historic home in Dorset, Connecticut, anymore. I am in a hot, dusty saloon with a name like the Silver Dollar or Last Chance, and somebody is about to end up dead on the floor.*

But who?

Hangtown said it again: "Good-bye, princess." His finger tightening on the trigger . . .

"No, Father . . . !"

"Hangtown, don't—!"

"Drop it! I'm warning you . . . !"

And an animal roar came out of the old man—

And Takai made her move—a sudden, desperate lunge for that trapdoor—

And never made it.

He blew her away. The sheer force of the Barrett's blast flinging her hard up against the wall, her chest torn wide open. What slid ever so slowly down the wall to the floor was no longer a person, let alone a gorgeous and deeply, deeply troubled one.

Des still had her Sig-Sauer aimed right at the old man. But she hadn't fired a shot at him. Couldn't. She was frozen there, a stricken expression on her face.

Mitch couldn't move a muscle either. He could barely breathe.

As for Hangtown, he calmly laid the Barrett flat on the table, went over to the butler's tray by the desk and poured himself a brandy from a leaded glass decanter. Then he raised his glass to what had once been his younger daughter and in a deep, solemn voice said, "Good fight, good night."

Mitch never got a chance to speak to Wendell Frye again.

The great artist had told him that when the will to live is gone, a person can go very fast. Hangtown went very fast. A massive heart attack killed him two days later. The page-one obituary in Mitch's newspaper called him a "colossus of twentieth-century art." Hangtown never had to stand trial for Takai's murder. He was never even formally charged. He was already a man of leisure by then, taking his nice long. dirt nap.

He didn't even have to leave his beloved farm. He was

buried there later that week among his forefathers in the family's cemetery overlooking the river, right alongside his Gentle Kate. Moose and Takai were laid to rest there at the same time. It was a small private ceremony. Some of Moose's schoolteacher friends were there, as were a few members of the art academy faculty. Greta Patterson was there with Colin. Jim Bolan was there. So was Takai's ex-husband, Dirk Doughty, whose bags were in his car—he was driving home to Toledo right after the funeral. And Mitch was there. He'd brought Sheila Enman along with him, as promised.

As Mitch was driving the old lady to the ceremony, he told her about Moose's quest to discover the secret ingredient in her chocolate chip cookies.

"If only she'd asked me," Mrs. Enman lamented sadly. "Gracious, I *would* have told her."

"Of course you would have," Mitch agreed. "It's the sour cream, right?"

Mrs. Enman smiled at him enigmatically, but remained silent. She would not tell *him*.

This was Dorset, after all.

Melanie Zide was buried later that same day in the town cemetery. No one came.

CHAPTER 14

The skeletal remains of the young sculptress known as Crazy Daisy were found in a shallow grave under a tree, a stone cairn marking the spot. Mitch had been told about the grave by Hangtown, but chose to keep the news from Des until after the funeral. Des found this both curious and upsetting. She could not believe he had kept silent. But she did not hassle Mitch about it. He had just buried his friend. He had told her when he was ready. And that would have to do for now.

Soave tried to find out who Crazy Daisy really was. A dental mold was made, a DNA sample taken, the FBI informed. Word was put out through the media. But she matched no missing person report filed in 1972, and no relatives stepped forward now to claim her. Truly, she was a lost soul, gone and forgotten. After a suitable waiting period she was reburied in the Dorset town cemetery in a proper casket set inside a sealed concrete burial vault, according to Connecticut state law. Her headstone read simply DAISY, SUMMER OF '72.

Funeral costs were paid for by the Patterson Gallery.

Des did have to be debriefed up in Meriden about the Takai Frye shooting by a lieutenant from Internal Affairs. She told him what she'd walked in on after she and Soave found Trooper Olsen dead at the front gate: Wendell Frye pointing the loaded Barrett at his daughter, Mitch Berger standing there alongside of her, unarmed. She said that she'd ordered the old man to drop his weapon but that he'd opened fire before she could get a single shot off. She did not raise the question of whether she'd held her fire too long. The lieutenant did not raise it either. He had what he needed, including Soave's unequivocal backing of her actions. Besides which, Wendell Frye was dead anyway. Case closed.

After the debriefing, she ran into Soave on his way into the old headmaster's house, the red brick mansion with the slate mansard roof that was home to the Central District's Major Crime Squad.

Soave grinned at the sight of her and said, "How did it go in there?"

"It went. Thanks for watching my back."

"Hey, that's what teammates do," he answered emphatically.

They lingered there in the parking lot for a moment, the barking of German shepherds serving as steady background noise. The state police's K-9 training center was located there on the secluded hilltop campus, as was the world-renowned Forensic Science lab.

"Where's little Tommy?" she asked.

Soave made a face. "I got him transferred to arson. My brother said I should have spoken up sooner. I put in for somebody smart. Maybe I'll get lucky this time, huh?"

"You never know. Maybe you'll even get a woman."

He leaned against his cruiser, smoothing his see-through mustache. "Des, I think maybe I've got a better handle on you now than I did before. What do you think?"

Des considered this for a moment, Soave glancing at her unsurely. He was trying. He really was. She couldn't slap him down. Understanding was too precious a commodity, no matter the history or the circumstances. So she smiled and said, "Rico, there's hope for you yet. Get yourself some decent threads, lose that caterpillar on your lip, and lil' Tawny will have herself quite some catch."

"What, you don't like my mustache?" he demanded, flabbergasted.

"That's correct."

"Why didn't you say something before?"

"It's your face, wow man."

"Des, are you honestly happy down there in Dorset?"

"I am, Rico. That's where the real job is."

Soave stuck out his hand and said, "Let's stay in touch this time, okay?"

"Deal," she said, shaking it firmly.

"Yo, would you come if I invited you?"

"Come where, Rico?"

"To the wedding."

"I wouldn't have to be a bridesmaid, would I?" Des loathed bridesmaid dresses. They were always made out of something pink and shiny, and made her look like one of Count Dracula's girls.

"Nah, Tawny's got like a million sisters and cousins."

"In that case," Des replied, "I'd be proud to come."

She got there at ten o'clock.

She did not want to take a chance on being late. Nor could she bring in another officer. Not if she wanted to keep this off the books. She did consider calling Soave, but decided not to. Even though he'd said all the right things, she was still not sure if she could trust him. She had to be sure on this one.

So she called Mitch. He brought his truck, as well as a half dozen six-by-eight-inch panes of glass, a tin of glazing compound and a putty knife. They sat there on watch together in his cab. He'd parked about halfway down the block, close enough to keep an eye out. Her own ride was stashed well out of sight.

"Are you *sure* we're not partners?" he asked her.

"Totally."

"Still, you have to admit that this is getting to be a habit."

"I wouldn't go that far."

"At the very least, I should get an honorary badge."

"Tell you what—if you'll stop flapping your gums, there's a Darren doll in it for you. Now listen up—once this breaks I want you out of sight. You're not to get involved, understood?"

Mitch said he understood.

"Is there anything else we need to go over?"

"Yeah, we haven't discussed how pretty you look in the moonlight," he said, beaming at her. "Aren't you going to say anything about how *I* look in the moonlight?"

"White. You look awfully white." She glanced at her watch and said, "Okay, let's split up. Anything goes down from your end, you signal me with your flashlight, deal?"

"Deal." He solemnly stuck out his hand so they could shake on it, Des wincing from his grip. "Hey, what's wrong with your hand?"

"Nothing," she growled, flexing it, feeling the soreness. "I ran into something, that's all." Which was entirely true. Nose cartilage qualified as something.

They split up, Mitch taking up a post in the bushes around back, with a thermos of coffee and his leather jacket for warmth against the late-October chill. If the Mod Squad tried to get in from that side, he would spot them. Des had chosen a spot for herself behind a privet hedge in front of an historic mansion on the other side of the street, two doors down. From there she could keep her eyes trained both on the front of the building and on Mitch. She'd also scored herself a spare set of keys. When she needed to go in, she'd be ready.

She flashed her light at Mitch to let him know she was in position. He flashed his back. Then she settled in for the wait, her hands stuffed deep in the pockets of her heavy wool pea coat. Her thoughts were on him. There had been a bit of strain between them ever since that night Hangtown shot Takai. They had not talked about it. They needed to. But now was not the right time.

It was Mitch who spotted them first, shortly after one o'clock. When Des saw his signal she immediately took off across the street, sprinting up the path to the front of the building. Swiftly, she unlocked the front door, shutting it softly behind her. Now she stood in the darkness of the front hallway with her ears pricked up, waiting for the sound that she knew would come next. Because a ground-level window was the obvious way in. All they had to do was break a single pane, reach inside and unlock it. There was no security alarm to worry about. She stood there poised on the balls of her feet, waiting, waiting . . .

And then she heard it—the sound of glass breaking. It was down the hall to her right. She darted in that direction, pausing in the darkness at each open door she came to . . . Nothing . . . nothing . . . still nothing . . . until she'd reached the room at the end of the hall. And could hear them hoisting themselves in the window, one after another. Des waited there just inside the doorway with her hand on the light switch. Waited until they were all safe and snug inside.

That was when she flicked on the glaring overhead lights and said, "I understand this is where the Claire Danes Fan Club meets."

There were five of them altogether, Ronnie and four other boys. All of them wearing those same dark hooded jackets they'd had on when she spotted them at the market. All of them cradling as many family-sized bags of potato chips in their arms as they could handle.

Naturally, they totally freaked at the sight of her standing there in that classroom with them. And they did exactly what most frightened fifteen-year-old boys would do under the circumstances—throw the bags of potato chips in the air and run, stampeding down the corridor toward the front door. She let them go.

With the exception of Ronnie, that is. Ronnie she grabbed and held, her hand clamped around his skinny arm as he struggled to get free, his bags of chips falling to the floor at his feet. Ronnie with his peach-fuzz goatee and his gangsta sneer. Ronnie with his red bandanna and his falling-down jeans.

It was Ronnie who she wanted.

The classroom they were standing in was familiar to her, Des realized. It was Moose Frye's classroom. Ben and Ricky's classroom, with the same tiny desks and the same

uplifting motto stenciled on the wall above the blackboard:
A GOOD BOOK IS A GOOD FRIEND.

Her eyes fell on the bags of potato chips that were heaped
on the floor. Thirty bags of them at least. She found it sur-
prising and upsetting that these small-town kids knew the
dirty little secret about America's favorite snack food—it
was a highly effective accelerant, pure grease, that left no
telltale residue behind. Dogs that were trained to sniff out
accelerants got nowhere with chips, and chemical tests
turned up zilch. She thought only the pros knew this. Must
be out on the Internet, she reflected unhappily. She would
have to tell the arson squad.

Now she turned her cold gaze on Ronnie, who continued
to struggle feebly in her grasp. The kid was frailer than a
week-old kitten. "You were going to burn down this school,"
she said to him accusingly.

"Ricky told you, didn't he?" he demanded, his head
cocked at her insolently. "I'll kick his ass."

"Ricky didn't have to tell me, you moron. I've been on to
you garbageheads for a couple of weeks."

He said nothing in response, just stood there trying to
strike a gangbanger pose. For such a smart kid he sure was
pathetic.

She took a gentler tone. "Do you want to try to explain
this to me, Ronnie?"

"Why should I?" he said, jabbing himself in the chest
with his thumb.

"Because I have some latitude here, that's why. I can look
upon this as some high-spirited local kids throwing a rock
through a school window. *Or* I can see it as breaking and en-
tering, which is a felony, coupled with attempted arson,
which is major-league bad news. We're talking serious time,
Ronnie." She paused, letting this sink in for a moment. "It's
up to me to decide which way to go, and that depends totally
on how you behave over the next few minutes."

He reached into his jacket for a cigarette and stuck it between his teeth. "You want me to do you a solid, is that it?"
he asked, fumbling for a light.

She swatted the cigarette from his mouth, sending it flying halfway across the room. "I want you to *talk* to me."

"Well, I'm not giving up the rest of my boys," he shot back. "You *can't* make me do that."

"Use your head, dope! I just laid my own two eyes on them—I can make them from their school photos." Des shook her head at him in disgust. "I'm wasting my time here. You're just a lame-assed punk. I'm running you in." She started for the door with Ronnie in tow.

He panicked. "No, wait! W-we can work this out. What . . . what do you want to know?"

"I want to know why."

"We thought it would be cool," he answered simply.

"You thought it would be *cool* to burn down Center School? Man, what are you on? Because I have *got* to get me some of that."

"Not a thing," Ronnie insisted. "Never when we go out on a mission. That's forbidden."

"So this is the 'real' you talking?"

"Absolutely. And this is something we gave a lot of thought to, okay? We thought it would serve 'em right, okay? All they keep doing is *arguing* about this place. Jerking us around. Pretending they care about us when they don't. We're sick of being jerked around. We're sick of them telling us they want what's best for us. They don't. So we thought we'd show 'em just how we feel, okay?"

Des glanced around at the aging classroom. "You hate this place, is that it?"

He let out a nasty laugh. "I hate everything."

"Then I really don't know how to talk to you, Ronnie," Des said regretfully. "Because if you truly believe what you're saying then you're coming from the same moral place as a terrorist. You're not fit to live among other people. Come on, let's go."

"Where are we going?" he wondered, wide-eyed.

"You don't ask the questions. I do."

She ushered him outside through the front door and flashed her light three times at Mitch. Their go-ahead signal.

His job now was to repair the window and clean up the broken glass—with luck, the school would know nothing about this in the morning. Her job was to lead Ronnie Welmers to her cruiser, which she'd parked in the lot behind town hall.

She put him in the front seat and got in next to him behind the wheel. "Okay, it's time to deal," she said, looking him right in the eye. "For starters, the Mod Squad is history. I know who you are and where you live. Anything happens again—graffiti, antics, *anything*—all five of you go directly to jail. And I am *so* not goofing, understand?"

He nodded, swallowing. "What else do you want?" he asked, his reedy voice soaring an octave.

She started up her cruiser, pulled out of the parking lot and headed north on Dorset Street in the 2-A.M. stillness. "I want you to be a man instead of a punk. I want you to be responsible."

"For what?" he asked, watching the road carefully, desperate to know where she was taking him.

"For your little brother. And those ladies next door. They've got themselves a problem. And I'm going to tell you straight up what it is—your dad, in case you didn't know it."

"I know it," Ronnie said quietly.

"What's his story, anyway?"

"He's a dead man walking. His business is in the toilet. He's bitter, broke, horny. Plus he's a total ass." Ronnie sneaked a hopeful look at her. "Word, did you break his nose?"

"Why, what did he say?"

"That he got hit in the nose with a golf club, by accident."

"Works for me," she said, straight-faced.

"You have it wrong, you know. He's not hot for Phoebe. He's hot for Mrs. Beddoe."

Des glanced over at him in surprise. "How do you know that?"

"Phoebe told me."

"You two are friends?

"Kind of."

"Why did your dad give Ricky that black eye?"

"Because Ricky talked back to him."

"Ricky told me *you* gave it to him."

"No way. I love the little turd. All we've got is each other. He's just afraid the law will come down on Dad and we'll end up in some foster home."

She thought this over as she steered her cruiser up the Old Post Road in the darkness. "You like Phoebe a lot, don't you?"

"I mean, yeah . . ." he answered uncomfortably. "But they're grooming her for the big leagues. She'll go off to Yale, marry a lawyer."

"You could do that. Go to Yale, *be* a lawyer."

"I'm not that smart."

"Word, I used to be married to a Yale Law School graduate—they aren't that smart." She glanced across the seat at him. He looked incredibly young, riding there next to her. They always looked younger when they were in custody. And smaller. "From now on, Phoebe's family to you. If I get one more phone call from that mother of hers, I'm busting you for tonight's antics, understand?"

"Does this mean you're not busting me now?"

"Depends. Do you realize the enormity of what you almost did?"

"Why are you asking me that?" asked Ronnie, frowning.

"Because if you don't, then I'll have to run you over to the Troop F Barracks in Westbrook, where they'll lock you up in a cell for the night with the rest of the trash. Man, are they going to love that smooth white flesh of yours. In the morning you'll be arraigned at New London Superior Court on—"

"I understand," Ronnie said urgently.

"*What* do you understand?"

"What I almost did tonight. How heavy it would have been."

"If your father steps out of line again, I want to hear from you. He lays a hand on you or your brother, he gets busy with the Beddoe ladies, you pick up the phone and you call me."

"You want me to rat out my own father to the police?"

"Not to the police, to me."

"God, this is too freakin' weird."

"Life *is* freakin' weird. Get used to it." Des came to a stop by the stone pillars at the foot of Somerset Ridge. "Up to you, big man. Either we deal or we head for Westbrook. What's it to be?"

"I'll call you," he said hoarsely.

"Smart move," she said, easing down the road toward his house. "I knew you had it in you."

"Damn," Ronnie Welmers marveled, shaking his head. "You're not very nice, are you?"

"That's where you are way wrong," Des said, flashing a smile at him. "Remember this day, sweetness. Remember it often. Because I am the nicest person you will ever meet."

CHAPTER 15

Des was out there enforcing the seventy-five-foot limit when Mitch pulled into the firehouse parking lot. The polling place was mobbed. Voters lined up out the door all the way to Dorset Street. Dozens of vocal demonstrators crowded the curb with save our school and WE CARE signs. It seemed as if every registered voter in town had shown up to weigh in on the future of Center School. And, quite possibly, the future of Dorset itself.

Mitch tried to wangle a smile out of Des as he eased on past her into a parking space, but the resident trooper had her game face on. All he got was a curt nod.

"Quite a lovely girl, isn't she?" Sheila Enman spoke up from the seat next to him, her eyes twinkling at Mitch.

"Yes, she is, Mrs. Enman," he said, watching Des in his rearview mirror as First Selectman Paffin approached her with his hand stuck out and a broad grin on his face.

"One helluva caboose on her, too," the old lady observed, craning her neck for a better look. "Me, I *never* looked like that in trousers."

The polls closed at eight o'clock. The tally, which was posted on the town's Web site later that evening, was surprisingly lopsided. The thirty-four-million-dollar school bond proposal failed by a no vote of 3,874 to 2,175. The Center School would be spared.

Mitch was positively elated. He liked Dorset just the way it was.

One of the reasons the no vote was so resounding was Wendell Frye's generous bequest to the town. In the fine print of his amended will Hangtown had pledged one-half million dollars to Center School for the construction of a world-class art studio complex for Dorset's young people. The money was not transferable to a new school facility—if the town tore down Center School, the bequest would be voided.

Even in death, the old master's voice was heard. And heeded.

The day after the election Bob Paffin officially said, "Thanks, but no thanks" to the parcel of land on Route 156 that Bruce Leanse had wanted to donate for a new school. The first selectman also announced that he would be forming a committee comprised of town committee leaders and school board members to find out exactly how much it would cost to renovate and enlarge Center School. Chairing the committee would be Colin Falconer, who would be restored to his post as Dorset's superintendent of schools after completing a two-week medical leave. Colin was officially reprimanded for engaging in a "pattern" of inappropriate relationships, but the town leaders could not bring themselves to fire their troubled school superintendent.

The likelihood of a huge, expensive lawsuit if they did may have had something to do with their decision, though they denied this vehemently.

By chatting up the locals at the market and the hardware store, Mitch gathered that the prevailing feeling around town was that Babette Leanse had overreached—in her zeal to build the new school she had behaved in a reckless, irresponsible manner that was most definitely not Dorset. They were also convinced that her husband had known all about her unsavory scheme to oust Colin, in spite of her insistence that she had purposely kept him in the dark about it. The Leanses simply could not persuade a single soul in Dorset to believe that they did anything without joint, careful calculation. No one believed them. No one.

Meanwhile, the word around town hall was that any future development proposal that Bruce Leanse brought before the planning, zoning or wetlands commission would be viewed most unfavorably. In short, the Brat was toast in Dorset, Connecticut. The Aerie, his self-proclaimed revolution in continuous living, would have to be built somewhere else. And it *would* be built, because people like Bruce Leanse didn't quit. They kept right on going.

In fact, he was already gone. When Mitch phoned him for a quote he got a phone machine message that said to try his New York office instead. Intrigued, Mitch drove up to the Leanses' hilltop house and discovered they had cleared out. The house was vacant. And Ben was no longer enrolled at Center School—he'd been transferred out.

Mitch spent almost all of his time in the days following Hangtown's death trying to pull all of the pieces of his magazine article together. The Sunday magazine's editor, who was labeling it "A Grisly Tale of one Famous Family's Mutual Assured Destruction" wanted it as fast as Mitch could deliver it.

Mitch was still pounding furiously away at it when Jim Bolan came bouncing across the causeway one blustery afternoon in his rusty old pickup, Sam the German shepherd riding next to him in the cab. Stashed in the back of the truck, under a tarp, was the completed copper tower.

"He wanted you to have this thing, son," Jim informed him, dragging deeply on a Lucky Strike. "It ain't in his will or nothing, but he told me so right to my face. Day before he died." Jim dropped the tailgate and carefully lifted out the six-foot-tall copper fountain. "He was real emphatic about it, on account of you helped him make it and all. Even made sure he signed it—etched it right there in acid, see?"

Mitch stared at the great man's signature, nodding dumbly. He could not speak.

"I guess I don't have to tell you it's kind of valuable," Jim mentioned. "Last piece he ever did. Miz Patterson can sell it for you if you ever—"

"Never," Mitch said hoarsely. "I'd never sell it."

"Up to you, son," Jim said easily. "It's yours. Want to crank her up?"

They filled the twenty-gallon copper holding tank in Mitch's bathtub and set it in the center of the living room. The copper tower stood smack in the center of the tank, stabilized by the weight of the water. A submersible pump went right into the tank. Jim connected it to the tower's skeleton of copper tubing with a short length of plastic hose. As soon as Mitch plugged it in he could hear the pump burp and gurgle. Within a few seconds it had pushed the water all the way up to the top of the tower. Then, slowly, it trickled down through the hundreds of nooks and crannies in between the copper boxes as it made its way back down into the tank to be recirculated again and again.

Mitch stood there watching and listening, transfixed. So did Jim. There was something positively hypnotic about Hangtown's copper tower. Something timeless and magical. Mitch couldn't put his finger on what it was exactly. Maybe there were no words to describe it, he reflected, because it touched him in a way that had nothing whatsoever to do with the intellectual side of his brain. He only knew that he was in the presence of great art.

"What will you do with yourself now?" he asked Jim as the two of them stood gazing at it reverently.

"Same as before," Jim answered. "Take care of the place. Watch his back. He wrote it into his will—I'm live-in caretaker for the rest of my natural days, if that's what I want. And I guess it is. Right now, I'm helping Miz Patterson catalog all of the pieces he never disposed of."

"If there's anything I can do, just yell," Mitch offered. "And if you ever feel like stopping by some night to watch *Celebrity Deathmatch*, my door's open."

"Likewise, son," Jim said warmly, clapping Mitch on the

back. "I haven't got me no cable TV, but you want to come by for a beer, you don't need to call. It's just me, Sam and Elrod the pig now."

"Well, at least you won't be alone," Mitch said, smiling at him.

Jim's lined, leathery face fell. "No, I won't be alone. There's plenty of ghosts there on that farm. Too damned many ghosts, you ask me."

"I think we should make a special pact in honor of Hangtown," Mitch said as they lolled there together in the sparkling new bathtub, sipping ice-cold Moët & Chandon.

Des had moved into her new house that morning. The place still smelled of fresh paint, but it was extraordinarily bright and airy and clean. Awesome view of the lake, too.

"Pact?" Des's eyes were shut, her ankles resting lazily on Mitch's shoulders. She seemed a bit more at ease now that she had her own digs for herself. And those eight furry boarders of hers were in her own garage instead of Bella's. It had bothered her, not being settled. "What kind of a pact?"

"I think we really should try to grow one day younger every day for the rest of our lives. What do you think of that?"

"I think," she replied, "that it sounds like a plan."

"More potato chips?" Mitch reached for the jumbo bag on the edge of the tub.

"Man, how can you keep eating those things?"

"What else am I going to do with them?" he asked, shoving several into his mouth. "Besides, I never got paid in one-hundred-percent grease before. I could get used to this."

"Well, don't," she sniffed. "Or I'll have to put you on a diet of carrot sticks and five-K runs."

Mitch had discovered her at her easel when he got there, working on a portrait of Takai Frye in death, her chest blown open by the Barrett, her beautiful face frozen in a final scream. It was truly horrifying, but it was how Des coped.

So she drew while Mitch labored over a printout of his article, and some time after midnight they popped open the champagne and collapsed in her tub together.

"Why didn't you do it?" he asked her quietly. "Why didn't you shoot Hangtown?"

"Baby, I've thought about that a lot," she replied, staring down into her long-stemmed glass of bubbly. "And I really don't know."

"Maybe I do."

Her face tightened. "Okay, let's hear it."

"Deep down inside you felt he deserved to live and Takai didn't."

"She deserved a trial," Des pointed out. "She had a right to a trial. She didn't get one."

"She got what was coming to her, and we both know it. That's why you didn't pull the trigger."

"Maybe so," Des conceded. "But don't ever tell anyone that. Because I'm supposed to protect them all, regardless of how I feel about them. If I showed a preference that would make me, I don't know . . ."

"Human," he said, grinning at her.

Her almond-shaped green eyes narrowed at him. "And that's okay with you?"

"Of course it is. If you weren't human, then I wouldn't be able to love you as much as I do."

"*Damn*, I wish you wouldn't say things like that," she said, her voice clutching. "It's just not . . . fair. You could at least *warn* me, okay?"

"Okay," he said, stroking her smooth, slender calf. "Look, I'm sorry I didn't tell you about Crazy Daisy. Hangtown told me about her while I was acting as a journalist, and that made it confidential. I didn't like keeping it from you, believe me."

"He told you that day the Deacon came for dinner, didn't he?"

"How did you know?"

"You had something heavy on your mind when you came in the door. You weren't all there." She reached for a washcloth and dabbed at her face with it. "Let's say Hangtown didn't die. Let's say he's still alive . . ."

"Okay . . ."

"Would you still be putting that in your article?"

"I honestly don't know," Mitch confessed, sipping his champagne. "He wanted me to. All I kept thinking about was how it would change the way people looked at his art. Change it for all time. And for what—something that happened thirty years ago?"

"A girl died, Mitch," Des reminded him.

"Believe me, I know that," he said, watching her. "You're not okay with this, are you? Me not telling you about it."

"Nooo, I'm cool," she said slowly. "Deciding what's right isn't that simple, no matter how much we want it to be. I mean, if there's one thing I've learned at the art academy, it's just how many different shades of gray there are. But if you're feeling guilty, I know how you can make it up to me . . ."

"Go for it."

"How would you like to mentor a troubled teenaged boy? He loves movies, he's incredibly bright. He's also a garbagehead with an attitude, but put seventy-five pounds and a pair of baggy khakis on him and, whoop-dee-damn-do, he's you."

"This is Ronnie the Mod Squad kid, am I right?"

"You are."

"I take it the first selectman is pleased that you shut them down?"

"Hey, I'm Dorset's new fair-haired girl," she cracked. "So what do you say—will you give it a try?"

"I can't say no to you. Why is that?"

"I can't imagine why," Des said demurely, caressing him with deft, knowing fingers under the water. "What would you think about Bella moving in here for a while? Until she finds a place of her own."

"I think it would be great," Mitch replied enthusiastically.

Her eyes searched his face carefully. "You do?"

"Absolutely. You'll feel better about spending more time

at my place if you know that she's here watching your charges. Plus we'll get a good, honest brisket dinner every Friday night. Major sandwiches with the leftovers. Of course, I'll have to grow us some horseradish . . ."

"I'm serious, Mitch."

"So am I, girlfriend. I'd be thrilled if you never spent a single night here. Stay with me out on Big Sister. We should be waking up in each other's arms every morning. We should be *together*. What do I have to do to convince you of that?"

She fell into a guarded silence for a moment, her body tensing next to his in the tub. "You liked Moose, didn't you."

"Sure, I did."

"No, I mean you *liked* her."

Mitch gazed at her in astonishment. "Why do you say that?"

"Maybe I can read your mind sometimes, too."

"What a scary concept."

"It isn't pretty, now that you mention it. Are you sorry how things turned out?"

"I'm sorry that she's dead, if that's what you mean."

"It's not," she said, leveling her gaze at him. "And you know it."

Mitch let out a sigh of sheer frustration. She still didn't believe they were for real. Was still protecting herself against getting hurt. "If you're wondering whether I'm sorry that you and I are together, the answer is no, you hardheaded doofus. Sooner or later everybody has got to believe in something. And somewhere along the line—I don't know when, I don't know how—*you* are going to have to believe in *us*. I sure as hell do." He reached for her hand, his fingers intertwining with hers. "Okay . . . ?"

Her eyes were shining at him now. She swallowed, and in a husky voice that sent shivers through his entire body, Des Mitry said, "Boyfriend, it's way more than okay."

There was no lollygagging in the feathers on Big Sister Island. Not in July. Not when the sun came beaming through the skylights in Mitch's sleeping loft at five-thirty in the morning. Not a chance. These days, Mitch Berger, creature of the darkness, got up when the sun got up.

And he loved every glorious minute.

He loved the cool, fresh breezes off of Long Island Sound that wafted through his antique post-and-beam carriage house, no matter how hot and sticky the day was. He loved the blackberries that grew wild all over the island and the fresh vegetables that he had brought to life in his own garden. He loved mowing his little patch of lawn with an old-fashioned push mower, which had to be one of the great, lost pleasures of the modern age. He loved parking his pudgy self in a shell-backed aluminum garden chair at sunset, cold beer in hand, waiting for Des to come thumping across the rickety wooden causeway in her cruiser. He loved the bracing dips in the Sound they would take together. He even—and this was the truly amazing part—loved those disgustingly healthy dinners of grilled fish, brown rice and steamed vegetables she would cook for them.

If he didn't know any better, Mitch would have sworn he was turning into somebody else.

Every day he learned something new about the sun-drenched natural world around him. Goldfinches are attracted to sunflowers, hummingbirds to the color red. The male osprey stays behind to teach the fledgling how to fly while the female migrates south on her own. Many of these things he had learned from Dodge Crockett, unofficial head of the unofficial walking club Mitch had fallen in with at the beginning of the summer—four local men who hiked the three-mile stretch of beach that ringed the Peck Point Nature Preserve every morning at seven, so as to exercise, bird watch and chew each other's ears off.

There was no getting around this: Mitch Berger, lead film critic for the most prestigious and therefore lowest paying of the three New York City metropolitan dailies, was in a male-bonding group. Or so Des called it. Mitch simply described it as four Dorseteers who liked to walk together, eat fresh-baked croissants and discuss life, love and women—three subjects they freely admitted they knew nothing about.

Besides, today he had a serious career-related matter to discuss with Dodge.

At the sound of Mitch stirring around in the kitchen Quirt came scooting in the cat door for his breakfast. Quirt, who was Mitch's lean, sinewy hunter, liked to sleep outside during the summer on a bench under the living room bay window. Clemmie, his lap cat, still preferred the safe confines of the house, but slept downstairs in his armchair as opposed to upstairs on Mitch's bed, snuggled into his collarbone. Mitch had grown accustomed to her being there at night and missed her terribly, but he had also come to understand cats and the high priority they placed on their own comfort. When autumn blew in, and Clemmie felt the need for Mitch's considerable body warmth, she would return to his bed as if she'd never left.

Right now, she yawned at him from his chair and stretched a languid paw out toward him, which was her way of saying good morning.

Mitch was otherwise alone this morning. Des had taken to spending three or four nights a week with him, the rest at her own place overlooking Uncas Lake. Bella Tillis, her good friend and fellow rescuer, had moved in with her on a trial basis, which meant Des could stay over with him and not fret over her own furry charges.

While Quirt hungrily munched kibble, Mitch squeezed himself a tall glass of grapefruit juice. As he drank it down he stood before his living-room windows that overlooked the water in three different directions, savoring the quiet of early morning on his island in the Sound. A fisherman was chugging his way out for the day. Otherwise, all was tranquil. He dressed in a faded gray T-shirt and baggy khaki shorts. Shoved four blue tin coffee mugs in his knapsack, along with an eight-ounce plastic water bottle filled with that see-through low-fat milk Des had him drinking—he himself vastly preferred whole milk of the chocolate variety. But Des was absolutely determined that Mitch take off some excess poundage this summer. And a determined Des was no one to trifle with. Ever since she'd turned his kitchen into a No-Fry Zone, he'd gone down two whole waist sizes.

He started out the door, binoculars around his neck, and headed down the footpath lined with wild beach roses and bayberry toward the causeway that connected Big Sister with Peck Point. The island had been in the Peck family since the 1600s. It was 40 acres of blue-blooded paradise at the mouth of the Connecticut River, just off Dorset, the historic New England village. There were five houses on the island, a de-commissioned lighthouse that was the second tallest in New England, a private beach, dock, tennis court. Mitch had been only too happy to rent the converted caretaker's cottage, and to eventually buy it. During the cold months he'd had the whole island to himself. Right now, one other house was in use—Bitsy Peck, his garden guru, was living in the big Victorian summer cottage with her daughter Becca.

Not a day went by when Mitch didn't tell himself how extraordinarily lucky he was to be here. He'd been a total wreck after he lost Maisie, a Harvard-trained landscape architect, to ovarian cancer when she was barely thirty. He had needed somewhere to go and heal. And it turned out that somewhere was this place. Slowly, he *was* healing. Certainly, Des Mitry's arrival in his life was a huge reason why. So was his determination to plunge himself headlong into new experiences—for Mitch Berger, a socially challenged screening-room rat, walking in the sunshine every morning with three men who he'd only recently met qualified as a huge leap into the unknown.

He could see them waiting for him there at the gate as he crossed the narrow quarter-mile wooden causeway—a trio of middle-aged Dorseteers in sizes small, medium and large. Will Durslag, who towered over the other two, was the fellow who'd brought him into the group. Will and his hyperkinetic wife, Donna, ran The Works and Mitch was a huge fan of their chocolate goodies, or at least he had been until Des put him on his diet. Standing there in his tank top and baggy surf shorts, knapsack thrown carelessly over one broad shoulder, 34-year-old Will looked more like a professional beach volleyball player or Nordic god than he did a jolly chef. He was a tanned, muscular six-feet-four with long sunbleached blond hair that he wore in a pony tail. Early one morning, Mitch had encountered him on the bluff hiking with Dodge Crockett and Jeff Wachtell. Introductions had been made, a casual invitation extended. Next thing Mitch knew he was not only joining their little group every morning but looking forward to it.

It was a loose group. If you were there at seven, fine. If you couldn't make it, that was fine, too. No explanations required. There was only one rule: You could not take yourself too seriously. Any subject was a legitimate topic of conversation. The group had no name, though Mitch was partial to the Mesmer Club in tribute to *The Woman In Green*, one of his favorite Basil Rathbone Sherlock Holmes films. Not that he had bothered to mention this to any of them—they would not understand what he was talking about. They had not, for example, grasped the origin of the *Rocky Dies Yellow* tattoo on his bicep.

"Good morning, men," he called out to them.

"Another beautiful day in paradise," said Dodge, his face breaking into a smile.

"*Ab-so-tootly*," piped up Jeff, an impish refugee from a major New York publishing house. Jeff ran the Book Schnook, Dorset's bookstore.

They set out, walking single file down the narrow footpath that edged the bluffs. Beach pea grew wild alongside of them. Cormorants and gulls flew overhead. Dodge set the brisk pace, his arms swinging loosely at his sides, his shoulders back, head up. Mitch fell in behind him, puffing a bit but keeping up. When he'd first joined the group, Mitch could barely cut it. He was definitely making progress—although his T-shirt was already sticking to him.

Dodge was far and away the oldest of the group. Also the wealthiest. He came from old Dorset money, had been a second-team All-American lacrosse player at Princeton and remained, at 54, remarkably vigorous and fit. Dodge was also the single most rigidly disciplined person Mitch had ever met in his life. So disciplined that he never needed to wear a watch. Thanks to his strict, self-imposed regimen of daily activities Dodge always knew within two minutes what time it was. What made this especially amazing was that Dodge had never held a real job in his life. Didn't need to. And yet he was never idle. Each day he awoke at six, walked at seven, lifted weights at eight, read the *New York Times* and *Wall Street Journal* at nine, attended to personal finances at ten and practiced classical piano at eleven. After lunch, the remainder of his day was given over to meetings. Dodge was president of the local chapter of the Nature Conservancy, as well as commissioner of Dorset's Historic District. He served on the Wetlands Commission, the executive board of the Dorset library and the Youth Services Bureau. Some years back, he had also put in two terms as a state senator up in Hartford. A few of the old-timers around John's barber shop still called him Senator.

And yet, Dodge was no tight assed prig. Mitch had heard him do some pretty amazing things with *Great Balls of Fire* on that Steinway of his. Mitch enjoyed being around the man every morning. He was good company, a good listener and, somehow, he made Mitch feel as if walking with him was the highlight of his day. Dodge also possessed a child-like excitement for life that Mitch truly envied. Hell, the man's whole life was enviable. He had health, wealth, a beautiful renovated farmhouse on ten acres overlooking the Connecticut River. He had Martine, his long-legged, blonde wife of 26 years who, as far as Mitch was concerned, was merely Grace Kelly in blue jeans. Between them Dodge and Martine had produced Esme, who happened to be one of the hottest and most talented young actresses in Hollywood.

And the reason why Mitch needed to speak to Dodge this morning. Because this was by no means a typical July for Dorset. Not since Esme Crockett and her actor husband, combustible blue-eyed Latino heartthrob Tito Molina, had rented a $3-million beachfront mansion for the summer. Tito and Esme, each of them 23 years old, were the biggest thing happening that summer as far the tabloids were concerned. She was a breathtakingly gorgeous Academy-Award winner. He was *People* magazine's Sexiest Man Alive, not to mention a man given to uncontrollable bouts of drinking, drugs and rage. Just within the past year Tito had served two stints in drug rehab, 30 days in a Los Angeles County jail for criminal drug possession and been sued twice by tabloid photographers for his violent behavior toward them in the street outside of the couple's Malibu home. Their arrival in Dorset had sparked debate all over the village. Esme was one of Dorset's own and the locals were justifiably proud of her. This was a girl, after all, who'd gotten her start on stage in the Dorset High production of *Fiddler on the Roof*. From there she'd starred in a summer revival of Neil Simon's *I Ought to Be in Pictures* at the Ivoryton Playhouse, where she was spotted by a top New York casting director. He was searching for a young actress to play an under-aged Roaring Twenties gun moll in the next Martin Scorcese crime epic. Esme won not only the part but an Oscar for Best Supporting Actress. Now she was one of Hollywood's top draws.

But Dorset also cherished its decidely *Un*hampton low profile, and Esme and Tito had brought a media army with them, along with stargazers, gawkers and more gawkers.

The village was positively overrun by outsiders, many of them rude and loud—although none ruder or louder than Chrissie Huberman, the high-profile celebrity publicist whom the golden couple had imported from New York to run interference for them.

"Oyster catchers at three o'clock, Mitch!" Dodge called out, pausing to aim his binoculars at the rocks down below. Dodge had a bristly gray crewcut, tufty black eyebrows and a round face that frequently lit up with glee. He was no more than five-feet-nine but was powerfully built, with a thick neck, heavy shoulders and immense hands and feet. He wore a polo shirt, khaki shorts and size-15 hiking boots. "Two of them, see? They almost always travel in pairs."

Mitch focussed his own glasses on one of them. It was a big, thick-set bird with a dark back, white belly and the longest, flattest orange bill Mitch had ever seen. "Wow, a cartoon shore bird. What a hoot."

"Not to mention a dead ringer for my Uncle Heshie," said Jeff as they resumed walking. "I wonder if he cheats at cards, too." Jeff was an odd little puppy of a guy in his late 30s who had a habit of sucking in his cheeks like a fish whenever he was upset, which was pretty much all of the time lately—he was in the middle of a rather ugly divorce. Jeff had moppety red hair, crooked, geeky black-framed glasses and freckly, undeniably web-like hands. He also happened to walk like a duck. Jeff possessed even less fashion sense than Mitch. Right now he had on a short-sleeved dress shirt of yellow polyester, madras shorts and Teva sandals with dark brown socks.

"Raccoon poop at nine o'clock," Dodge warned them so they wouldn't step in the fresh, seed-speckled clump on the edge of the path.

The path cut down through the bluffs toward the beach now, and they started plowing their way out to the end of the Point's narrow, mile-long ribbon of sand. It was a very special ribbon of sand. At its farthest tip was one of the few sanctuaries in all of New England where the endangered piping plovers came to lay their eggs every summer. There were two chicks this season. The Nature Conservancy had erected a wire cage to protect them from predators. Also a warning fence to keep walkers and their dogs out. One of the walking group's assignments every morning was to make sure that the fence hadn't been messed with in the night. Kids liked to have beer parties and bonfires out there and sometimes got rowdy.

"You know what I was thinking about this morning?" Dodge said, waving to an early morning kayaker who was working his way along close to shore. "I've traveled all over the world, and yet I would never want to live anywhere but here. Why is that?"

"Open up your eyes, Dodger," Jeff said. No one else in the group called him Dodger—so far as Mitch knew, no one else in the world did. "It's awful damned pretty here."

"If you ask me," said Will, "it's Sheffield Wiggins."

"Old Sheff Wiggins? My god, I haven't thought of him in ages." To Mitch and Jeff Dodge said, "He used to live in that big saltbox across from the Congregational Church."

"You mean the cream-colored one?" asked Jeff.

"That's not called cream, my friend. That's called Dorset Yellow."

"I've seen that same color all over New England. What do they call it if you're in, say, Brattleboro?"

"They call it Dorset Yellow."

"Okay, I think we're drifting off of the subject," Will said.

"You mean this wasn't a story about paint?" Mitch said.

"Yes, what *about* Sheff? He's been dead for an honest twenty years."

A faint smile crossed Will's lean face. He was a good-looking guy with a strong jaw and clear, wide-set blue eyes. Yet he seemed totally unaware of his looks. He was very modest and soft-spoken. "Sheff's sister, Harriet, called my mom about a week after he died. This was in January and the ground was frozen, so they had to wait until spring before they could bury him. My dad used to dig the graves over at the cemetery, see." Will was a full-blooded swamp yankee whose late father had done a variety of jobs around Dorset, including serving as Dodge's gardener and handyman. Will was only a kid when he died. Dodge gave Will odd jobs after that and became like a second father to him. The two remained very close. "Anyway, Harriet called my mom to tell her that Rudy, Sheff's parakeet, had died . . ."

"Honest to God, Will," Jeff interjected. "I can't imagine where this story is going."

"She wanted to know if my mom would keep Rudy in our freezer until the spring so that he and Sheff could be buried together."

"You mean in the same casket?" asked Mitch, his eyes widening.

"I do."

"And did your mom . . . ?"

"She did. And, yes, they are. Buried together, that is."

"How old were you, Will?" Jeff asked.

"Ten, maybe."

Jeff shuddered. "God, having that parakeet in my freezer all winter would have given me nightmares. What color was it? Wait, don't even tell me."

"My point," Will said, "is that Harriet Wiggins thought nothing of calling up my mom to ask her. And my mom didn't bat an eyelash. *That's* Dorset."

"In other words, everyone in town is totally crazy?" asked Jeff.

"I like to think of it as totally sane," said Dodge as they trudged their way out to the point, the sun getting higher, the air warmer. The tide was going out. Dozens of semipalmated plovers were feeding at the water's edge on spindly little legs. "Martine was talking about you last night, Mitch."

"She was?"

"They desperately need tutors over at the Youth Services Bureau. All sorts of subjects—history, English, math."

For weeks, Dodge had been trying to convince Mitch to join up with some local organization or another. Already, Mitch had turned down a chance to become recording secretary of the Shellfish Commission. Not the sort of thing he could see himself doing. It seemed so Ozzie Nelson. But

Mitch was coming to understand that getting involved was part of the deal when you lived in a small town. Will Durslag served on the volunteer fire department. Jeff was a literacy volunteer.

"We have a bunch of really talented kids in this town, but they're just not motivated. Would lighting a fire under one of them be your kind of deal?"

"Maybe. I mean, sure."

"Great. I'll get you an application."

This man was relentless. Still, Mitch greatly admired his commitment. Mitch could hear a helicopter zooming its way toward them now across the Sound, moving low and fast. A news chopper from New York. All part of the Esme-Robbie circus. Another day, another breathless new inquiry. Here was yesterday's: Did she or didn't she just have a boob job? Inquiring, very small minds wanted to know.

Mitch sped up so as to pull alongside of Dodge, the other two falling in behind them. "I wanted to give you a head's up," he told him, puffing. "My review of Tito's new movie is in this morning's paper. I panned it. I hope that won't be awkward for you."

"Don't worry about Tito. He's much more level-headed than people give him credit for. Besides, I'm sure you were your usual tactful self."

"Tactful is not exactly the word I'd use."

Tito's movie, *Dark Star*, was in fact Hollywood's hugest, loudest clunker of the summer, an ill-conceived $200-million outer-space epic that the studio had held back from its Fourth of July weekend opening because preview audiences were laughing out loud in all the wrong places. It was so disastrously awful that Mitch had called it, "The most unintentionally hilarious major studio bomb since *Exorcist II: The Heretic*." He went on to say, "Tito Molina has such a pained expression on his face throughout the film that it's hard to tell whether he wants to shoot the aliens or himself."

"I really like this kid," Dodge said. "I didn't expect to, not after everything I'd read about him. But I do. And I don't just say this because he's my son-in-law. He has a broken

wing is all. Can't fly straight to save his life. That doesn't
make him a bad person. You'd like him, Mitch. I sure wish
you'd reconsider my invitation."

Dodge wanted him to join them for dinner one evening.
Mitch didn't think that socializing with performers was a
good idea for someone in his position. "I'd love to, Dodge,
but it wouldn't be appropriate."

"Sure, I understand. I just think you'd enjoy his company.
He's one of the most intuitively brilliant young men I've
ever met."

This in spite of Tito's famously troubled childhood in
Bakersfield, California. Tito's father, a Mexican migrant
worker, was killed in a bar fight when Tito was seven. His
Anglo mother, a schizophrenic, was in and out of state men-
tal hospitals until she committed suicide when he was thir-
teen. He took to living on his own after that, often in
abandoned cars, and survived by dealing drugs. His big
break came when a Britney Spears video was being shot at
the Bakersfield high school that he'd recently dropped out
of. A girl he was dating auditioned for a bit role. He tagged
along with her. The video's director was looking for a bad
boy from the wrong side of the tracks to play the bare-
chested object of Britney's sweaty affections. One look at
Tito's intense, smoldering good looks and he got the part.
The video was such a hit on MTV that Tito shot straight to
teen-dream stardom, acting in a succession of edgy teen-
angst dramas—most notably the highly successful re-make
of the greatest teen-angst drama of them all, *Rebel Without a
Cause*, in which he stepped into James Dean's almost
mythic shoes and, somehow, made them his own. It was
Esme who was cast in the Natalie Wood role. They fell in
love on the set, fueling the picture's on-screen heat, and
married shortly thereafter.

Inevitably, critics were labeling Tito as his generation's
James Dean. Mitch was not one of them. He believed that la-
bels were for soup cans, not artists. He only knew that when
Tito Molina appeared on screen he could not take his eyes
off of him. Tito had an untamed animal quality about him,

an edge of danger, and yet at the same time he was so vulnerable that he seemed to have his skin on inside out. Plus he had remarkable courage. Mitch was completely won over after he saw him conquer Broadway as Biff Loman to John Malkovich's Willy in an electrifying new production of Arthur Miller's *The Death of a Salesman*. As far as Mitch was concerned, Tito Molina was simply the most gifted and daring actor of his generation.

"He and Esme are like a pair of special, golden children," Dodge said. "When I see them together, hand in hand, I think of Hansel and Gretel on their way through the woods to grandmother's house. They absolutely adore each other, and she's been able to help him some with his rage. And their publicist, Chrissie, really does try to put a smile on his public face. But it's a challenge. He's just such an intensely unhappy person."

"He's an actor," Mitch said.

"So is Esme, and she's not like that. She's a sweet, big-hearted girl. A total innocent. I just . . . I hope he doesn't hurt her. He isn't faithful to her, you see."

"How do you know this?" Mitch asked, glancing at him.

"I just do. You can always tell—like with Martine," Dodge said, lowering his voice confidentially. "She's not faithful to me. She has a lover."

"I'm so sorry, Dodge," Mitch said, taken aback.

"These things happen over the course of a marriage," Dodge said, his jaw set with grim determination. "I sure wish I knew what to do about it. But the unvarnished truth is that I don't."

"Well, have you spoken to Martine about it?"

"Hell, no. What good would that do?"

"Communication is a positive thing, Dodge."

"No, it's not. As a matter of fact, it's highly overrated."

They were nearing the tip of Peck Point now. The osprey stands that the Nature Conservancy had erected out in the tidal marshes were no longer occupied. The ospreys had nested and gone for the season. Mitch did spot two blue herons out there. And the two rare, precious dun-colored piping-plover chicks were still in residence in their protective enclosure, tiny as field mice and nearly invisible against the sand.

He and Dodge inspected the cage and warning fence as Jeff and Will caught up with them. A fence stake had worked its way out in the night. Dodge pounded it back down with a rock as Mitch swabbed his face and neck with a bandanna, wondering why Dodge had chosen him to confide in about Martine. Why not Will? The two of them were so much closer.

Mitch opened his knapsack and got out the mugs and plastic milk bottle, his stomach growling with anticipation. From his own knapsack Will produced a Thermos of his finest fresh-brewed Blue Mountain coffee and a bag of croissants he'd baked before dawn. Will was up every morning at four to oversee his extensive baking operation. The beach constituted his only break from the punishing 14-hour shifts he worked.

There were two driftwood logs with plenty of seating room for four. Jeff filled the tin mugs from the Thermos. He and Will took their coffee black, Mitch and Dodge used milk. Dodge passed around the croissants. Then they all sat there munching and watching the killdeer and willets poke at the water's edge for their own breakfast.

Mitch chewed slowly, savoring each and every rich, flaky bite. His diet restricted him to one croissant, and he wanted to make the most of it. "Honestly, Will, you're a true artist. What's your secret, anyway?"

"Nothing to it," Will said off-handedly. "I've been making these ever since I was working in Nag's Head. My partner in those days gave me the recipe."

"You two owned a place together there?"

"No, not really," he replied.

Which Mitch had learned was typical of Will, who was perfectly friendly and polite but could be rather vague when it came to career details. Mitch knew he'd attended the Culinary Institute of America and had led the *Have Knives, Will Travel* life of an itinerant chef up and down the East coast before he hooked up with Donna, who was working in the kitchen of the same Boston seafood place at the time. Donna was from Duxbury. After they married, Will brought her home to Dorset and they'd moved into the old farmhouse on Kelton City Road that he'd inherited from his mom. This spring they had pooled their considerable skills to open The Works, a gourmet food emporium that was housed in Dorset's abandoned piano works. The food hall was the biggest piece of an ambitious conversion of the old river-front factory that included shops, offices and luxury water-view condominiums. Dodge had helped finance the venture, and it was proving to be a huge success. Already it had attracted Jeff's Book Schnook.

Jeff could not have been more different from Will—every detail of his life was fair game for discussion, whether the others wanted to get in on it or not. The little man was a walking, talking ganglion of complaints. Inevitably, these complaints centered around his estranged wife, Abby Kaminsky, the pretty little blond who happened to be hottest author of children's fiction in the country—America's own answer to J. K. Rowling. Abby's first two Carleton Carp books, *The Codfather* and *Return of the Codfather*, had actually rivaled the Harry Potter book in sales. Her just-released third installment, *The Codfather of Sole*—in which Carleton saves the gill world from the clutches of the evil Sturgeon General—was even threatening to outsell Harry.

Unfortunately for Jeff, Abby had dumped him for the man who'd served as her escort on her last book tour. Devastated, Jeff had moved to Dorset to start a new life, but an ugly and very public divorce settlement was looming on his personal horizon. At issue was Abby's half-boy, half-fish hero. There was a lot about Carleton that struck people who knew Jeff as *familiar*. Such as Carleton's moppety red hair, his crooked, geeky black-framed glasses, his freckly, unde-niably web-like hands, the way he sucked his cheeks in and out when he was upset. Not to mention his constant use of the word, "*ab-so-toot-ly*." Though Abby vehemently denied it, it was obvious that Carleton was Jeff. As part of their divorce settlement, Jeff was insisting she compensate him for the contribution he'd made to her great success. Abby was flatly refusing, despite what was sure to be a punishing public-relations disaster if their divorce went to court. To handle the publicity fallout, Abby had hired Chrissie Huberman, the very same New York publicist who was handling Esme and Tito. As for Jeff, he was so bitter that he refused to carry Abby's books in his store, even though she outsold every single author in America who wasn't named John Grisham.

"Hey, I got a shipment of your paperbacks in, Mitch," Jeff spoke up, chewing on his croissant. Mitch was the author of three highly authoritative and entertaining reference volumes on horror, crime and western films—*It Came From Beneath the Sink*, *Shoot My Wife, Please* and *They Went Thataway*. "Would you mind signing them for me—you being a local author and all?"

"Be happy to, Jeff. I can stop by around lunchtime if you'll be there."

Jeff let out a snort. "Where else would I be? That damned bookshop is my whole life. I'm there twelve hours a day, seven days a week. I even sleep right over the store in a cramped little—"

"Two-bedroom luxury condo with river views," Will said, his eyes twinkling at Mitch with amusement.

"Plus I have to drive a rusty old egg-beater of a car, so the locals won't think I'm getting rich off of them," Jeff whined.

"Which, correct me if I'm wrong, you're not," Mitch pointed out, grinning at Will.

"Damned straight I'm not," Jeff said indignantly. "Listen to this, I had to give an old woman her money back yesterday. It seems I recommended a thriller to her and she hated it. Oh, she read every single word of it all right, but she pronounced it garbage. Stood there yelling at me in my own store until I paid her back. It was either that or she'd tell all of her friends that I'm a no-good bum. Barnes and Noble can afford to be so generous. Me, I'm barely hanging on. I don't know what I'll do if things don't pick up."

"But they *will* pick up," Dodge told him. "You're already building customer loyalty and good word of mouth. Start-up pains are perfectly normal. The Works felt them, too, and now it's doing great, right, Will?"

After a brief hesitation Will responded, "You bet."

Which Mitch immediately found intriguing, because if there was one thing he'd learned about Dorset it was this: Often, the truth wasn't in the words, it was in the pauses.

"Sometimes I feel like I'm not even in the book business at all," Jeff grumbled. "I'm in the *people* business. I have to be pleasant to strangers all day long. Yikes, it's hard enough being pleasant around you guys."

"Wait, who said you were pleasant?" asked Mitch.

"By the way, Dodger, Martine did me a real solid—she's so popular with the other ladies that as soon as she joined my Monday evening reading group they all wanted in. I may even add a Tuesday reading group, thanks to her. Best thing that's happened to me in weeks. You'd think with all of these media people in town I'd be selling books like crazy, but I'm not." Jeff drained his coffee, staring down into the empty mug. "Did I tell you they're trying to buy me off?"

Mitch popped the last of his croissant in his mouth. "Who, the tabloids?"

"They want me to spill the dirt on Abby. Every time I say no they raise the ante—it's up to two hundred and fifty."

"*Thousand*?" Will was incredulous.

"And I've got plenty to spill, believe me. Hell, I've known her since she was typing letters for the children's book editor and I was the little *pisher* in the next cubicle."

"You're still a little *pisher*."

"Thank you for that, Mitchell."

"My yiddish is a little rusty," Dodge said. "Exactly what is a *pisher*?"

"She loathes kids, you know" Jeff said. "Calls them germ carriers, poop machines, fecal felons. . . . She hates them so much she even made me get a vasectomy. I can't have children now."

"I thought those were reversible in a lot of cases," Will said.

"Not mine," Jeff said. "My God-given right to sire children has been snipped away from me—all thanks to the top children's author in America. Nice story, hunh? And how does the little skank repay me? By boning that-that glorified cab driver, that's how. I swear, every time I see a box of Cocoa Pebbles I get nauseated."

Mitch and the others exchanged an utterly bewildered look, but let it alone.

Dodge said, "Any chance you'll take them up on their offer?"

"I'm flat broke, man. I might have to if she doesn't give me what I want."

"Which is . . . ?"

"Twenty-five percent of the proceeds from the first book. My lawyer wants me to aim for the whole series, but that would be greedy. I'm not being greedy. I just . . . I deserve *something*, don't I? I nursed that book along, night after that. I read every early draft, helped her refine it and craft it months before she ever submitted it."

"Plus you *are* Carleton Carp," Mitch added. "That ought to be worth something."

"I am not a fish!" Jeff snapped, sucking his cheeks in and out.

Dodge, the human timepiece, climbed to his feet now, signifying that it was time to start back for his eight o'clock weight training. Mitch wondered if the man was ever late.

"You'll never do it, Jeff," Mitch said. "You'll never sell out Abby to the tabloids."

Jeff peered at him quizzically. "Why have you got so much faith in me?"

"Because you still love her, that's why. No matter how upset you are, you could never hurt her that way."

"You're right," Jeff admitted, reddening slightly. "Abby's the only woman I've ever loved. I'd take her back in a flash. Answer me this, Dodger, what's the secret?"

"To what?" Dodge asked.

"You and Martine have been together all these years, you've got a terrific thing going on—how do you do it?"

Mitch watched closely as Dodge considered this, the older man's face betraying not one bit of what he'd just revealed to Mitch. "Jeff, there are so many things that factor into it," he answered slowly. "Shared values, common interests and goals. Affection, respect, tolerance. But if I had to narrow it down to one word, it would be the same one that's the secret to a happy friendship."

"What is it?" Jeff pressed him.

Dodge shot a hard stare right at Will Durslag before he replied, "The word is trust."